Leaving Egypt

By: Paula Sadok

Part One: 1959
Chapter One

Sarah was dreaming of date palms in Cairo when the pain woke her. Her eyes opened wide and she knew instantly what was wrong. She put her hand between her legs and felt warm liquid. Ya'allah, she cried, not again. She tried to get out of bed quietly. Her husband, Eddie, was sleeping beside her and she didn't want to wake him. Slowly, she rolled over but another pain ripped through her abdomen and pushed her back down. She could feel the blood flowing out of her, wanted to make it to the bathroom before it came out. The baby. Her baby. The second baby she was about to lose.

Sarah willed herself out of bed despite the cramps, bunching her nightgown between her legs as she stumbled to the bathroom. She turned on the light and sat on the floor, back against the wall, knees bent, grabbing two towels to catch the life that was about to slip away from her again.

She had seen her aunt, a midwife, do it once in Egypt, heard a woman scream in the middle of the night, her frantic husband banging on the door to their apartment. The midwife, hastily woken, took her young niece to assist her, coming to the rescue of the woman, calming her, cleaning her, burying the baby.

But here there were no midwives close by. Here there would be an ambulance, a hospital, machines and tubes devoid of privacy and humanity. Here there would be men in white coats who spoke a language she barely understood. Sarah couldn't bear that so she waited on her own.

She sat on the cold linoleum floor. Its pattern—swirling yellow, green and beige blobs pretending to be cheerful flowers— was so ugly it would blush with shame should it stand next to the granite in her father's home in Cairo. The floor was so cold beneath her thin, wet nightgown, the chill creeping into her in this bathroom with no window, with no soft light of the sun, only garish florescent lights to hurt her eyes. And what were these towels she held in her hands pretending to be cotton? Cotton was smooth and soft and comforting at home, not this fabric sand paper that she held to swaddle the lifeless form of another baby she would never have and never hold and never be able to love.

She bit her tongue so as not to scream when another pain sliced through her body. Her head smacked against the wall as the pain snapped her back into an arch and her pelvis made ready to expel the baby. Despite her best efforts, she screamed and Eddie ran into the bathroom. When he saw his young wife in a pool of her own blood, he swooned and held the doorpost, trying not to faint.

"Sarah," he said, "let me call an ambulance this time."

"No. No ambulance. I don't want to go to the hospital. Go back to bed."

"Let me help you."

"No. Go back to bed. I'll be fine."

Eddie didn't listen to his wife. He sat next to her and held her while she screamed, and after the baby came, he helped her clean up.

"You were past three months?" he asked.

"Three months and one week," she replied. He said he would call the Rabbi to arrange the baby's burial.

Sarah tried to stand, and Eddie lifted her, putting her gently into the bathtub, where she was too tired to stop him from washing her. After she was clean, he drained the tub and refilled it to let her soak.

"I'm going to get you clean towels and a clean nightgown."

He left her in the warm water, and she cried, softly, slowly, as the fear returned. The bathtub was white porcelain and she traced her fingers up and down its smooth ledge as her toes played with the chain on the plastic stopper. She stared at the dingy yellow bathroom walls and the ugly floral border the landlord had chosen to match the floor. Staring into daisies on paper, she could almost see laughing faces hidden in those flowers, and the longer she stared at them the more they began to move. Soon the flowers were dancing around the bathroom, dancing and laughing, laughing at her. For she was eighteen years old and had suffered two miscarriages, and the flowers laughed that this was only the beginning of her suffering.

Tears silently flowed down her face as her fear grew, as she considered her possibly rotten womb. She dipped her fingers in the tub and lifted them, watching the droplets fall back into the bath, watching the water ripple around them.

She looked at the sweating walls, beads of condensation sliding from the ceiling to the floor. She dunked her head under the water to see how long she could hold it, if she could hold it, if she could follow her baby to wherever it had gone.

Eddie returned to the bathroom with fresh towels. He cleaned and scrubbed the bathroom floor, which somehow added to her humiliation—just another way she couldn't be a proper wife. She sank her head lower into the water, unable to watch her husband on his hands and knees.

Eddie finally stood up. He gathered the soiled linens into a bag.

"Put them in the hamper," Sarah said. "I'll wash them tomorrow."

"I'm throwing these away," Eddie said. "I'll bring more home. You don't need to look at them again."

"Haram," she said. "It's a waste."

"It's haram for you to look at them," he said as he walked out.

When he returned, he drained the tub and lifted her out. He covered her in towels and dried every inch of her body, wrapping her in a robe. He pressed her body against his and held her, and she thought of how lucky she was to have a husband who didn't throw her out after she lost two of his babies. She let him lead her to the bedroom, remove her robe, dress her in a clean nightgown. He helped her into bed, covering her with blankets, tucking her in, sitting by her side, stroking her back. Then he got into bed himself and held her, pressing himself into her. She held the arm he had wrapped around her waist and prayed he wouldn't leave her as she fell into a dreamless sleep.

The next morning, Sarah woke at 6:30 as usual, as though nothing had happened the night before. She did not need an alarm clock to wake her; she just woke with the sun as she had in Egypt. She was used to sleeping with the curtains open to relieve the oppressive heat, and when the sun came up, she roused herself and went about her morning chores. It was the same when she moved to New York.

Quietly, she moved Eddie's arm aside and got out of bed. She took clothing from her closet and went to the bathroom where she washed herself, dressed, arranged her hair, and put on her make-up. Her father had told her that a good wife always looked perfect while she served her husband. She should not even have one hair out of place while she poured his coffee.

Having dressed, she put the pot on the stove to boil water for Turkish coffee. She went outside to get Eddie's paper, passed the bag of soiled linens he had left by the door. She didn't look. She ignored the pains that still scratched at her insides. She was his wife. She had her duty.

When Eddie's alarm clock went off, she had already finished toasting his Syrian bread on the fire. She sliced a few pieces of cheese for him and put black and green olives in a bowl. For herself, Sarah made a cup of tea, which she drank with a few pieces of kaak. She turned on the radio in the kitchen, and Johnny Cash's voice filled the room. Eddie liked to listen to the news in the morning, so she changed it to his usual program. The announcer was saying something about President Eisenhower when Eddie entered the kitchen.

"Sarah, you should be resting," he said.

"I'll get back into bed when you leave for work."

"But you're all dressed and ready to go out."

"Then I'll get undressed again after you leave, Eddie."

"I'll call Rosette and ask her to make dinner for us tonight."

"I don't want her to know," she said.

"I'll tell her you're running a fever."

"Fine."

"And, Sarah, I'm making you an appointment with the doctor."

"I don't want to go."

"But I want you to go."

Sarah nodded and slumped into her chair, covering her face with her hands.

"God will take care of us, Sarah," Eddie said, kissing the top of her head. "Put your faith in him."

Again, she nodded, and waited for him to leave. And when he did, guilty sobs wracked her body.

God was taking care of her: He was giving her exactly what she deserved.

Chapter Two

One week after God took her second baby, Sarah sat in the
doctor's office. Eddie had pleaded with her to go with one of her sisters-
in-law, but Sarah refused.

"I'm sorry, Mrs. Salama," he said, "but I don't have very good
news for you."

Sarah had never been alone in a room with a man who was not a
close relative. She had never been in a room this white, or with this
particular smell. All this shiny white wanted to be clean so badly, as
though by denying everything color and by superimposing this eerie
glow, the place would seem safer. Instead it was a vacuum, a space in the
void with no nutrients to sustain life.

The room was quiet except for the ticking of a large wall clock
behind Dr. Rosenberg's head. Next to those were his framed diplomas.
He had gone to important schools, she could see; Eddie would only send
her to the best doctor.

"It appears that you may not be able to bear children."

So calmly, he said those words. As though he had said he was
sorry her head hurt, or it was a shame how tired she was.

"No children?" she asked, taking a deep breath.

"Maybe not."

"What is this maybe? Yes children, or no children?"

"I don't think so."

"So, no?" She tried to keep her voice calm.

"It's not impossible, but it is unlikely."

He tried to explain. He said something about her uterus and
something about its walls, but her English wasn't good enough and the
whys were not important.

Sarah felt herself shaking as she put on her gloves.

"Mrs. Salama, do you understand me?"

She nodded. Taking another deep breath, she smoothed her hair,
straightened her hat, and stood up.

"I'm sorry."

"I am...I may...I can go?" she stammered as she made her way toward the door.

"Yes. I'm very sorry."

He was sorry? After putting her on the cold table, after putting her feet in stirrups, like she was an animal, after he stuck things inside of her in shameful ways, after that cold clamp, to hold her open, after violating her in that bright white room, all he said was he was sorry. Women didn't have to be humiliated this way in Egypt. And in Egypt, if a woman could not have a baby, time told her, not some old man in glasses with certificates whose words she couldn't read, pretending he was sorry while essentially telling her she was worthless.

"Mama," her heart called out. "Beg Him to forgive me."

In the bathroom, Sarah collected herself, rebuttoning the back of her pale yellow dress and fluffing out the full skirt. She smoothed her hair and straightened her hat and reapplied her rose-colored lipstick. Rosette was meeting her at the Syrian grocery store on 65th Street. Rosette was seven years older than Sarah and, lacking a biological baby sister, had adopted her sister-in-law Sarah as her own.

Rosette looked beautiful as always, in a striped boat-neck blouse and pleated skirt. Her blonde curls fell out of her hat as though by accident, but Sarah knew she had pinned them that way for effect. Short bangs curled on her forehead. Sarah thought of her own hair, wondered if the curls she had set were falling, and ran her hands over them, hoping they weren't frizzing. As she walked over to Rosette, she twirled a strand around her index finger.

"Where have you been? I've been waiting for ten minutes."

"I'm sorry, I got..."

"Come, look, they have beautiful tamarind plants here. We'll spend the next two afternoons making *tamerhindi*, yes? Shavuot is next week, we'll need it," Rosette said, as she led Sarah through the store by the hand.

Leaving Egypt

Shavuot was the holiday when God gave them the Torah, when He was kind enough to give the guidelines for behavior in every situation. Sarah had planned to announce her pregnancy to her family over the Holiday. Jewish custom dictated that pregnancies should not be announced before the end of the third month, as most miscarriages occurred in the first trimester. Silently, Sarah thanked God for this beautiful rule that had saved her so much shame.

Walking through the Middle-Eastern grocery store, she stared at barrels of olives, black and green, some spiced with crushed-pepper flakes. Other vats contained pickled radishes and cauliflower, colored bright pink with beet juice. Stacked on the shelves were bags of freshly baked Syrian bread, six flat-pocketed loaves to a bag. Other shelves contained semolina flour, cracked wheat and sesame seeds. Jars of grape leaves and tahini paste sat beside bags of dates and pistachios. In the refrigerator section were white Syrian cheese and figure eight packages of twisted cheese with black seeds.

This was Sarah's favorite store. It carried all the foods they needed for their cuisine, their food being such an integral part of the identity as a community. It was so hard to find those ingredients in any American store, and when she had first moved to New York, she had been confused upon seeing the kosher sections in the local market. What did these Ashkenazim eat? Some kind of fish loaf in jello, pickled fish, preserved meats, potato and noodle puddings. And they had been labeled Jewish? No Jews she knew ate that.

In one corner of the store, Rosette sorted through tamarind plants. Making tamerhindi, the tangy sauce essential for so much of their food, was not something Sarah was up for. It required two days of intense labor, cleaning the tamarind plants, and boiling them, straining them through cheese cloths, allowing them to cool overnight and then repeating the process several times until it reached the desired consistency. They would most likely work in Rosette's house, surrounded by her two young children, Rosette dispensing advice the entire time. Sarah said nothing but hoped Eddie might be able to help her with an excuse later.

"What are you making for dinner tonight? I'm making rice and kiftes, shall we work together?" Rosette said, when she returned with the plants in her hand. Rosette stopped to look at her young sister-in-law. "Look at you, so pale, so thin, you look like you're starving. You'll never be able to make a baby if you don't have meat on your bones."

Sarah bit her tongue so hard she tasted blood. She would not say anything to Rosette. Scorn was better than sympathy.

"No, sorry. I promised Eddie I'd make dairy for dinner."

"Oh. But we can work together anyway. I'm sure we'll find something to make. And by the way I have something to tell you."

"What?" Sarah asked.

"I'm pregnant again. Isn't that majnoon? I told Elie we're going to have to sleep in separate rooms after this."

Sarah smiled and held back tears. "Mabrouk," she said, kissing Rosette. "I'm running out of spices. I'm going to go pick out a few bags."

Rosette found her at the spice station with tears running down her face.

"It will happen soon, ya rohi," she whispered, embracing her crying sister.

"No, it's nothing," Sarah said, forcing a smile. "The allspice is very strong today."

I need to get away from her, she thought. From her love, and her mothering me, and her friendship. Can you be strangled by love? And then: guilt. Rosette is so good to me, adopting me as her own little sister, the sister I never had, the mother I long for. And yet, there is jealousy. Four years of marriage and two children, a third on the way. What blessings does she have that I lack? Why do I lack them? How can I gain His forgiveness?

"I'll go to the butcher and then I have an errand or two to run," Sarah said. "Why don't you pick up your clothing from the dry cleaners, and I'll meet you back at your house in a few hours?"

Rosette's faced registered hurt and shock, but she was both wise and kind enough not to argue.

Leaving Egypt

So Sarah walked down the block that was the focal point of their community: the synagogue two avenues over this way, the mikveh one block down that way, all of the stores where they shopped, where she ran into fellow Middle Eastern Jews, from Syria, from Egypt, the kosher stores catering to them and to their Ashkenazi neighbors, and the pork stores for their Italian ones.

The mikveh: the rainwater bath where she cleansed herself ritually every month, where she would go again to cleanse herself after her lost baby, immersing again and again into the sanctified waters, and still she was unclean.

Bensonhurst. Three-story red brick buildings, devoid of history, new and drab, lacking the grandeur, the maturity of Cairo. No broad boulevards. No elegant apartment buildings with balconies, broad arches and beautiful molding. All looking the same. Not the contrast of Art Deco and Rococo and Neo-Classical like she was used to. No Nile. No grounds like the gardens of Gezira, once Khedive Ismail's own botanical gardens, later opened to the public. No trees heavy with mangoes and tangerines, no jasmine trees to perfume to the city. And weather so cold in the winter, so dark, when little needles of ice pricked her skin under her coat, so unlike the beautiful breezes coming off the Nile.

Everyone speaking English, all kinds of strange accents: Yiddish, Italian and Arabic. No sounds of French, no Ladino, no Greek. On the streets they sell hotdogs, not Koshary or Ful. Old men playing chess in the park with timers, instead of the leisureliness or yelling of backgammon. And cigarettes with their foul odors instead of the sweet aroma of fruit-flavored tobacco emerging from water pipes. And no cafes to speak of. Bensonhurst.

Where Sephardic Jews were the minority, Ashkenazi the majority, and everyone thought that if you were Jewish you were one of them. Those Jews had such different names, such different ways of doing things. They prayed so differently, pronounced Hebrew such that she could not understand it, and had their own language, Yiddish, that she had been outraged to learn meant Jewish. Those Jews didn't even know her kinds of Jews existed. They hadn't accepted them, thinking they were

14

lowborn backwards members of desert culture. Imagine that! Jews from the ghetto in Poland thought less of them for being from Cairo!

There were Ashkenazi Jews in Cairo, but few of them and they kept to themselves. And here, they looked down on her kind as though they rode here from the desert on their camels, when Sarah spoke three languages, and her mother had spoken four, and all they spoke was that crazy mishmash of Old German and Hebrew.

What is this place?

Thinking these thoughts, Sarah longed for water. From their old apartment, they had beautiful views of the Nile and one of her favorite pastimes had been a stroll along the Corniche. Especially after her mother died, with Elie, and even after Elie married and moved out of Cairo to the suburb Heliopolis, he visited her once a week for their regular walk.

There was no Nile here, but there was a boardwalk, there was the ocean. Maybe watching the waves roll in would calm her as watching the felucca boats, their white triangular sails almost glowing in the sun, almost shimmering in the soft Egyptian light, had once calmed her when she was back home.

Boarding the bus, she headed for Coney Island. When she arrived, she walked along the boardwalk. Here, they used planks of wood, drab slabs nailed down, instead of the rosy-colored, intricately patterned concrete blocks that paved the Corniche. And the ocean was so vast, so uncontained; one could lose one's sense of place in it. The Nile gave her a better sense of proportion. Because even walking the streets of Zamalek, on the island in the middle of the Nile where she lived, she could see the shimmering lights of the hotels across on the other side. She could cross Gezira Bridge, that large steel structure, the entrance on each side flanked by pairs of lions standing proud in front of granite pylons from Aswan, dotted with lampposts that glittered on the river at night like a bracelet on the wrist of the Nile, lighting the way for her to get off her island, and into the rest of the city, to the glamorous hotels, Shepheard's or the Semiramis. But here, in Brooklyn, by the ocean, she was stuck were she stood. She could see no lights on the other side. Only this vast expanse of violent, angry water that would drown her should she get too close.

She sat on a bench on the boardwalk, her back to the cafes and restaurants and people.

I want to go home, she thought, but home no longer exists. All the people that made it home were no longer there, not just her parents, but everyone, aunts, uncles, cousins, friends, scattered to the winds, to Europe and Israel and South America and Australia. Even if she did go back to Cairo, even if she could, the Nile would still be there, but it would no longer be home.

This is my new home. Where I am filled with feelings as foreign to me as this land.

Jealousy.

Jealous of Rosette for having more than her, angry with herself for being jealous of Rosette. Her sister. Her surrogate mother. And she was jealous.

Honor your father and mother. One commandment she had broken. And today another: Do not covet your neighbor, but she was filled with coveting.

How could she begrudge Rosette anything? Of all the people who had given to her? Rosette! Her oldest brother's wife. Elie, who had assumed the role of head of the family, not a role he wanted, but one that had been forced upon him. And Rosette, as his wife, taking the role of family matriarch, not one she had asked for, but one she carried with such elegance and grace, especially regarding her husband's orphaned and childless baby sister.

As close as Sarah was to Rosette, so much of her wished to be closer. To cry on her shoulder, to weep in her lap, to confess all of her fears and insecurities, to have her waiting by her closet every morning telling her what to wear. Having been an adolescent girl surrounded by men, Sarah had no mother to teach her how to dress. It was Rosette, even back in Cairo, who had taken her to buy fabrics. It was Rosette who took her to the dressmaker; it was Rosette who had argued with her father for more money to dress his daughter properly. It was Rosette who taught her to pluck her eyebrows into thin crescents over her eyes, to paint her lips on like a bow, to powder her face. And here, in this new home, she continued in that role, taking Sarah shopping, helping her to select skirts, blouses, hats, shoes, and gloves.

A wall existed between them, and Sarah knew it was she who perpetuated it. Rosette was as available to Sarah as Sarah would let her be. And yet, something kept Sarah from letting Rosette be exactly what Sarah needed. Today, she knew. It was jealousy. Rosette had both of her parents, and none of the guilt, and two children with a third on the way. She had lost her life back in Egypt, too, but she had her whole family in Brooklyn, and she had created her own family here as well. As much as she loved her, Sarah could not forgive Rosette for having everything she wanted. And Sarah knew she was wrong. A sinner. Do not covet your neighbor.

But I am filled with coveting.

Honor your father and mother.

I should walk to the ocean to throw away my sins. I should walk into the ocean and let the waters cleanse my sins.

Still, she sat on her wooden bench, watching the beach, watching the sand, watching the waves and the water, filled with longing, waiting and praying for answers.

How fitting to be struggling with this now. This week. With Shavuot on the way. Shavuot: the holiday where God gave the Jews the Torah, the rules, the code of conduct for life on earth. And also, Sarah's birthday. A very unhappy nineteenth.

Picking her birthday was like picking an identity: one according to the Arabic calendar, another according to the Western calendar, and a third according to the Jewish calendar. It was the Jewish calendar date she chose to celebrate. Chose it because it was on the holiday, because it was her father's favorite holiday: how proud had he been to have his daughter born on the day that God addressed the Jews directly for the first and only time.

God was addressing her now. What was He saying?

It was not just a judgment. No, that holiday was Yom Kippur. He was reminding her of the rules: the guidelines He had given to His people. The step-by-step instructions to life that she had tried so hard to follow, had been so grateful for so many times. But now was He punishing her for the times she could not abide?

"*Adonai, Adonai, El rahum v'hanum, erech apaim, v'rav hesed v'emet!*" Her heart cried out the attributes of God, chanted again and again on Yom Kippur as they begged forgiveness. Our Lord, Our Lord, a merciful god, slow to anger, and full of kindness and truth.

This could not be just a punishment. There had to be a lesson. Some trial she had to pass, some cleansing ritual to bring her closer to God, to make her worthy of bringing a child into the nation of His chosen people.

Shavuot: After God took His children out of Egypt, He summoned them before Mount Sinai and made them His nation, spelling out their purpose, choosing them to live by a system of ethics that defined them among the other peoples of the earth.

But the first exodus had been a blessing. What of the second? What of her own?

Cairo in flames. Jews murdered in streets. Deemed foreigners despite living in Egypt for generations. Tortured. Imprisoned. Rounded up. And then expelled. Forced to leave, surrendering all assets to the state, given no compensation, allowed to leave with only two suitcases and so little money they could barely buy bread. Where were the miracles there?

And her father left behind.

Honor thy father and mother.

But the rules have saved me so many times. Do not forsake Him. Do not forsake them. We do not know heaven's designs, her father always said. We are human, and not meant to comprehend. God understands that we are too frail, too filled with our own pain and longing to know the right way and He shows us. He gave us the greatest gift ever given to mankind, her father always said: love, moral clarity and guidance.

18

God is just, Sarah told herself. I will be my father's daughter. I will believe.

She remembered her mother's death, so sudden, they were blindsided by the loss. Sarah wanted to run to Giza and fly head first off the tallest pyramid. Her father had not been able to speak for two days. But the laws dictated that they sit shiva, surrounded by their family and their community, watching them so they could do nothing rash.

The laws told them how to mourn, by covering mirrors, tearing their clothing, and refraining from bathing. They could not listen to music, could not be entertained, only surrounded by those closest to them, and after one week, God compelled them to go on with life. The rules instructed Sarah to assume her mother's responsibilities in looking after her father and her six brothers. The rules forced out her grief by making her know that there was work to be done and it was her responsibility to do it.

Though her father had not wanted to leave Egypt, he instructed his sons, just in case: If they come for me, you will take your sister and go to your mother's cousins in Italy or my cousins in New York. Do not wait for me. Use whatever influence this family has left to get me out, but not from here or they will come for you, too.

What could have been a moral dilemma had been avoided. God's instructions: Honor thy father, and that was what they had done.

When she lost the first baby she had been home alone, cooking. She hadn't known what the pain was then, but sat and held her belly, rocking back and forth, praying, until her body expelled a tiny ball of human tissue.

What do you do with this lifeless, bloody mass that your body has killed? How do you honor the life it almost had? How do you grieve? God gave the answers. A fetus that small had to be buried, but mourning customs were not observed. A woman and her husband had to refrain from intimacy until a week after the bleeding stopped, when she would cleanse herself in the ritual bath. And there, in those waters, He would absolve her, and absolve her body, and make her ready to try again.

How could anyone know how to function, forgive, continue living without those rules? How lost would they be without them?

I will have faith in God. I will follow His rules. I will make my father proud. I will persevere through the trials He puts in my path.

Tired of watching the ocean, she stood up and walked away.

Sarah remained lost in her thoughts as she took the bus back from Coney Island to Bay Parkway. She walked until the butcher shop, a big black and white sign that read, "Goldberg's Glatt Kosher Meats."

The store was crowded with women, two of them pregnant, all placing their orders for the holidays. Mr. Goldberg sang along with Frank Sinatra on the radio as he sliced and packed meat. Sarah stood in line and waited her turn. In front of her, an Ashkenazi woman with short blonde hair and blue eyes stood holding the hand of a blonde, blue-eyed boy. Sarah smiled at him. He smiled back and looked down shyly. Then he looked up and puckered his lips into a fish mouth. Sarah did the same and the boy laughed. He couldn't have been older than three. He fidgeted, wriggling his hand out of his mother's.

"Moshe, hold still," she said.

He flushed, then looked back up at Sarah, who crossed her eyes and stuck out her tongue. He laughed again and looked away.

As he looked down, Sarah caught sight of the butcher's work space, the big wooden board, covered in fresh blood and flesh, and in the corner, crumbled up, a pile of bloody towels, the red blood turning to black stains on the white linens. She couldn't stop staring. The boy giggled and waved as he and his mother exited the store. It was Sarah's turn to order.

"What can I do for you, Ma'am?" the butcher asked.

Sarah stared at the bloodstained linens.

"Ma'am can I help you?"

Sarah continued to stare.

"You feeling okay, lady? You need a glass of water, or something?

Finally, she heard him. She stammered, "Four pounds of chop meat," and reached for her wallet.

"Sorry, lady," he says. "Yiddish I can do. That one I don't speak."

She had been speaking in Arabic, had forgotten her English.

Don't cry in the butcher shop.

She held up four fingers and pointed to the pile of ground beef.

"Four pounds of chop meat?" he asked.

She took a deep breath. She nodded.

"Three dollars and twenty cents," he said.

She took another deep breath and bit her lip. Then she handed him the money, grabbing the meat and the coins she didn't bother to count, and ran out of the store before the tears spilled down her face.

"Hey lady, I'm sorry. I didn't mean nothing by it," he called after her.

Chapter Three

Rosette had purchased two jars of grape leaves and decided that since the two women were together, they would stuff and roll grape leaves for dinner the next night. The kiftes took four hours to cook anyway, the meatballs flavoring the lemon-based tomato sauce, and it would be foolish to sit in the kitchen and do nothing for all that time, so they would make yebra as well. Anyway, she had reasoned, they hadn't spent much time together lately and it would nice to catch up.

"All right," was all Sarah said.

"What's wrong with you today?" Rosette asked. "You haven't disagreed with me a single time today! I feel like I'm spending the day with Frieda!"

Frieda was Rosette's cousin, famous for never having an opinion of her own.

Sarah smiled. "I guess I'm just tired. I haven't been feeling well lately."

"For how long? Is it bad in the mornings? Maybe you should go see a doctor."

"No, it's not that."

"Don't say no. You never know."

Sarah thought about the doctor and wondered what she would tell Eddie.

Usually Sarah enjoyed working at Rosette's house. She had a good radio with strong speakers and a phonograph with a wonderful collection of Arabic records from Raschid's Record Store on Atlantic Avenue. That day, they listened to Abdel Halim-Hafez.

Rosette's kitchen felt inhabited, the spice jars full, the room always fragrant. Rosette had taken the time to decorate, filling the room with flowers, be they silk, dried or fresh, all of them red, Rosette's favorite color. The colors in her kitchen were drab: beige Formica countertops and dark wood cabinets and a brown and beige linoleum floor.

"And no light," she always complained, pointing to her small single window that overlooked the driveway. "Remember how light flooded our apartment in Cairo?"

To compensate, she had folded brightly colored linen napkins, samples from her husband's store, into flowers, birds and other beautiful designs, and tacked them all over the kitchen.

There were always other women in Rosette's kitchen, cooking, eating, gossiping, complaining. Most of them still spoke French nixed in with Arabic with a smattering of English words, but some spoke perfect English, and it was the French that they stumbled over.

"This song always reminds me of your father," Rosette said as she shaped chop meat into torpedo-shaped meatballs.

"Really," Sarah replied. "Why?"

"We danced to it together at my wedding," she said quietly. She wiped her hands on her apron. "I think Elie has given up. I think he thinks it's been too long."

Sarah said nothing.

"I heard him on the phone with Moise a few days ago. He said there's just no communication between the Israelis and the Egyptians. He said he tried working with the Americans, but after all these years, he's just presumed ..."

"I don't know what to think," Sarah said finally. "I just pray for God to take care of him, wherever he is."

"I'm sorry. I shouldn't have said anything. We have to keep hoping and praying. Inshalla you'll hear something soon. Inshalla this time next year, he'll be here playing with his grandchildren."

Grandchildren. No children. No grandchildren. What would she tell Eddie?

When the women finished working, Sarah collected her belongings and made her way home in time to prepare for the end of Eddie's day. Walking home, she tried to guess what Eddie's reaction could be. He could leave her. He could take another wife. It was her duty to bear him children, and if she could not, it was perfectly within the realm of propriety for him to find someone who could. She might even suggest it to him; she doubted he would do so on his own. She had six older brothers. One of them, whether one of the three who moved to Israel or the three in New York with her, would be able to take her on and she could work for them. Then she could make herself useful, then she could make her life worth something. Instead of being barren. Childless. Dried. Lacking.

Holding her still rounded stomach in her hands, Sarah was reminded of a story she had learned in school and began looking through the bookshelf for the Torah. When she and Eddie had married, all of her brothers had arranged to have a set of beautiful leather-bound Hebrew books sent from Israel as a wedding gift for the young couple. The gift comprised the complete volumes of the Old Testament, the complete Talmud and a shelf of prayer books for every possible holiday and occasion. She found the book of Genesis, the story of Sarah, and began to read.

"Now Sarai, Abram's wife, had borne him no children."

Sarah, under the reading lamp on her kitchen table, read out of the leather-bound book of Genesis given to her by her brothers. The power of names, she thought. How fitting that she should be called Sarah, she thought, the woman of the house for six brothers, unable to bear sons of her own. Sarah searched for instructions within the text.

Sarai the matriarch had been unable to bear any children to her wealthy and powerful husband. Other than his nephew, Lot, there was no direct heir to his fortune. Though it was so common for men in that time to do so, Abram had never taken another wife. Perhaps it was his faith in his God, who had repeatedly promised that he would be father to many great nations, that kept him from marrying another. Perhaps it stemmed from a sense of fidelity so uncommon in those times; perhaps it was because of true love for his wife.

"Sarai said to Abram, 'See now the Lord has restrained me from bearing, consort now with my maidservant; perhaps I will be built up through her.'"

Being a truly loving wife, Sarai could not bear to see her great husband Abram without a son. If Sarai the matriarch had given her husband another wife, shouldn't little Sarah Salama do the same for her husband? Leave him and allow him to try with someone else?

But then the message became unclear. After Sarai's handmaiden, Hagar, bore Abram a son, Ishmael, Sarai became jealous.

"The outrage against me is due to you! It was I who gave my maidservant into your bosom, and now that she sees that she has conceived, I became lowered in her esteem. Let God judge between me and you!"

If Sarai the holy matriarch could not handle her own jealousy, how could Sarah? What was the Torah saying here? Should Sarai have been punished for her lapse in judgment? Was she wrong for giving her husband the chance to have a child and then sending that child and his mother into the desert to die? Was Abram at fault for letting her?

But, then God changed their names, Abram to Abraham, Sarai to Sarah, and in changing their names, changed their fate. Sarah, at the age of ninety, conceived a child to Abraham at the age of one hundred. Sarah gave birth to Isaac, who in turn fathered Jacob, who then fathered the twelve sons who became the twelve tribes of Israel.

"God remembered Sarah as he said, and God did for Sarah as he had spoken. Sarah conceived and bore a son unto Abraham in his old age."

What was the lesson? Sarah asked herself again. That it would be wrong to leave Eddie? That it should be his decision? Or that she should wait, as did her namesake, until God was ready to answer her prayers?

Both Sarah and her son Isaac's wife, the matriarch Rebecca, had been barren, and God had not ignored their prayers. He waited till the time was right, purified their souls with prayer and faith and then rewarded them. The message was clear. It was not for her to decide. She would pray and she would wait. She would leave the matter of another wife with Eddie. She would leave the matter of a baby with God.

Chapter Four

The last time Sarah saw her father was in late November 1956. She had been sitting in her mother's favorite chair, rose-colored, Louis XV-style, stiff-backed and stuffed, with elegantly curved arms and legs, in her mother's favorite corner of the apartment, right by the terrace, where the sunlight was strongest. When she looked up from her spot she could see the Nile, and on cool Fall days, feel the breezes coming off the river. Knowing their days in Egypt might be numbered, she tried to indulge in simple pleasures, reading *Le Comte de Monte Cristo*, again, when she was interrupted by three loud knocks on the door. She rose to answer it, but her father stopped her.

"Sarah, go upstairs," he said, the fear in his voice palpable.

Sarah looked at her father with questions in her eyes, questions that seemed to anger him.

"Sarah, upstairs, right now."

"Baba, who is it?"

"Why do you ask so many questions? Just do what you're told and go upstairs."

Sarah walked towards the stairs at the back of the apartment, and hid around the corner so she could hear what was about to happen.

Her father opened the door.

The preceding week had been marked by fear, by the sounds of sirens signaling air raids, as Egypt was pounded with rockets. Cairenes huddled in bomb shelters as British, French and Israeli forces united to punish Gamal Abdel Nasser for nationalizing the Suez Canal.

Many, including all six of Sarah's older brothers, were secretly thrilled. Surely Nasser was no match for the powers of Europe. And it served him right, the brazen upstart, removing the king of Egypt and forcing him into exile, ending a dynasty that had lasted 150 years. They hoped that after Nasser was gone, life as they knew it could resume.

King Farouk had been far from a model leader but he and his father Fouad, in fact all the monarchs of the Mohammed Ali dynasty, had modernized Egypt, taken a poor country in Africa and recreated it as a modern state. The monarchy had loved the Jews, invited them in, encouraged their enterprises, and maintained close ties to the community, sending royal delegations to the main synagogues in Cairo and Alexandria on the High Holy days. In return, those same Jews founded Egypt's finest hospitals, largest banks, and most glamorous department stores.

Though many Jews lived in Egypt for generations, almost none were granted Egyptian citizenship. Few foreigners were, and because a curious set of laws called "The Capitulations" made it easier to do business with a foreign nationality, most didn't try. Still, the Jews of Egypt were coddled, a protected minority, loved and valued foreigners. To those same foreigners, it seemed like Nasser intended to destroy everything about Egypt they held dear.

Before Nasser, Sarah's brother Murad was an executive at a major Egyptian bank. After the coup, his boss, an Italian Jew, was exiled because of his close ties to the monarchy. Though Murad was horrified to see his boss go, he was promoted to the vacant position, and filled it successfully until new laws were enacted. Slowly, all his skilled managers were replaced because the new laws required seventy-five percent of employees in each company to be of Egyptian nationality, regardless of education or experience. Finally, Murad was fired, his job given to the new owner's nephew, a twenty-year-old boy who used to walk the streets of the city with a cart, selling vegetables.

Close family friends saw their fortunes reversed overnight, the prosperous reduced to paupers, everything they had built taken. Murad was one of the lucky ones because their father had managed to hold onto his own factory. Regretfully, his father fired a young Jewish clerk and hired his son Murad in his place. But they knew it was only a temporary solution and the climate of fear grew worse by the day.

The previous four years seemed surreal. It started on a fateful day in January 1952, when a confrontation between British soldiers and Egyptian policemen in Ismaliya left fifty policemen dead. Sarah and her family were cut off from the news. They were sitting shiva for their mother, who had died of influenza. They weren't allowed to read the paper or listen to the radio, and so they had no idea that Egyptians had taken to the streets to protest the British occupation, to protest the monarchy and the wealthy foreigners who ran the country. They only found out that the protest turned violent when they could see Cairo in flames from their windows. On what was later called "Black Saturday," mobs stormed the streets, looting and burning, attacking British interests, torching the famous Shepheard's Hotel to the ground. Somehow, the tide turned against the Jews, and people chanted, "*idbahu el-Yehud*"—death to the Jews—as they turned their ire toward Jewish businesses and killed Jews in mobs on the streets.

"God had mercy on your mother," their father said, his clothes torn, his face unshaven. "At least she didn't have to witness this."

Several months later, on July 23, 1952, the Free Officers led by Nasser and Mohammed Naguib staged a coup, and just three days later Farouk and his entourage set sail aboard the no-longer-royal yacht to Italy. A republic was established. Egypt was ruled by Egyptians for the first time in centuries.

The Jews of Egypt were terrified. They had seen how Egyptians viewed them on Black Saturday and, years earlier, during the riots that followed Israel's declaration of independence. The holocaust in Europe was fresh in their minds; they knew what happened to Jews who stayed too long in places they weren't wanted. Many left, but many stayed, hoping against hope to hold on.

With the onslaught of war came a barrage of rumors.

Though no one told a young Sarah anything, she overheard her brothers gossiping. There would be retributions, they said. Nasser had long wanted to expel all the French and English and Jews. Now he would have a reason.

Finally, Sarah asked her brother Elie if the rumors were true, if they were in danger. She knew he was the only one who might give her an honest answer. One night, Elie and his newly married wife were over for

28

dinner, and Sarah managed to get him out of the room as Rosette tried to calm everyone's nerves by playing the piano.

Elie, the firstborn son, was named after his father's father. Elie was jinngi—red-haired and green-eyed. He had inherited his father's family's looks along with their name.

"They are true," he said. "The government is nationalizing property belonging to Jews and arresting community leaders."

"But why the Jews?" she asked. "We're not Israelis."

"It's all the same to Nasser," he replied.

"How can they do that?" she asked, shocked.

"They're using the war as an excuse," he said. "They've issued a proclamation that all Jews are Zionists and enemies of the state. They're accusing them of spying for Israel."

"But that's a lie," Sarah said. "If we were Zionists, we would have already moved to Israel."

"I don't think Nasser really cares," said Elie. "If he had no problem nationalizing the canal, why would he care about stealing property from Jews? We're not even citizens."

"But Mama's family has been here for over a hundred years!" Sarah sat on her bed, looking at a framed picture of her mother's family, taken at an aunt's wedding at Shaar HaShamaim, Cairo's most important synagogue.

"He doesn't care," Elie said. "We have no papers; we've never had papers."

"So what do we do?"

Elie opened his hands, raised them in the air, and shrugged. "Either we wait and see, or we leave before they kick us out."

Sarah shook her head. "Baba will never leave."

"I know. It's too bad. We should just go to Israel and start over."

"But we'll have nothing."

"We'll have our lives and we'll have our families. That's enough."

Through those nights, Sarah heard Elie arguing with their father, trying to persuade him to leave. Her brothers Murad and Moise agreed.

Leaving Egypt

Their father refused. He had already left Syria, the country of his birth. He had built a life in Egypt.

"I'm not a young man anymore," he said. "I don't have the energy to build a business again. And what do I do with all that I have worked for here? Leave it for the *fellaheen*? No. It's mine. I earned it. Maybe you don't want to stay to inherit it, but I'm not giving it up."

When Ezra, Zaki, and Jacques told him they feared for his safety, their father was intractable.

"This is not the first time we've heard this talk!" he yelled. "How are all of those families who left when Israel was created? My cousin lives on a kibbutz in a metal shack with no running water. He wakes up at five in the morning to pick mangoes. Do you want to pick mangoes Zaki? Maybe your tailor can make you overalls in silk! And how about all those people who left when they got rid of Farouk? 'They'll kill all the Jews,' they screamed! Well, we're still here, aren't we?"

The brothers relented but their whispering led Sarah to believe they were making other plans. Then one day, her brother Moise announced that he was sending his wife and son to Italy. His wife's family, the Guindis, held Italian passports from generations back. He feared for them, he explained, and though they had only distant relations in Italy, those cousins had agreed to take them in. He planned to stay in Egypt with his father for the time being but did not think it safe for his wife. Adele had pleaded with him to go with her, but he decided to stay a little longer. Adele was afraid, he explained, because she would not be allowed back into Egypt once she left. But for the sake of their son and their unborn child, she had agreed to go at once.

Next Murad announced his plans. His wife, Ninette, held French citizenship and her family was leaving. They had only been married a year and he did not want to send her to Paris alone. Zaki, Jacques and Ezra were not sure what to do, but they were afraid for their safety. They held a family conference, listing the names of the Jews they knew who had been arrested or had disappeared. Their father said the same thing he had been saying all along: "You are all grown men and I can't stop you from leaving but I'm staying here."

30

The knocks on the door were therefore not at all shocking and all the more terrifying; it was this terrified curiosity that prompted Sarah to disobey her father by listening in on things he tried to protect her from, an act of defiance she would regret for the rest of her life.

Her father answered the door. From her hiding place, Sarah could see three men in uniform.

One of them asked, "Are you Saleem Mizrahi?"

"I am," Saleem said.

"You will come with us," said another.

"Just give me a moment to inform my household," Saleem said.

"You will come now," said the first voice.

Saleem tried to argue for a few more moments, but one of the guards must have grabbed him because he said, "Take your hands off of me. I am a respected member of the community."

"You are *kalb ibn kalb*," Sarah heard him say—dog, son of a dog. How dare they? "You are under arrest. You will do exactly as you are told."

"And what is the charge?" Saleem asked.

"You are a well-documented Zionist," said the officer. "Now we go."

Sarah snuck around the stairs to get a better view of the men who were taking her father so she could inform her brothers. As she did, an officer saw her and said, "What a pretty little daughter you have, *kalb*. Perhaps we'll take her as well and have some fun with her."

"She is not my daughter," said Saleem. "She is just a servant girl."

"All the same," said the officer. "I'm sure we can find some reason to detain her." The other officers laughed. Sarah shook, unable to move.

Saleem turned around to look at Sarah, wearing an expression she had never seen before. He turned back to the officers and spat in one's face.

"You will not touch a single member of my household, you filthy Arab pig," he shouted at the officer, lunging at him. The officer swiftly grabbed his baton and hit Saleem over the head, a blow so strong it knocked him to the ground.

"Baba!" Sarah screamed.

"So she is his daughter. Let's bring her in."

"Sarah," he yelled in Hebrew, "go upstairs at once and lock yourself in my room. Listen to me this time. Now!"

Sarah ran upstairs as fast as she could. One of the officers said, "See, he speaks Hebrew. The spy passes coded messages to his daughter!" She heard the crack of the baton on her father's body again, and then another, and then a third, followed by a low moan, and the sound of a body being dragged from her house.

Locking herself in her father's room, she secured the large bolt that had been installed a few weeks earlier. He had known they would come for him. He had known they would try to hurt her. He had tried to protect her and he was beaten for it. They beat her father. She made them beat her father. Sarah hid in her father's wardrobe in terror, hands over her ears, blocking out sounds, praying: God forgive me.

Chapter Five

One of the last days Sarah spent with her mother was in the autumn of 1951, a beautiful day when Farouk was still king, before the fires, before the revolution, before she had any idea how quickly her life could shatter.

Sarah and her mother Esther, Terra to her friends, sat in the kitchen, surrounded by bowls of melted butter, chopped pistachios and walnuts seasoned with sugar and cinnamon, and trays of filah dough in sheets and shreds. Saleem's niece, Shefiya, was engaged to be married and Terra promised to prepare two desserts for the swanee, a party where the groom's mother sent gifts to the bride.

"Today, I'm going to teach you to make baklawa and kunafa, like your grandmother Sarah taught me to make in Aleppo," Terra said.

"Nonna didn't teach you how?" Sarah asked.

"My mother? No, sweetheart, I've never seen your Nonna cook once in her life. I'm not sure she knows how to light the stove."

At the kitchen table, a twelve-year-old Sarah wore a pink cotton calf-length sleeveless dress and sandals, and her mother wore a full navy skirt, covered by an apron, along with a white eyelet blouse. Her dark glossy hair was pinned back, and pearls adorned her neck.

Taking a sheet of filah, she showed Sarah how to layer them, one at a time, until there were seven layers, brushing each layer with butter before adding the next sheet. Next, they spread the crushed pistachio mixture over the dough. Then, they covered the pistachios with another seven layers of dough.

"Now this is the hard part," her mother said. "I ruined many trays while your Sitto was teaching me, but she was always wonderfully patient."

She sliced the trays in perfectly spaced diagonal lines, going in both directions, until she was left with a sheet of diamond-shaped pastries. Next was the syrup: Terra brought water and sugar to a boil, splashed in some fresh lemon juice and removed a bottle of rosewater from the pantry.

"Look how little maward you use," she said, holding the bottle. She took two toothpicks, dipped them into the rosewater then dipped them into the syrup.

"That's it, or else the taste is overpowering."

Sarah nodded and wiped the sweat from her forehead with the back of her hand. With a kitchen towel, Terra wiped the nape of her neck and top of her back under her blouse. She looked at the shredded filah on the table and the cheese for the kunafa.

"Should we make the kunafa today? No, it's just too hot. Let's go to the cinema so we can sit in the air conditioning."

They took a taxi to Cinema Metro in downtown Cairo, where they sat for half the day in the delicious cold of the air conditioning. Later, Sarah couldn't remember what picture they saw, only that it was a romance, because they always made her mother cry.

After the movie, they walked down Adly Street, past Shaar HaShamaim Synagogue. The large concrete building was decorated in a neo-pharonic style, with art deco palm trees and Jewish stars carved into the walls, evoking the long history of the Jews in Egypt—though many of the 80,000 Jews who lived in Egypt had moved there in the past century, there had been a continuous Jewish presence in Egypt for the previous 2,000 years. There, behind the gates and under the large, stained-glass windows, a laughing crowd loitered at the base of the steps.

"I think I heard something about a bar mitzvah," her mother whispered, as she smiled and waved to those she knew.

They continued to Groppi Garden and sat outside in wicker chairs, on mosaic floors, under the shade of trees, as the late afternoon air turned cooler. Sarah's mother sipped a cappuccino, while Sarah ate an éclair.

As they sat, Eddie Salama walked in with a pretty young girl Sarah had seen before at some wedding or bar mitzvah or something. She couldn't place her, but it didn't matter: Sarah hated her.

Eddie was twelve years older than Sarah, a friend of her brother Zaki's. Though they had barely exchanged ten words with each other, she was secretly in love. The girl's back was to Sarah, and Sarah could see her long dark hair hanging down the back of her white cotton dress, her slim waist accented by the pale blue sash tied around it.

Terra noticed her daughter staring. "They must have just come from the party," she said.

Sarah barely paid attention to her mother. She fixated on Eddie as he laughed and smiled and looked at the girl.

"Stop staring, Sarah," her mother said, laughing. "It's rude. What, do you like him?"

Look at his dark brown eyes and hair, she thought. Look at his broad smile, the way his eyes crease when he's laughing. He doesn't even know I'm alive. I wish he would just notice me.

At that moment, he saw her and waved.

Sarah turned a shade of red brighter than her mother's lipstick. She waved back. Her mother turned and smiled warmly.

"See that's what you get for staring," she said. "But at least you have good taste. He'll probably be off the market by the time we start looking for you, but inshalla you'll marry a nice boy like that."

Sarah pulled a strand of hair out of her barrette and twirled it vigorously.

"Stop, honey, you'll ruin it," her mother said, pulling her hands away from her hair. "Don't worry," Terra continued, "Baba will find a nice boy for you to marry."

Sarah giggled. "Like the one Nonno found for you?"

"Touché," Terra replied, laughing. She took a long sip of her cappuccino. Staring off into the distance she said, "I promise you, Sarah, I'll make sure the husband your father finds for you is more suitable than the one mine tried to find for me."

"Tell me the story, again," Sarah said.

"Again?!" she asked.

Sarah nodded. "And tell me with Baba's side, too."

When Terra was sixteen, her father tried to marry her off to the son of a family friend. That he was almost twice her age didn't bother her; the age gap between her sister and brother-in-law was even larger and they were the happiest couple she knew. No, there wasn't anything wrong with him in particular. He was nice and respectful, from a good family and financially stable. He wasn't bad looking or lacking in manners. He was just, well, boring.

Terra's father kept trying to make the match, her mother gently encouraging her, her sisters telling her she could do much worse, but Terra knew that being in a marriage with this man would be like eating food without salt: hardly the end of the world, but what good is life with no flavor?

Then she met Saleem and marriage to bland boy was out of the question.

By the time Saleem Mizrahi was born, in 1902 in Aleppo, Syria, the opening of the Suez Canal had all but wrecked his family's textile business. For hundreds of years, the Aleppo Mizrahis had operated a trade through the caravans, importing silks from China, cashmere from India and damask from Persia. Camels would arrive at his father's warehouse in the Khan-il-Ghimrog laden with fabrics from the Far East to be sold in Aleppo or sent on to new destinations along the Silk Road. But it was cheaper to ship than to carry by camel, and slowly their business dried up. They tried sending a cousin to Manchester, England to open an import outpost, but financial crises struck Syria again and again, and by the time Saleem was old enough to work, there was no work to be found.

Saleem hadn't wanted to leave Syria, where his family had been important for generations, but as the Ottoman Empire crumbled, great changes took hold of the Middle East. Jews living under Ottoman rule, in Constantinople, Baghdad, Beirut, Jerusalem, Damascus and Fez, found their destinies a little more tenuous. The Young Turk Revolution strove to reform the empire from corruption, but among their reforms was mandatory conscription for all young men. Life as a Turkish soldier meant no kosher food, labor on the Sabbath, the desecration of every tenet of Judaism that Saleem held dear.

His cousins and brothers dispersed to the far corners of the earth, to Buenos Aires, Panama, Paris, Milan and New York. All intended to work until they could save enough to live well in the land of their birth. But letter after letter arrived bearing instructions and tickets for wives and children to follow to these far-away places. Saleem couldn't bear moving away from his family, from everything he knew to an entirely new world. Instead, he went to Cairo, a twenty-four-hour train ride away, so he could return, and easily. He went to where he spoke the language, was familiar with the custom. Saleem was an Arab, after all, and didn't know how he would find the Americas.

Egypt had been calling to the Jews since the days of Mohammed Ali, the Albanian general in the Turkish Army, who dared to challenge the Ottoman Sultan and crown himself King of Egypt and Sudan. The soldier who founded a dynasty strove to revolutionize Egypt, to create a European outpost in Africa. He opened Egypt's arms to those with western education, sent his brightest young subjects to European universities. His successors continued his plans, rebuilding Egypt using French architecture, Italian aesthetics, and German engineering. The dynasty was so eager to distance itself from Africa, re-invent itself in the mold of Europe, that the fifth in line, Khedive Ismail, bankrupted the nation with his overreaching expansion plans. His British creditors stepped in and brought Egypt under Her Majesty's fold. Though the Egyptian monarchy remained, Egypt was now administered by England. The learned, the wealthy, those thirsting for an economy of opportunity flocked to Egypt.

When Saleem arrived in Cairo in 1924, it was as though the twenty-four-hour train ride had taken him to another world. He had never seen a telephone, never seen an electric light. He had never used indoor plumbing. At first this world frightened him and he thought to return to Syria. But there were no opportunities in Aleppo, no jobs, no way for a young man to work his way to success. And besides, as always, the local population blamed the Jews for the economic depression. Here in Cairo, in this Paris on the Nile, a young man had a dizzying and overwhelming array of options.

Leaving Egypt

Saleem was amazed by how few people actually spoke Arabic. He heard a confusing mishmash of Greek, Turkish, Armenian, Spanish and Italian, in addition to French, Egypt's *lingua franca*.

Back in Syria, Saleem had studied for a few years in an *Alliance Israelite Universelle* school, a school funded by wealthy French Jews to teach Enlightenment values to the Jews of the Middle East. He was grateful for this broken French; without it, gainful employment would have been impossible.

He settled in the Daaher neighborhood with other Halabi— Aleppoans—so he could pray with them at the Ahaba ve Ahva synagogue. During morning prayers, he met an old family acquaintance who helped him get a job in his field. Within a week, he was employed at the Jewish-owned Cicurel's department store, buying the fine fabrics his family used to import.

And there he saw her. Religious, traditional, Syrian Saleem fell in love with cultured, secular Terra Moreno. She was bijhenan, had the kind of beauty that could make a man crazy.

"The first time I saw her," he always said, "I knew. She was standing with another girl, picking out gloves. I was in the middle of a conversation with my boss. The words flew right out of my mouth and I just stood there, staring. Later, I asked my cousin who she was. I said, 'That's my future wife,' and he laughed. 'Go tell her that and see how she spits in your face.'"

But she didn't spit; in fact, she swooned. Her parents forbid the courtship, so Terra saw him on the sly.

"He's a nothing. A nobody. A clerk in a store," her father said when she finally told him. "An immigrant, an Arab Jew, of all things," he said, when she was the daughter of a wealthy, prominent Ottoman family, one that had been in Egypt for over a hundred years. But even as they snuck around, he treated her formally and with respect. His goal was marriage, not some illicit affair.

Saleem was dazzled and amazed by Cairo's nightlife. Dancing and gambling and endless arrays of exotic cuisine. And women. Women wearing makeup, and women showing cleavage, and women laughing

38

loudly and flirting and beckoning. In Aleppo, the only women out at night were those of ill repute. A less devout Jew may have succumbed to Cairo's temptations, but not Saleem. First, he found the woman he wanted, courted her only as a prospective wife, and then with her as his guide, he sampled the delights of this opulent new world. He grew to love this new world as he grew to love this young woman, the excitement of both experiences inextricably linked.

For Saleem, Terra embodied Cairo's charms. She took him to the theater and the opera. After, she insisted on dancing in the one of the city's many nightclubs where she taught him tango and foxtrot, and later, when she was starved from all the dancing, dragged him to one of the city's many patisseries for dessert. On hot days, Terra loved to cool down by packing a picnic basket and hiring a boat and captain for the day, drifting down the Nile, reveling in the breezes while chatting and snacking on dried apricots and roasted pistachios. She was so carefree, so excited, so eager for the next adventure. What a contrast to his mother, Sarah, who spent all day, every day cooking. Back in Aleppo, they were treated to musicians at a furrah, a celebration of some milestone like a wedding or bar mitzvah or brit milah. Here in Cairo, Terra expected to enjoy live music every night, either as an orchestra played waltzes while they danced, or an Arabic band played as they watched belly dancers gyrate well into the middle of the night.

"He'd never been to the cinema," her mother recounted. "Or the theatre. And his French was horrible. But I taught him. I got to open new worlds for him. I loved it."

"She barely spoke Arabic. And she wasn't religious at all," her father always added. "I got to show her the beauty of our tradition, the richness of Judaism."

After two dizzying months, they eloped to Aleppo, stopping in Alexandria to be married quickly in a Rabbi's office, because Saleem would not spend the night with Terra until she was his wife. Terra's family was so connected that none of the rabbis in Cairo would have married them without alerting her parents.

Leaving Egypt

Saleem had told Terra about Aleppo, but nothing he said could have prepared her for what she saw. The twenty-four-hour train ride had been like traveling back in time. Aleppo, Halab in Arabic, was an ancient city, which, according to legend, derived its name from the patriarch Abraham, who had stopped to give milk—*halab* in both Hebrew and Arabic—to weary passersby. The Jewish community in Halab dated back to the time of King David and Jews still lived within the narrow alleys of the old city as they had for almost 3,000 years.

After their train arrived in Baghdad Station, Saleem hired a porter to carry their luggage to Bab-il-Faraj, a square in the city's center. Situated on the square was Baron's Hotel and the Hotel du Park, virtually the only hotels in Aleppo; Orodsi-Beck, a tiny Austrian department store; a post office and a telegraph office.

There was one striking feature to the square: a large clock tower, sixty feet high, with a clock on each side, one telling European time, the other Arabic time. Saleem explained to her that twelve o'clock marked sundown in Arabic time.

"We should send your parents a cable," he said. When Terra looked surprised he continued, "I doubt we'll find a phone anywhere."

From there, they continued down the narrow, winding cobblestone alleys that led to Bahsita, his parents' neighborhood. How archaic, she thought. This ancient, dusty city was like something out of Arabian Nights. How unlike the broad boulevards of Cairo, like the hand of time had somehow forgotten Aleppo. As they walked, Terra looked up and saw the wooden balconies with ornately carved panels that defined Aleppo's architecture. Other than that, the outsides were drab and ugly.

"Don't let it fool you," Saleem said, seeing her grimace. "The insides of many of these homes are quite beautiful. They just look like this on the outside not to provoke the 'ain," he said, referring to the evil eye.

Finally, they arrived at his parents' house. The house was actually a collection of rooms surrounding an inner courtyard called a *hohsh*. In the center of the courtyard stood a cistern and what looked like—no, it couldn't be—an outhouse. Saleem explained that his family used to occupy all the rooms around the hohsh, a sign of wealth, but as their fortunes dwindled and their sons moved away, his father had invited his brothers and their wives and remaining young children to share the hohsh. Now three families lived there, occupying one or two rooms each, depending on their means.

They arrived to a whirlwind of activity, women running this way and that, cleaning, pumping water, cooking. The courtyard was filled with the aromas of Aleppo: tamarind, apricots, cinnamon and allspice. Terra could smell the meats cooking, the rice boiling, the pine nuts roasting and the dough frying and she realized how hungry she was. Before she could eat or drink, a woman she presumed was her mother-in-law screamed and slapped her hands to her face. She ran over to Saleem, this woman dressed in a long robe that covered everything but her face, threw her arms around him and covered his face with kisses. Once satisfied with showering affection on her son, she turned to her daughter-in-law, and kissed her as well. "Hilweh," she said over and over again—pretty.

In a fit of excitement, she yammered on and on, but Terra could barely understand her: Terra spoke Arabic horribly. In her home, she had grown up speaking French. Occasionally, they spoke Italian. She understood Ladino from her grandmothers, though she didn't much speak it. She could communicate a bit in Greek, as it seemed that Greeks owned all the grocery stores in Cairo and one needed some Greek to shop. Arabic was her weakest language, spoken only with her servants, and it was the language in which her mother-in-law addressed her now.

"Shoof, shoof," her mother-in-law said—look, look—dragging Terra by the hand to the salon and showing her a bale of exceedingly fine silk fabric. Then, she brought her another bale and fingered some beautiful lace. After, she showed her a magazine from Paris with dress patterns, urging her to select one, telling her a seamstress was standing by. The pattern Terra selected met with clucks of approval by the women who surrounded her. Finally, they ushered her to the room she would share with Saleem.   Terra could hardly conceal her dismay. An ancient-looking rug covered the floor, along with a low couch that must have come from the same era. In the center of the room stood a low table covered with a large tray, surrounded by cushions for sitting. An armoire adorned the wall next to a small empty alcove. There were no lights, just a kerosene lamp. No bathroom, just a chamber pot. No running water, just a jug that had been filled from the cistern outside.

"There are no real beds," he said apologetically. "My parents have them, from many years back, when they were wealthy, but we'll have to sleep on these." He pointed to several mattresses stacked in the corner.

They have no running water, she thought. No phone and no electricity and no beds. Surely, she could not live in such a place.

Her new husband embraced her. "I'm sorry," he said. "We'll be back in Cairo soon. I promise."

Though they had been married in Alexandria, Saleem and Terra had yet to consummate the marriage—they had boarded a train immediately after Saleem signed the ketubah and put a ring on Terra's finger. Before they could be intimate, she would have to immerse herself in the mikveh—the ritual bath. But to prepare for the mikveh, she must be immaculately clean, and in this country with no running water, that required a trip to the hammam. Saleem was in the process of explaining this to his bride when the women of his family were upon them, pulling Terra away again.

As Terra entered the hammam, she was impressed for the first time since arriving in Syria. The grand structure was a paradigm of Ottoman architecture, with an enormous dome in the center and vaulted ceilings. In the middle of a large room was an octagonal marble fountain. Women lounged on couches sitting on the platforms that lined the room. Behind those platforms, curtains draped over Ottoman arched doorways, concealing the hot rooms. Saleem's mother Sarah led Terra into one of these rooms, where they sat in the steam until Terra thought she might faint.

An attendant then entered the room, poured hot water from the stone basin over Terra, removed her robe, and scrubbed her body with a mohair mitten, removing all the grime accumulated from her travels and readying her for her husband. By the time the woman finished, Terra was so relaxed she thought she might drift into sleep right there. Sleep would have to wait, though, because her attendant rinsed her off, wrapped her in a robe, and led her back into the central room, and then into a cooler antechamber.

Terra noticed that the female bathers who had been there when she entered were gone and only Saleem's family remained. The ladies lounged, drinking schraab, a juice made of orange syrup, and smoking, to her shock, a sheesha. In Cairo, only the Arab men smoked the water pipe; a lady would never dare.

Two women sat her down on a couch and began ululating and singing, as her mother-in-law walked into the room holding a tray of gifts—a swanee. The tray contained two bags that Saleem would later tell her were henna and a rose-scented clay shampoo. Sugared almonds in pastel colors were artfully arranged to highlight the most important gift on the tray—a triple-stranded pearl necklace with a flower-shaped clasp studded with diamonds. Terra could hardly conceal her delight, and seeing this, her mother-in-law clapped her hands again, smiling broadly.

After more singing and dancing, more schraab and sheesha, Sarah took Terra to the Jewish ritual bath, where she threw in a pinch of henna for good luck.

The next day, Friday afternoon, was the wedding, a simple ceremony that took place in the courtyard. Since they had already been married, it was more like a performance for the benefit of Saleem's family. The following night was the nobeh, Arabic music party, when friends and family were summoned to the Mizrahi family's hohsh for a feast of Syrian foods and a night of dancing and merrymaking. It was unlike any wedding Terra had ever attended and she loved watching the old men flicking their wrists, performing comical dances with glasses filled with water on their heads.

Finally, they were allowed to spend the night together; finally, they were indeed husband and wife.

On their first day after the wedding party, Saleem went off to his father's office in the Khan, and Sarah took Terra by the hand, excitedly showing her the new Primus stove. When Terra looked dumbfounded, Sarah explained that kerosene was the newest thing; they no longer had to cook over charcoal. When Terra failed to reply, Sarah asked her what her mother used at home. Terra had no idea. She had never been inside the kitchen.

"But what does your mother do all day?" Sarah wanted to know.

"Shop, see her friends, visit family," Terra offered.

Sarah shook her head and muttered something Terra didn't understand. Finally, she looked at her daughter-in-law and said, "Someone's got to teach you to cook or else my son will starve."

And so the lessons began. They ground wheat into flour and pounded flour into pita loaves, sending them off to the baker's. They stewed apricots for hours, the sticky sweetness making Terra nauseous. They cleaned tamarind plants, boiling and straining, and repeating the process again and again. They rolled dough into sheets paper thin, then folded and stuffed them with meat or rice or vegetables. They ground meat and sautéed it with allspice and cumin. They boiled rice and lentils and mixed in caramelized onions. They stopped cooking only long enough to eat and then they started cooking again.

Early in the afternoon, a servant boy appeared, and Sarah packed food into interlocking metal containers, sending the men in her family lunch. When the boy returned, Sarah dictated a grocery list and sent the boy shopping.

"Why don't I go to the market for you?" Terra asked, longing to get out of the house. Sarah looked at her as though she had gone mad. "Women are never seen at the market," Saleem explained later. "It just isn't done."

Terra felt trapped, until one day, her mother-in-law addressed her in French. "I learned a little French in school but I don't remember much. Perhaps you'll help me practice?"

Thus began a game, where they alternated languages by the hour, Terra teaching Sarah French, and Sarah teaching Terra Arabic. As they conversed in two languages, Terra learned to appreciate her mother-in-law's wicked sense of humor, to feel her longing for the children who had

44

left home, to admire the strength she displayed in keeping up appearances as their family's fortunes sank lower and lower.

But the big surprise was Shabbat. After a week wholly dedicated to the creation of food, Sarah stopped on the Sabbath. And on Sabbath afternoon, their friends stormed the house and played cards for hours and hours. Their game was a form of whist called Solo, and Sarah was clearly the best player on the table. Sarah let Terra watch her play, and the morning after, recounted hand by hand, recalling each card revealed and discarded, explaining to Terra why she played the way she had and how she had been able to anticipate the other players' moves. Sarah may have been a brilliant cook but her true genius lay at whist.

During their French mornings and Arabic afternoons, Sarah taught Terra about food, family and cards. At night she taught her how to relax with her narghile. After a long day of work in her hot kitchen, Sarah ended every day in her salon, stretched out on the divan, smoking from her water pipe. It was a ritual Terra came to love. Though Terra greatly missed her life in Cairo, she was sad when it was finally time to leave Sarah behind.

A cable had arrived from Terra's parents, saying they accepted the marriage and wanted her home. She thought her husband would keep them in Aleppo longer, but Saleem hadn't realized how hard it would be to live without the modern comforts of Cairo. Also, as he looked at the members of his community, he remembered that there was no room to grow in Syria. If one was poor one stayed poor, and even his family, which had once been rich, had little to offer for him. No, he would take his bride back to Egypt, to a land teeming with opportunities. He would work as hard as he could to build a life for them, to provide for his wife in the way she had been raised, to build a business he could pass on to his sons, and along the way, to send money to his parents, so that they would not succumb to the poverty that seemed destined to otherwise overtake them.

The Mizrahis saw them off as they once again boarded the train in Baghdad station. Sarah wept as she hugged and kissed her son and her new daughter. "Allah ma'ak" was all she could bring herself to say—God go with you. Before they boarded the train, she handed Terra a valise. A tear slid down Terra's face when she opened it and saw what it contained.

Young Sarah never tired of hearing that story, and her mother Terra never tired of telling it.

"We had a big wedding when we came home. A beautiful party with so many gifts. But the best gift I got was the one your Sitto Sarah gave me. When I saw her narghile in the suitcase, I knew she approved.

"It was a special time for us," Terra said, finishing her cappuccino. "Hiding out in Aleppo, living with your Sitto, learning to cook Syrian food, learning Arabic by listening to her friends gossip. You think your aunties are bad, you should have heard what these women talked about."

"Weren't your parents mad?" Sarah asked.

"They were. They thought your father was after their money. But your father never took anything from anyone. He worked hard to build his business. The one time he took money from my father, it was a loan, and he paid him back within two years. But don't even think about that. Your father and I will find you someone good, someone you'll love as much as I love Baba. I promise."

Chapter Six

Terra was not there to keep her promise to her daughter. A few weeks after their afternoon at Groppi Garden, she died of influenza. One night she took to her bed with a fever, only to leave it three days later in a white sheet.

Saleem wanted to call the doctor.

"It's nothing," she said. "Bring me some water and let me sleep. I'll be fine."

Her fever continued to worsen.

"I'll get in the bath," she said. "No need for a doctor."

But the bath failed to cool her raging temperature and she seized. By the time the doctor came, her heart had stopped and it was too late. Who could imagine a woman so vital could be conquered by something as banal as the flu?

Saleem sat at the edge of her bed unable to move. He barely blinked as tears flooded his eyes and poured down his face. Something inside of him closed; an almost imperceptible shuffling of tissue hardened him, his eyes growing sharp, his jaw setting into an expression that would never again relax into a genuine smile.

In the years to come, Sarah legitimately worried over the husband her father would find for her. He barely let her leave the house. Rosette offered herself as a chaperone and Terra's sisters screamed their disapproval, but Saleem kept his young daughter under close watch.

At twelve, she was too afraid to argue with him but as she grew older and saw her friends and classmates go to parties and have the fun that was the right of teenage girls in the most glamorous city in the world, she bristled. She began with lies of omission. "I'll be at Racheline's house," she said, neglecting to mention that Racheline's older brother and his friends would be there, too. Then she moved to white lies. "Racheline's mother will be at the cinema with us," when in reality she was only dropping them off.

That was as far as she had gone until the day they came for him. Though Elie tried to tell her otherwise, Sarah felt responsible for their missing father. Elie had found her after their father was taken, curled in a shivering ball in the floor in the back of the closet. He had heard her sobbing, coaxed her out and held her, calmed her till she could tell him what happened.

"It's all my fault," she screamed.

"It's not your fault," he said, holding her.

"He hit them to protect me. And they beat him for it. God knows what they're doing to him now."

"Sarah, they were coming for him anyway. They would have beat him anyway. They don't need a reason. I promise you, it's not your fault."

Though Elie tried to reassure her, Sarah could not forgive herself. He tried to distract her with daily walks along the corniche. As they made arrangements to leave, he took her to her favorite spots in Cairo to say good-bye, but this only exacerbated her grief, as she felt the full burden of her guilt, that her actions caused her whole family to leave their home.

"Nasser is causing us to leave our home," Elie said. "Most of the people we know are leaving. Many of the ones we know have already left."

Within a week of their father's arrest, the Mirazhi sons and daughter boarded a boat to Marseilles, filled with other Jews who shared their plight, where they tried to decide where to go, waiting for visas to see who would take them. Three of the Mizrahis decided on Israel, three on America, and Sarah had to choose between them. These siblings, who had never been separated for more than a few days at a time, would now live oceans apart, unsure if they would ever reunite again.

Refugees from Egypt flooded Brooklyn, those who came earlier doing their best to help the newcomers adjust, those newcomers amazed at how quickly and drastically their lives had become unrecognizable.

When they arrived in New York, Sarah couldn't believe the cold. Gusts of wet wind froze her face and ears and hands as they walked the streets of Bensonhurst, looking at apartment after apartment to see what might suit them. In Cairo, the siblings had lived in a fancy neighborhood, in a large luxurious space. In New York, they finally settled on a one-bedroom basement apartment. Because Elie and Rosette were the only married couple, they slept in the bedroom. Sarah slept on the couch, and her brothers Zaki and Jacques slept on thin mattresses on the floor.

In Cairo, they had servants, so that even after Terra died, their maid, Fatima, ran the household. In New York, Rosette and Sarah worked all day, cleaning the apartment, washing clothes and cooking food. Back home, they ate meat several times a week, but in this new life, Rosette boiled every last bit of flavor out of chicken bones and scrimped so they could eat beef on Shabbat. Before, holidays began with trips to the dressmaker, picking out fabrics and ribbons for fancy new frocks. But now, Sarah sewed patches onto pants and jackets and her own dresses shone from being ironed too many times.

In Egypt, their father had owned a factory and, even as times grew tough, was able to employ his sons. In New York, the brothers walked for days, visiting every relative of every acquaintance they had, until someone took pity and gave them a job. Where they had been managers or executives before, each brother swallowed his pride more with every rejection until he took whatever job was offered, even stocking shelves at a five-and-dime.

Elie's lot improved the fastest, a mercy from God, as his wife was expecting, and didn't know where she would put the baby. After he was promoted, they moved out into their own tiny one-bedroom apartment, the baby later sleeping in a drawer padded with third-hand blankets. Sarah thought she would have to find work as well to make up for the loss in rent money, but Zaki reconnected with an old friend from Egypt who offered him a position in his new business.

With a little bit of luck and a lot of hard work, their lives improved gradually over the next year, and the brothers began to talk of finding a husband for their sister. When her brothers suggested Eddie Salama as a match for her, Sarah took it as her mother's intervention, her mother's way of reassuring her that everything would be all right, that a divine hand guided everything and there had been some purpose to all their loss and suffering.

Leaving Egypt

Eddie and his family had left shortly after Terra died, in the winter of 1952, after the fires, after their uncle and one of his sons had been killed by a looting mob, thirsty for Jewish blood.

And yet, could there be a happy ending? That Eddie left Egypt with nothing, and, being impoverished, needed a few years to be financially secure enough to marry, at which time, Sarah Mizrahi had magically ended up living in the same neighborhood, in Brooklyn, as him? That her brothers were arranging a match with his parents? Could this be her mother's way of telling her she was forgiven? That it wasn't her fault, that she was just an instrument in God's unknowable plan?

Elie smiled when he told her about the Salamas, reminding her that they had been neighbors in Zamalek, a suburb of Cairo situated on an island in the Nile. That they prayed at the same synagogue, that Eddie's family had its roots back in Aleppo, like her father. As though she had forgotten a single detail about him or his family.

Now, five years after their last meeting, he and his family were coming over for dinner. Elie didn't need to explain; Sarah knew that dinner was tantamount to a test for both sides. While her future in-laws evaluated her, she would form an opinion of them and then give or deny consent to her brothers to further the courtship. As though she needed to think about it.

Sarah spent days cleaning the house, scrubbing the walls and floors, beating the carpets and fluffing the pillows. For eight hours a day she worked, cleaning in the morning, and preparing Middle Eastern delicacies all afternoon, before she stopped to cook dinner for Zaki and Jacques. A neighbor lent her a record player and some Oum Kalthoum records. She scrubbed the narghile, the new one purchased in New York, the one they used for company, and bought fresh tobacco and apple tea to serve after dinner.

The Salamas were scheduled to arrive at 7:00 pm on Monday. By nine o'clock Monday morning, Sarah had everything under control. The two-bedroom apartment she shared with her two unmarried brothers was immaculate. All the salads had been prepared, all the food had been assembled and was ready to go into the oven an hour before her guests arrived. She had placed the serving plates and utensils in the living room. There was a bottle of arak in the fridge. The narghile was set out in the middle of the room, stuffed with tobacco. The coals, coal plate and tongs were in the kitchen. Only she had no idea of what to wear.

Rosette had gone shopping for Sarah, arriving at eleven that morning with a knee-length wool skirt and matching silk blouse, taking care to highlight Sarah's womanly figure while displaying unquestionable modesty.

As Sarah waited, she brewed Turkish coffee and baked the baklawa for dessert.

When they arrived, these old family friends she had not seen in years, she sat on the sofa with her hands in her lap, trying hard not to curl her hair around her finger. Eddie joked with her brothers, especially Zaki, whom he missed after the many years apart. He smiled at Sarah, addressed comments towards her and finally asked her questions, to which she replied with one-word answers. Her mind had gone blank and later she would berate herself thinking of all the clever and witty things she should have said.

Because she couldn't speak, Sarah kept her hands busy, serving the mezze: several salads and tangy finger foods. She refilled plates when they were empty, poured drinks, cleaned, and then cleared the table to bring out coffee and dessert. She lit the coals in the kitchen and brought them to the living room to place on top of the narghile. As she worked, she heard snippets of conversation.

"She is an excellent cook."

"She runs this house by herself."

"She never complains."

"He has a good job."

"He is honest and works hard."

"It's time for him to find a wife."

"Our families have been connected for years."

"I think this will be a good match."

"I think this will be a good match."

Leaving Egypt

As Sarah worked, showing her abilities, showing her obedience, proving herself, she noticed Eddie was not paying attention to the conversation. Instead he watched her. And when she caught him watching her, he smiled with a kindness that made her blush.

When she had eight plates in her hand, he stood up to help her. She blushed again.

"Please sit. I can do it. Thank you."

Eddie insisted. His father said nothing.

In the kitchen she whispered to him, "You shouldn't be in here."

"Sarah," he said, "they're practically promising us to each other and we haven't had a moment alone."

"That's the way it's done. We should go inside."

"One minute," he said, taking her arm. She gasped. "You've barely said a word all night. I know this must be scary for you. But I remember what a sweet girl you were in Cairo. And I'm amazed at the woman you've become, in spite of everything. And before my family says it to your family, I want to say to it to you. I would be honored if you would consider me for your husband."

Later that night, after clearing the dishes and cleaning up after her guests, Sarah contemplated smoking what was left in the narghile.

"When you are a married woman," Terra used to say, "you'll have more responsibilities than time. But at the end of the day, you must take some time to relax."

Terra used to finish her day seated in her favorite upholstered chair with daintily carved legs, beneath the framed needlepoint of a cornucopia of fruit, and beside the large window of the apartment that overlooked the Nile. There she smoked her narghile, the one her mother-in-law Sarah had given her at the end of her honeymoon in Aleppo, a symbol of Sarah's approval of her new daughter-in-law.

"It's not a sheesha," Terra would say, answering her daughter Sarah's question for why she called it by a different name than then they did on the streets of Cairo. "Sheesha," she would explain, "is for the men outside, in public, down in the coffee shops. Narghile is from your

52

grandmother Sarah, a gift from one lady to another, to be smoked in private as a reward for a long day's work."

In her wide skirted dress and heels, pearls strung around her neck, crown of dark curls around her face, Terra was the picture of glamour to young Sarah. Sitting in her own kitchen in Brooklyn after her future in-laws left, Sarah thought she would always remember her mother that way: Young, beautiful, relaxed and smiling.

Wanting to share this moment with her mother, Sarah decided against the narghile in front of her. From the top shelf in the small closet in the hallway, she removed a small suitcase, which contained two of the few things she had taken from Egypt. One was an old, frayed, sepia-tinged photograph of her parents at their official wedding in Cairo, months after they had really married. The second was her mother's narghile, a gift from Sarah's namesake, last touched in Egypt. It was unlike her, so impractical, when all they could take was one suitcase, and hers was filled with a framed photograph and her mother's old water pipe. Elie had yelled at her for being so foolish. But it was the wisest decision she had ever made. Instead of taking underwear, which they had plenty of in Israel or America or wherever they were going, she took a piece of her mother, a comfort, a means of channeling her spirit. This was the first time she allowed herself to look at it. This was the first time she felt capable of using it. In her heart, Sarah smiled to her mother and thanked her for keeping her promise.

But three years and two miscarriages later, Sarah wasn't sure her marriage was a gift from her mother. Maybe it was part of her punishment: to have what she prayed for only to lose it.

Alone again in her kitchen, she thought, "An eye for an eye." She had disobeyed her father: she would never be a mother.

Part Two: 1978

Chapter One

In the years that followed, Eddie did not forsake Sarah, and neither did God.

Long after she had given up hope of having children, she became pregnant with Marcelle. When she realized she was pregnant again, Sarah was overcome with a feeling of dread. She felt the telltale signs, her breasts swelling, her womb cramping. She delayed going to the doctor, afraid of what he would say.

After she was a month late, she relented.

When the doctor confirmed her suspicions, she wept.

"I've seen many women have healthy children after going through what you did," he said. "Try to be happy. Nerves are bad for the baby."

But Sarah couldn't relax. Memories of lying on the bathroom floor flooded her mind. She wasn't sure she could endure it again.

Walking home from the doctor on that brisk November morning, she again wondered what she would tell Eddie. Why upset him again, lift his hopes when they were sure to result in pain made far worse by raised expectations? Surely, he had noticed she hadn't separated herself from him as she did every month during her period. Surely, he noticed she had not gone to the ritual bath. Would he confront her or wait for her to tell him?

As the weeks went on, he said nothing, only looked at her with eyes too afraid to show joy. But by the fourth month, he came home one night with flowers. He took a vase out from the cupboard, filled it with water, and placed it on the table as she served him dinner.

Sarah knew he knew but said nothing. She waited for him to speak as they ate.

"This time will be different, Sarah," he said, from across the table.

"I don't want to talk about it," she said. "It'll bring bad luck."

The next night he came home with a gold hamsika, a five-fingered hand pendant on a gold chain. "For good luck, Sarah," he said, as he came behind her while she was washing dishes, putting the chain around her neck.

"To ward off bad luck," she said.

"Think only of the good, ya rohi," he said, his arms moving around her waist as he kissed her on the neck.

"Let's not talk about it," she said. "Let's pretend it isn't happening for now."

"I love you, Sarah. You are the best wife a man could ask for. For the rest, whatever God has in store for us will be."

During the fourth and fifth months, she and Eddie never discussed the baby. They smiled more, they laughed more, they made love more, but they never discussed the family they might finally be able to begin. When Sarah's belly became round, Eddie rubbed it as she lay in bed beside him.

They kept the secret as long as they could. Sarah bought bigger clothes, complained to her friends that she was getting fat, joking that years of fried food finally caught up with her. One day, cooking in Rosette's kitchen with Rosette's cousin Esther, and Esther's husband's cousin Frieda, it became impossible to hide.

"Sarah," Rosette said casually, as they created bulgur wheat shells, stuffed with seasoned chop meat. "Don't you think there is something you should tell us?"

Sarah smiled and looked at the floor.

"It's not like we haven't noticed," said Esther.

Sarah kept smiling.

"Don't leave us out of all of the fun," said Frieda, pulling on Sarah's sleeve.

"The baby's due in June," Sarah said, wiping her eyes with the back of her hand.

Sarah's pregnancy progressed; each day seemed like a miracle. Then, finally on June 27, 1961, Marcelle arrived, a final push followed by a gush of liquid, the sweet sound of her scream. Ages passed before the nurses finished cleaning and weighing her, until they brought her into the recovery room, where Sarah held Marcelle's tiny wrinkled body in her arms. She should have been exhausted from the labor, but a burst of adrenaline shot through her, and Sarah spent hours rocking her infant daughter, reveling in every stretch and squirm and yawn.

After they brought Marcelle home, Sarah found herself unable to sleep despite her exhaustion. She rushed into Marcelle's room constantly, standing over the crib, watching her baby's chest rise and fall, making sure her daughter was still breathing. As the months passed, she learned to relax, to accept the blessing she had been given, to enjoy the little love of her life.

She cradled Marcelle in her arms, rocking her in a chair, singing the French lullabies her mother sang to her. Long after Marcelle fell asleep, Sarah held her, unwilling to put her down, unwilling to let the moment end. Eddie often found her, still sitting in the rocking chair, holding a sleeping Marcelle while she sat, head tilted back, sound asleep.

As she watched her daughter smile and crawl and learn to sit up by herself, Sarah finally felt settled in America, invested in the country where she lived: with the birth of this child, she had created a new home. Her daughter wasn't Syrian like her father or Egyptian like her but American. The way her father had found a way to become Egyptian, she would have to find a way to become American.

How proud she felt to have the Kennedys in the White House. Sarah and her friends loved Jackie—as they called her, as though she were their friend—and were proud to be represented by such an elegant lady. They gathered together and watched, enraptured, when Mrs. Kennedy let reporters into the White House, telling them that everything in the White House should be the best, that the history of the White House, and by extension, America, was important, and needed to be told.

That notion comforted Sarah, who came from a place where history began. But unlike Egypt, America had a bright future.

Until the lights of the future were trampled upon on. Sarah would always remember the date of her next miscarriage; it was the day before Kennedy died. As she and Eddie sat in front of the television set for days, she wondered what they had done, moving to this crazy country where a man could shoot the president, and days later, another man could shoot the shooter.

Eddie, her always calm husband, so visibly afraid, worked hard to project confidence, to blame her fear on the hormones, to make her watch as President Johnson was sworn in, Jackie Kennedy by his side, to show the continuity, to show that America would not be like Egypt, plunged into chaos when violent forces removed her ruler. Kennedy's assassination, horrible though it was, gave Sarah cover. This time, she could cry in the street over her lost baby. Everyone else cried, too. She could cry sitting at Frieda's table on Shabbat as another friend announced a pregnancy or showed off a new baby, a curled up ball swaddled in a cradle.

"Those poor children," she would say. "Growing up without a father."

People just nodded their heads and patted her back. "This is a terrible time for our country." Only one person said, "Who knew our Sarah cared so much about politics?"

A year later, in 1964, when Marcelle was three, Sarah became pregnant for the fifth time. By then, the thought of losing another baby was more than she could bear. After Marcelle, she began to hope again, hope she dared not feel this time. But the first month went into the second and the second into the third, and before she allowed herself to believe that she was being blessed with another child, the doctor announced she had a son. A son who almost killed her with toxemia, a son whose birth had necessitated a partial hysterectomy, but a son all the same. A daughter and a son. A girl and a boy. Marcelle and Charles. Not one miracle, but two.

Egyptian custom dictated that the first son and first daughter in a family be named after their paternal grandparents, the second son and daughter after their maternal grandparents. So she named her children after Eddie's parents, Charles and Marcelle, in Hebrew, Chaim and Mazal—Life and Luck—not the worst names a mother could give her children.

Sarah and Eddie, once united only by the bonds of matrimony, were now united by the bonds of family. Sarah surprised herself by being less formal around her husband. She surprised herself by sometimes being too tired and too busy to be perfectly kempt. Her dinners were more casual and she even began asking Eddie to pick up groceries from the store on the way home. But Eddie never complained. It seemed he loved his disheveled, flustered wife even more than he had loved his perfect and organized wife.

Some days he came home and found his young wife so exhausted he couldn't understand what she said. On those days, he smiled and kissed her forehead and led her to bed the way he would one of his children.

"Sarah, you need to rest. Take a nap, and I'll feed the children."

"Dinner's on the stove," she whispered. She felt him stroking her hair as she drifted away.

On one of those nights, she shocked herself by waking him, long past when the children were asleep. Her body needed this man, needed to love this man, who so actively loved her every moment. Her own desire surprised her but she could not control it, and her husband's ardent responses begged her never to try.

The morning after that first night, after the first time she had released herself upon him, she kept her back to him in the kitchen. She served him breakfast without speaking a word, looking at the floor as he smiled at her. She fussed over Marcelle, feeding her though she was almost four years old and liked to feed herself.

As she stood up to tend to a baby boy who wasn't calling out to her, Eddie said softly, "You know Sarah, Maimonides writes that anything that happens between a man and his wife behind closed doors is holy and sanctioned by God."

Sarah looked at the floor and smiled. "Who am I to argue with him?"

As the years passed, Sarah struggled with what it meant to be an American. Was it to eat white bread instead of pita? Potatoes instead of rice? Roast instead of mechshe? Back in Egypt, the fancy ladies followed the latest fashions from Paris, but what was she to say when Eddie appeared in her living room in a polyester leisure suit, or Charles insisted on growing his sideburns down the side of his face, or Marcelle never styled her hair, instead wearing it long and loose down her back?

She was certainly grateful for this country that had taken her in and given her a new life, but what chaos reigned! Most nights, she caught snippets from the news reports as she stood leaning against the wall that separated the kitchen from the living room area. Eddie watched Walter Cronkite on CBS religiously, as regularly as he went to synagogue on Shabbat.

"Turn the television off," she would say. "Your dinner's getting cold."

"Just a few more minutes," he would reply, watching updates from Vietnam.

Soon Sarah cooked dinner earlier and joined him. Watching a report on so-called "Flower Children," she looked at her own babies, Marcelle then six, Charles two, grateful they were too young to participate in this horrible "free love." Imagine, running away from your parents' home, living on your own before marriage, all together and all having sex. From what would she have to shield her own children when they came of age?

Watching riots in Detroit and Newark, and the assassinations of Martin Luther King, Jr. and Bobby Kennedy, Sarah feared for her children's safety.

"Has this country gone crazy?" she asked Eddie. "Will we have to leave here, too?"

He calmed her. "Sarah, my sweet, the whole world's gone crazy. These young people, these hippies and yippies, they're not so bad. One day, they'll grow up and get jobs."

Sarah looked at her children playing, Marcelle and Charles stacking blocks on top of each other so Charles could knock them over, and hoped they would always be this innocent. The world had gone crazy, the world kept going crazy, yet despite all the insanity, they stayed safe. Somewhere in their pocket of America, they could simply watch the madness, and not have to participate. They could live how they wanted, and not have the chaos forced upon them. They could be two immigrants raising two children, and as long as they worked hard and kept out of trouble, they could protect their babies from the bedlam.

They seemed to have found a way to do it. The Community, the Syrian Jews of New York, seemed able to be both American and traditional. When Eddie, and later Sarah, had arrived, the Community that embraced them was Syrian, but now it included refugees from Egypt and Lebanon. They took care of each other, bringing food when a new baby was born, raising money when someone was sick. Through charities and schools and the sheer will to resist complete assimilation, they formed an enclave where they could maintain both identities, American and Middle-Eastern Jew. They wore the latest fashions, danced in the hottest discothèques, ate in the finest restaurants (even if they didn't order meat). But on Shabbat, they were with their families, they prayed in synagogue, and when it was time to marry, it was from one of their own.

When they lived in Bensonhurst, many were friends with their Italian neighbors; they found they had much in common. But as the Community grew, it became more insular, moving to the Midwood area of Brooklyn, spreading out around Ocean Parkway. By the time Eddie and Sarah could afford to buy a house, it was 1973, and they purchased a modest, semi-attached three bedroom on East Eighth Street just off Avenue S. She knew ten of the families who lived on her block; two she knew from as far back as Cairo. It cost them every penny of the $12,000 they had managed to save, but Sarah loved it.

She had a husband, two children and a house. It felt like everything was going right. She was sure God had long forgiven her, sure her crimes had not been as severe as she imagined. Sure her father, who could not have possibly survived more than a year or two in Abu Zabaal prison, was reunited with her mother, smiling down on her from heaven.

Until the day the phone call came.

And then she wasn't sure of anything.

Chapter Two

Be a lady: the sum total of her mother's instructions. The sum total of all conversations had by mothers in the Community with their daughters. The throwback to Arab culture, the importance placed on a woman's outward representation of her family by her behavior. Be a lady. Uphold the family honor.

Young women like Marcelle knew there were many rules under this code of conduct; they were constantly reminded by their mothers. Especially during times like these, when she was sixteen and in a summer house on Bradley Beach, New Jersey, for the express purpose of finding a husband.

Though her parents had been talking about renting a beach house for as long as she could remember ("Like when we went to Alexandria," her father would say. "Or those wonderful weekends in Port Said," her mother would reply), it was not lost on Marcelle that the first summer they actually rented the house was the first summer she was officially allowed to date.

Not that she minded, though. Brooklyn was dead on the weekends. Everyone in the Community (said by all with a capital "C," as though it were the only community in the world) went to Bradley. Those whose families didn't rent houses, like her best friend Ruby, tried to find someone to stay with on weekends. Marcelle had the attic room, large with low ceilings, and for the first half of the summer Ruby came up every Friday afternoon.

Ruby and Marcelle had known each other since third grade, since Marcelle knocked a jar of paint onto Ruby's lap, resulting in an eruption of ashamed tears from an eight-year-old Marcelle.

"Don't worry," Ruby had said. "I don't even like this dress. My mommy thinks it's pretty, but I hate it because it has no pink."

From that day on, the two girls were inseparable. They slept in each other's houses, grew up with each other's families, shared clothes and frustrations and any bits of information they could find about the real life their mothers spent so much time hiding from them.

One hot Friday afternoon, Marcelle and Ruby decided to play a game: to write down the rules, to see how many they could find. The list seemed endless, and yet many fell into the same categories.

This was what they came up with:

1. Always look beautiful. Don't go outside without full make-up, perfect clothing and styled hair. In fact, forget the part about not going outside. As soon as you wake up, and before you go downstairs to serve your husband and children breakfast, make yourself look perfect.

2. Be shaatra, an excellent homemaker. Your food must be delicious and your home must be immaculate at all times. Always expect that someone will drop in, so make sure nothing is ever messy, you always have pastries and cookies in the freezer that you can take out at a moment's notice, and that you look perfect even though you weren't planning on leaving the house (see rule #1).

3. Family comes first, and community comes second. These are your priorities. Don't let anything get in the way of them. Don't embarrass your family, especially not in the eyes of your community.

4. Don't be rude to anyone, even if they deserve it. Be the better person (especially if the person being rude is a man).

5. Don't tell anyone your private business. Nobody needs to know.

6. And, most importantly: Stay a virgin until marriage. No man wants a woman who's been with another man.

"Of course, it's fine if the guy's been with another woman," Marcelle said with a scowl.

"Well, someone should know what they're doing, no?" Ruby replied.

Marcelle lay on her bed and Ruby was sprawled out on a makeshift mattress on the floor. They had tried sharing the bed, but Marcelle inevitably hit Ruby in the face during the night.

Between the two girls, the brown shag carpet was covered in clothing, jeans, tops and mismatched pairs of shoes, from which they assembled the perfect outfits on the nights they went out. Lipsticks and eyeliners, blushes and eye shadows fought for space on every surface of the dark wood furniture with hairsprays and brushes and curlers and hair dryers. Sarah yelled every time she walked into the room. The girls would clean up, and then recreate the mess the following night, as they went to yet another party or out on another date.

It was hot; both windows were open and two fans blew air around the room. On a record player in the corner, Donna Summer sang about the fate of "Bad Girls."

"What would we do if there were no rules?" Marcelle asked. "Who would we be?"

"What is the opposite of a lady?" Ruby asked.

"A slut?" Marcelle replied. "A pothead?"

"A slob," Ruby said. "A selfish slob who never has to worry that 'it doesn't look nice,' or 'what will people think'."

"We could be disco queens," Marcelle said.

Ruby picked a red sequined halter top off the floor. "Looks like you already have a little disco queen in you."

"You know what I mean."

"I know. We could party at Studio 54. Do some," and here she began to sing, "White lines, through my head. Get higher baby." Marcelle laughed. Ruby continued, "or some 'Lucy in the Sky with Diamonds.' Psychedelic groove," she said, fluttering her fingers in front of her face. "I know some people who do that."

"All guys, right?" Marcelle said. Ruby nodded.

"I would backpack through Europe," Marcelle said.

"Oh! Like in _The Drifters_," Ruby said. "I want to come!"

"Okay, in my next lifetime when that's actually possible, I promise to take you with me."

"Maybe we'll go with our husbands one day," Ruby said. "Anyway, I hope so, cause our mothers don't care what American girls do. No way they'd let us go."

"But we are American girls!" Marcelle said.

"You know what I mean," Ruby said. "That's just our way. And really, do you want to change it? Do you want to be like the girl in

Saturday Night Fever? Having sex in his car with all his friends watching? And when they're done, he asks what her name is?"

"Of course not," Marcelle said, shrugging.

Ruby was probably right. Marcelle would rather live in the security of the Community than be out and alone in the world, though how nice would it be to be anonymous? To walk down the street and know no one was watching you because no one knew who you were? To not have so many rules in place, such a strict code, so many expectations? To not always wonder what others think, to leave life to chance, to be open to possibilities, to be completely free. Yet that freedom was also the absence of security, the absence of the family and friends she had known her whole life, who would always care for her, even as they judged her.

Sometimes she watched television programs about young teen girls who had no one to care for them, and the terrible things that happened. How they were abused by men, how they were raped, or beaten. Or about people who had suffered tragedies, losses and became homeless. Marcelle knew that could never happen to her. Because even now, if her family lost everything, if her house burned down, there were so many people who loved them who would take care of them. Someone in the Community would find her father a job. Someone would put them up until they could have a place to live. Some volunteers would deliver food baskets to them, as she had done, many times, for other Community families less fortunate.

She would never be old and dying alone. Her children would live close by and come to see her. If she never had children (God forbid), her nieces and nephews would come, and even if she had absolutely no one, which she could hardly imagine, Community organizations arranged hospital visits to the sick and lonely. She would never be alone, she would never be neglected, as long as she followed the rules. For a sixteen-year-old Marcelle, following the rules seemed a small price to pay for that kind of security. Still, there was a price.

"I'm thirsty," Ruby said, breaking Marcelle's chain of thought.

Marcelle and Ruby wandered downstairs in search of iced tea when they heard shouting from the living room.

"I'm telling you, the Shah is gone. He won't last another year," Eddie said.

"Not a chance," said another voice. "The Americans will never allow it."

"That's what we said about the British and King Farouk. And look what happened there," Eddie continued.

"It's not the same thing at all," the other voice continued.

"Ach, you young people. You never learn from history. You never know a thing."

Before Marcelle got to the living room, she recognized the voice of Nathan Hazan, her cousin Gabriel's best friend. Nathan was of average height and build, olive skinned and brown-eyed. He had shaggy dark hair and wore a wide-collared polyester shirt with a yellow and orange print over bell-bottomed jeans. Somehow, with a little help from Gabriel and his wife Jeannie, Auntie Rosette had convinced him to join them in the house for weekends. He was twenty-six and unmarried and Auntie Rosette decided he needed to join the social scene, the other young Syrians and Egyptians hanging out on the beach, making plans for Saturday night.

Renting a house for the summer was beyond Marcelle's parents' means, so they split it with Auntie Rosette and Uncle Elie. The house had four bedrooms. Her parents slept in one, and Rosette and Elie, another. Gabriel, Jeannie, and their baby Elliot were in the third, and Rosette and Elie's remaining single children crowded into the fourth room. Marcelle had the attic, which suited her just fine, and Charles slept on the daybed in the den. When Nathan came, he shared the den with Charles, sleeping on the mattress that pulled out from under the daybed.

 Marcelle always wondered if Auntie Rosette's plan was to make a *buzrah*, a match, between the two of them. Marcelle had known Nathan for years, but had never exchanged more than a few words with him. She found him stuffy and pretentious, always talking about books and arguing politics with her father. Frankly, she resented him, taking her place by her father's side as they watched the news at night.

Back in Brooklyn, Marcelle would come home from school and help her mother prepare for dinner until the news came on. Then Eddie would call her from the living room, "Marcelle, it's starting," and they would watch together.

Previously, when Eddie had gone on his rants, Marcelle had just listened, absorbing and filing away. But this Nathan character came and challenged him. How dare he question her father?

When Eddie extolled the virtue of thrift, telling Marcelle to save instead of spending on frivolous things, Nathan countered, "Why? With the rate of inflation, your money's worth less tomorrow than it is today. Better buy it on credit and lock in a price before it goes up."

Eddie shook his head. "Don't listen to him," he said to Marcelle, laughing.

One night, when Nathan wasn't around, Eddie turned to Marcelle after the broadcast and said, "Always pay attention to what's going on in the world."

Usually she would have just nodded, but that day she thought for a moment and asked, "Why?"

Eddie's voice softened. "Because we are Jews, *ya binti*. Sooner or later, they stop wanting us. You have to recognize the signs so you can leave on your own terms."

"We'll never get kicked out of America," she said. She couldn't fathom it.

"Never in my wildest dreams did I think I'd leave Egypt," he replied.

From Yom Kippur of 1973 on, from the day eight Arab countries attacked Israel on her holiest day, Eddie insisted that his daughter learn about the world. Marcelle was eleven then. Charles was only seven, and Sarah tried to shield him. "There will be plenty of time for him to know what the world is like," she said over Eddie's protests. "He can live in the land of innocence a little longer."

But even Charles knew. They had cousins in Israel, several of whom were old enough to be in the IDF. One of Sarah's brothers in New York tried to talk to one in Israel each day, reporting to the family. All of

Eddie's siblings were in New York, but several of his cousins were in Jerusalem and two of his oldest friends lived in Haifa, and he anxiously awaited news from them.

In 1967, Eddie had been sure he made the right decision, choosing America over Israel, but once again, this decision was confirmed. He felt guilty for choosing his safety and the safety of his children, so he donated whatever he could to Israeli charities, especially during times of crisis. He knew that wasn't enough, but short of sending his children to the Army, nothing would be. So he watched. And he waited.

That summer in Bradley, Eddie was particularly obsessed, watching the demonstrations in Iran. Every day there were reports of protests and riots and strikes. The people were angry. Something was going to happen. Even on Shabbat, they waited for Cronkite to finish his broadcast before Eddie began Kiddush.

And then there were reports of the Jews. As in Egypt, many of the poor Jews left Iran after Israel was created. Anti-Zionist sentiments led to riots in the streets, and the 70,000 poor Iranians who left felt they may as well be poor in a country that wanted them. But the upper and middle classes stayed. They felt protected by the Shah, in the same way Sarah's family had felt protected by King Farouk. But when reports of wealthy Jews leaving in droves reached Eddie, no one could convince him that the Shah's days weren't numbered.

"Always watch the Jews!" he said. "How a country treats its Jews, that's how they'll be treating everyone else in a few years. When they invite the Jews in, that's someplace you want to go. It will prosper. But when they kick the Jews out, the fanatics are on their way. Look at Spain in the Middle Ages, and look at Egypt and Iran now. Our whole way of life is gone. The Jews of the Middle East in the Middle East? It's over. Communities thousands of years old are finished! The only Middle Eastern Jews now are in Israel, where they're a minority and the Ashkenazim are in charge. Ach. The irony."

"No matter where we are, we're the minority," Nathan said.

68

"And what about me?" Marcelle asked. "I'm an Arab Jewish woman. A minority within a minority within a minority."

"Women aren't a minority," Nathan said.

"Not technically," Marcelle countered, "but we're treated like one, so we may as well be."

"You allow this kind of talk in your house?" Nathan said to Eddie.

Eddie beamed. "What can I say? My daughter is interested in the world."

Nathan muttered something under his breath about the damned feminists, but his smile belied his anger.

Another night, Eddie talked about saving for the future. He told the story of how he built his business, how he climbed out of near poverty after arriving in America, and urged Marcelle to share those values.

"But by what you just said, it would be wiser not to do that, after all. You're just waiting for them to kick us out and take all our stuff anyway," Marcelle said.

Nathan practically hooted.

One might have expected Eddie to be angry, but if Eddie loved anything, it was a good debate. "Close, but no cigar," Eddie replied. "I said you have to watch in case they come to take everything. If you can leave before it happens, on your own terms, sometimes you can take what little you have with you." Then they would break out the backgammon board, and the screaming would get even louder.

In the beginning of the summer, nights began with a trip to the kitchen, where her mother and aunt played cards. They sat by the big bay windows at a white table with wicker chairs. The green vine pattern on the wallpaper border matched the chair cushions. There her mother would approve of her outfit, but beg her to put on some more makeup. Then Sarah would send her and Ruby off to the beach saying, "Go meet a nice boy from a nice family."

"A nice Egyptian boy," Auntie Rosette would say, winking.

As though on cue, her mother would snap, "Syrian is fine, too. Her grandfather was from Aleppo."

"Yes, but Egyptian is still better."

Auntie Rosette would try not to laugh as she watched Sarah's face morph into anger, lips and nose scrunched together, eyes narrowed, glance piercing as a laser, as though it could cut right into her. A look that terrified Marcelle. But Auntie Rosette just laughed.

"You shouldn't make that face, Sarah. It makes you look very ugly."

Then would yell at each other in French, which Marcelle didn't understand, probably screaming obscenities, until Sarah collapsed into laughter.

Marcelle remembered Nathan walking in during one of those exchanges.

"They do this all the time," she told him. "Apparently, it's fun for them."

He found it amusing, too, part of why they loved him so much.

Since they were all going to the same beach and the same parties, and neither of the girls had a car, Nathan drove them. Inside his Cadillac, they argued over what to play. Ruby had a KC & The Sunshine Band 8-track, but Nathan said they would hear enough of that once they got to the party and insisted on _Led Zeppelin IV_. True to Nathan's predictions, Marcelle could hear the disco music blaring as soon as they arrived. She would grab Nathan's hand, trying to coerce him onto the dance floor. But Nathan was always careful to distance himself from Marcelle and Ruby so boys didn't think he was dating either girl. He introduced them to his friends as Gabe's cousin and her friend. He actually encouraged other boys to flirt with her. She quickly realized she hated it.

Much more than the parties, she enjoyed driving back and forth, especially when Ruby got a ride home from some guy she had been talking to and Marcelle had Nathan all to herself. Then he would tell her about school. He had gone to college, and gotten a law degree, from Columbia University of all places. It was rare in their world. She was so impressed by him. She wanted to learn everything he knew, and she wanted him to teach her. She wanted his complete attention, and realized she would have to try harder to get it.

Her outfits became showier. Sarah always complained that Marcelle didn't spend enough time on her looks. Like many girls her age, she wore her curly brown hair long and loose. But that summer, despite the ubiquitous sea-air inducing frizz, Marcelle took pains to straighten her hair. She pinned it in a wrap around her head; she cut layers and tried to blow it out, imitating Farrah Fawcett; Sarah even walked in on her one day kneeling beside the ironing board as Ruby ran the iron over sections of her hair.

Where Marcelle had been content to wear her bell-bottom jeans and a t-shirt, she now wore dresses, high-waisted halters that highlighted her slim hips, strapless dresses with ruffles to accentuate her smallish breasts, a strapless, one-piece, belted jumpsuit that showed off how slender she was, while highlighting curves she didn't really have.

She wore more make-up, ran kohl around her eyes, used mascara, wore lipstick in neutral colors rather than just Vaseline to make her lips shiny.

Sarah noticed and was pleased. "What's this change I see in you? Why do you care all of sudden? Who did you meet?"

Sarah knew it was Nathan, though, because Marcelle wore these outfits around the house on weekends, in particular a strapless terry cloth number that Eddie almost outlawed. (I'll tell her she has to wear a bathing suit under it, Sarah counter-argued.)

While Marcelle fell for Nathan, Ruby met Jimmy, the man she would soon marry. Jimmy stayed in Brooklyn for the weekends, so Ruby stopped coming to the shore. To entertain Marcelle in Ruby's absence, Nathan brought her his books from college, from the Core Curriculum, and introduced her to Plato and Homer and Aristotle and Virgil. He courted her through books, with ideas.

She was his eager student, reading each book during the week while he worked in New York, ready to discuss it by the weekend. She read his underlined passage two and three times, trying to understand why he underlined them. She read the notes in his small, careful handwriting in the margins many times over, wondering if he remembered what he wrote, and if those were his own ideas or the main ideas of his professor's lecture. Through his books, he opened up worlds for her. Other boys made her feel pretty, but he made her feel smart. He let her know that education wasn't a foolish pursuit for a woman, but could actually make her more interesting to a man, and more interesting to herself.

They came home earlier from parties, left later for the beach. Instead of meeting people, they sat on the veranda in white wicker chairs, drinking iced mint tea, talking philosophy and listening to the waves roll in.

Marcelle remembered the night he asked her the question that would haunt her for years.

She hadn't felt like going out. Too many parties; too many of the same people. Why should she keep meeting boys who kept asking her out, whom she kept turning down, because she wanted to be with Nathan?

Nathan stayed home, too. He said he was tired of the parties as well. Loser, she thought, this is his cowardly way of spending time with me without owning up to it and calling it a date. But Marcelle wanted to be with him and beggars couldn't be choosers.

It was one of the nicest nights of her life, warm and humid with a delicious breeze off the ocean, sitting on those same wicker chairs, the porch illuminated by short candles in tall glasses, and she thought this might be the most romantic thing she had ever experienced.

They were quiet for a while: all of a sudden they had run out of things to say.

And then he asked her, "Marcelle, who are you?"

She didn't even know what he was asking her. "What do you mean, who am I? What kind of question is that?"

"I mean, you. Separate from all your relationships. Not your father's daughter or your brother's sister or a member of the community. Just you. Who are you?"

"I don't think you can separate them. Those things shape me."

"But you also shape yourself. Who do you want to be?"

She had no answer.

Never one to be patient or subtle, Auntie Rosette pressed Nathan one morning over breakfast. Marcelle was late coming down, and Rosette must have thought she was still sleeping. Hiding in the hallway, Marcelle overheard their conversation.

"Nathan," she said, with the voice of a woman who has been bursting for weeks to say what she is about to say, "I don't understand you. You spend all day on the porch talking to Marcelle, but you don't ask her out. What's wrong with you? She's a good girl. Pretty and sweet and smart enough for a boy like you. She'd make an excellent wife. You're getting old, you know. Twenty-six and still single. Gabriel has a baby already. What are you waiting for?"

"You're right," he said. "She's a great girl. I like her a lot, but she's so young. She's never dated anyone before. And I'm ten years older than her. I think I need to give her time to see what's out there."

"But you're playing with her head, spending all that time with her."

"I'm sorry if it looks like that. We like spending time together, but I really think it would be better for her if she went on a few dates before she gets serious with anyone."

"But what if she gets serious with someone else before then?"

"Then she isn't meant for me."

Auntie Rosette scowled and huffed.

He laughed, "Okay, then you'll tell me and I'll break it up and make her mine."

Marcelle wanted to run in the kitchen, screaming to him to make her his immediately, but Auntie Rosette would have killed her.

Marcelle waited, still refusing to date until another night when she suggested that she and Nathan take a stroll along the beach. As they walked, she brushed her fingers against his until finally he took her hand. And when they stopped walking to turn back in the direction of the house, she inched closer and closer to him until finally, he kissed her.

"I've been waiting for that all summer," he said.

She giggled. "So has everyone else in the house."

After that night, they were officially a couple. Everyone in the house was happy about it, especially Eddie. Finally, Eddie found a match for his ability in backgammon.

"Your Uncle Elie isn't a very good player," her father had once confided in her. "I have to let him win every so often just so he'll keep playing me. But Nathan, he's a good player. A very good player." He smiled and took her arm. "A very good boy, that Nathan," he said. She blushed.

When they returned to their house in Brooklyn, the political discussions continued as did the heated backgammon games. Nathan was a regular on Shabbat.

"Doesn't your mother miss you?" Sarah asked him one night.

He smiled. "She knows it's for a good cause," he said.

Nathan rushed over on the night the Camp David Accords were signed, joining Eddie, Sarah and Marcelle, as they all watched the news, the parents smoking their narghile, Eddie drinking arak, watching as Begin, Sadat and Carter shook hands, announcing peace between Israel in Egypt.

"Never in my life did I think I'd see this moment," Sarah said.

"Does that mean you'll get to go back?" Marcelle asked.

"Would I even want to?" Eddie asked. "Will they give me back my house? Will they give me my father's business?"

"Still," Marcelle continued, "to see the place you grew up. Where you spent your childhood?"

"That place doesn't exist anymore," Eddie said.

"I'd go," said Sarah, her voice a whisper. "I'd go pray by my mother's grave. I'd go find my father's bones and bury them."

Eddie hugged Sarah and kissed her on the forehead. "This is why a man needs a wife. They have a wisdom we do not."

Nathan looked at Marcelle and smiled. She smiled back.

Who am I? she thought. What a stupid question. You know exactly who I am.

Chapter Three

The day before the phone call came, Sarah went about her life as usual, playing mahjong with her friends, planning a fundraiser for the community.

"We will make a cookbook," Sarah announced, proud of herself.

"I'm not making no cookbook," said Frieda.

"Why not? It's the perfect idea. Especially for young married girls," said Esther.

"Those are my mother's recipes, and I learned them the hard way, and I'm not giving nobody those recipes," Frieda replied, adjusting the sleeve on her peasant blouse.

"Not even to raise money for the school, Frieda? The school where you sent all four of your sons?" Sarah asked quietly, raising her eyebrow.

Frieda looked at the faces of the other women in the room. Sarah noticed that Frieda avoided her eyes. Rosette and Esther were quiet.

Sarah continued, "It could be a wonderful project. It could be on every *swanee* table. We would help young brides feed their husbands, and raise money at the same time. We would make sure that even though we no longer live in Egypt and in Syria, our community will still eat our foods. But Frieda," Sarah said, looking her squarely in the eye, "if you refuse to do this, we have to respect you. But now it's on you to come up with a better idea."

Sarah knew none of the other women had a better idea, and if one of them did, it would certainly not be Frieda.

"But they're my recipes. They're my mother's recipes. I don't want everyone else to know exactly how I make it. Then they won't be mine anymore."

Rosette laughed. "Frieda, don't be ridiculous. I plan to leave out an instruction or two in my recipes. Everyone we gather them from will, too."

"Rosette!" Sarah exclaimed, "I didn't expect that from you!"

"Why not? Our mothers' mothers didn't hand them little books with neat instructions, and our mothers certainly didn't hand them to us," Rosette continued.

"That's right," said Frieda. "These girls can figure out a few things for themselves. We don't have to give everything away."

"But this book is not about these girls, like you keep calling them. It's for the school. It's for our sons, who study at the school. If the recipes are bad, no one will buy it."

"No one said anything about bad recipes," said Esther.

"That's right," said Frieda. "They can be good recipes, just not our perfect secret recipes."

Rosette laughed. "Please, my daughter-in-law is lucky if she gets those. Anyway, Sarah, don't you always say learning from mistakes builds character? Look what we are doing, robbing these girls of character-building experiences."

It was Frieda's turn to host and the women were in her living room. They sat around the square card table she had purchased ten years earlier when they began to have their weekly game. With their children in school all day, they found themselves with more time on their hands and, instead of spending every one of their meetings cooking, decided to do something only for themselves.

"So I have news," said Frieda, beaming.

"Your daughter's pregnant?" asked Rosette.

"No. My daughter-in-law. She's just entered her fourth month. She's due in early August."

The ladies kissed their friend and wished her *mabrouk*. Frieda's oldest daughter Linda already had three small children, but this would be the first for her son Danny and his wife, Fortune.

"I love being a grandmother," said Esther. "So much more than I love being a mother. So much less work." Esther had five children and now five grandchildren from her two married daughters.

"I know," said Frieda, "at least you can give them back when they bother you."

"They never bother me," said Rosette.

"Exactly. Because you can give them back," said Frieda.

Rosette and Esther laughed. Sarah said, "I guess I'll find out soon enough."

At thirty-eight, Sarah was the youngest of the group. Esther was the oldest at forty-six, and Rosette and Frieda were both forty-five.

"Your kids are still so young."

"Charles is only fifteen, so we have plenty of time for him, but Marcelle, she's almost eighteen, and she's been dating Nathan for eight months now."

"So she's almost ready. I was sixteen when I met Joey, and we got married when I was seventeen," said Esther. "How old were you when you got married?"

"Almost seventeen."

"So, it's almost time, no?" Esther continued

"I don't know. Maybe all the girls, they get married too young," Sarah said.

Frieda looked appalled. "What else are they going to do?'

"Maybe Marcelle should study a little while before she gets married."

"You want her to finish high school? I guess I understand that," said Rosette.

"And what if she wants to go to college?" asked Sarah.

"Why would she want to go to college?" asked Frieda.

"I don't know. So she has something for herself."

"Sarah, are you turning into one of those, what are they called, those feminists?" Frieda continued.

Rosette giggled as she discarded a tile. "Of course! Just last week she burned her bra."

Sarah gave her a dirty look. "What kind of question is that? I only want what's best for my daughter."

"What, to go to college, so she can meet people who aren't in the community?" Frieda fumed.

"A lot of people in the community are sending their children, their girls also, to Brooklyn College. I don't see what would be so bad about it. We always talk about doing things for ourselves, and having things for ourselves. Maybe we should give those things to our daughters, too," Sarah said.

"Sarah has a point," Esther said. "Look how much more we have than our mothers had. Some of our grandmothers couldn't even read. Maybe it's better if our daughters have even a little more than we had. College, hah. I think I was in high school for two years, maybe."

"You'll see what happens, you send them out into the world, and they're exposed to things. No," Frieda shook her head. "Better to keep them close."

"Yeah, but I know what it really is," Rosette said, her hand on Sarah's arm. "She's your only daughter and you waited a long time for her. You don't want to see her go so soon."

Later that night, Sarah's mind filled with memories as she prepared the halawa: three cups of sugar, two cups of water and two teaspoons of fresh lemon juice, their Egyptian maid Fatima's recipe for the solution to unwanted hair. In the weeks before they left, Sarah's brothers scrambled around Cairo making arrangements, leaving Sarah alone with Fatima. So that Sarah would never forget her Egyptian ways, would never forget her, Fatima watched Sarah ruin batch after batch until she learned to make it herself, as Fatima shed farewell tears for the family that had so long employed her.

When Sarah was a girl, she would sit in the kitchen while Fatima waxed her mother's legs. Sarah remembered her mother one afternoon, after Fatima had finished, dressed in a pale blue suit and heels, off to the charity luncheon on behalf of the flood of Jewish immigrants from the war in Europe, a luncheon she had planned and a charity she co-chaired.

"Always give back to your community," her mother said, staring in the mirror. "If God gives you more than He gives others, it's your responsibility to share," she said, rouging her cheeks and powdering her nose.

As a young girl, Sarah didn't pay as much attention to her mother's words as she did to her hair, dark brown and glossy, pulled back into a chignon, her dark brown eyes lined with kohl, her fair skin, her sophisticated clothing. Was there a more glamorous woman in the world than her mother, dressed-up and ready to do important things?

"Can I come with you, Mama?"

"When you turn sixteen, you'll work with me. Like all the women in my family. But now you're too young." Terra smoothed her hair and straightened her hat.

On the way out, she kissed her young daughter, and said what she always did when they parted. "Be good, cheri."

Be good, Sarah thought, pouring the halawa into the sink, letting it cool, and going to get Marcelle. The instructions my mother gave me. Have I followed them correctly? What will I give to my daughter?

Upstairs that daughter was reading a copy of *Fear of Flying* that she found at the used bookstore on Kings Highway and rethinking the marriage that had begun to seem inevitable. As Isidora Wing had her first "zipless fuck," Marcelle wondered if she would ever want something like herself. What if Nathan wasn't any good in bed? She wouldn't know until the wedding. What if he was fine in bed, but she wasn't satisfied being married to him? What if she just wasn't satisfied with marriage?

There were many great things about Nathan, like how well he fit into her family, and how much her father loved him. But there were not great things about him as well.

Like, he didn't like to dance at all. When Marcelle heard disco music she couldn't help but move her body. She felt sexy and alive, just like ABBA's "Dancing Queen" (after all, she was only seventeen), and she was really good at it. But Nathan hated to dance. He took her to nightclubs where they sat motionless at a table, watching others shake their groove thangs on the dance floor.

"I feel like a fool," he said, when she begged him to try.

"Well, I feel like a fool just watching these other people have fun."

"Fine," he said, "let's go someplace else."

What kind of life would she live with someone who never danced? Would she spend a lifetime of weddings and bar mitzvahs staring longingly at the dance floor as her old, stick-in-the mud husband decided to leave just as the real party started?

On the plus side was their shared love of books, and the way they talked about ideas.

Then again, the last time they were at the used bookstore together, and she picked up copies of *The Feminine Mystique* and *Fear of Flying,* he sniggered.

"Why would you want to read that nonsense?" he asked, instead handing her a copy of a book by John Updike about a man who leaves his wife for another woman who gives him a blow-job. Why would he want her to read about men feeling trapped, but not women? Two days after they shopped together, she returned to the store alone with the Updike book (which, despite herself, she enjoyed), buying the ones she had wanted in the first place.

He asked her who she was, expected an interesting answer, but she couldn't be sure he was interested in the full answer, or only the answer he wanted to hear.

Marcelle was reading more of Isadora's adventures in a sexual landscape she would never experience while sitting on the floor of her room. She heard her mother come upstairs and quickly shoved her copy of *Fear of Flying* under an issue of Ms., which then went under her bed. She grabbed another magazine, this time an old issue of Glamour, and opened it.

"Marci," Sarah said, poking her head into her daughter's room. "It's time to do your legs, no? It's been a month?"

Marcelle looked up from the magazine she was pretending to read and raised the bell-bottom of her jeans. "Yeah, I guess, so."

"The halawa is ready. Come. You want to listen to music?"

"We always do. Layla Murad?"

"No, you can bring your Bee Gees if you want."

Marcelle raised her eyebrows. Sarah hated the Bee Gees. "How about the Carpenters?" she asked. "You halfway like them."

Marcelle put the record on, while Sarah readied the kitchen, clearing her cutting boards and utensils from the kitchen table and covering the wooden surface. She hung sheets over the doorways into the kitchen, and taped newspaper over the cutout in the wall that was a window into the dining room. The ladies needed their privacy. When she was finished, Marcelle climbed on top of the table and Sarah began stretching the halawa onto the skin of Marcelle's calf, rubbing it vigorously and then pulling it off, repeating the motion two or three times over every part of skin until there was no hair left on her daughter's leg.

"Mom, I'm getting old enough to do this myself," Marcelle said.

"When you get married...." Sarah answered, guessing Marcelle felt odd about being in her underwear in the middle of the kitchen at her age.

"Sometimes it seems like that's the answer to everything with you. When I get married, I can smoke, when I get married, I can wear whatever I want, when I get married I can do my own legs. What if I never get married?"

"Why would you say that to me?" Sarah clucked her tongue and shook her head.

"Forget it." She rolled her eyes and looked down. "Here, you missed a spot."

"Roll over, honey, onto your stomach." Marcelle complied.

"Ma, I have to tell you something," she said, chin resting on forearms crossed in front of her.

"Go ahead."

"I think it might be getting serious with Nathan." Marcelle turned to see her mother's reaction.

"You've been dating eight months. That's a long time," Sarah said. "I only dated your father for four months before we got married."

"Yeah, but there are things I'm still not sure about."

"No one's ever completely sure," Sarah said. "And no one's perfect, Marci, remember that. Not him, not you. Everyone has things about them we don't like, but you have to ask yourself, are these things a big deal or not. And if they're not a big deal, you learn to live with them."

Marcelle nodded. "But what if I decide I can live with them, and then later I can't."

"Like what, Marci? What are we talking about here?"

Sarah continued her waxing.

"Nothing," Marcelle said. "I guess it's stupid."

"*Haram* that you never got to know my parents. You could see from them, two people who could not have been more different, but they were so in love with each other. Nathan is a good boy. He'll be a good father and a good husband. He'll always take care of you. Try to focus on the important things."

"But what if it doesn't work out?" Marcelle asked. "What will I do if it doesn't work out?"

"I don't know, Marci, I guess we'll figure that out if it happens. But he's a good boy, Marci. A very good boy. And it's a beautiful thing, to build a life of your own."

Marcelle turned onto her side.

"Have you been talking about marriage yet?" Sarah continued.

"Yes and no. It's come up. Like we're both going in that direction, but it hasn't been decided yet."

"So you're not in any rush."

"No. He hasn't proposed yet."

"Well, he better not. Not till he sits down and has a talk with your father. But until then, you can think about what you want to do. Finish high school. Go to college if you want. Even start before you get married. Who knows, maybe you won't even like it. But if you do, there's no reason you can't go to college and be married."

"Nobody does that," Marcelle said.

"Since when do you care what everybody else does? If that's what you want, do it. That's for you to decide. And if you decide to marry Nathan, that's for you and Nathan to decide together. But I told you, I think it's good for you to go to college. So you can have something to fall back on. Just in case."

"In case what?"

"Oh, sweetheart, we never know what kinds of crazy things are going to happen in this world," Sarah said, finishing up.

Marcelle sat up and looked at her mother, smiling, grateful. "And I'll always have my family. Right, Mom? That's what you always say. Married or not married, I'll always have my family."

Sarah smiled and kissed Marcelle on her head. "That's right," she said.

But sometimes things can happen to your family.

They can die or leave or disappear, never to be heard from again.

Until, one day, they come back.

Chapter Four

Sarah's hands shook as she replaced the phone on the cradle. He was alive.

After all these years—how many years had it been? She was sixteen when she saw him last, and now, twenty-three years later, when they had long given up hope, they learned he was alive.

Moise was the one who found out, but Elie was the one who called her. Called her just now, on a regular Tuesday morning to tell her that their father was still alive, that he was being released from prison in Egypt, that he would fly to Israel to join her brothers, who would be collecting him from the authorities.

Alive.

They hadn't heard of anyone lasting that long in those prisons. He had been held at Abu Zabaal. On the ridiculous charge of being a Zionist, of all things. Her father, who had loved Egypt as his homeland, more than the land of his birth, who had refused to leave even as it became obvious that they had to. Taken out of his house in handcuffs and imprisoned for being a Jew.

Standing motionless in her kitchen, Sarah thought she should feel something. Anything. She waited for a surge of emotion but none came, so she did what she did best—kept busy. Elie and Zaki and Jacques were on their way: she must prepare breakfast. Turn the oven on. Take the sambousak out of the freezer to bake. Pour the juice. Put on the coffee. Slice cheese, cut tomatoes and cucumbers, warm the bread. A busy woman is a good woman. Be good, Sarah, be good.

What if they want tea? And I have kaak in the freezer, too. It's good I'm always so prepared. Prepared for what? How could I prepare for this?

And then her hands continued to shake, enough that she feared the knife she held. She needed to sit. She needed to relax.

But she couldn't relax. They were coming over. He was coming home. What home; which home? Here to New York, or to Israel? Where would he go? With whom would he stay? Stop thinking; start acting; get to work, Sarah; be good.

In her second freezer, in one of the many food-filled Tupperwares in Ziploc bags, were Syrian pastries: Sambousak with cheese, filah with spinach, kaak, graybeh. She would serve them all.

After turning on the stove, she lined baking sheets with parchment paper, her still- shaking hands gently placing pastry after pastry on them. Then the crystal dishes came out of the pantry and vegetables and fruits from the refrigerator. Put on the water for coffee and tea. Start slicing. Stop shaking.

She washed produce, peeled cucumbers, sliced tomatoes, warmed pita bread on an open flame, and arranged everything neatly on crystal, stopped for a moment to admire her work. What's wrong with me that I admire my work? My father's alive. Then she went back to slicing, this time oranges, and cut her finger with the sharp blade. Instinctively putting her finger in her mouth to stop the bleeding, she felt no pain. Nothing compared to this.

Get a band-aid, she told herself, then back to work. Fishing through her record collection she found her favorite, Charles Aznavour. Listening to the record, played so many times that the sound crackled through the speakers, Sarah longed for her childhood in Egypt. For the smell of freshly roasted pistachios in the air, for strolls along the Corniche el-Nile, for the Nile herself, and Arab men in gallabiyahs asking if she wanted a carriage ride. She longed for the sight of her parents embracing, kissing Shabbat Shalom after she and her brothers had listened to her father say Kiddush before the Friday night meal. For the warm weather, for the soft-bright light, for palm trees and terraces with Nile views.

She missed her mother.

Oh Mama, I thought he was with you. All this time I thought he was with you. That was my comfort.

Her mother's narghile was in the kitchen, kept where Sarah could see it, a daily reminder of home. Turning on the stove, she placed a piece of coal on the flame. She filled the clay bowl with apple tobacco, and then removed the red-glowing coal from the flame with tongs, placed it on the tobacco and waited till she heard it burn and saw it smoke, and inhaled the smoke, breathing a sigh of relief, because it smelled like Egypt, and she called out in her heart to her mother.

The doorbell rang.

When Sarah opened the door, she found Elie's green eyes red and swollen with tears. As they embraced, she felt the hard glass of the bottle in his hand against her back.

"What is that?" she asked.

"Arak," he said.

"It's ten o'clock in the morning, are you crazy?"

Elie laughed and sniffed loudly. "And what's that I smell? Tobacco? It's ten o'clock in the morning, are you crazy?"

Kissing his cheek, Sarah led him into the living room.

"Come," she said. "Let me make you a plate. Will you at least eat before you open that?"

"Always feeding everyone. Always thinking about food." His eyes smiled.

She emerged from the kitchen with platters of food. After setting them down on the coffee table, she returned for plates, cutlery, napkins and cups.

"What do you want to drink?" she asked.

"Arak," he said.

Sarah scowled. "I meant, coffee? Tea? Juice?"

"We're celebrating Sarah. Drink with me! If ever there was a time for you drink, it's today!"

"Elie, it's ten o'clock in the morning!"

"And if it was three you would have some? Please. You've never had a drink in your life. I'm your oldest brother and I say we drink. Don't worry what Eddie will think. Your father's coming home after twenty-three years in prison. When your husband gets home, he'll join us!"

"Fine, but first tell me exactly what Moise said."

"No, first finish your glass, then another, a toast to our father's health, and then I'll tell you everything."

86

"Baba would kill us!" Sarah said.

"Well, he's not home yet," Elie replied.

She drained her glass. The sweet licorice burned its way down to her stomach, warming her insides, easing the churning that had begun when Elie called. But it wasn't enough, the fist in her gut kept kneading, so she drank another shot and then another.

"Aayim!" he said, glass lifted. The Arabic word for life.

"Aayim!" she said, clicking her glass on his.

"Now tell me everything," Sarah implored.

Elie complied. In a tiny footnote to the Egyptian-Israeli Peace Treaty, a long-forgotten Jewish prisoner named Saleem Mizrahi was released. Moise was the oldest member of the family in Israel, so Moise was the one they called. Their father was alive. He was weak, but he was well, and the Egyptian authorities had agreed to turn him over to the Israeli government. He would be returned to his family in a week, after a team of the best Israeli doctors examined him. They would provide him with medical care for as long as he required.

Sarah held her hands over her heart. She shook her head in disbelief.

"Why didn't you call me right away?' Sarah asked.

"You can blame your dear friend Rosette," he said, draining yet another glass.

"She's your wife first."

Elie nodded. "My wife said if I came over in the middle of the night I might give you a heart attack. Best to wait until first thing in the morning."

"What about Jacques and Zaki?"

"I had to tell you first."

"You haven't called them at all?"

"I called them before I came. They're on their way, with another bottle of arak. This one will be finished by the time they get here."

Just then the doorbell rang again.

Elie rose to answer it, leaving Sarah to press fingers over the bridge of her nose. She looked around the room as if seeing it for the first time: the dark brown carpeting, the dark green walls, the wine-colored crushed-velvet sofa. It was so unlike her mother's elegant salon. The room and its colors were somber, where her mother's had been airy. The heavy wood furniture was crude and gauche, where her mother had chosen French period pieces, gracefully curving chairs on elegant spindly legs. Her mother had thin, woven Persian rugs, but Sarah had opted for the thick shag carpeting everyone was using at the time. He would hate this room. He would hate this place.

The narghile was on the coffee table; she reached for it, coal still lit, inhaling the apple tobacco, sucking deeply, and drawing it down into her lungs. But this time she drew too deeply, and it sent her into a fit of coughing, the smoke becoming a hand that squeezed her windpipe.

Jacques and Zaki looked shocked as the walked in to find their baby sister gasping on the floor.

Elie waved his hand. "It's my fault," he said, still in Arabic. "I got her drunk. We have a reason to celebrate. Baba is coming home!"

Sarah caught her breath and rose to hug her brothers. She felt Zaki's chest heave while she held him, saw Jacques wipe his eyes with the back of his hands. Only Elie seemed elated, as though he wanted to dance and toss sweets into the street.

"Come sit," she said, gesturing to the coffee table laden with food. Jacques took the cushions off her couch and put them on the floor.

"Do you mind?" he asked before reclining on them. She shook her head.

Zaki copied him. "Syrian style," he said, as he, too, reclined on cushions on the floor. "It only seems appropriate."

Elie poured more arak, and repeated the few details he knew. They toasted their father's health and well-being.

"To our father," said Elie.

"To our parents," said Zaki.

"To our mother," said Jacques, eyeing the narghile. "That's Mama's isn't it? You never let us use this one."

"It's a special occasion," Sarah said. She lifted her glass, "To Mama."

88

"Our Italian mother," said Elie, a wink in his eye.

Zaki rolled his eyes. "Again with this conversation? Elie, you know as well as I do, she never set foot in Italy."

"Zaki, you and your details," said Elie, punching his brother in the arm. "You know she held an Italian passport."

"Well, I held an Italian passport, I grew up speaking French, and now I live in America, and I still consider myself Egyptian," Jacques said.

"Unlike our Sarah, here, who fancies herself American," Elie said, this time jabbing Sarah in the arm.

Sarah smiled halfway and looked away.

"What an unlikely pair, they were, our Mama and Baba," Jacques said.

"He suffered so much when she died. We all did," Zaki said. He looked at his parents' wedding picture, which Sarah kept framed on an end table. He held the photo in his hand, gently running his index finger over the image of his mother's smiling face.

"But he was so strong," Jacques continued. "Remember how he took us to see Oum Kalthoum after our mourning was over? He hated to go to concerts. But she loved it. He celebrated her spirit with us that night, to tell us she would always be with us.

"And then remember what he said after she died? That God had mercy on her, sparing her the sight of Cairo burning. That alone would have killed her."

"But she was Italian, right?" said Zaki. "Dahilak, Elie! She was Egyptian, through and through."

Her brothers were laughing now, in their familiar rituals of teasing, only Sarah couldn't let herself participate. Her father was alive. Her father who had been in prison for most of her life. Her father, whom she had thought dead. Her father. He was alive.

"To our parents," said Elie, refilling their glasses. "Rest in peace to our mother, and to our father, Allah ma'ak!"

Chapter Five

When Marcelle got home from school that day, she was eager to talk. She needed her mother's advice.

The night before, after her mother waxed her legs, Nathan picked her up for a late-night run to Spumoni Gardens, which turned out to be a mistake. While sitting in his car eating Spumoni—that amazing half-ices half-ice cream concoction—she and Nathan had their first real fight.

She was halfway through the *Feminine Mystique* and wondered if Betty Freidan was right. Her mother seemed happy and fulfilled by her life as a housewife. Almost all the women she knew did. But what if it was the secret nobody talked about, and everyone secretly hated their lives? She knew very few women who worked in the Community, and all of them did so because they had to. She wondered what Nathan, college educated Nathan, would think.

"Of course I don't want my wife to work," he practically yelled. "Who's going to raise the children? The maid?" He seemed shocked that she had asked the question.

Marcelle was equally shocked by his answer. "But what if she was really good at something?" she asked. "What if she had something she really loved?"

"As opposed to her children?" he said. "Our children wouldn't be important enough for you?"

"I'm not talking about us," she said. "I'm talking in the abstract."

"What do you mean in the abstract? We've been dating for eight months. When you ask me to think about my future hypothetical wife, who else would I think of but you?"

Marcelle went back to eating her ice cream. She licked the cone, careful not to let the droplets spill down the sides.

"Where is this coming from anyway?" Nathan asked. "Why are you bringing it up? Is there something in particular you want to do?"

"No. I just don't understand how you tell me I should go to college, and you tell me I'm the smartest woman you've ever met, but then you don't want me to do anything with it."

"Marcelle, who said I don't want you to do anything with it? Education has an intrinsic value. Just having an education is important. And anyway, what I want you to do is raise our children. It's the most important job in the world. Certainly more important than the stupid shit I do all day."

Marcelle looked down. Lately, it seemed she couldn't even explain herself to Nathan. He out-argued her every time, making her feel foolish whenever she challenged him. She got so upset, she lost her words.

"Go to work," he said, shaking his head. "A Syrian wife has the best life. She doesn't have to worry about anything. Her husband takes care of everything. I wish I could be a Syrian wife. Work? Please! Why don't you go to work for a few weeks? You'll see how lucky you are, not having to go, every day, for the rest of your life."

Marcelle focused on her ice cream. She tried to eat, but she lost her appetite. Instead she focused on the music. As if on cue, Mick Jagger reminded her, "You Can't Always Get What You Want." She inched away from him in her seat

"Hey," he said, moving closer, stroking her hair. "Are you angry at me? Are you upset? Look, we don't have to decide anything yet. You haven't even finished high school. You're so young! You have so much to learn."

Well what do you expect? And why are you dating a girl ten years younger than you? Can't get a woman your own age? Or do you just like being the older, wiser know-it-all?

"I'm really tired," she said. "And I still have some reading to do for school tomorrow. Can you please take me home?"

"Marci, we don't have to know all the answers yet," he said, his hand caressing her thigh.

Her leg stiffened. "Please, just please take me home."

She hadn't slept well that night, hadn't been able to concentrate all day in school. When Ruby asked what was wrong, she was barely able to verbalize it. She wanted to talk to her mother. Was this one of the things she could live with, one of the things they could work through, or something she shouldn't ignore?

"Mom," she called, opening the door, throwing her jacket and backpack on the table. "Mom, are you home?"

The house reeked of tobacco, not just from the narghile, but from cigarettes, too. Had her uncles been over? A horrible scratching noise filled the room, and she walked over to the record player, where the needle circled the inner core of the record. As she turned it off, she noticed her mother sleeping on the couch. The smell of arak overpowered her as she leaned in to check if her mother was all right.

Marcelle had trouble processing what her senses told her to be true. Here was her mother, passed out drunk, in the middle of the day. It was like entering some awful made-for-TV movie.

"Mom?" she asked, sitting beside her, gently shaking her, "Mom, are you okay?"

Sarah rubbed her eyes and yawned. Then she patted herself down—head, face, chest—as though making sure all her parts were still there.

"Marci," she said. "Oh, Marcelle. I love you so much, I love you so so much." And here she began to weep. Sarah burrowed her head in Marcelle's lap and held her daughter, crying. "I love you so much, my baby." Her body heaved with sobs.

"I love you, too," Marcelle replied. She had no idea what to do.

"Are you okay?" she asked, and immediately chided herself. Of course she wasn't okay. "What's wrong Mom? How can I help you?"

Sarah just kept crying. Marcelle remained at a loss.

"Do you want some tea?" Marcelle asked. Sarah was always offering tea. It was her remedy for everything.

"No," Sarah said. "Coffee. Make me some Turkish coffee."

Marcelle extricated herself from her mother's grip and walked towards the kitchen. Halfway there, she turned around and rushed back to the couch. She hugged and kissed her mother. "I love you, too," she said. "I love you so much, too."

In the kitchen, she found the little mug-sized pot with the long diagonal handle used for Turkish coffee. She filled it with water and put it on the stove. As she waited for the water to boil, she heard her mother crying softly on the couch. Marcelle peeked around the wall to survey the scene. There had been a feast. The table was covered with small plates. Empty platters lay on the coffee table with scraps of filah dough, scattered sesame seeds, a few dried-out slices of cheese and vegetables. Most of the couch cushions were on the floor, and an ashtray overflowed with cigarette butts. Her uncles had definitely been there. But in the middle of the day?

They had been listening to Charles Aznavour and smoking her late grandmother's narghile. It looked like a celebration. But then there was her mother, drunk (drunk!) and crying on the couch. Marcelle had no idea what to make of it. She thought to call Auntie Rosette, but then realized the water was boiling.

Marcelle spooned coffee and sugar into a glass and added hot water. She also poured a glass of cold water. When she returned to the living room, Sarah was sitting up, straightening her clothes and patting down her hair.

"Here you go, Mom," Marcelle said. Sarah sipped her coffee.

Together they sat in awkward silence. Marcelle tried as best she could to wait for her mother to speak. She realized this was probably not the time to discuss her fight with Nathan.

"Here," Marcelle said finally. "The narghile is still lit. Why don't you smoke a little? It'll make you feel better."

Marcelle handed the wooden mouthpiece over to Sarah, stroking her hair while she smoked.

"You know who this belonged to originally?" Sarah asked, holding the pipe towards Marcelle: a test, her next action contingent upon the correct answer.

Marcelle nodded. "Jiddo's mother, Sitto Sarah, who you were named after. She gave it to your mother the first time your father took her to Aleppo to meet his parents. It was how Sitto told them she approved of the marriage."

Nodding her head and smiling, she passed the mouthpiece to Marcelle, asking, "You want?"

Marcelle nodded. It was the first time Sarah had ever offered. Marcelle understood what it meant.

"Slowly," Sarah said. "Slowly pull the smoke into your mouth so you can taste it. Like apple, yes? It's sweet."

Marcelle nodded.

"Now hold the smoke in your mouth and taste it. Not like those tacky cigarettes where they pull in and out, so quickly, with no enjoyment. Like people who eat too fast, you know?"

Then Sarah smiled, looking at her daughter. Marcelle's cheeks were full, like when she had the mumps as a little girl. "Now swallow, gently, and now you blow it out. No, no, through your mouth," and smiled again as she saw the smoke come out of Marcelle's nose.

"But you blow it out of your nose, Mommy."

"Yeah, but I didn't start that way." Sarah stared off, out the big bay windows in the living room, at nothing.

"Did Nonna show you how?"

Sarah nodded. "Right before she died."

Turning to Marcelle, she smiled. "My mother was a good woman. A good mother."

Marcelle squeezed Sarah's hand, then rested her head on her mother's shoulder, running her arm around her waist. "So is mine," she said.

Marcelle offered to clean the living room so Sarah could freshen herself up and get dinner started. She could hear the water running in the bathroom when Charles came home.

"What's all this?" he asked, gesturing to the mess.

"I have no idea," Marcelle answered. "I just walked into it and now I'm trying to help Mommy out."

"Well," Charles said, "I need you to help me out a little, too."

She handed Charles a stack of dishes, "You scratch my back…"

"Yeah, yeah," he said, as they walked into the kitchen together.

"Listen, I was talking to Nathan last week," he said. Marcelle's heart dropped into her bowels just at the sound of his name.

"And he said that Lenny Sayegh" —the Community's most prominent Arabic music band leader—"is an old friend of his. He was going to find out if Lenny would teach me the oud in exchange for being his roadie over the summer."

"His roadie?"

"Yeah, you know, hauling around his equipment, hooking it up, putting it away."

"You know how to do that?"

"I'll learn. Anyway, that's the easy part. The oud is the hard part. But the hardest part is Dad. You know he's not going to like this."

The oud, the Arabic lute, was a particularly difficult instrument. If Charles wanted to learn the oud, apprenticing Lenny would be a priceless opportunity.

"So what do I have to do with this?"

"Use your feminine charms to get Nathan to make it happen. And then stop Dad from killing me when I tell him."

Marcelle scowled. The last thing she wanted was to talk to Nathan. And right now she didn't want to ask him for anything.

She said as much to Charles.

"You can't break up with him," Charles said. "At least not till you get me this gig!"

Marcelle snapped at Charles's behind with a towel.

"Ow!" Charles yelled. "For what it's worth, which is clearly very little," he rubbed his hand where the towel hit, "I think that's a great guy you got there. I wouldn't mind too much if he stuck around."

Marcelle smirked. "Yeah, like I need my kid brother's permission."

"I wasn't giving my permission. I was giving my opinion. But who cares what baby brother thinks." He stuck out his bottom lip and made it quiver, pretending he was about to cry.

"Oh, stop it," she said, laughing. "The next time I talk to Nathan, I'll find out, okay?"

Charles hugged Marcelle so hard, she was taken aback. "Thanks, sis," he said, and walked out of the kitchen to his room.

Nathan, Marcelle wondered. What to do about Nathan?

Upstairs in her bedroom, Sarah smoothed her hair and freshened her make-up. Staring at her reflection in the mirror, she saw olive-colored skin with fine lines on the forehead, almond-shaped green eyes, lined with dark, thick eyelashes, and crow's feet in the corners. Her full mouth rested between two light crescent-shaped lines. Her thick curly hair had been straightened and colored brown at the beauty parlor.

How I've aged since the last time he saw me. How I look like my mother did at my age. What will he see when he sees me?

By the time Eddie arrived, Sarah had rehearsed her speech in her head a hundred times. How could she tell her family? She had the feeling that it should be perfect, that it would be one of those family milestones, one of those stories that gets told over and over again, weaving its way in to the fabric of a family's history.

She was anxious to hear their reactions. Would they be happy? They never knew him. They'll think they're supposed to be happy, but will they be? Then the churning returned. Am I?

Stop.

Walking down the stairs she put her smile on, kissed her husband warmly. If she couldn't feel it, she would fake it.

Kissing her in return, Eddie smiled and put his arm around her as they walked into the dining room. A large oval cherry mahogany table stood at the center of the room, on top of a dark green rug. Around the table stood eight plush chairs, upholstered with deep rose-colored fabric. The walls were painted a pale yellow. On one wall hung a painting of the Nile, and on the other stood a cherry mahogany breakfront, where Sarah displayed her prettiest pieces of china and crystal.

I have made a beautiful family, she reminded herself. I have raised wonderful children.

Just then, Charles ambled out of his room. His tousled hair and wrinkled clothes suggested he had fallen asleep. As he walked past his father, he grunted a hello and sank into his chair.

"Fall asleep again?" Eddie asked. He took his place at the head of the table while Sarah and Marcelle brought platters of food.

"Yeah," Charles said, scratching his head.

"Did you call Mr. Mosseri today?" Eddie continued.

"Yeah," Charles said.

"And?" Eddie asked. "What did he say?"

"Nothing," Charles said. "No one answered the phone in the store."

"Did you think to walk over there?"

"Come on everyone, go wash your hands so we can eat," Sarah said. Please, she cried silently, not today.

Eddie looked at his wife as though about to speak, but thought the better of it. They all washed their hands, and Sarah placed the bread and salt on the table for hamotzi. Hoping to soften him, she smiled at Eddie. He did not smile back. He blessed the bread and passed it around the table.

"Let me make you a plate," Sarah said, still smiling too brightly. She inhaled deeply, about to begin.

But just as she sat, Eddie continued. "Charles, did you think to walk over there and talk to Mr. Mosseri in person?"

"Uh, no, I didn't."

"Did you try to call anyone else?"

"The only person you told me to call was Mr. Mosseri," Charles said, moving lentils around his plate.

"So, that's it? You think that making one phone call a day is how you find a job?"

Charles sulked into his seat; Marcelle reached over to squeeze her brother's hand.

"Let's not argue over dinner," said Sarah. "Let's enjoy our time together. As a family. Eddie how was your day?"

"Fine. It would be better if I knew my son had a job for the summer."

Charles's face reddened, and Sarah saw Marcelle squeeze his hand again. They exchanged a look and Marcelle shook her head. Charles squeezed her hand back.

"School ends in a few weeks and he still doesn't have a job. Sits home all afternoon and sleeps," Eddie said. He flicked his wrist in Charles's direction. "Thinks he's a prince, this one."

"Dad, the thing is, I don't want to work for Mr. Mosseri," Charles said.

"Oh. Okay. Is that all? You don't want to work for Mr. Mosseri. Oh, fine. Why don't you play in the street all the summer? Maybe go to the beach every day. Sound good?"

Oh, no. He's doing his sarcastic voice. He came home in a bad mood and now he's going to set Charles off. Not today, Eddie. Not today.

But Eddie continued. "In life, we have to do a lot of things we don't want to do."

Rolling his eyes, Charles said, "You get to do what you want to do. You're your own boss. You don't have to work for someone you can't stand."

Eddie slapped both hands on the table, so hard the flower vase shook. "I get to do what I want?" he yelled. "Yes. Now that I am forty-five years old, and I have worked hard every day of my life, I get to do what I want. After I spent years doing things I didn't want. Do you think I wanted to come here as a pauper and work as a clerk for my cousin in a linen store when I was supposed to inherit my father's factories? Do you think I wanted to leave Egypt so I could do that?"

Charles rolled his eyes once more. "Here he goes with Egypt again."

Eddie's nostrils flared, his eyes bulging.

"Charles, honey, show some respect," Sarah interjected, her voice soft.

"I didn't mean to be disrespectful," he muttered into his food.

"Yes, you did," said Eddie. "And I will not tolerate that during our dinner. You're finished eating. Go back to your room."

Sarah couldn't place the emotion registering on Charles's face; it was deeper than anger.

"Charles, you will leave your plate here."

"Eddie, honey, he didn't eat anything." Not now, Eddie. I want my whole family here when I tell the news.

"Maybe hunger will teach him some respect."

"Eddie, please, he'll behave from now on, won't you Charles?"

"Sarah, stay out of this," he yelled in Arabic, and then returning to English, "Charles, to your room. Now!"

Charles left the table and slammed the door to his room. The rest of the family continued eating in awkward silence. Sarah wanted to ease the tension, but thinking of nothing to say, looked to Marcelle, hoping she might be able to put Eddie in a better mood.

But Sarah noticed that Marcelle was not in the best of moods herself. Had she been like that all day? Had Sarah been too preoccupied to notice?

Eddie cleared his throat. "So," he began, "how is our friend Nathan today?"

Marcelle dropped her fork. "Fine," she said.

"When will we get to see him next?" Eddie continued.

"I don't know," Marcelle shrugged.

"Fine. I don't know," Eddie said. "What kind of answers are those? I would think you'd show a little more enthusiasm when I ask about your boyfriend."

Marcelle threw her fork down. "Why do you only care about Nathan? Why don't you ever ask about me? I'm here right now. And I'm not fine. And you know what?" she yelled, "I'm not hungry either." She pushed her chair away from the table so hard she shook the flowers in the vase again. She stormed off to her room and slammed the door.

Eddie looked dumbfounded. "What's wrong with her?" he asked.

Sarah was furious. "What's wrong with her? What's wrong with you! I cook this dinner, for my beautiful family, so we can all eat together, so we can share a beautiful meal, and you chase both of our children from the table! What's wrong with her?" she said, her voice mocking his. "What's wrong with you!" she screamed.

And like her daughter before her, she pushed her chair away, stomped up the stairs and slammed the door to her room.

Eddie sat alone at the table incredulous. He shook his head and took his plate to the living room. There, he placed it on the coffee table. He turned on the TV and played with the dial till he found something he liked. *Charlie's Angels* was on.

Upstairs, Sarah sobbed in her bed. This is not how I wanted today to be. This was not what I wanted. Look what I did. Look how I screamed at Eddie. How could I do that to him? What would my father think? Twenty different threads of thought leapt into her mind, where they tangled into a ball of despair, and no cogent words found their way out of her mouth. Instead she moaned.

She heard Eddie watching TV downstairs. If only he would come to her. If only she could go to him.

There was so much to say, but the emotions—happiness, fear, guilt, relief—swelled in her throat like a bad infection, raw, red, cutting off air, so she choked on them, unable to speak. Crying harder, she shook her head. She was so ashamed of herself she hid under her blankets. She tried so hard to be a good wife and mother, the way her father had taught her, her father who was coming home, and now because she could not control her children and could not please her husband, she could not tell them. Sobbing in bed alone, she cried herself to sleep.

Chapter Six

Sarah never got to tell Eddie the news. Zaki called later that night after Sarah fell asleep. Assuming Eddie already knew, he quoted prices for plane tickets to Israel, asking when Eddie planned to leave.

In the following weeks, Sarah had trouble sleeping. Eddie found her sitting in the living room, staring blankly out the window night after night.

"Come to bed," he said.

"All this time he's been alive," she replied, still staring out the window.

"Isn't it a miracle?" Eddie said.

"We just kept living as though he were dead, and all this time he's been alive."

"Sarah. Sarah. Look at me. Look at me," Eddie said. She turned to face him. "Your family did everything they could do and now they got him released. Come to bed."

"Why? I can't sleep."

"At least try. I'll hold you as long as you need. We can talk about this more, but just come to bed."

"I don't want to keep you up, Eddie. You have to get up early for work."

"Really, Sarah, we've been married for over twenty years. If I can't stay up with me wife when she needs me, what's the point?"

Eddie took her hand and led her to the bedroom. He laid her down on the bed, fluffing her pillows and adjusting her blankets, tucking her in as he smiled down at her. He ran his hands through her long brown hair, brushing his fingers on her face and down her neck.

"Would it help if I made you some tea?" Eddie asked.

"I can do that myself. I don't want to keep you up any more."

Eddie smiled. "You'll have your father back in a few days, but until then, you're my little girl, and I'm going to take care of you."

Sarah laughed. "I can keep being your little girl. I took care of him."

"I'm going to make you some tea. I'll be right back."

Sarah rearranged herself so she was sitting up and tried to remember her childhood. Squinting her eyes to reach the back of her mind, Sarah tried to reconstruct her father's face in her memory. She remembered green eyes, the same color and shape of her own. They were both small in stature. She stood at five foot one inch; he couldn't have been taller than five-five. She had her mother's smile, people used to say, so her mouth wasn't his, but as far as she could recall he had a neatly trimmed black beard on his face, so she wouldn't have known what his mouth looked like anyway. She tried focusing on his other features, his nose, his ears, his forehead. It was long and sloping, she remembered. She had loved that part of his profile as a child, thinking of how much fun it would be if she could shrink herself and slide down it.

Eddie returned with two hot cups of mint tea. He sat beside her on the bed and set the tea down on the nightstand.

"You were concentrating. What were you thinking?" he asked.

"I can't remember what he looks like," she said.

"Ah, it's all right, he'll look completely different now anyway," Eddie said, trying to make her laugh.

"The only picture I have of him is my parents' wedding picture. He hated posing for pictures; my mother used to argue with him to get in the picture all the time, but he refused. He was so stubborn."

"He is so stubborn, my love, he's still alive."

"I keep thinking of him in the past tense. I've been thinking of him in the past tense for years already. Like he hasn't been here. And all this time, he's been alive, and I've been living my life without even thinking about him."

"You thought about him all the time. I know you did."

"But I just left him for dead. I didn't sit shiva, but I may as well have."

"You did what he told you to do. You left Egypt because he told you to. You took care of your brothers like he would have wanted. You got married. You had children. You did everything he would have wanted."

"I could have thought about him more. He was sitting in a prison cell and I was playing mahjong with my friends. We had holidays and weddings and bar mitzvahs without him. We just kept living like he wasn't there."

Sarah sipped her tea as she looked at Eddie. She had read in a magazine that people tended to marry people who were like their parents. She had laughed when she read it and laughed in her head as she looked at Eddie now. The two men could not possibly be more different. Imagine, her father bringing her tea. She couldn't remember him ever doing that. Eddie was so warm and kind and affectionate. Her father was stiff and formal and cold.

How could she be thinking that of him now? Why did her mind only send her negative memories? She tried to think of something good. She tried to think of a tender moment. She knew there were many but why couldn't she remember any?

"What are you thinking? All of a sudden you look very upset."

"I can't remember anything good. I can only remember how hard it was."

"Do you want to tell me about it?"

"I don't want to say bad things about him."

"But maybe if you just start talking you'll remember something good."

Sarah stared at the pale blue wallpaper as she thought. Next she shifted her eyes to the dark blue rug. The memories evaded her. Finally, she stared at the pictures on her nightstand, and saw one of her and Eddie dancing at Charles's bar mitzvah.

"He used to take her dancing at Covent Garden a few times a month. I remember how beautiful they looked, him in a suit and cravat, and her in a dress and pearls. He didn't even like dancing, but she loved it. He did a lot to please her. He loved her dearly. When she died, he became a completely different person. He was much stricter, much more concerned about how other people viewed us, just more severe all around. I think she opened him up, kept him light. He barely went out after she died. Just to work and to synagogue. He was completely devastated."

Eddie smiled. "That's a beautiful thing to remember, Sarah, how deeply he loved your mother."

Sarah smiled and nestled into Eddie's chest. He wrapped his arms around her, squeezing tightly.

"I love you."

"I love you, too."

That night she had a dream. She was in her old apartment in Cairo, except it was smaller than before. She could not stand upright without banging her head on the ceiling. She knew she had to make dinner, as her brothers would be coming home soon, but she had no groceries in the house. She put on her shoes and her jacket to go to the market, but upon opening the door to the house she saw that the street had collapsed and there was no way for her to get to the road. She went back into the house, crawling on her hands and knees, and remembered a tale about a young girl who was at once too big and then too small. She knew she needed mushrooms to make herself smaller. She looked inside the pantry for the mushrooms, but after crawling into the kitchen, she found herself too small to reach the pantry doors. She jumped up and down, but every time she fell a crack opened in the floor, and she had to stop because she was afraid to fall through. All of a sudden, she heard her father's voice calling her from the other room. He was hungry and wanted to eat. She stood up and tried to walk through the kitchen door to the living room so she could tell him there was no food. She felt the floor moving and the ground gave way beneath her. She began to fall. She tried to call out to her father but her voice wouldn't come out. She heard him calling her again; she heard his footsteps moving towards the kitchen. He was coming to save her. She saw a huge figure hulking in the doorway. He was her father; she knew that, but he looked nothing like him. He looked around the kitchen for her. She wanted to scream, "I'm here," but her voice still would not come out. He didn't see her. She was too small and shrinking more and more quickly. She felt herself fall through the floor, her voice finally coming, and she screamed as she fell, but he had already left the room and didn't hear her.

She woke with a start. Eddie was sleeping peacefully beside her. She wanted to wake him, knew he would want to be woken, but didn't know what she would say. That she was afraid to see her father? What kind of person is afraid to see her father after all these years?

When Sarah woke the next morning, the dream was still on her mind. Her feelings confused her, and not knowing how to respond, she decided to keep her day as busy as possible. There was never a shortage of work to be done, and she would throw herself into it today. "Be like Mama," she thought. "Just keep busy. Baba would approve."

After making breakfast and sending Eddie off to work and Charles and Marcelle to school, Sarah inventoried her kitchen. Then she opened the freezer and examined the marked Tupperware containers to see what foods she could prepare today and freeze for later. It was just after Passover. The freezer was mostly empty because she had had to rid herself of all leavened food products before the holiday began. Now was time to refill it again, in preparation for the next holiday, Shavuot. Amazing, she thought to herself, that my father's own exodus should come at the same time of year that God took us out of Egypt. Is there a message here?

After making her shopping list, Sarah stepped out into the warm spring air. The flowers in the garden would need planting soon, and she made a mental note to call the gardener when she returned home. Holding her car keys, Sarah looked at her brand new Lincoln Town Car. Eddie had wanted to buy her a Jaguar, but she told him it was too fancy. She walked down the front steps of her house, stopping to notice how large it was, how beautiful. Feelings of pride and shame commingled as she stared at the structure in front of her and the shiny new car in the driveway. All this time they had been living an affluent life and her father had been going through God knows what, in conditions she could not even imagine. What would he think when he saw them?

Leaving Egypt

She put the key in the car door, but changed her mind, deciding instead to walk. They only lived a few blocks away from the main shopping street, yet she always drove. How lazy she had become in America.

Sarah walked down her tree-lined Brooklyn street, marveling at the tall brick houses, many with porches, all with tiny front yards, thinking of the life her fellow community members had made for themselves since the first group of them arrived more than sixty years earlier. So much had changed, and yet the basic mores—family, community, religion—stayed the same. Her father would be proud of the way the community established itself, that she knew. They lived close to one another so they could walk to the homes of their friends and family on Shabbat and holidays, so they could celebrate and relish their culture in a melting pot they refused to be put inside.

But what about her children? They were going to be shocked. They were so Americanized. How would her children react to her traditional father? How would he react to them?

When she arrived at the grocery store, she was not surprised to see three women she knew picking out spices, boxes of filah dough and jars of grape leaves. They stopped speaking when she walked in and ran to embrace her.

"We heard the wonderful news," said Linda.

"You must be so happy," said Allegra.

"God has blessed you, and the entire community," said Shirley.

Sarah smiled, enjoying the closeness of their community, and how fast word traveled among a group that lived with and for one another.

"David saw Abe in knis this morning. He came home and told me right away. I can't believe it,' said Shirley.

"When are you going to see him?" asked Allegra.

"Is he moving to Brooklyn or staying in Israel?" asked Linda.

"Sarah, I myself heard this morning. Mabrouk," said Ralph, the owner of the store, as he walked out from the back room of the store. "Me and Grace are so happy for your family."

106

"Thank you all so much," said Sarah. "We're all going to Israel in a few weeks over Shavuot. The doctors say he needs a little more time before he's ready to see everyone, so we can't go right away. And we don't know where he's going to live right now, but they say he's not strong enough to make that decision yet."

She herself didn't know how she felt about him moving to Brooklyn. At least Israel would be a little more familiar to him. Also, where would he live? He could certainly not live alone, and she, being a daughter and not a daughter-in-law, was the only person who really should be tasked with caring for him day-to-day. Eddie would not object, but would she?

Her father would require so much more than her husband did. No more easy dinners, no more asking Eddie to help with the dishes. None of her friends' husbands helped them at all in the kitchen. Sarah knew how lucky she was to have Eddie and his modern ideas. Her father would never approve. Men and women had their separate places. For now, hers was in the grocery store, buying semolina and bulgar wheat.

The other women kissed her goodbye when they finished shopping. Holding her groceries, Sarah approached the register to pay.

"It's on the house," said Ralph.

"Absolutely not," said Sarah. "My father would never allow it."

Ralph laughed. "Then give the money to sedaka in his name. For me. So that he should be healthy and live long."

Sarah took twenty dollars out her purse and put it in the sedaka box that Ralph kept on the counter. Reading the label on the box, she saw that the money went to a community organization where she volunteered twice a week.

That he should be healthy and live long, Ralph had said. She hadn't even thought of that. What if he died right away? What if he was too sick to move? What if he only had a few more weeks? I'm a horrible person. I'm a terrible, ungrateful daughter, that all I can think about is how hard it will be for me if he comes to live with me. I should give more sedaka right now so God will forgive me for the sins in my mind. But what if he does die? What would have been God's purpose in keeping him alive all these years if he is going to die as soon as he is freed? Why am I questioning God? Why am I killing my father in my mind?

Continuing her walk on Kings Highway, Sarah came to Jacob's butcher shop.

"Hello, Sarah," said Jacob, "Mabrouk! Elie stopped in yesterday to tell me the news."

As she selected chop meat and veal pockets, Jeannie approached her.

"Sarah," she said, hugging her, "I've been calling you all morning. Some of the girls decided to throw a sebbet for your family this Shabbat. We're all so excited for you. We're inviting everyone. They all want to celebrate with you. This is so wonderful!"

"What are we making? I have some laham b'agin in the freezer, and I was going to make more today," Sarah asked.

"Don't be ridiculous. Marlene organized everyone, and we're doing everything. You should just relax and enjoy."

Sarah was overwhelmed again by the solidarity her people felt with her. Then she was overcome with shame that everyone else seemed happier than she did.

Jeannie and Sarah walked out together, Jeannie to her car and Sarah continuing along one more block to the vegetable store.

"Why are you walking?" Jeannie asked, as she got into her car. "Is something wrong with your car?'

"No," said Sarah. "It's nice outside. I felt like walking."

"But how can you carry all of those bags? It's too heavy for you."

"No, I'm fine. Don't worry."

Jeannie offered again to drive her, but Sarah declined, wanting to be alone. Then she ran into Rosette in the vegetable store.

Rosette hugged her. "Sarah, isn't this wonderful?"

Sarah stiffened. "Yes. It is. Wonderful."

Rosette stared at her. "What?" she asked. "Something's wrong. Is there something Elie didn't tell me?"

"Nothing's wrong."

"Sarah Salama, I've known you for almost thirty years now, and I can tell when you're lying to me."

"Rosette, I promise you, there is nothing wrong."

"Then something's wrong with you. What it is, honey?"

"Nothing. Rosette, I don't want to talk about it.'

"Are you afraid to see him?'

"I don't want to talk about it."

"Because I would be if I were you," Rosette said, squeezing a tomato. "You don't know who he is anymore, and he doesn't know you. What's he going to think when he sees his little girl all grown up? Will he realize you're an adult? What will he think of Eddie, the kids?"

"How is it that you know everything? It's really irritating."

Rosette laughed. "I don't know everything. I just know you. And so does Elie, and so does Eddie. You don't have to do this alone; don't insist on it."

"Let's not talk about it anymore."

"Fine. Let's pay and then go home. Why are you carrying so many bags? Why didn't you put them in your trunk?"

"Because I decided to walk."

"Then I'm driving you home. There's no reason for you to be carrying around all that heavy stuff by yourself."

Rosette went to the register, leaving Sarah to marvel over how lucky she was.

Chapter Seven

Sarah closed her eyes and dug her fingers into the sides of her seat. This was her second time on an airplane. Last time, she flew from Paris to New York, terrified of the unknown future that awaited her. This time, her fear lay in confronting her past. Last time, she had her brothers next to her. This time, she was alone, as Eddie insisted she take the soonest flight available; he would follow with the children in a few days.

Sarah wondered what her father would think about her coming without her husband. She opened her purse and sorted through the contents: a lipstick, a compact mirror, pictures of her husband and children, a prayer book and a little brown bottle of Valium that her doctor had so kindly prescribed for the flight. Valium, to help her relax he said, probably make her sleep, he said. To keep me from thinking too much, she thought.

Moise picked her up at the airport in Tel Aviv. Though they spoke every week and sent photos and letters regularly, they hadn't seen each other in several years.

"There are things you should know before you see him," Moise said, as they began the hour-long drive to Jerusalem.

"What kinds of things?"

"You should be prepared. I don't want you to show your shock in front of him."

Sarah nodded.

"It's going to be hard, Sarah. He's not the way we remember him. His memory is spotty. Some things he knows clearly; other things have been completely erased from his mind. He doesn't like bright lights, he limps, and he won't let us see him undressed. He has a nurse who bathes and clothes him, and she won't tell us why. He made her promise. The doctors assure me they're only scars. They see him once a week. They promised to tell me if anything needs attention."

Moise took one hand off the wheel and lit a cigarette. Sarah bit her lower lip and began fidgeting with her hair.

"You still do that when you get nervous, ah? You did that even when you were a little girl. Don't be afraid. He's still our father. We're still lucky to have him alive."

"I think I need one of those, too," Sarah said.

"Since when do you smoke?"

"I don't really. Just from Mama's narghile. It helps me relax."

Sarah closed her eyes as she inhaled, still chewing on her lips as she exhaled through her nose. Will he be able to forgive me? she wondered. When I ask him, will he know why I need forgiveness?

"Something else you should know," Moise said. "Don't light a cigarette in front of him. He'll freak out."

"But he used to smoke."

"It's not about the smoking. That's fine. Just not cigarettes."

"Moise, I don't understand. Why not?"

Moise sighed. "I think they burned him with them."

God have mercy on us. She bit her lip so hard she tasted blood.

When they arrived, the nurse, Ofra, said he was sleeping. She cautioned Sarah not to wake him, but Sarah couldn't wait.

"Please," she begged. "I've spent twenty-three years thinking he was dead. Please, can I just look at him?"

"That's fine," said Ofra. "Just be quiet. He's very easily startled."

She opened the door to the bedroom and found him sleeping on the floor in the fetal position. He looked so small, curled up like a wrinkled infant, his face grey and deeply lined. He wore wool pajamas and thick socks and was swaddled by two blankets even though the room was not air conditioned and the temperature in Jerusalem in May hovered around seventy-five degrees. The room was completely dark and when the light from the hallway passed into his room, he stirred and began to whimper.

"Why is he on the floor?" she whispered to Ofra.

"He won't sleep on the bed," Ofra replied. "He hasn't slept on a bed in many years. Please close the door before the light wakes him."

Sarah closed the door but as soon as the door clicked into place, she heard him scream, a terrible, terrified wail, more animal than human.

"Oh my God. Oh my God, what did I do?" Sarah cried.

"It's not your fault," said Ofra. "He screams like that whenever he wakes. I just didn't want you to hear that right away." She put her arm around Sarah. "Go in there and comfort him. He'll be so happy to see you. Just please, move slowly. He's afraid and needs to be soothed."

Sarah opened the door again, and slowly closed it behind her. "Baba," she said softly, "Baba, it's me, Sarah. Baba, it's Sarah, it's your daughter, your baby girl, Sarah." Kneeling slowly beside him, she gently stroked his head, the way she had so many times with her children.

"It was just a dream, Baba, it was all just a bad dream."

His body stiffened at her first touch, then relaxed as she rubbed her hand up and down his back. Eyes closed, he sighed, his breathing returning to normal until he seemed to be asleep again. Lying down beside him, she nestled her head into his chest, holding him around the waist, her hand still running up and down the small of his back. He stirred again, this time lifting his arm and putting it around her, and like that, holding each other, lying on the floor, father and daughter fell asleep.

When she woke, after what could have been a few moments or a few hours, Sarah felt her father's eyes on her before she saw him. Looking into what used to be his sharp green eyes, now cloudy and bluish from cataracts, she thought she saw a smile.

"Terra," he whispered. "Is it really you?"

She shook her head unable to speak. He touched her face, stroking her cheek, and staring at her intensely. She held his hand with her own and brought it to her lips.

"It's been so long, Terra. I thought I'd never see you again," he said.

"Baba, it's Sarah. It's your daughter. Sarah. Baba, it's me, your baby girl."

He looked confused. He thought for a moment and recognition flashed over his face. "Sarah," he said. "But you're so old."

Laughing through her tears, she said, "It's been a long time, Baba. I grew up. I'm married now. I have two children."

"Two children," he said. "How old are they?"

"Charles is fourteen and Marcelle is seventeen."

"Two children," he said. "Two children. Who did you marry?"

"Eddie Salama."

"Charles and Marcelle Salama. I used to know them, yes?"

"Yes. They lived in Zamalek with us. They left Cairo in 1948, Baba, do you remember? They were among the first to leave."

"My only daughter and I wasn't there to see you married."

"Elie, Zaki and Jacques were there, Baba. They took care of me."

Saleem nodded his head as tears formed in his eyes.

"You are a good wife, Sarah? A good mother?"

"I try, Baba. I try to be good like you taught me."

"This is good Sarah."

"Let's get up, Baba, let's go inside and sit down with everyone else."

"Soon, Sarah, soon. I have waited a long time for this. Give me a little longer." Nodding her head, she held him closer. She wanted to beg him for forgiveness right then and there, the words "I'm sorry" repeating again and again in her mind, getting louder each time, but she decided to give him some time, to wait a while before making him remember things he would rather have forgotten. Instead she just allowed the feeling to overcome her, her soul begging forgiveness from a higher power instead of the only person who could grant it.

When he was finally ready to join the family in the other room, Sarah helped him stand. "Should I call Ofra?" she asked.

"Who's Ofra?" he asked. Sarah wondered if she got the name wrong.

"Your nurse, Baba. Should I call her?"

"Why do I need a nurse? I have my daughter."

Sarah faced him and put her arms underneath his to lift him up, but when her arms pushed against his underarms, he screamed.

"What's wrong, Baba? Does it hurt?"

He kept screaming. Ofra came running into the room.

"What happened?" she asked. Sarah explained that she had tried to lift him.

"Don't touch his armpits," Ofra said. "And don't touch the soles of his feet."

"Why not?" Sarah asked. Moise, who was standing at the door, shook his head and mouthed, "later."

Ofra lifted him from the waist and he put his arm around her. She led him slowly out of the room. He looked at her, confused. "Who are you?" he asked.

"I'm your nurse, Mr. Mizrahi. I am here to take care of you."

"What's your name?"

"Ofra, Mr. Mizrahi. You can call me Ofra."

"Are you married Ofra? I have six sons. Three of them are unmarried."

"Sorry, Mr. Mizrahi, I'm already married."

As she led him out of the room, Sarah whispered to Moise. "Hasn't Ofra been with him all week?" she asked.

"Yes," said Moise. "He has that conversation with her at least once a day. She's wonderfully patient with him."

Sarah started to cry. "What did they do to him?"

Moise held his baby sister. "Don't ask me that Sarah. I'd rather you didn't know."

Soon after, Moise's wife Adele began to prepare dinner. Sarah went into the kitchen to help her.

"Sit," she said. "You've been on a plane for twelve hours and this is not an easy day for you."

"Thanks, but I can't sit still. Give me some vegetables to chop. I need to keep my hands busy."

Sarah sliced vegetables for salad while she and Adele asked after each other's children. Adele was kind enough to focus on small talk.

114

Sarah set the table for the five of them: plate, salad plate, fork, knife, spoon and glass. She arranged the napkins in pretty shapes on the plates, fussed at keeping everything symmetrical.

The family sat down to eat. Moise honored his father with the seat at the head of the table. Adele rose to serve Saleem, but Sarah stopped her, pleading, "Let me." She unfolded the napkin and placed it in his lap. She poured him a glass of lemon water, moved his salad plate to the left of his entrée plate. She filled the salad plate with vegetables, hummus and ripped a warm pita into four pieces, placing them on the table. Then she filled his dinner plate with chicken, rice and string beans. She put the salad fork on the salad plate and the knife and fork on the entrée plate. Finally, she sat in her seat and made a plate for herself.

"Be'te'avon," said Moise. Good appetite.

The family began to eat and Sarah noticed her father staring strangely at the food. He looked at the shiny silverware for a moment, pushed it away and began eating with his hands, scooping his fingers into the hummus and putting them in his mouth to lick clean. A combination of disgust and pity filled her as she watched him eat his chicken, grease pouring down his fingers and dribbling down his chin as he ate. Table manners used to be so important to him.

He looked at her and smiled. "Terra," he said. "This is delicious. I am a lucky man to have a wife like you."

Sarah put her fork down on the plate. "Baba, it's Sarah. I'm Sarah, your daughter."

"Sarah?" he asked, looking at her confused, "But you're so old."

Swallowing hard, she forced a smile. "It's been a long time, Baba. I'm married. I have two children. Their names are Charles and Marcelle."

"Who did you marry?" he asked.

"Eddie Salama, Baba. His parents are Charles and Marcelle Salama. They lived near us in Zamalek. They left Cairo in 1948, remember?"

"I wasn't there Sarah. My only daughter and I wasn't there. And the Salamas, such a fine family. What must they think?"

She started to speak, but Moise shook his head. Instead, she put her hand on his, rubbing his arm. Once again, she wanted to beg for his forgiveness, but not here, not at the table, not in front of everyone. He would not like that, her father, who was always so appropriate.

Suddenly, he belched loudly. "My compliments to the chef!" he yelled. "No one is a better cook than my Terra. Where is she? Where is my wife?"

Sarah looked at Moise, but he nodded reassuringly. He didn't remember.

"She's resting, Baba. She'll be awake again soon."

"She works very hard," Saleem said, nodding his head. "A woman's work is never done. My Terra deserves a rest."

His eyes clouded as he stared down at his plate. He lifted more rice and string beans into his mouth, spilling sauce all over his shirt. Then he looked as though he had had a revelation. He forgot he was eating. Food dripped out of his mouth as he said, "She's gone. She's been gone for many years now. God rest her soul, my Terra is gone. There was never a better woman; I was lucky to have her for so long." He began to cry. "Terra, my Terra, I miss you so much."

Sarah rushed to his side and held him. He wrapped his arms around her, sobbing onto her chest; half chewed food oozed out of his mouth as he babbled, "Terra, my Terra, I miss you." His face clouded over again, and he lifted himself off her. He looked at the mess he had made all over Sarah and said, "Sarah, you should be ashamed of yourself coming to the table looking like that. Go clean up."

"I'm sorry, Baba," she said. "I'll go clean up right now."

"Didn't I teach you anything?" he said. "I taught you how to be a good woman. I taught you to be like your mother. Haram, Sarah. Ibe. You do your mother's memory disrespect. You were blessed to have her face; everyone knows you're her daughter. Do not shame her memory."

"I'm sorry, Baba. I'm sorry I shamed you. I'm sorry I didn't listen to you. I'm sorry that I never learned. I'm sorry. I'm so sorry. I'm so sorry." She fell to her knees and wept on him. I'm sorry I didn't listen. I'm sorry I made them beat you. I'm sorry I made them think you were a

116

spy. This is all my fault. I'm sorry. It's all my fault. I'm sorry, I'm sorry, I'm so sorry.

He couldn't absolve her; he didn't remember why she needed absolution. In that moment, she realized there was only one way to earn his forgiveness: by living exactly as he would have wanted. Every action of her life would honor him, so that when his soul rose to heaven, so that when he had the kind of clarity his tortured mind would not allow him now, he could look down on her from above and be proud. And forgive her.

"Get up and wash yourself, Sarah," he said. "Look how you've made my shirt all dirty. Now I'll need to change, too. Moise, I need a new shirt. Sarah, get up. For once, will you listen to your father?"

As she stood up, she swore she always would.

Chapter Eight

When she was fifteen, sixteen, even after she started dating Nathan seriously, Marcelle's mother had always told her to go to college, to study, to have the tools she needed to stand on her own two feet, just in case. But everything changed when she was seventeen, after her grandfather came back from the dead. That's how Marcelle referred to it: his resurrection. He died, came back to life, then died again. Those three months he was alive changed everything.

Her mother flew to Israel and stayed for a month. The rest of the family was supposed to follow, but her mother told them to wait, he couldn't handle the whole family just yet. Marcelle heard her father and aunts and uncles discussing whether they would bring him to New York, but when Sarah returned to Brooklyn, he was not with her. He was too weak to make the trip, she said, but the doctors hoped he would be well enough by the middle of the summer.

He was going to live in New York, with them. She and Eddie had the most room, Sarah explained one night when her brothers were over, with only two children, and one who was about to get married anyway. Regardless, Sarah continued, she was Saleem's daughter: the responsibilities of his care should fall to her, not a daughter-in-law.

At first, Marcelle was none too pleased to be informed of her impending nuptials. What happened to there not being any rush? It wasn't like her grandfather was going to move into her room. Apparently, he couldn't go up and down stairs. In fact, all the brothers were contributing money to have an extension built onto the back of the house, which would become her grandfather's bedroom.

Marcelle tried to talk to her mother, but Sarah was too busy finding excuses to yell at her. All of a sudden, Marcelle's jumpsuits and halter-tops were not allowed, even though Sarah had complimented her on the clothes when she came home after buying them on Orchard Street.

Now she said, "Put some clothes on! What kind of girl walks around like that, half dressed?"

Their neighbors, Marcelle's Italian girlfriends, with whom she had grown up, were discounted.

"Spend time with your own kind," Sarah began to say. "There's nothing like a Syrian."

Dreams of college were all of a sudden replaced with, "Get married. Your husband will let you go to college. Get married. Get married."

What happened to a woman having something of her own to fall back on? Her husband would let her? Since when did she have to ask his permission?

Sarah had always been very traditional with regards to her Judaism, even if she fudged on some of the details. Their kitchen was kosher, but they didn't always eat in kosher restaurants. Just eating kosher ingredients was enough. But once her father came back, Sarah yelled, "Don't eat there and don't eat that."

It was like living with an alien. Gone was her mother who was engaged with the world, interested in ideas, wanting her daughter to outshine her, to have what she never had. Now she was pushing her into everything she had once warned her to avoid.

When she wasn't being lectured, Marcelle's heart broke for her mother. She heard Sarah crying in her room when she thought no one was home, heard her pacing in the living room at all hours of the night, saw her lips move as she sat alone in the kitchen preparing food. Was she talking to herself or praying?

"Do you know what he kept saying?" Sarah asked Marcelle one day, as Marcelle helped her chop vegetables for a dinner salad. "Over and over, he kept crying, because he couldn't be at my wedding. Because I'm his only daughter and he couldn't be there to see me married."

Then her face shone with hope as she looked at Marcelle: it was clear she had been thinking what she was about to say for a while. "But he could be at yours, ya rohi; he could see his granddaughter happily married." She wiped tears out of the corners of her eyes.

Marcelle didn't know how to respond to her mother so she looked to her father for guidance. It was hard to get any time alone with him, as Sarah had taken to fussing over him constantly, bringing him his slippers and his newspapers and hovering over him in case he should express a desire for anything.

"I have to admit," he said, "it was nice at first, but now it's driving me crazy."

Father and daughter were in the car, Marcelle having used a driving lesson as a pretext for getting him out of the house.

"Now, shift into reverse, honey, we're going to practice parking."

"She's driving you crazy by bringing you stuff? Dad, she's completely forgetting that she brought me up in America and not in the old country."

"It's not even the old country, ya binti. She's remembering the way her father brought her up, like they were in his old country, in Aleppo. Your Nonna fought with him over that, you know. She wanted your mother to be a cosmopolitan woman like she was. But she died young, and your mother only remembers what her father taught her."

"You knew my Nonna?"

"Sure. Your uncle Zaki was a good friend of mine and we were also cousins by marriage. She was an amazing woman. Strong, capable, free-spirited, but always, always a lady. Your mother was so young when she died. I've often thought what a shame it was that I knew your grandmother longer than her own daughter did."

Eddie put his hand on Marcelle's forearm.

"Listen, Marci, this is very hard for her. She's a mess. She has no idea what she's doing, and you're going to have to have some patience with her."

"Dad, she wants to burn all of my clothes and marry me off immediately."

"But you want to marry Nathan, don't you?"

"I think so, but I'm not one hundred percent sure."

"No one's ever one hundred percent sure. And you know, your Nonna may have been a fancy lady, but she was married by your age."

"So I should get married just to calm my mother down?"

"Marci, no one's asking you to do anything you don't want to do. I'm just suggesting you do it a little sooner than you may have planned as a kindness to your mother. Really, just try to imagine what she's going through."

Ruby agreed. By then, she was already married and wanted Marcelle to join the club.

"Come on, we've always done everything together. Now let's do this. And we could have babies together, and take them to the park together..."

"That's a great reason to get married," Marcelle retorted. "So we can do it together."

"Shut up," Ruby said, hitting her lightly on the arm. "You love Nathan. He's a great guy. So what if you hurry it up a little?"

Her mother had always put her children first. Maybe it was now time to return the favor. Marcelle saw images of her mother's tear-stained face, heard the echo of slippers on the kitchen floor at night. Everyone expected that she and Nathan would marry, everyone kept telling her how great he was. And Nathan was a modern man. Sort of. Wasn't she just being selfish by putting off the inevitable?

Marcelle continued to fight for a while, sneaking out of the house in jeans and a button-down shirt, leaving her pretend outfit at Ruby's house, where she changed into her slinky strapless dress, but Nathan didn't approve.

"I don't want you lying to your mother on my account," he said to her one night when they were out to dinner.

"She's going crazy, Nathan. She raised me in New York. She sent me to public school, now she expects me to be the way my grandfather was in the old country?"

"Still," he shook his head. "I don't want to be involved with you lying to her."

"Whose side are you on?" She glared at him, pouting.

He brushed a strand of hair off her face. "It's not about sides, Marci. It's about respecting the woman I hope will be my mother-in-law one day."

"That's another thing. She wants us to get married now. This minute."

He smiled and took her hand in his. "So let's get married."

Marcelle felt a pang in her stomach. How could he be so sure?

"What about college, Nathan?" she said, squeezing his hand. "I wanted to go to college."

"So let's get married," he said, squeezing hers back, "and you can wear your halter dresses to class and distract all your professors so bad they can't teach."

She laughed a little, but the serious expression returned to her face. "I don't want to get married because we're being pushed into it."

A week later, days before her eighteenth birthday, he asked her father for her hand in marriage, and that Friday night, during Shabbat dinner with her family, he proposed.

It was so disappointing.

They sat at the table, her parents, Charles, and Nathan. And somewhere between dinner and dessert he put a ring on her finger.

No flowers.

No candles.

No romance.

A chaste kiss on the cheek because her parents were watching.

A marriage borne out of a sense of duty; let's get it done before Jiddoh dies. The moment a girl waits for her whole life, over in a flash, as unromantic as signing a contract, a precursor of what was to come.

That was the reason she gave herself, later that night, when instead of feeling excited, she lay sobbing in her bed. She knew something had been lost. There was one night, though, one summer night, when all that she wanted seemed possible.

The waves rolling in from the beach.

The candles flickering in their glasses.

A question she still couldn't answer.

Activities supposedly for Marcelle's benefit consumed everyone around her. Her mother and aunts and all their friends cooked constantly, making mountains of food for the series of parties to precede the wedding. Marcelle was shuttled from boutique to dressmaker to shoe store to be properly outfitted for all the events. First, there was the meeting of the family, which should have been twenty or so people, but ballooned to over a hundred. Then her bridal shower. Hardly the intimate affair she imagined sharing with her girlfriends, the shower was instead combined with a swanee—a table of gifts from her mother-in-law—displayed for all to see: jewelry, fur, silver, a lace negligee hand embroidered from Italy. One hundred and fifty of her mother and mother-in-law's closest female friends and relatives were invited to admire the gifts. An engagement party followed, a night of dinner and dancing so elaborate, it may as well have been a wedding. All that was missing was the Rabbi. And her grandfather.

Her grandfather was still in Israel. The man for whose benefit was all this pomp and circumstance was not even there to experience it. He would be well enough to travel in time for the wedding. That was what the doctors kept assuring Sarah. But it was already almost August and the wedding was set for Labor Day weekend. As the days passed, he was still not cleared for air travel. Sarah become more and more nervous, pacing, planning, cooking and above all, yelling.

Marcelle was hardly calm herself. She was getting married, she was scared and she needed her mother's normal calm demeanor to help her overcome the fear. But her mother had turned into an automaton, irrevocably programmed into planning mode, who could only say, "get married."

Her father was hardly better; he was as caught up in the wedding madness as everyone else. He loved being congratulated on the street. He loved being patted on the back in synagogue as everyone wished him "Mabrouk!" Their relationship regressed, and instead of treating her like his intellectual sparring partner, he kept hugging her with tears in his eyes, telling her how proud he was of her for marrying Nathan, what a wonderful wife she was going to be. It amazed her that a man who could go on for hours about the implications of Iran's becoming an Islamic Republic could not handle the exchange of more than a few platitudinous statements when it came to the most important decision his daughter was about to make in her life so far. As far as he was concerned, they had already talked and the matter was settled.

The next person she tried was Auntie Rosette, but Auntie Rosette was so busy running triage on Uncle Elie that she had no time for her niece. Even Charles was unavailable, and that was Marcelle's own fault. Just like he asked, she had gotten him an apprenticeship with Lenny Sayegh, who convinced her father to let Charles work for him by significantly discounting his fee to play at Marcelle's wedding. Charles was out all night with Lenny, who played at practically every party in the Community. He slept well into the day and when he woke he rushed out the door for his daily music lesson. A flurry of activity surrounded Marcelle and she stood lonely and confused at the center of it.

Ruby was the one who gave her "the talk." The night before Ruby's wedding, her older sister had sat her down and told her everything she would need to know.

Everything Sarah had told Marcelle about sex could be summed up in three words: Don't until marriage. That and, "No man wants to marry a woman who isn't a virgin." Even before her wedding night, when her mother was supposed to prepare her, her mother said nothing.

Though poor Mommy, Marcelle thought, with no mother and no sisters, who was there to talk to her?

When Ruby returned from her honeymoon, she invited Marcelle over to her new apartment, served her coffee and cookies on her new table, and put an ashtray right on the table because her mother wasn't in the other room to yell at her. As they smoked their first not-hidden, right-at-the-kitchen-table cigarettes, Ruby's big blue eyes shone as she gave Marcelle all the details.

"The first time hurts like hell. You might not bleed. I didn't, but I was in so much pain, Jimmy knew I was a virgin. The second time was all right. The third time," she laughed, "well, the third time was a lot of fun. It's the best part of being married. You know, not having to make yourself stop."

Days crept by and still Saleem hadn't arrived. Ten days before the wedding Saleem suffered a massive heart attack. He survived, but barely. Sarah wanted to go to Israel immediately, but how could she with her daughter's wedding only days away? She screamed into the phone when she found out, a deep animal howl that echoed in Marcelle's room upstairs, drowning out any last shreds of protest.

Marcelle ran down the stairs to find her mother huddled on the floor, her head between her knees, a sound of desperate pain pouring out of her soul. Marcelle sat next to her mother and held her. She pulled her into her arms and hugged her tightly.

"We'll send him pictures, Mom. Imagine how happy he'll be when he gets them. They'll help him recover. And then maybe Nathan can get some extra time off and we can take our honeymoon in Israel. So we can go see him. Maybe we can all go together."

Sarah kept sobbing, kept wailing, kept killing Marcelle with her grief.

"It'll be okay, Mom, he'll be happy just to know that I got married, right? Maybe we can call him from the wedding. Maybe we can let him hear the music and imagine being with us."

Sarah burrowed her head into her daughter's chest. What kind words she spoke. What she didn't know was that Saleem would have no idea who Marcelle was if he didn't see her with Sarah. That if they just told him about the wedding, it would not register, that if she went to see him in Israel, he would stare at her with empty eyes. No, it didn't work if he couldn't come. It wasn't worth it. All of this, all that she wanted to give him, was for nothing. She held onto Marcelle and cried harder. All her work was for nothing.

Leaving Egypt

Marcelle held her mother's heaving body and swore she would do anything to take her pain away. She chastised herself for being so selfish, for thinking only of her own needs when her mother suffered so greatly. It wasn't like she was being sent to the old country to marry a man she had never met. It was Nathan. She loved him. She had chosen him. It was just not on her terms. In the face of her mother's pain, so what?

She swallowed all reservations, and focused on the day. It was to be a beautiful, elegant wedding, white roses everywhere and candles, and a dress made of silk sateen, overlaid with lace embroidery, and three hundred friends and family coming to celebrate with them, Lenny Sayegh playing Arabic music and a DJ later to play disco music for the young people. It would be a fun night, a lovely night to look back on. Who knew, maybe Nathan would even dance.

Then Saleem died the night before the wedding. With the end came a silence more deafening than the howling that came with the news of his illness. The call came on Saturday night, the wedding set to take place the next day, on Sunday, a day when Sarah and her brothers would begin their shiva, their mourning period, during which they could not bathe or watch TV or celebrate or go to parties with live music like the wedding that was scheduled for that day.

They could not cancel. Eddie called the rabbi who said that the wedding had to go on, that they would find a loophole for Sarah to attend, even if briefly, but she would not be allowed to dance with her daughter or her friends or her brothers, as they would all be in mourning, too.

Nathan came over and took Marcelle upstairs, where he held her in her bed. He had never been allowed in her room before. That night no one noticed.

"I know this wasn't what you wanted. I hope this horrible tragedy won't mark the start of our marriage tomorrow. I hope you can find a way to be happy about us, even though you're in pain for your mother."

Marcelle cried in his arms, too confused to think. Was this a sign? Was her grandfather telling her something? Should she just call it off?

But Eddie said no. The rabbi said no. Sarah said no.

So on Labor Day 1979, Marcelle and Nathan were married. And after the wedding, they went to the shiva. And after the shiva, they went to a hotel where all the confusion and anger and rage and lust and excitement stretched Marcelle from the inside out, so that her skin felt like it would explode, and her husband, her new husband, took her in his arms and brought her to their bed, and expertly with his hands and with his mouth, brought her to release, and then made love to her, and then despite the pain and the blood that came with her first time, made her relaxed enough, released enough to drift into sleep.

And sleep she did, sleepwalking through the first month of her marriage, the week of her mother's mourning, the setting up house, the grief that hung over everyone, until a fear began to build, a fear that woke her one morning to a pain that burst from deep within her breasts and her belly and she realized that in all of this sleepwalking, they had forgotten about birth control, and then ran to pharmacy to buy a kit, and then peed into a cup, and used a dropper to transfer it to a vial and waited for two hours for the black ring to form, the ring that told her her dreams of college were over.

Nathan came home that night to find her vomiting in the bathroom. He mistook her tears for joy and pulled her into an embrace that crushed her deep into his chest.

"I am so happy, my love, I am so happy. I could not be happier. We have to call your mother. This will change everything for her."

Marcelle continued to cry, stopping only to vomit again.

"Oh my love," Nathan said, kissing her. "Oh, my love. We are going to be so happy."

Part Three: 1989

Chapter One

On a cold winter morning at six a.m., Marcelle stared at her face in the mirror, toothpaste on toothbrush, hand suspended in front of her face, and asked herself the same question Nathan had asked her years ago: Who are you?

At sixteen, she hadn't known the answer; she had barely understood the question. But now, at twenty-seven, the question hung over her head, and the answer remained as elusive as ever.

Mechanically, she moved the bristles over her teeth. Back and forth. Up and down. Top teeth. Bottom molars. The rote answer filled her mind. Wife for almost ten years. Mother of three children. Syrian-Egyptian Jew. Daughter. Sister. Community member.

Minus the wife and mother, it was the same answer she had given Nathan years ago.

On that summer night, sitting on her aunt's porch, listening to the waves roll off the ocean and onto the Jersey Shore, he had responded, "But I know all that. Who are *you*?"

A collection of categories, she answered, brushing her hair, and pulling it into a ponytail. Categories that come with duties, the answer continued as she washed her face and applied moisturizer. Walking down the stairs to turn up the heat and put on the coffee, she thought, someone who makes everyone's life run smoothly. But what about your life, the voice in her head she had named "The Grand Inquisitor" asked. To which her resigned self responded, chuckling, that is my life.

The Grand Inquisitor continued. What is that life made of? Heh, heh, she thought. That life is made of food.

Pushing questions out of her head, she pulled her bathrobe tight around her body and poured herself a cup of coffee. Nathan's doctor told him skim milk, sweet and low, but Nathan was still sleeping, so Marcelle added cream and sugar. And a cigarette.

She had to hide them. Ladies didn't smoke, Mom said, and certainly not in front of their children. Somehow Mom's two-foot-high water pipe didn't count as smoking. They were under the sink, behind the cleaning products, in the box of brillo where no one else would look. Because who else scrubbed the stove with steel wool?

My favorite time of the day, she thought, inhaling. Everyone is here, everyone is sleeping, and I can watch the night slowly fade as the morning lights up my kitchen. The big bay windows looked out onto the pathetic patch of grass they called a yard in Brooklyn, but the light and the image of the snow-covered bushes were soothing. As were the greys of the granite and the blues of the cabinets, slowly changing hues as the room grew brighter. These few moments of solitude before the day began recharged her. No one asking for anything, expecting anything, needing anything, demanding anything. Just a few moments, alone, with herself, her thoughts, and her silence.

And her voices.

What a nut job I am, she thought, naming voices in my head.

The Grand Inquisitor: a new voice, or one long dormant, reawakened by her crazy questions or perhaps the source of them?

Staring at her grey granite countertops, Marcelle noticed the neatly lined glass mason jars, containing coffee, tea, sugar and flour, glimmering with sunlight. She knew her favorite time of day was over.

She stubbed out her cigarette and drank her last sip of coffee. Time to get back to reality, she thought. But why isn't this your reality, the Grand Inquisitor asked?

Putting the Turkish coffee pot on the flame for Nathan, and removing pancake mix from the pantry, she answered, because there's everyone else to take care of.

Everyone else began to stir upstairs, and her silence was broken by the sounds of her baby's cries coming through the monitor with echoes of the alarm going off again to wake Nathan.

She mixed the pancake batter quickly in a big silver bowl, took out plates and little forks, and went back upstairs to wake her children.

Lauren first, because Lauren took longer to get out of bed and usually needed a second waking. Her father's daughter, eight-year-old Lauren liked staying in bed, and her mother hated taking her out of it.

Deep breath. Try not to start the morning out yelling. And taking hold of Lauren's arm, she gently shook, "Lauren, honey, it's time to wake up."

"Noooo," a deep moan that would soon turn into a yell as Marcelle kept shaking, kept saying, gently, "Lauren, honey, it's time to wake up."

"Five more minutes," she said, rolling over to make her point.

It's like a script, Marcelle thought, the same lines every day, and she went down the hall to wake Jack. Her six-year-old, as sweet awake as he was asleep, moved his tongue around his mouth and rubbed his eyes. He smiled.

"What's for breakfast?" he asked, through his yawn.

"Pancakes," she said.

"Yummy," he said, scratching his head.

Then back to Lauren. Marcelle could hear the water running in their bathroom, and Sarah crying in her bedroom. Steeling herself for the fight with Lauren she wished, just once, that Nathan would take the baby out of the crib, change her diaper and bring her downstairs. But their roles were clear; he was the breadwinner, she was the homemaker. Couldn't those lines be blurred once in a while?

"Lauren, get up. I have to go make breakfast."

"Five more minutes," Lauren whispered.

Keep your patience.

"Do we have to have this fight every morning?" Marcelle said.

Lauren rolled over and pulled the blankets over her head.

Patience was lost. She yanked Lauren's arm.

"Get up NOW!"

"You're so mean!"

"I'm awful, I know," Marcelle replied, as Lauren got out of bed.

Next, Marcelle went to Sarah's room. Your greatest joy is in your children, her mother always said, and that joy was embodied in sweet
130

Sarah's smile. She stood in her crib, her messy curls a cloud of brown fuzz surrounding her round, smiling face.

"Mommy!" she yelled, holding her arms out.

At least one of my daughters is happy to see me, Marcelle thought, lifting her baby out of the crib. Laying her down on the changing table, Marcelle cleaned her and blew raspberries on the smooth softness of Sarah's belly. She took delight in the adoring eyes that studied her, giggling from the feeling of vibrating lips on her skin.

Sarah sat calmly as Marcelle brushed her hair and put it back, cleaned her face with a wet washcloth and put booties on her feet. Nathan didn't like to see his children looking dirty or messy. Nor his wife, for that matter.

Baby on hip, Marcelle checked Lauren and Jack's rooms to confirm they had gone downstairs. Then to the bathroom to feel the bristles of toothbrushes, making sure they had been used. Time to make pancakes.

Nathan sat at the kitchen table in his striped pajamas with his tousled black hair reading the newspaper.

She leaned in to kiss his cheek.

"Honey," he said quietly, "maybe next time you should make breakfast before you wake them up."

She sighed loudly and rolled her eyes as she sat Sarah in her highchair. Last time they had complained that breakfast was cold. You just can't win. They were lucky she didn't feed them cold cereal in the mornings, like other mothers did.

But not her mother. When Marcelle was young, Mom had always appeared at the breakfast table dressed, her hair done, her makeup on, to serve them hot breakfasts that they never appreciated, either. Her mother was the kind of woman incapable of doing anything half way; the table had always been set before breakfast and included fresh fruit and pastries or cookies in addition to whatever she had cooking on the stove. God, how had she managed to be so perfect all the time, so patient and so happy to do it all?

Questions to ponder another time, when she didn't have children to feed and dress and put on a bus for school.

Eat something, she told herself, you haven't been eating enough lately. Using a spatula, she lifted the remaining four pancakes out of the frying pan and onto her plate.

"Mommy!" yelled Jack. "Lauren just threw her food at me." Marcelle turned around to see Lauren's green eyes wide open with glee, as she stared at globs of syrupy pancakes in her brother's curly hair.

"Lauren! Why would you do something like that?" Marcelle asked. Goddamn it, is this child's mission in life to drive me completely out of my mind?

"Sorry, Mommy," she said, as she tried to hide her smiling face under her napkin.

"Say you're sorry to your brother, and then go stand in the corner while the rest of us finish eating our breakfast."

"I don't want to stand in the corner!" she yelled, banging her hands on the table.

Marcelle looked to Nathan for support. He hid behind his newspaper.

"Go, now, or no TV for two days." She pointed her spatula at the corner, a look on her face that told Lauren she wasn't kidding. Lauren pouted and walked to the corner.

After she had been standing there for two minutes, Nathan, no longer hiding behind his paper said, "Okay, Lauren, that's enough. You can come back to the table now."

Marcelle shot him a dirty look, but he didn't notice.

"Well, it's time to get dressed. Let's go upstairs," she said.

"But I'm hungry!" yelled Lauren.

"Marci, let her finish her pancakes," Nathan interjected.

"She doesn't have any left on her plate, Nathan. Remember, she threw them at Jack?" she said.

"Aren't there any more?" Nathan replied, head back in his paper.

"Other than the ones I'm eating, no."

"Well, then Lauren, I guess you'd better learn to behave yourself next time. Now go on upstairs and get dressed."

Why does she listen to him, Marcelle wanted to know, as she watched her daughter silently make her way from the table. One word from him, spoken calmly, without raising his voice, was enough to mobilize armies, yet she could be standing there, screaming at the tops of her lungs and the response was the same she'd expect in a clinic for the deaf.

Shaking her head, she grabbed a child in each arm and dragged them up the stairs. After dressing them (and cleaning Jack's hair), she dressed herself, dragged them both back down the stairs, checked their backpacks, stuffed in their lunches, put on hats, jackets and gloves, and got them out the door in time to hear the bus driver honk his horn.

Nathan, now neatly combed and dressed in a dark suit, was on his way out the door as Marcelle made her way back in.

"Have a nice day, honey," he said, kissing her on the cheek.

She stiffened.

"What's wrong?" he asked.

"Nothing," she huffed, and started to walk past him.

He held her arm. "Marci, did I do something wrong?"

Exhaling sharply, she stared at the carpet.

"If you don't tell me when I do something wrong, I'm going to keep doing it. What is it?"

He spoke in the tone that annoyed her most, that measured patience one used when speaking to a child or an idiot.

"Marci?"

"Fine," she said. "I wish you would pay attention to what goes on in this family. You just sit there absorbed in your newspaper while the kids drive me crazy."

"What! You handled everything perfectly. It didn't seem like you needed me."

"Yeah, it seemed like that because you were hiding behind your goddamned newspaper!"

"What's this really about, baby? You haven't been you in a long time."

"Don't blame this on my mood. I hate when you do that."

Nathan looked like he was about to lose his temper but he took a deep breath and calmed himself down. Does he always have to calm himself down? Can't the man just yell once in a while?

"Listen, I really have to go. Why don't we talk about this tonight?"

"Fine," she said, continuing to admire the carpet.

"I love you," he said, his voice rising at the end, as though he were asking a question.

"Uh huh. I love you, too." Good thing the carpet was pretty.

Finally he left. She was alone with Sarah; the house was hers. Welcoming the silence, Marcelle pondered her day. What to do? So many possibilities and yet they all seemed the same: shop for food, cook with her mother, cook with Ruby, or cook alone. Other alternatives were: clean the house, do the laundry, reorganize the pantry, or possibly, get her nails done.

All things her mother would approve of.

What she really wanted was to deposit Sarah in her playpen so she could take a nap.

Instead, she sat on the couch. Sarah hobbled about, playing with her dolls and occasionally screaming, "Baby!" evidently not knowing she was one.

Your joy is in your children. Your joy is in your children. She looked at Sarah and tried to feel joy.

"Yummy yummy?" Sarah said.

"You're hungry?" Marcelle asked. Of course she's hungry, you idiot. You haven't fed her yet.

Sarah nodded.

"Well then, we should feed you," she said, walking into the kitchen.

"Yummy yummy!" Sarah yelled, as Marcelle put on her bib and sat her in her high chair.

There must be something wrong with me.

Sitting in her kitchen with her daughter, Marcelle mechanically shoved a spoon into an eager mouth. Wrinkling her nose, Sarah made a "ffffhhhh" sound as yogurt dribbled down her chin. With her chubby hand, she attempted to wipe the wetness off her face. It was adorable. Marcelle didn't feel adoring.

"Mommy!" Sarah exclaimed, as Marcelle used a napkin to clean her face. Banging her hands on the table, Sarah giggled and yelled, "Mommy, Mommy, Mommy!" then sucked her teeth into her bottom lip and released: her way of blowing a kiss.

Your joy is in your children.

Smiling a thin smile, Marcelle blew a kiss back. And counted down the minutes till she could put Sarah down for a nap.

How did I get here, she asked herself. How did I get to the place where I'm just trying to muscle through every minute of the day?

It wasn't always like that. Once upon a time, Nathan's every word had delighted her as much as it now annoyed her. Once upon a time, she had been able to watch Lauren playing for hours with her toys, finding her every gesture amusing, adorable, even more entertaining than *The Cosby Show*.

One afternoon, when Lauren was two, Marcelle had covered the kitchen of their small apartment in white paper, dressing her daughter in a onesie and herself in an old white t-shirt and gym shorts.

She made a palette of primary colors on a piece of cardboard, and dipped Lauren's hands into red and blue paint, pressing them on the paper in the pattern of a heart.

Lauren laughed and clapped her hands.

"Mommy paint!"

Marcelle dipped her hands in the paint, mixed white and red to make pink, and drew a rose on the canvas.

"Flower," she said.

"Flower," Lauren repeated.

After rinsing her fingers in water, she made brown by mixing yellow, red and black, and painted a tree on the canvas next to the flower.

Lauren clapped her hands again and then slapped them on her face. Then, realizing she was wet, cried, "Mommy, dirty."

Marcelle sang to distract her while she cleaned off her face with a wet one, but Lauren kept crying and she pointed to the paint on her onesie.

"That's okay, baby," Marcelle said, drawing a heart on her t-shirt. "We can paint our clothes."

Lauren smiled and smeared her hands on the canvas. Reaching for her mother, she made handprints on Marcelle's shirt.

"You want to decorate Mommy?" Marcelle asked.

When Lauren nodded, Marcelle lay down on her back, letting Lauren paint her stomach.

After smearing paint all over her mother, Lauren said, "Paint you," so Marcelle traced a rainbow on her shirt and drew a heart around her belly button.

"No," Lauren laughed, "paint *you*!" Lauren confused her pronouns, couldn't keep "you" and "me" straight.

Marcelle understood, and drew a heart on Lauren's belly. Lauren giggled. "More!"

When Nathan came home, he found his two favorite girls laughing and covered in paint. He stripped down to his boxers and undershirt and joined them, asking Lauren to decorate his shirt with her paint-covered little fingers.

"Mommy paint," she yelled, so Marcelle drew smiley faces on Nathan's shirt. And then she yelled. "Daddy paint you!" and Nathan looked confused until Marcelle reminded him of Lauren's pronoun confusion and he drew a shining sun on his daughter.

Marcelle's eyes welled with gratitude, looking at her family, their love for each other painted all over their sleeves, all of them dressed in white, the blank canvas of a family they could color however they wished.

There, on that messy floor, covered in splatters of primary colors, Marcelle and Nathan knew they were the luckiest people ever to form a family, and that night, after they washed the blue and red and green out of their daughter's hair, and after putting her to bed, showered together, allowing the paint to drip off their bodies and form a rainbow down the drain, they dried each other off, and went to bed, and made Lauren a brother, so sure that the only thing to do with this amazing love was to create more people to share it with.

Sarah babbled to herself as she stacked her blocks on top of each other and then laughed as she knocked them over. Marcelle watched and yelled at herself for remaining on the couch.

The phone rang.

She didn't want to talk but she walked to the kitchen to answer it.

It was Nathan. "How's your day going so far, honey?"

"Fine," she said, leaning against the wall. "Playing with blocks."

"Nice," he said, "I just called to say hello."

"Hi," she smiled, staring at the picture of him holding Jack on the refrigerator.

"And that I'm going to be working late again tonight."

Silence. Big surprise, she thought. Marcelle twisted the phone cord around her finger. Good thing I have a picture or I'd forget what he looks like.

"I'm sorry, baby. I know this isn't easy for you. This case is a nightmare."

More silence. More cord twisting and untwisting.

"I love you, Marci."

Her finger touched the glossy paper, tracing the outline of his face.

"I love you, too," she said. She closed her eyes and cradled her forehead in her hand, pressing her fingers into her temples.

I hate my life, she thought.

Chapter Two

Just when Marcelle was sure she couldn't feel any worse, Sofia entered their lives, her perfection highlighting Marcelle's every flaw. Sofia was Marcelle's age, glamorous, educated, a career woman, and about to marry Marcelle's little brother Charles.

(He's marrying an older woman? all the old ladies yelled.)

Sophisticated Sofia had been born in Milan, where her parents settled after their exodus from Egypt. She had lived there until she was seven and then relocated to New York. Though Italian was indeed her first language, it seemed positively contrived to Marcelle that her perfect and unaccented English was sprinkled with words like "*bongiorno*" and "*ciao*" and "*grazi*." Marcelle wanted to slap her every time. She also wanted to slap Sofia every time she rubbed her education in their faces saying, "Oh when I was at Barnard studying Italian," or "When I was taking my classes in economics." But what made Marcelle angriest was when Sarah, her mother, always so critical, always rushing Marcelle off to marry and breed and feed, complimented Sofia, saying how wonderful it was for women to be educated, how important it was these days for a woman to be able to be independent.

At her baby brother's meeting of the family, on the night that he proposed, Nathan had to tell Marcelle four times to wipe the scowl from her face.

Is it wrong to hate the bride? she had wondered.

When you barely know her?

And you're celebrating her engagement?

To your little brother?

Yes, part of her said.

Well I do anyway, the rest of her retorted.

And if you must hate her (the reluctant part continued), shouldn't you at least know why?

Was it her name? Sofia. With an eff.

It's just so pretentious, part of her said.

But she was born in Italy, another part of her answered. And she hardly named herself.

Was it her beauty? Her hazel eyes and long black hair? Or her stomach, her breasts, her ass, still nice and firm and devoid of stretch marks because she hadn't given birth to three children?

Was it the constant praise her mother seemed to lavish on Sofia, despite never being able to find a kind word for Marcelle? Sarah complimented Sofia's food, saying Sofia made the best Molkhiyah—a traditional Egyptian soup—that she had ever tasted. Sarah always criticized Marcelle's (too salty, too watery). Sarah loved everything Sofia wore, even suggested to Marcelle that Sofia take her shopping for some new clothes. Marcelle had been furious, but instead of directing her anger at her mother, Marcelle displaced her resentment on her unsuspecting sister-in-law.

Sofia called Marcelle, time and again, telling her that she was only working part time that spring in order to prepare for the wedding. Marcelle screened her calls, making faces at her new answering machine as Sofia invited her to lunch yet again.

"Actually," Marcelle told Ruby one afternoon, as they listened to Sofia leave yet another message, "she's the reason I got the answering machine to begin with. So instead of making excuses every time she gets me on the phone, I can just ignore her calls." The two women were in Marcelle's kitchen, making two hundred mini spinach tarts for Sofia's bridal shower the following week.

"You're evil," Ruby said, filling a tart shell with a sautéed spinach and cheese mixture. "Honestly, how bad can she be?"

Marcelle shuddered. "Awful. I can't believe Charles is marrying an old woman like that. And do you know she was engaged once before? He can have anyone he wants. Why would he want someone who couldn't get anyone else?"

"She's not old. She's our age!" Ruby said.

"Yeah, and I have three children already and you're on your fifth!"

"Seriously, Marce, you better get cracking or you'll never catch up."

"I don't want to. You have too many kids."

"You don't have enough. Jack needs a brother."

Marcelle snorted.

"Very ladylike," Ruby said. "I'm sure your mother would love it."

Marcelle shot Ruby the evil eye. "Are you going out of your way to piss me off today?"

But Ruby just laughed. "After all these years, honey, it's not like I have to try that hard."

Marcelle smirked as she counted the tarts on her baking sheet.

"I wonder if she's even a virgin," Marcelle said, placing a tray into the oven. "Maybe that's why the former fiancé dumped her."

"Do you know why it ended?"

"No. Charles wouldn't tell me. But I can think of a few reasons."

"Do you realize how mean you're being?" Ruby asked. "You sound like one of those horrible old ladies telling stories about people. We hated them when we were single. Don't become one of them now. You know you're going to have to see her for the rest of your life. At least give the poor girl a chance."

I really should, part of her said.

But you know you're not going to, the rest of her answered.

Her mother noticed it. Her mother noticed everything. "Why don't you invite Sofia to your canasta game?" Sarah would ask.

"Because we're already four, Ma. What are we going to do with a fifth?"

"Fine. Well, why don't you ask her to go shopping with you for your dress for the wedding? This way, I can watch Sarah and you can relax while you shop."

"Thanks, but Ruby said she'd come with me."

Sarah scowled and muttered in Arabic.

"You could at least try to like her," she mumbled, under her breath, in English.

140

Marcelle pretended not to hear.

Charles tried, too. He told her about the books Sofia was reading, books he knew Marcelle had read and enjoyed. Marcelle expressed frustration that none of her friends would form a book club; Charles said Sofia would love for Marcelle to join hers. He talked about her love of reading, of culture, how she enjoyed museums and the opera. These were all pursuits Marcelle wanted to cultivate but had no one in her life who shared that desire, save Nathan, who was always at work. Finally, in Sofia she could have a partner. Finally, she could have a sister. He had been so excited upon meeting Sofia, thinking that his older sister would love her, he had said. But every time Marcelle declined an invitation she could hear the hurt in his voice.

Why am I doing this? she asked herself.

Why do I hate her so much?

Marcelle had always considered herself a nice person, a good person, someone a friend could rely on. She watched two of Ruby's kids for a week so Ruby could go to Mexico with her husband. She always said yes if one of the other mothers in her carpool needed her to cover a turn. She volunteered for the PTA bake sale and donated money to charity. But these were all things that came easily to her, didn't require her to try or to work hard. The Sofia situation was the first one that left her struggling. For the first time in her life, Marcelle was purposely being mean. She knew she was wrong, yet she had no desire to stop.

Not that I owe her anything, part of her said.

But what about Charles?

What about Charles? Her little brother, born when she was four years old, old enough to remember loving him, wanting to play with him and trying to feed him (making a huge mess in the kitchen in the process). Charles, whom she respected and admired. The talent in the family. The non-conformist. The free spirit. Whom Marcelle had always supported.

Leaving Egypt

It was Marcelle who facilitated his music career, connecting him with his teacher, convincing their father that it was a good idea. After Charles excelled at the oud, he decided to learn bass guitar. Over their father's objections, he moved out of the house, into an apartment in Park Slope, playing with a blues band in the Village, and later spending a year touring around the country. Marcelle was the only member of her family who went to see him play at CBGB's, dragging Nathan along with her because he wouldn't allow her to be alone in the Village in a bar. She mediated between him and their father, helping Charles develop his business as a wedding musician, while supporting his other endeavors.

Her father was furious that Charles moved out of the house.

"It isn't our way," he said. "He shouldn't have left till he found a wife!"

"Daddy," she said, using her calming voice, the one that always worked on him and never worked on her mother, "lots of boys in the community are moving out now before they get married. It isn't so bad."

"Those other boys aren't my son," he said. "I don't care what they do. This isn't right."

When Charles decided to bum around Europe for a year, sleeping in hostels and playing in jazz clubs, Marcelle defended his choices to their livid father.

"You raised him well, Daddy. He's just getting a few things out of his system before he settles down."

"And what if he doesn't? What if he never grows up? Never gets married? And then, what if he marries out? Some not religious girl, not from our community?"

He couldn't even bring himself to voice the possibility that Charles might marry a non-Jew.

"You just have to have a little faith," she said. "Because at this point, the more you fight him, the harder he's going to fight back."

So when Charles brought Sofia home, a religious Egyptian Jew from a family they knew, everyone was overjoyed.

"You were right," her father said, "I should have listened to you all along. My wise-beyond-her-years daughter." He beamed, looking at his son and his future daughter-in-law.

Yes, everyone was overjoyed.

Everyone but Marcelle.

Chapter Three

Many years after Terra's swanee party in the Aleppo hammam, Sarah and Rosette shopped for Sofia's. The custom's origin—to send the future bride the fee for the mikveh—would have been impossible for an outsider to guess should one have attended the party. Gifts displayed on the swanee table included fur, jewelry, perfume, leather accessories from Italy, imported linens and lace, and, most importantly, the white peignoir for the virginal bride to wear on her wedding night.

Of course, the money for the mikveh was not forgotten: fifty-five dollars were often placed on the inside of an exquisite leather wallet or handbag. The number five, often signified by a hand pendant called a hamsika, was used to ward off the 'ayin—the evil eye. However, to display the $55 to everyone there would be an insult, a presumption that they were jealous people who were giving the 'ayin. Therefore it made more sense to hide it in the wallet, so it could be there for protection without making anyone uncomfortable.

Sarah and Rosette had already selected the handbag to hold the cash when they found themselves in a lingerie shop on Kings Highway, trying to choose a wedding night peignoir from among the many white lace and silk options the shop girl had laid before them.

"The lacework on this is beautiful," said Rosette, holding a short negligee with gossamer thin silk. "And this silk is so soft. I think you should get this one."

"I don't know," Sarah said. "It's a little too sexy. A little too see-through. Maybe this one," she said, lifting a silk sateen night gown.

"That one's so modest she could wear it outside the bedroom," Rosette huffed. "What about this one?" She lifted a longer chiffon and lace gown with a matching robe.

"That's definitely better," Sarah said. "But how am I supposed to know what she'll like? How am I supposed to know if Charles will like it?"

"I thought the same thing when I was buying swanee gifts for my daughters-in-law. But you know what, you try to buy something you think they'll like, but most importantly, you buy something you'll be proud to display to her family. Something that says, 'I think highly of your daughter and bought high quality, classy gifts befitting a proper lady.' And anyway, isn't Marci supposed to find out a few things for you?"

Sarah shook her hand, "My daughter will barely talk to her. I'm embarrassed by how mean she is! Here is this lovely young lady—okay not so young—coming into our family and my daughter, my twenty-seven-year-old daughter, a mother to three children, acts like one of her babies."

"Maybe they had a fight you don't know about?'

"No. I asked Charles. He called to ask me to talk to Marci. That conversation didn't go well."

Rosette just shook her head and sighed, though Sarah suspected Rosette knew the real reason. Sarah did, or at least she thought she so. Marcelle was jealous of Sofia because Sofia was getting the kind of attention a bride should get. Sofia would have months of parties, adoration and attention heaped on her. She would be celebrated in a carefully orchestrated series of affairs that would culminate in a beautiful wedding, planned to perfection.

What she would not get were a haphazard series of rushed and disorganized gatherings, thrown together by force as if to put a check in each box, to get them over with quickly so they could move on to the wedding, so a man she had never met and would never know might take some solace in knowing his granddaughter was married. A man who died the day before the wedding, casting the betrothed in a shadow of grief, and depriving the bride of her mother, the person supposed to advocate for her, guiding her through this life-altering transition. Sofia would not go from her wedding to a funeral, would not spend the week of her honeymoon in a house of mourning, would not have to sublimate her own happiness lest it be inappropriate in a house filled with ineffable loss. It would be bad enough to watch her own sister get the experience she had been denied, but to watch her mother fuss and fawn over a sister-in-law was a slap in the face to Marcelle, and Sarah didn't know how to handle the situation.

The obvious thing would have been to have a talk with her daughter, to apologize for what Marcelle went through but explain that Sarah couldn't very well ignore her new daughter-in-law just because she had not been there for her daughter. That wasn't fair to Charles, and anyway, one had to be on one's best behavior with a new in-law. The mother-in-law/daughter-in-law relationship was ripe for conflict, as Rosette had warned her many times, and it was very important to set the proper tone early. But who could talk to Marcelle these days?

Rosette led Sarah down the street to the jewelry store, where they would pick a necklace and bracelet. Sarah thought pearls were appropriate.

"Absolutely," Rosette concurred, winding the long strand around her fingers and holding them up to the light to look for imperfections. "Plus, a long strand of pearls is a beautiful way to decorate the table. You can drape it over the fur, you can wind them over the linens, you can lace them through the gloves. Anyway, pearls are a gift for a classy lady. Like I said, you can't go wrong with that."

Sarah looked at a few different strands. "I think Marci's still upset about what happened at her wedding."

Rosette looked shocked. "Sarah, you could have hardly prevented that."

Sarah shook her head. "No, not Baba dying. The whole thing. That I wasn't there for her. What a crazy person I was. I didn't even talk to her the night before the wedding. I didn't even tell her what to expect. She must have been so scared."

"Sarah, you can beat yourself up for this as long as you like, but what you really have to look at is how nicely everything turned out. Look what a beautiful life she has now. How much does a bad wedding matter when everything that came after it was so good?"

Sarah nodded her head. Yes, when Marcelle was first married, it did seem she had the perfect life: loving husband, baby on the way, her house full of friends and relatives.

Sarah often thought about how happy she would have been to have a life like that in her youth. Marcelle's biggest blessing, though, lay in something she had never had to experience, something that had haunted Sarah's early years as a bride: loss.

Ten years earlier, when Sarah awoke from the slumber of her grief, she relished in visiting the house of her newly wed daughter. So many things pleased her when she did. Marcelle was shaatra. Even in pregnancy, she kept her house immaculate, and when the house wasn't full of the smell of cookies baking or chicken roasting, the lingering scents of lemon or pine told Sarah how Marcelle had spent the morning. Her house gleamed and she glowed. Sarah had never expected that she would become pregnant so soon, but Marcelle was radiant, full and bursting with life.

Looking at her daughter, Sarah reassured herself that everything always happened for the best, but shortly after Lauren was born, Sarah realized that something had changed between her and Marcelle. First, she thought it was just the fatigue of childbirth followed by the exhaustion of early motherhood. Of course, Marcelle wasn't herself; of course, all she wanted to do was sleep when Sarah came over to help.

But there were signs, tiny signals, that an irreparable damage had been done to their relationship. As a girl, Marcelle had always asked her mother for advice, but now as a wife and mother she turned to Ruby with parenting questions. Instead of calling to ask for Sarah's recipes, she bought the community cookbook when it was printed.

"I don't understand why this upsets you," Marcelle said. "I paid for the book as a donation to a charity you work for. I'm supporting you, here."

But Sarah knew that wasn't it. She wasn't sure if Marcelle knew, but she did.

Sarah tried to make amends, to apologize, to set things right between them, but every time Sarah tried to talk to Marcelle, she made it worse. It wasn't that Marcelle rebuffed her; it was that she refused to admit she was angry. Refusing to admit it made it impossible for them to move past it, and it wedged its way between them, like the root of a tree under the sidewalk that displaces the concrete until finally it cracks.

And they were cracking.

After Jack was born, Sarah saw Marcelle let herself go. She barely wore makeup. She rarely got her nails done. Once, when the two sat drinking tea in Marcelle's house, her raised pant leg revealed a calf covered with hair. Sarah was aghast. What kind of husband wants a wife who looks like that?

Sarah tried to choose gentle words, saying, "Sweetheart you look so pale, go put some color on your face," and Marcelle would get angry, yelling that her mother was always judging her.

When Marcelle came to her mother's house with her hair a mess and specks of food on her clothes, Sarah was embarrassed for her. "Ya rohi," she would say, "when you have small children, you have to check yourself before you leave the house. You were always getting food on me when you were little. I used to feed you in my slip and a bathrobe. I'd leave my dress by the door to put on when we left, or in case someone came over."

Marcelle refused to hear the love in Sarah's advice. Instead she would stare down into her tea. "Well I'm sorry we can't all be as perfect as you, Mom."

But Sarah wasn't trying to get her to be perfect. She knew she wasn't perfect. She was just trying to wake her up. Let her see what she was becoming.

When Sarah offered to babysit so Marcelle could get her hair done, Marcelle just cried. "I'm exhausted. I don't want to get my hair done. Why don't you offer to babysit so I can sleep?"

So Sarah did. She babysat. She brought over food. She played with her grandbabies while her daughter napped and then tidied up before she left. Marcelle would wake up, and hug her, saying, "Thanks, Ma," but there was something missing from her embrace. The physical gestures were there, but the emotions behind them were gone. Marcelle knew she ought to feel gratitude, but something prevented her from being able to take freely from her mother.

Instead, an almost antagonistic relationship developed between the two of them: Sarah did things to help Marcelle, which Marcelle resented, which made Sarah feel freer to criticize. If she was giving Marcelle so much help, she figured, she had the right to speak her mind. Of course, as Marcelle saw it, help shouldn't come with a price tag. If her mother wanted to help her, she should do it without preconditions.

Over the years, their relationship grew worse. At first, Sarah tried to do even more. But Marcelle seemed angry, perceiving her help as an insult, as though Sarah were taunting her, telling her she could not take care of her family by herself. Increasingly, she refused to take things from Sarah. Soon the two were like the Americans and the Soviets living out their own version of the cold war: measure met counter-measure, move provoked counter-move, neither side admitting what they had done, neither side owning its aggression.

"I can take care of myself," Marcelle would say. The problem was, she couldn't.

Of course, it grew harder with each child; Sarah remembered that, but after baby Sarah was born, it felt like Marcelle had given up. Marcelle's house was always a mess, even after the kids had gone to sleep. Sarah often invited the whole family over for Shabbat dinner, partially to help, but also because she didn't enjoy eating Marcelle's food anymore. It was like she wasn't paying attention when she cooked. Sometimes the chicken was overcooked. Sometimes the soup was too salty. Often the dishes didn't go together—there was no sense to be made from the combinations of food she decided to serve. Sarah knew that she had taught her better.

Even Eddie, who was never one to complain, said, after one particularly disappointing meal, "Sarah, I think you need to go over to help her. It tasted like she cooked that in her sleep."

But that was not all Eddie said, and Eddie was in a position to know. He and his daughter still had a fine relationship. He often dropped by Marcelle's house on his way home after work. He would play with Lauren and Jack, try to help Lauren with her homework. Sometimes he would offer to bathe the kids while Marcelle cleared their dinner. Somehow, she didn't resent his help. He tried to continue their habit of watching the news together. He would often bring over newspaper or magazine articles for her to read, curious about her opinion.

"What do you think about this George Bush?" he asked. "Do you think he'll be as good a president as Reagan? Do you think he'll get along as well with Gorbachev?"

If she said, "Daddy, I don't have time," he would say, "Sit down, read it now. I'll go bathe the kids. Your mother refuses to talk politics, your brother only cares about music, and your husband is always working. You're my only hope."

But after Sarah was born, Marcelle barely participated in their conversations. She lacked the energy and confidence to form an opinion, no matter how much Eddie egged her on. "Daddy, does it really matter?" was all she could muster.

"Our daughter is very unhappy," Eddie said after coming home from one such evening with Marcelle. "I'm worried if we don't intervene, she'll fall into a depression."

Sarah raised an eyebrow.

"I saw a special about depressed mothers on 20/20," Eddie continued.

"But what does she have to be depressed about?" Sarah asked, exasperated, as she served him dinner. He was starving. The only things to eat in Marcelle's house were cereal, frozen pizza and some tasteless pasta dish.

"That's not the point," Eddie said. "We have to help her."

"It's not like I don't try," Sarah said. "She has to learn to help herself. She has to pull herself out of bed every day and attend to her responsibilities. She can't mope around like a crazy woman. She has children to think about."

They were sitting at their kitchen table. Since the kids moved out, they rarely used the dining room.

Eddie tried to calm Sarah down. "Don't be so critical. She's having a hard time."

"But from what?" Sarah wanted to know. "What is a hard time? We had a hard time Eddie; things were hard for us. I would have given anything to live her life when I was younger. She does not have a hard life. She just feels sorry for herself. And she's still mad at me after all these years, whether she knows it or not."

"You're her mother, Sarah," he said. "You have to help her."

"She's a grown woman, Eddie."

"It doesn't matter. You're still her mother."

Sarah slumped down into her chair. "Eddie, I swear, if I knew how to help her, I would."

Eddie wanted to watch *Crossfire* on CNN, so the two moved to the living room. They showed a clip of Ayatollah Khomeini, thundering his fatwa against Salman Rushdie, ordering his death for *The Satanic Verses*.

Watching Khomeini scream on television brought Sarah back ten years, when that same angry man refused the pleas of President Carter to let American hostages come home, when she was held captive to her grief, when her father was finally, irrevocably dead after being a prisoner for so many years.

Was it better that he had been freed after so long to spend a few months with his children, or would God have been more merciful to let him die years earlier? Had all the years of suffering been worth the few months of freedom he had in the end?

She remembered ten years earlier, right after he died, watching the families of the hostages on the news, watching the hostages themselves on television, in a tape of a Christmas party that their captors had made. Americans tied yellow ribbons around trees. They never tied ribbons for her father. Their lives didn't stop the way the lives of the Iranian hostages' families seemed to stop.

When the Mizrahis got Saleem back, it was nothing like what she would later see on TV. He wasn't only thinner, with more facial hair, but he was a lifetime older, twisted and turned in both body and soul, and only in very rare moments on very lucky days, a semblance of the same man. She had offered up her daughter in the hopes of awakening him, had sacrificed her daughter on the altar of her guilt. Then he died anyway, unaware of what she had tried to give him, the penance she had

151

tried to make. In trying to save her father, she had lost her daughter, and in ten years had not found a way to win her back.

Chapter Four

Marcelle had just put Sarah down for a nap when she heard Charles's voice on the answering machine.

"Marci, pick up," he said. "I just got off the phone with Mom. She told me you were home."

She ran to grab the phone. "Hey, Charles," she said, stalling to think of an excuse. "I was..."

"Don't 'hey Charles' me. I'm very upset with you. We need to talk."

"Okay," she said. "What about?"

"You know what about. I expected this from our parents, maybe, because she's a little older and a career woman and independent. From them, maybe. But never from you. Anyway, I don't want to talk about this on the phone."

"Fine," she said, trying to keep the shame out of her voice. "When are you coming to Brooklyn?"

"I live in Brooklyn, Marci. I'm here right now."

"You know what I mean."

"Yeah, the tiny little universe all of you live in. No, you come to Park Slope. Tomorrow. I'll be home most of the day."

She agreed. Hanging up the phone she felt her heart beating faster. Realizing she was clamping her hands on her granite countertops, she picked them up and saw the moist handprints her sweating palms had left behind. She sensed an ugliness inside of her, a feeling of being very, very young and having done something very, very bad. But then she thought of Sofia again, and try as she did, she could not suppress the feeling of hatred that rose along with the mental image.

Who is this horrible person I'm turning into?

The next day, Marcelle dropped Sarah off at Ruby's house, Ruby patting her back reassuringly and wishing her luck. She drove to Park Slope, down tree-lined Ocean Parkway, admiring the leaves as they began to fill the branches again, to the Prospect Expressway, exiting on Fourth

Avenue and driving down the scary avenue where her brother lived. His apartment, the second floor of a walk-up on Fifth Avenue and President, was across the street from the shadiest bodega she had ever seen, one that sold two dusty cans of Goya beans and no milk, and was closed half the afternoon. A pockmarked, nervous man usually inhabited the doorway of the adjacent building. That was, if he wasn't pacing back and forth on the block talking to himself.

Marcelle remembered the first time she had seen the apartment, how she had yelled at him. Why hadn't he moved into one of those nice buildings off Seventh Avenue? Why live here, next door to what looked like a crack den?

"Do you want to pay my rent?" was all he answered.

Though he had lived there for over two years, Marcelle still hadn't gotten used to it and rarely came to visit him. That April morning, though, she had no choice.

Anxiously, she waited for him to answer the door, rehearsing an invented defense in her head, and a promise to try harder. She knew how thin her words sounded, and that was before they even left her mouth.

The door opened. It was Sofia. Shit. What was she doing there? Were they already living together?

Sofia raised an eyebrow. "Hi Marci," she asked more than said.

"Oh. Um. Hi Sofia. Uh, is, uh, Charles here?"

"Oh. No. He's in rehearsals all day."

"Really? He was supposed to meet me here."

"That's odd. He didn't say anything about it to me. Well, there's no need to stand in the street. Why don't you come in?"

Marcelle tried to think of an excuse, but realized there wasn't one she could make. She had, after all, planned on being there all afternoon.

Well played, baby brother.

Following Sofia upstairs, Marcelle noticed she was in bleach-stained sweatpants and a Poison t-shirt. Her hair, normally so perfectly styled, was in a messy careless bun, held in place with a black sparkled scrunchy.

"Please," Sofia said, leading her into the living room. "Have a seat."

She gestured to the couch, a hideous crushed velvet green affair that had clearly been a hand-me-down from someone who realized the seventies were over. A freshly poured glass of wine sat on top of a cheap wooden coffee table, the legs so uneven that two of them had folded cardboard of varying thicknesses wedged underneath them. The windows were open, and a fresh breeze filled the room, but underneath it, Marcelle could smell the fetid scent of an apartment that had not been cleaned in a while.

"Would you like a glass?" Sofia asked.

Marcelle shook her head, feeling confirmed in her suspicions. What kind of woman drinks wine at one o'clock in the afternoon?

"Some tea, then?" Sofia asked.

"Uh, sure. Thanks."

Sofia left the room and Marcelle wondered what on earth they would talk about. While Sofia was certainly being polite, all the unanswered phone calls and ignored invitations had clearly had their effect.

Marcelle tried to think of an explanation, but she didn't have one.

I never called you back because I hate you.

But then another voice, taking the shape of Sofia's, asked, "But what did I ever do to deserve your hate?"

Nothing. She knew that. They both knew that.

Marcelle felt awkward sitting on the couch, waiting, so she went to the kitchen to see if she could help. Something made her stop before she entered the doorway. She wasn't sure if it was the shock of the music: loud, angry and metallic. Marcelle had always imagined Sofia listening to opera or Beethoven, not this sort of music that greasy-haired kids in tattoos and leather listened to. She had expected Sofia to be immaculately clean, so she was shocked by the piles of dishes and empty takeout containers, the sour smell of old garbage. What surprised her most was the ashtray filled with lipstick-stained cigarette butts and a pack of Parliaments sitting on the table.

Sofia stood in front of an opened window, her hand stuck outside of it, holding a cigarette.

"Sofia?" Marcelle said.

Sofia jumped and turned around, dropping the cigarette into an ashtray on the window sill, the back of her hand flying to her face to wipe her eyes.

When Sofia turned around, Marcelle saw the black smudges on her face, the bloodshot eyes.

Marcelle felt frozen, the ice spreading inside her, freezing and squeezing her gut. She had known all these weeks that her actions were causing Sofia pain. She had relished in it. But facing that pain was too much

Marcelle walked to the table and lifted the pack of Parliaments. She heard a sharp intake of air, and then a sigh of relief when she took out a cigarette and asked, "Do you mind if I have one, too?"

"Not at all," Sofia said.

She made space by the window, where Marcelle joined her.

"What is this music?" Marcelle asked.

Sofia smiled. "Nine Inch Nails. Charles hates it, but it helps me when I'm in a certain frame of mind."

"Yeah, like me and smoking. Nathan hates when I smoke," Marcelle said. "I can usually only have one when I'm home alone. And my mother? Huh. Don't ever smoke in front of her. Even if she's smoking out of her narghile."

"Your mother scares me," Sofia said.

"She scares me, too," Marcelle said, "but she seems to love you."

"She said that?"

"No, but she never criticizes you. She criticizes everyone. Especially me."

"Maybe it's one of those reverse things. She only criticizes people she loves."

"Nah. She pretty much leaves Charles alone, too."

Sofia shrugged and inhaled.

The teakettle whistled. Sofia stubbed out her cigarette and turned off the flame. She removed the last two clean teacups from the pantry and filled them with mint leaves, pouring the hot water on top. Marcelle joined her as she made her way to the kitchen table, trying to silence her critical voice as Sofia just pushed all the dirty cups and plates out of the way.

Marcelle inhaled deeply over her teacup, taking in the scent of the dried mint leaves.

"Hey, are you okay?" she asked, her hand lightly grazing Sofia's forearm.

Sofia shrugged and sipped her tea. "It doesn't matter," she said.

"You look really upset," Marcelle said.

"And you care all of a sudden?"

Marcelle gasped and widened her eyes.

"I'm sorry," Sofia said. "I shouldn't have said that."

Marcelle smiled and looked down. "No, I deserved that. But I really do care, even if I've been bad about showing it."

Sofia sipped her tea again. "I'm so tired of the constant criticism."

"What do you mean?"

"My mother and my aunts. That's why I'm here all the time. They drive me crazy. This is the only place I can get some peace."

"What do they say?"

"For years, it was that no good Egyptian boy was going to marry me. Because I was too old. Or too independent. Even now, they tiptoe around Charles, telling me to push up the wedding, yelling at me for taking six months to plan it. As though he'll change his mind any minute. Come to his senses and realize what a mistake he's making. Do you know how hard it is to be twenty-eight and unmarried in this community? You may as well be dead. People pity you. Right to your face. They ask you what's wrong with you that you're still single. Like you wanted to be single! I mean, I love my job, I do, but what I really want is to be married, to have a family. Do you know how many guys I dated before I found Charles? Do you know how many guys there are in this community who want their wives to be docile little creatures living in the house? Stupid, silent and pregnant."

Marcelle was silent. Like me, she thought.

"I guess you don't," Sofia continued. "You got lucky to meet Nathan when you were so young. To be married to someone who wants to hear what you think and respects your opinion. Charles told me how Nathan was always bringing you books, arguing politics with you. I guess in the end we're both lucky, marrying open-minded men."

Marcelle was sure she was going to cry.

"Sometimes I'm afraid they're right, though. That Charles is going to wake up, realize he's only twenty-five, and decide he wants some eighteen-year-old."

Sofia noticed.

"What's wrong," Sofia asked. "Did I say something wrong?"

Marcelle shook her head.

"Did I do something wrong? You know, before? Did I mess up in some way?"

Marcelle shook her head again.

"Because I really thought we'd get along. The way Charles talks about you..."

"You should hear what he says about you. He isn't going anywhere. Believe me. I would know. You make him really happy."

"So then why do you...?"

"I don't know," Marcelle said. But she did. She had always known but was too embarrassed by her own pettiness to admit it to herself.

Marcelle half smiled and shook her head. "You know last year Lauren came home from school crying. She had made friends with this girl Sally and Sally's friend Grace wouldn't stop teasing her and calling her names, and I told her that Grace was just jealous of her because of her friendship with Sally and that's why she was so mean."

"You think I'm going to take Charles away from you?"

Marcelle shook her head and looked down. She lit another cigarette, trying to find her words. It seemed so stupid, so embarrassing to say out loud. Sofia had barely moved, barely breathed, while waiting for her to answer.

"No," she said, looking Sofia in the eye. "It's just that," she shook her head and looked down again, "I always wanted to go to school, to have a career."

"So?" Sofia said, putting her hand on Marcelle's arm. "I don't understand. Why don't you?"

Marcelle shook her head. "It's too late. What am I qualified to do?"

"So go to school," Sofia said.

Marcelle shook her head. "I can't do that."

"Why not?" Sofia pressed. "Your older kids are in school, your younger one will be next year. Ask your mother to help you. What else is she doing all day? Honestly, how much cooking can one person do?"

Marcelle shook her head and stared at the ashtray filled with cigarette butts.

"Marci," she continued, "you can't wait for people to give you things. If you want something, you have to make it happen."

Marcelle shook her head again and decided it was time to go. She hugged Sofia, repeating her apology and promising to get together again soon.

Later that night, Marcelle's mother called. "I hear you need some babysitting," Sarah said. "I can give you a few hours on Tuesdays and Thursdays. Get back to me on the times you need."

Soon after, Charles dropped by. "This is from Sofia," he said, handing her a wrapped package. "I told you she wasn't so bad."

Marcelle tore off the wrapping paper to find a catalogue of Brooklyn College's classes for the summer session.

"Tell her she's amazing," Marcelle said, eyes tearing as she thumbed through the pages.

"I tell her all the time," he said, a smile forming in his brown eyes. He handed her the phone. "Why don't you?"

Chapter Five

Angie was a bad influence. At least that's what her mother would have said had Marcelle brought Angie home when she was young. Marcelle imagined her mother's reaction to the story Angie was telling her, and then wondered what kind of almost thirty-year-old (oh, hush, you just turned twenty-eight) woman with three children still thinks of everything in terms of her mother.

Turning her attention back to Angie, she focused on the story.

Angie, a beautiful twenty-three-year-old Italian girl, with dark curly hair and kohl-lined brown eyes, squinted behind her oversized glasses in the summer sun, as she told her classmate and new friend Marcelle the sordid details of her sexual encounters with the two men she was currently sleeping with.

"Fucking, Marci," Angie would correct her. "'Sleeping with' sounds so genteel."

And Marcelle would blush, and Angie would laugh and say, "God, I feel like the Grand Whore of Babylon talking to you."

During one of their many lunch time conversations Angie said, "Come on, I know you're the happily married lady, but you have to have one sordid story from your past. Just tell me."

Marcelle laughed. "After listening to you, I sort of wish I did, but I don't."

"How is that even possible?" Angie yelled. "What about prom night? You went to your prom, didn't you?"

"Yeah," Marcelle replied. "But I went with Nathan. And Nathan already knew he wanted to marry me, and he respected me too much to push me into having sex."

"What, he needed to push you? You didn't want to have sex?"

"I did," she said, a half smile creeping onto her face. She averted her eyes and then shrugged. "But I was raised to wait until marriage. And I started dating Nathan when I was sixteen, and he was my only boyfriend, and I married him less than two years later, so when was there time?"

160

"Well, I was raised to wait until marriage, too, and look at me."
Angie gestured to her low-cut shirt, her ample cleavage proudly on
display. She took a drag off her cigarette. "Wow, a virgin bride. You're
my Sicilian grandmother's wet dream."

So little separated the two women on the surface. They were both
in their twenties, both born in Bensonhurst, though now Marcelle lived in
Midwood, both first-generation Americans, the children of immigrant
parents deeply rooted in the values and traditions of their home
countries, committed to keeping their families together and their
daughters in their cultures.

"And both utterly obsessed with food," Angie would laugh.
Because even she, who had moved into her own apartment over her
mother's screams, who never wanted to get married, who gagged at the
thought of children, could make pasta from scratch and a red sauce so
good it made men weep with joy.

Angie seemed so free. Unencumbered by a husband and
children, somehow oblivious to her overbearing mother, Angie sat on the
green lawn of Brooklyn College's campus, smoking and cursing and
commenting on the "fuckability" of each man who walked by, while
wearing see-through lacy clothing that showed her bra, and some of what
was in her bra, without being remotely embarrassed.

Marcelle, on the other hand, wore a prim white and pink cotton
sundress, lowered her voice every time she said "shit," and smoked
discreetly, hiding the cigarette behind her back when it wasn't at her lips,
furtively glancing about should one of the many passersby be someone
who knew her family.

It was summer semester, and though she knew several other
people from her community who were students at Brooklyn College, most
of the ones she knew were away at the Jersey Shore for the summer.
Marcelle and Nathan had stayed in Brooklyn that summer because, after
ten years of dreaming about it, Marcelle had finally decided to go to
college. Though Marcelle had always been sure that her mother and
Nathan would object to her shirking her responsibilities as wife and
mother, they had been incredibly supportive. Maybe they had finally

noticed she was losing it. Marcelle's mother had stayed in Brooklyn, too, picking up the kids from camp and watching the baby on the two days a week that Marcelle went to class.

Angie, an English major, was in both of her classes, taking her last four classes so she could finally graduate. She was supposed to have graduated the previous year, but had taken some time off to recover from a disastrous love affair. That Angie, who relished in the sharing of details, declined to do so regarding this episode, told Marcelle that those details must have been very painful, so she never asked.

"Sometimes I'm embarrassed to talk to you about this stuff," Angie said one day, as they sat sharing iced coffees in the campus café. The room smelled like old grease and fresh cookies. On the table next to them, two girls with teased hair played Bon Jovi's *New Jersey* on their boom box. Angie had been giving them dirty looks, but "Bad Medicine" was one of her favorite songs, so she stopped when it came on.

"Why? I have three kids, you know. It's not like I don't know how sex works," Marcelle said.

"Fine," Angie said, "then show me." She emptied the cigarettes out of the pack and onto the table. Circling her index finger and thumb around six cigarettes she said, "Frankie's is about this thick," and then taking two more, "but Peter's," she giggled, "Peter's peter is more like this. It's so big it hurts sometimes."

Marcelle widened her eyes, felt herself blush, giggled and looked down. The room was over-air-conditioned. She pulled her cardigan around her and rubbed her arms.

Angie dropped the cigarettes back onto the table. "So, show me, how big is Nathan's?"

Marcelle made her shocked face. "I can't do that. He's my husband."

"Oh, come on! This is what girlfriends are supposed to talk about."

"Not my girlfriends! You'll see when you get married."

"If I get married."

"Okay, if you get married. I can't talk about my husband that way."

"But if you can't talk about your husband, and you've only ever had sex with your husband, then you can't talk about sex at all. Where's the fun in that?"

Marcelle raised her eyebrows and shrugged. Then she grabbed one of the cigarettes off the table and lit it. Angie lit one, too.

She must think I'm such an old lady, Marcelle thought.

"You must think I'm such a whore," Angie said.

Marcelle laughed. "Not at all," she said. "In fact, I sort of envy you."

Angie laughed so hard she snorted.

"No really. I have no idea what else is out there. I think Nathan and I have good sex, well, when we have sex, but I have nothing to compare it to. Maybe it's terrible and I don't even know."

"Oh, sweetie, you would know if it was bad, trust me on that. And don't worry too much about what's out there. The chase is exciting, but once you get it, most of it sucks."

"I know, but there's something I'll never have again. Newness. Excitement. The chase. I gave that up at age eighteen. I'm married. It's over."

"See, that's what I love about you. For you, married is over. One of my girlfriends, Judy, for her 'I'm married' means 'I need to be discreet so he doesn't find out.' You're so good."

"No, I'm not," she said, as she looked around the room at the posters that papered the walls. "Justice for the students at Tiananmen Square!" screamed one. "Solidarity with Solidarity," proclaimed another. Another still showed a picture of Reagan shaking hands with Gorbachev, with a caption that read, "Mr. Gorbachev, tear this wall down!"

"If I were so good, I would join one of these causes," she replied, gesturing to the wall of activism.

Angie shook her head. "Those people aren't 'good.' They're just self-important. You, my dear, are the real deal."

Again, Marcelle averted her eyes, tilted her head and shrugged one shoulder.

And again that half-smile crept onto her face.

Because lately Marcelle wasn't sure she wanted to be good. Lately, the opportunity for being very, very bad had been dangled in front of her and, though she had expected herself to be disgusted by it, she was amazed to find herself excited.

So when Angie said things like, "Only one person for the rest of your life, I don't know how you do it," instead of answering, "I just do," Marcelle thought, "I don't know how either."

Just thinking that way shocked her.

Since when do I ask questions like that? she wondered.

You're married. You have kids. You don't have the luxury of wondering, what if...

Marcelle was scared she was obvious, that everyone around her could tell. She felt like a different person, like a fraud, like every time she thought of him, the faint beginnings of the scarlet letter A emblazoned itself on her forehead. As she blushed and giggled and balked at the thought of discussing Nathan's anatomy, she wondered about the anatomy of another man, and how that anatomy would feel if...Stop!

And then: shame. Was this why I went back to school? Was this what was missing in my life, making me miserable? And I found it by flirting with a stupid boy? Am I that shallow? Am I that much of a cliché?

He was going to join the Peace Corps. Was leaving for Senegal after exams, after graduation. In October (after the holidays, her mother's voice reminder her). They could have a brief, passionate fling, and then he would be gone for the next two years. Over, clean, no problem of him showing up at her house demanding she leave her husband.

A few weeks.

A few nights, even.

Oh, I would never.

But just the thought of it, the idea, filled her with exhilaration: the perfect point where excitement and fear meet.

164

She was afraid and excited.

She wanted to touch him. (Where? How much?)

Am I honestly capable of it?

Who is this person having these thoughts?

How did I get here?

Chapter Six

His name was Chris. Short for Christian. Christian Dane. (Though what a stupid name, she thought; it would be as silly as naming one of her sons Jewish.) He was in her writing workshop, and he had submitted a story, a romance, and it was clear that the main character, Mary, was based on her.

Late at night, the kids long sleeping, Nathan coming home somewhere between now and never, Marcelle sat on the black leather couch in her living room, reading his story and wondering why.

And did the other students in the class know it was her?

It wasn't even subtle. Reading his description of Mary's clothes, she had to laugh. He described Mary's shirt, red, off the shoulder with a wide black patent leather belt: it was her favorite. Marcelle laughed, sitting on the couch, looking down at the same shirt worn today, as in the story, with red, white and black plastic bracelets.

She didn't know if she should feel angry or embarrassed for him.

But it wasn't just her clothing. He had noticed her mannerisms. Mary drummed her right hand while biting on the nail of her left index finger when she was nervous, a tick Nathan teased her for all the time, something she was certain she had done when her classmates had workshopped her story two weeks earlier.

He described the time she had knocked his books off his desk during a heated discussion. He included the day she had walked into a glass door while talking to him in the hallway.

God, I am such a spaz.

Though embarrassed by his detailed recall of her klutziness, Marcelle found herself strangely flattered. But then again, mortified. Was he mocking her?

But he wasn't. Because Mary was "beautiful, a lady, an embodiment of the eternal feminine. And the light of life blazed from her face like the sun in the early hours of morning."

Dear God, isn't he embarrassed to write this tripe?

Marcelle wanted to call Ruby to read some of this to her, but the clock on the wall read 10:30. Anyway, that might be really mean.

Then again, he was the one who handed it out to the entire class.

"Craig saw in Mary everything he had ever dreamed of in a woman. Though he lay in bed with Lacey, the latest in an unending string of young beauties he brought to his bed, his heart only dreamed of Mary, his angel of purity, the one woman he could never hope to possess."

At this point she laughed out loud. The young stud, pining away for the unavailable woman, a modern-day retelling of knights and courtly love.

It was horrible. But it was also kind of sweet. Did he mean it? Was it a message? Or was he just using some of her actions because they perfectly described a beautiful, likeable, adorably absent-minded woman. Because that's who Mary was in the story. Was that who Marcelle was in real life?

Or was she just reading too much into it?

Did he like her?

How old am I, seriously? Does he like me? I'm married with three kids. This isn't third grade.

And yet... it was nice to feel noticed.

She remembered the first time she had spotted him in class: longish hair, an earring, wearing ripped jeans and a Metallica t-shirt. He wasn't the kind of guy she usually found attractive. After all, Nathan was a preppy lawyer.

He was objectively good-looking: dark hair, fair skin, blue eyes and six feet tall with broad shoulders and a slim physique. Marcelle chuckled when she noticed the other girls in class stare the first time he walked in. Sure, she had noticed him, too, and found him very attractive, but she did so in a platonic, married-woman kind of way (is there such a thing?). She appreciated what he had to offer to a woman in general, she just never imagined that she might be that woman in particular.

But there he was, telling her in a not-so-subtle message that he thought the same about her. It was unbearably romantic. It was also incredibly dangerous. What if...

Oh, this is ridiculous, I'm making this all up in my head.

She read the story again. With her pencil she scribbled notes all over the margins. Mary wasn't her at all, she decided. He had just done what all writers are supposed to do—stolen details from real life and twisted them into the story. He probably hadn't even done it consciously. Just noticed lots of things and remembered them as he created a character. Anyway, there was no point in this kind of useless thought. She had children to take care of. Who were sleeping now. And a husband who was working late, again. But what was the harm in dreaming? (Just a little, anyway.)

She was loudly yelling, "But I'm married" to Chris as they stood in an outside version of her classroom that was somehow taking place on the lawn of the synagogue where she had married. Then she rolled over and saw Nathan climbing into bed, trying not to disturb her. Wiping her eye with the back of her hand, she whispered, "What time is it?"

He kissed her forehead. "It's late, baby. Go back to sleep."

Nodding, she rolled back on her side. He pressed his body next to hers, holding his back to her stomach.

"I love you," he whispered into her hair.

"I love you, too," she half-sighed, as she adjusted her body to his in their bed.

"Go back to sleep, baby," he said.

So she did. And resumed her dream about Chris.

Marcelle wasn't the sort of woman who spent a lot of time on her appearance. As long as her hair was neat and her eyebrows groomed, she figured she had nice enough skin to go without make-up most of the time—something that drove her mother insane—especially when she went to school, where she was the oldest person in her class. Going fresh-faced made her feel younger, like she might just be a college student instead of a married mother of three.

That morning, though, she spent close to an hour in front of the mirror getting ready. She knew she always dressed nicely—at least neatly—to class. But had she ever worn make-up to school before? There were countless mornings where she remembered her mother's scorn as Marcelle arrived to drop off Sarah. ("Put some color on your face. You look so pale.") But were there mornings that she really had put herself together for school? Because if she never had, she didn't want to be obviously trying to look good for Chris now that she had read his story. Now that he had noticed her, now that she knew what he thought of her, she wanted to look even better, to earn the right to be looked at that way.

Staring at her reflection in the mirror, she decided on make-up. Maybe just a little eye shadow and some lipstick. But she knew she looked so much better when she wore eyeliner, so she applied some. Then she had to complete the look with mascara. She blew out her feathered brown hair and sprayed it with hairspray so it would stay big, instead of falling into the usual curls around her face.

Then she decided she looked ridiculous. She looked like she was going to a wedding, not to class.

So she washed her face and put her hair back into a banana clip, leaving only her bangs on her face, and wished she knew how to put on make-up so that it just made her look prettier instead of making her look painted.

But after looking at herself with no make-up she decided that just some lipstick and mascara might do the trick.

Now for clothes. She wanted something suggestive but not sexy. Something that made her stand out, but not something that made her look like she was trying too hard. Her off-the-shoulder red and white shirt was perfect, but he had described that in the story, and she didn't want him to think she had noticed. But then again, how was she supposed to not notice?

I should call Ruby, she thought. She's great at picking out these sorts of things.

Yes, but then what would I tell her, she continued. That I want to get all dressed up for some boy in my class who may or may not have a crush on me?

And then feeling ridiculous, she sat on her bed, hugging her knees to her chest, and looking at the pillows that still held the shape of Nathan's head. She snuggled into the pillow and breathed in his scent.

My husband, she thought. My husband. The man I love.

Whom I never see.

Who is always too tired to want me.

Shouldn't somebody want me?

Then she got off the bed and found a clingy black cotton tank that looked great with her jeans and a pair of dangly earrings.

She noticed him noticing her as she walked into class. She was purposely five minutes late so that she wouldn't have to talk to him before class started. The workshop came first, and then lunch, and then the literature class. She had started having lunch with him and some of her other classmates in the last few weeks, and she wondered how today would go.

When class ended, Marcelle made a fuss over her papers, taking longer than normal to get up from her desk.

"Hey Marci," he said. "I have to talk to you."

She looked up at him, a little afraid.

"Come," he said. "Outside. I don't want to talk about this in front of everyone."

As she gathered her papers, the voices in her head were in full panic, as was she.

Is he going to tell me he loves me?

Is he going to ask me to leave my husband?

What the hell is wrong with this guy?

What the hell is wrong me?

Together, they walked outside, onto the campus green. When no one they knew was around he grabbed her by the arms and said, "Marci, I am so sorry."

"Umm," she said, furrowing her brow. "Sorry?"

"Yeah," he said, combing his fingers through his hair. "That must have been so embarrassing for you."

"Embarrassing for me?"

"Jeez," he said. "Okay, let me explain. Remember when Professor Tare told us to write a character study of someone in the room. Well, you were sitting in front of me, so I used you as a basis and kind of took off from there. And then, because I'm lazy and didn't feel like creating another character, I put that crap into the love story exercise. I completely forgot it was my turn for workshop. I had another story I wanted to submit, but I didn't have a chance to type it up. The garbage I made you read was the only thing saved on my word processor."

Marcelle felt relieved.

And embarrassed.

And disappointed.

And embarrassed about being disappointed.

She forced a smile. "So why are you apologizing to me? You're the one who submitted that pitiful story."

Chris laughed and ran his fingers through his hair again.

"I mean, of course I'm mortified. The whole class thinks I'm in love with you. But I don't care about what they think about me. I just felt terrible about putting you in an awkward position. I could have at least warned you."

"Yeah, you could have done that. I was squirming, reading that on my couch last night."

"Well, sweetheart, if I were going to make you squirm, that's not how I'd want to do it."

Marcelle raised her eyebrows and slapped him on the arm.

"You can't talk to me that way; I'm a married woman."

"You see," he said, "that's exactly what I mean. If you think I'm in love with you, I can't tease you anymore. And you get so embarrassed; you're so much fun to tease."

"You and Angie both think I'm such an old lady. You both love to mock me."

"Please don't be offended. Look, you're a really cool person, and I'm happy that we've become friends, and I don't want to mess that up.

Leaving Egypt

Let me buy you a cup of coffee. Peace offering, okay? There's a great place I think you'll love a few blocks from here."

They arrived at the café. Chris was right: it was exactly the kind of place she liked. Oversized furniture, mismatched tables and chairs, odds and ends collected from various garage sales and arranged on the floor to look like a batty old aunt's oh-so-comfy living room. The place smelled like fresh ground coffee, and had various pastries and small dishes displayed in the counter. U2's *Joshua Tree*—the album currently on constant rotation on her brand new CD player—played in the background.

He smiled when he saw her reaction. "There should be a place like this on every corner," he said.

She laughed and nodded. "I love this song," she said, as "With or Without You," came on.

"Nah," he said. "I'll take Guns N' Roses over U2 any day."

"Well," she said, "just shows you what an old lady I am, cause I think they're just too loud and too vulgar."

"How old are you?" he asked.

Apparently too old and too married for a young stud like you, she thought.

"How old do you think I am?" she asked.

Marci! You're flirting with him. Stop it.

"I don't know. Twenty-four."

"Are you serious? I have three kids, Chris. I'm twenty-eight. How old are you?"

"Sorry, Grandma, I didn't want to say thirty-two and risk offending you."

Marcelle opened her mouth in a gesture of mock horror, and lightly slapped him on the arm again.

He laughed. "I'm twenty-four," he said. "I took two years off school to go traveling. After these two classes this summer, I'm done. Then off to Senegal."

After claiming two of the most comfortable looking chairs, Chris left with her coffee order.

172

Marcelle felt so stupid sitting in her chair, watching Chris get their drinks. How could she even think someone like him was interested in her? She watched him talking to the girl behind the counter. They were clearly flirting. She was leaning in to him, laughing, her back arched, her stomach pressed against the counter, her chest forward so her breasts were closer to his face. It wasn't the first time she noticed a woman responding to Chris that way.

More importantly, why would she even want him to be interested in her? What would she have done if he had told her he was interested? Run off with him? To Senegal? How ridiculous. She had heard stories of a few women in the Community running off with younger men and been furious with them. It was one thing to hate one's husband, quite another to abandon one's children. And she didn't hate Nathan at all. As much as her kids drove her nuts, she realized they were kids and that was part of their job. If it came down to it, she was capable of bare-handed murder in their defense. She would never leave her kids. She was too neurotic to let anyone but family baby-sit them.

Well, it's a good thing you feel that way, one of her voices said. Because nobody's asking you to go anywhere.

But even though I'd say no, another smaller voice responded, it would be nice if someone asked.

Chris sat back down beside her and handed her an enormous white mug. She took a long slow sip, hiding her face in the ceramic.

"So, three kids at twenty-eight, huh? Shotgun wedding?" he asked.

She laughed so hard, coffee came out of her nose. When she recovered, she said, "Yes and no. We got married in a hurry, but I didn't get pregnant till after the wedding."

"Why were you in such a hurry?" he asked. He leaned back into his chair, staring intently at her.

"It's a long, complicated story. There were circumstances beyond our control."

"But you had kids pretty fast."

"Yup. Lauren was born nine months to the day after my wedding."

"Nine months to the day?" he looked at her with disbelief. "And you know for a fact you weren't pregnant when you got married."

She nodded her head. "Positive."

"How could you possibly know?" he said, his tone mocking, leaning into her.

She sat up a little straighter. "Because you have to have sex to get pregnant, Chris."

"Oh," he said, leaning back into his own seat. Clearly waiting till marriage was something that had not occurred to him.

After a few moments of hiding in his own enormous mug he said, "So, tell me about your husband."

"Nathan? He's a lawyer. Ten years older than me. How should I describe him?" She smiled and flushed, and looked down at her coffee. Then she looked at Chris. "It's funny, everyone always uses the same term—he's a 'great guy'."

He held her gaze. "Do you not think he is?"

"No, he is," she said, nodding her head. "He's smart and kind and reliable. All the things a woman wants in a husband."

"You sound hesitant," he said, furrowing his brow.

"Do I?" she shook her head. "No, Nathan is definitely a great guy."

Marcelle looked off.

"I just wanted a little more time to be Marci before I became Nathan's wife and Lauren's mommy. Somewhere in taking care of everyone else, I lost myself. But that's why I'm here. This is my Marci-time. You know, because running off with my tennis instructor is really not an option for me."

"Oh no? Why not?"

"Duh," she said. "I don't play tennis."

"Duh?" he repeated, laughing. "Really, grandma?" He shook his head. "Well, I'm glad to be a part of your Marci time."

"Yes, my boring Marci-time. Let's talk about exciting things. You spent two years traveling? That's awesome. Where did you go?"

"Around the world. Twenty-three countries."

"Twenty-three countries! That's crazy! I want to see twenty-three countries."

"I took tons of pictures. I'm kind of an amateur photographer," he said. "Well, a little more than amateur. I've sold a few photographs to travel magazines."

"That's amazing. Can you bring them? I'd love to see them."

Chris smiled, and then kind of blushed.

"Sure, grandma," he said, patting her leg. "I'd be happy to show you my pictures."

Again, she lightly slapped his arm. "Yes, it can count as your community service. Humor the boring old lady with your fascinating life."

"Marci, there is nothing boring about you."

Now it was her turn to laugh.

"And you know what else, grandma, you're looking pretty fine today. When I get to be your age, I'm going to need the number for your plastic surgeon. Keep me looking like I did in my youth." He tilted his chin up, patting his hands on his face.

She giggled, shaking her head and looking down, trying to hide how alternately elated and horrified she felt.

What planet am I on?

Suddenly, she wanted to kiss him.

And then she wanted to never talk to him again.

He took a pack of Marlboro Reds out of his pockets. He lit one and stared off at the wall. That horribly annoying song, "Don't Worry, Be Happy," came through the speakers.

"Can I have one?" she asked.

"You smoke?" he asked.

"Just when Nathan's not around," she said, his name feeling awkward on her lips. And what else do you do when Nathan's not around?

Shut up.

They smoked in silence for a while. On her last drag, she exhaled loudly before stubbing her cigarette out in the ashtray.

"Thanks," she said, smiling. "I needed that."

Chapter Seven

Marcelle, Sofia and Angie sat in a bar in Soho. They had just gone to the newly opened Angelika Theater on Houston Street to see *sex, lies & videotape*. It was Sofia's idea; she thought it would be fun to take Marcelle out for a girls' night, but when Marcelle mentioned to Angie that they were going to see the film, Angie insisted on coming.

Angie and Sofia each got a kick out of the other, especially when it came to their outfits. Angie wore a black lycra mini-skirt and an off-the shoulder sleeveless gray, hot pink and white top, and though it was August, she had brought a boxy blazer to wear inside the theater.

Sofia wore a purple strapless knit dress that flared at the hips, where a large metallic belt hugged her figure. She accessorized with silver hoop earrings and ten slim but noisy metal bangles up her left arm.

Marcelle felt positively dowdy between the two of them, wearing acid-washed jean shorts with front pleats and a white short-sleeve button down shirt with shoulder-pads. She wasn't even wearing jewelry and realized she had barely worn make-up. She also hadn't spent too much time on her hair, so it hung flat down her face. Angie and Sofia had both done theirs: Angie's hair was curly and full, and she had probably used half a can of Aqua-net to get her bangs to stay in place. Sofia's bangs were softer and subtler, but even she had perfectly styled hair framing her face, while the rest of it was pulled back into a large bow at the nape of her neck.

Men all around them were staring at Sofia and Angie.

"I think it's time for me to get a make-over," Marcelle said.

Angie and Sofia both nodded their heads. "That's our next outing," Angie said. "Me and you, we're going to take her for some new clothes and a hair-cut."

"Okay, but let me pick most of the clothes," Sofia said. "You look great, but her mother might just drop dead if Marci walked into the house in a skirt that short."

Angie smiled. "Oh, yeah? Is she a little old-fashioned?"

Sofia and Marcelle both laughed.

"Are you kidding," Marcelle said. "I told my mother we were going to see *When Harry Met Sally* and that scandalized her enough. You should have seen her. 'Isn't that the movie where that woman makes sex noises in the middle of a restaurant.' The best part was that she didn't even say the word 'sex.' She mouthed it. Imagine if I told her we were seeing a movie that had the word 'sex' in the title."

"Oh, so you won't be telling her about the part when the woman masturbates on camera?" Angie says.

Sofia burst out laughing. "I'm not sure she knows what the word means. Proper ladies don't even do that in private."

Angie took their drink order: a gin and tonic for her, a Chianti for Sofia and a Diet Coke for Marcelle. Angie gave her a look.

"I'm driving," Marcelle said.

"One drink isn't going to get you drunk," Angie said. Marcelle shook her head. "Wuss!" Angie yelled.

When she returned with their drinks, Angie wanted to talk about the movie. "So I am clearly the extroverted Cynthia," she said. "I would totally make a tape, though I would probably not show my lady parts on it. You never know where that might turn up."

"Would you make a tape?" she asked Sofia. Sofia shook her head no.

"Why," Angie pressed. "Are you as innocent as our little Marci here?"

Sofia looked confused. Angie continued, "Will you be worthy of the white dress you'll be wearing at your wedding?"

Sofia flushed and took a sip of her wine.

"Shit, sorry. Did I go too far? I forget that you're marrying her brother," Angie said.

"No, it's okay," Sofia replied. "But my circumstances are different from Marci's. I'm ten years older than Marci was when she got married. Besides I was engaged before. And for work, you know, I travel a lot, so after my engagement broke off, I had a 'friend' in Milan who helped me get over my ex."

Angie grinned. "An Italian lover. Nothing better in the world..."

Marcelle drank deeply from her soda. This wasn't something she wanted to know, wasn't something she wanted to keep from her brother.

Sofia turned to Marcelle. "Look, it's not like Charles doesn't know. I told him he wasn't the first. He didn't care. And since I wasn't a virgin anyway, it didn't make sense to wait until after the wedding."

"Exactly," Angie said. "Try before you buy."

"Or end up like Ann," Marcelle said, referring to the movie's protagonist. "Essentially frigid because you've never had a proper lay."

"Hey," Angie said, "No one's calling you frigid. And you have had orgasms before, right?"

"Yes," Marci said, feeling the heat rise in her face.

She drank deeply from her Diet Coke again.

"Just not in a long, long time," she whispered to her soda.

Sarah had just finished her afternoon tea, when Marcelle and Sofia walked in, their arms laden with shopping bags. They had gone for haircuts, Sofia taking Marcelle to her very expensive coiffeur on 57th Street, followed by makeovers at Bloomingdale's. After, they had taken a taxi to Loehmann's, where the head buyer was a business contact of Sofia's, and bought Marcelle a new wardrobe.

Sofia had selected several sundresses, but instead of the loose-hanging night-gown tablecloth hybrid Marcelle usually preferred, these were fitted to her body. Everything Sofia chose highlighted Marcelle's figure.

"If I looked as good as you do after three kids, I'd be in lycra all day long!" Sofia exclaimed, as Sarah clucked approvingly, opening the bags and pulling out a pair of peach belted culottes that Sofia had paired with a light cream-colored cashmere tank top, and a black evening dress with a sweetheart neckline and a red sash that encircled the waist, folding into an enormous bow on the backside.

Sofia had also selected a bag of accessories. In it were lots of dangly earrings, several wide belts and bangle bracelets in every color.

"You look so beautiful, Marci," Sarah said. Marcelle giggled. "Nathan is going to be so happy to see you looking this good."

Leaving Egypt

Sarah left her guests on the couch and went to the kitchen to make more tea. There were so many things to be happy about. Her daughter and daughter-in-law were friends; her daughter was smiling and happy and finally cared about her appearance. She hadn't seen Marcelle like this since she first fell in love with Nathan.

Something must have happened between them. Married couples often separate and then come back together. It had happened so many times between her and Eddie. You get so busy, with the kids, with the house, with work, you forget that you were once a young couple who delighted in every inch of the other's body. And then pregnancy, and nursing especially, can make a woman feel more like a dairy cow than a creature worthy of sexual attention. It was so hard to come back to each other after that. Even though children could bring a couple closer in many ways, they could become more partners than lovers. Sarah was so glad to see that Marcelle and Nathan had come away from that path. Watching them together—together was the wrong word, it was more like watching them occupy the same space—had worried her tremendously. But now, what a relief, her daughter was smiling again. Could all of this have stemmed just from sending her daughter to school?

Sofia and Marcelle were giggling on the couch when Sarah returned with tea and graybeh—a ring-shaped sugar cookie topped with a pistachio. Just then, they heard a cry coming from the bedroom. Baby Sarah was up from her afternoon nap.

"I'll get her," Sarah said, pulling herself up from the couch.

"No way," Marcelle replied. "I haven't seen her all day. I'll get her."

Sofia and Sarah exchanged smiles while they listened to Marcelle cooing and kissing her baby. They laughed when they heard the loud sounds of raspberries and squeals of laughter from the baby.

"Thank you so much," Sarah said.

"For what?" Sofia asked.

"For helping me get my daughter back."

It seemed to all that Marcelle was back. She argued politics again with her father on the Shabbat table. She paid attention while she was cooking and the flavor returned to her food. She played with her children, wrestling with them and giggling, clearly enjoying them instead of feeling that they were a burden.

Walking home from one such dinner, after a particularly fierce debate over whether communism was finally failing, Eddie said to Sarah, beaming, "She's like her old self again."

Sarah smiled back at him, but she was worried. That night she watched closely for some signs of a renewal between Marcelle and Nathan, but she hadn't seen any. Oh, they were perfectly civil. They were kind to each other. They were good parents. But there was no spark, no chemistry. The signs of life Sarah had observed in Marcelle didn't come from any change in her relationship with Nathan.

Maybe it was just having something of her own that brought about the change in Marcelle. But Sarah knew her daughter, and she didn't think reading books was enough. It was something else.

She wasn't sure what it was, but her instincts told her it wasn't good.

Chapter Eight

Chris was by her side the moment class ended.

"Lunch?" he asked, grinning.

"Sure," she said. "I told Angie we'd meet her and Evan on the green at 12:45."

His grin slipped for a moment, and then firmly planted itself back on his face.

"Great," he said and, as she walked past him, grazed his hand on the small of her back. She stiffened and jerked herself forward.

That was a bit much, she thought, and shot him a look that told him so.

Half an hour later, her skin still tingled where his hand had been.

As they walked along campus, Marcelle noticed fliers stapled to trees and message boards advertising High Holiday services at the campus Hillel.

"The holidays are coming," they read. "Time to reassess yourself. Time to ask God for forgiveness for all you've done."

Time to reevaluate. To stand before God and be accountable for your actions. To commit to bettering yourself in the coming year. To ask for forgiveness for all you've done.

Have I done anything that needs forgiving?

She was strangely aware of Chris walking beside her, grinning, trying to accidentally touch her at every occasion, which alternately pleased and shocked her, and she wondered, can this be me? Who is this person walking beside this non-Jewish boy who likes me and is not my husband, whom I'm allowing myself to like? I'm not eighteen anymore, and there's too much at stake. What am I doing?

But the other voices chimed in, drowning out the voice of her conscience, screaming:

You haven't done anything.

You won't do anything.

You're allowed to feel alive, too.

And then the guilt: Was this why I went back to school? Is my mother watching my daughter two days a week so I can flirt like a single girl?

And then the next voice, the one she never let herself hear, the one that asked, is it possible for a man to work that late night after night after night? Who is working late with him, and exactly what kind of work is it?

No, not Nathan. Not my sweet, loving, loyal Nathan.

But if I can have these thoughts, can't he?

Angie and Evan were waiting on the green when they arrived, sitting on the grass under a tree and eating their lunch. They made a fine contrast, Evan in his preppy gear, khaki pants and navy and light blue striped polo shirt, and Angie wearing a skin tight v-neck shirt, cut low enough to show a hint of black bra. Evan's hair was cropped short and neatly combed, while Angie's was big and feathered and tied with a lace headband. Their voices were arguing, but their faces were flirting.

It reminded Marcelle of foreplay.

Did she and Chris look like that when they talked?

"What are you guys fighting about?" she asked, as she and Chris sat on the grass beside them.

"Genius over here actually thinks that raising taxes will create less revenue for the government. Okay, Mr. Wall Street. Okay, Mr. Savings and Loan."

"Angie," he said, "you are one hell of a woman, but you have no understanding of economics whatsoever."

As he said this, his pager went off. He looked at the number on the screen and said, "Shit. Oh shit. I gotta go."

"What happened," she said. "Stock market crashing?"

"No, wiseass. I'll tell you about it later." He kissed her forehead before he stood up and left.

Marcelle raised her eyebrows at Angie and Angie smiled and mouthed "later."

Chris was oblivious; he had been rummaging through his backpack from the moment they sat down.

"Digging for treasure?" Angie asked.

Chris looked up, holding three manila envelopes. "No," he said. "Better than treasure." He emptied the contents of one the envelopes on the grass.

Angie took one look and said, "Ugh. The last thing I need is to see more pictures of Italy. I'm going to go stalk Evan. Manicures Thursday?" she said to Marcelle.

Marcelle nodded, and Angie winked and walked off. Marcelle didn't like the suggestion on her face, so she ignored it.

You'll tell her later, part of her said.

There's nothing to tell, another part of her answered.

She returned her attentions to the pictures. A week earlier, Chris had presented another story to the class, one that was not about her, one that was not embarrassingly bad. It was about a young man backpacking through Europe, having lost his travel mates and running out of money himself, sleeping on a park bench in Prague one night, and wondering what to do to keep going. Marcelle had loved the story and, when she told him so after class, he revealed that the story was true. Again he promised to show her his travel pictures.

Now, a week later, as he tried to form a narrative from the disorganized heap of exotic images, Marcelle could barely contain her questions.

"Who did you go with?" she asked.

"It's kind of a long story. I was supposed to go with two of my buddies, Mickey and Jesse, but Mickey lost all the money he saved for the trip on a football bet so Jesse and I went alone. We were in Amsterdam, in this really cool hotel, where each of the rooms is themed after a different philosopher. Jesse ate too many magic mushrooms one morning. After he spent three hours fighting with the ceiling fan—he was cowering on the floor, holding his pillow between him and the fan—he ran out of the room and straight into one of those bike tour groups. A few of them swerved to miss him, but this one guy rode right into him and he fell and broke his ankle. Anyway, he had to go home, and I decided, screw it, I'm already here. I may as well see Europe."

184

"So you were alone?"

"Yeah."

"Weren't you scared?"

"Not really. I met people. It's easy when you're traveling. You meet people on trains, in hostels. You can tell who the backpackers are. We all look kind of dirty."

"I've always wanted to do something like that."

"It was the best experience of my life," Chris said. "When I was fifteen I read this book called *The Drifters*."

"By James Michener? I love that book."

"You too? It's one of my favorites. After I read that, I knew it was something I had to do. No matter what. I just had to go out there and see the world and find myself in it. And I did.

"I ended up being away for a little over a year. I didn't have enough money saved, but I found odd jobs here and there so I managed to make enough to live on. I was lucky, though. I made friends with this guy who lived in London. His father owned a grocery store. I worked for him as a stock boy. The pay wasn't great, but it included some basic food and a small room to sleep in on top of the store. And I got to go to the British Museum every day."

He showed her pictures from the museum, of the Parthenon friezes and the Egyptian obelisks.

"I saved enough from working in London to get to Australia. And after diving on the Great Barrier Reef and surfing on Bondi Beach, I worked on a fruit farm."

He picked up another picture of himself in overalls, holding a basket of apples, standing next to a very attractive blonde girl. Marcelle felt a pang: jealousy?

"Awful work," he continued. "Long, hot hours in the sun, but I made some friends who had great weed, and I saved enough to get to Thailand."

Then he found pictures of the Grand Palace in Bangkok, multi-colored jeweled statues and gilded tiered pagoda ceilings, all sparkling in the sunlight, Chris beaming with his arm around a pretty brunette.

185

"What was your favorite part?"

"Of the whole trip? Would have to be the pyramids."

"You've been to Egypt?" She almost jumped on him.

"I take it you want to go there?"

"Of course I do. I'm Egyptian."

"I thought you were Jewish," he said.

"Yeah."

"I'm confused. How can you be both Arab and Jew?"

"How can Angie be both Italian and American?" she answered, somewhat annoyed.

The confusion remained on his face.

"Both my parents were born in Cairo. They were pretty much kicked out. They were allowed to take two suitcases and almost no money. They had to start here from scratch."

He shook his head. "I didn't know that."

"Most people don't. But yeah, I don't really speak Arabic, but I understand it. And I love Arabic food and Arabic music. And Egypt wasn't the only Arab country with lots of Jews."

She shook her head. "Nobody knows about our history. There were a million Jews in Muslim lands before Israel was created. Most of them, like my family, got kicked out. Most of them lost everything they had."

"Okay. Okay. I'm sorry. You learn something new every day, right?"

"Yeah, so the next time you hear someone talking about how the Palestinians lost everything, remind them that there are two sets of Middle Eastern refugees."

Chris sat silently, leaning away from her, as though he were scared.

She looked at him, smiled, and shook her head again. "Sorry. God, I sound like my father. Years of listening to him and his friends. It makes me angry whenever I think about it."

"No," he said. "Don't be. I really didn't know. I can see why it would make you angry."

186

"So, what was it like, Cairo? My parents talk about it like it was the most beautiful city in the world. Like Paris on the Nile. And Alexandria. You should hear my father's stories. He used to go with his brothers for long weekends in the summer. He talks about the glamour, the nightlife, the way people dressed up to go out. He used to dance all night under the stars to bands that played everything from swing to tango. My mother was too young to have done that, and her father too strict to allow her out without her husband, but he remembers. Then he says it doesn't matter anymore. That even if he went back, it wouldn't be there. That all the people who made it what he loved were gone. He gets in these moods on Thursday nights. He'll take out his Oum Kalthoum records and listen to them so he remembers his youth. He tells me that Cairo shut down on Thursday nights to listen to her concerts on the radio."

While she spoke, Chris busily sorted through pictures, making a pile of the ones from Egypt.

"What you said makes a lot of sense," he said, handing her a stack of pictures. "It has a sort of faded glory. These big beautiful boulevards with these apartment buildings that would be at home in Paris except that they're covered in grime and haven't been painted in years. Cairo's shabby, and dirty and kind of crazy. The buses don't stop to let you on or off. They just sort of slow down, and you have to jump.

"That's the Corniche," he said, leaning close to her, his shoulder grazing hers. The picture was of a tree-lined walkway, the Nile gleaming in the distance. "And those are felucca boats," he said, pointing to a picture of white sailboats on the river at sunset. "The captains are everywhere, trying to talk you into a sunset ride; even if you've just gotten off the felucca belonging to the guy's cousin, he still tries to get you into his."

She smiled up at him. "It looks beautiful."

"Would your parents ever go back?" he asked.

"Not my father. He's still angry. He's never gotten over being kicked out of his home, never forgiven them for how his father suffered moving here, starting from nothing in his late fifties after he spent almost forty years building his business. I think my mother would, though. No matter how happy she is here, there's a part of her that's still homesick. I would love to go. To see where I'm from. To walk down the streets my mother walked down as a girl."

Looking at his pictures, she tried to insert herself into the scenes, seeing herself strolling along the Mediterranean in Alexandria, stopping by a street vendor for some sugarcane juice.

Or walking along the Seine in Paris or the Thames in London, or on a beach in the south of Spain.

She had always imagined herself taking these trips with Nathan. Nathan: the same person who answered, "Why can't we just go to Florida?" when she said, "Let's go see the world."

That night she would take those walks in her mind again.

Only they wouldn't be with Nathan.

Chapter Nine

Marcelle waited alone at the table for Nathan to come home. Their kids were long asleep and his dinner, roasted chicken with rice and peas, sat in a tin on the grey granite kitchen countertop getting cold. There she was again, alone in her kitchen. The beginning and end to each day. Except this day, for the first time in weeks, Nathan promised to be home before she went to bed to spend time with her.

The clock on the wall read 10:15. Marcelle was usually in bed by eleven.

She wanted a cigarette, but was afraid he would walk in as she was smoking, before she could wash her hands and brush her teeth to get the smell out.

But so what if I smell like smoke, she thought. I need something to keep me company. Does a husband who's never there get to tell his wife what to do?

Kneeling on the cold ceramic tile, she opened the kitchen cabinet and felt around for her cigarettes.

"What are you doing?" Nathan said.

Marcelle jumped and hit her head on the countertop.

"You scared the shit out of me," she said, sitting on the floor, rubbing her head.

He sat on the floor next to her and pulled her to him, kissing her head.

"It shouldn't scare you so much. I do live here, you know."

She nuzzled into his shoulder before looking up at him.

"Sometimes," she said.

"I know," he said, "I'm sorry about that. Let's sit at the table. Sitting on the floor is a sign of mourning. We're not in mourning, are we?"

One mourned when something died. One tore one's clothes and covered all the mirrors and sat on the floor for a week. Shouldn't they now mourn? For the death of their marriage? What kind of marriage was it when they were never together?

Stop being such a drama queen. He's right here right now. Enjoy your time together.

"I wish you would have called before you left," she said, removing the tin from the counter top. "I would have put your food in the oven and it would be warm already. We probably should get a microwave."

"What if they cause cancer? Don't worry about heating the food. I'm starving. I'll eat it as it is."

Marcelle transferred the food from the tin to a plate and placed it in front of her husband on the glass-topped kitchen table. He thanked her and commenced eating at warp speed. She watched him with amusement. Sometimes she forgot how adorable he was, with this dark brown eyes and thick eyelashes. He had thick eyebrows, which cut across his forehead in a straight line, punctuated by a brief stop above his straight, small nose. Nathan's wavy black hair, which he wore slicked back, was starting to grey at the temples, but it looked good on him. The little belly that had begun to grow on his otherwise compact 5'8" frame actually looked really cute. She often wanted to pet it, like he was her own private Buddha statue.

Though Marcelle studied her husband's every motion, his eyes barely left his plate. Poor thing, she thought, he probably hasn't eaten since lunch. He did that all the time, forgetting to eat. He got occupied and wouldn't realize till he was about to faint that he hadn't eaten all day. How well she knew him.

She knew exactly how he was going to eat his chicken—with a fork and knife until only scraps were left on the bone; then with his fingers, he would lift the bones to his mouth to suck the scraps off. He would leave off the skin because she was sitting across from him, and had been there when the doctor warned him about his rising cholesterol and his high blood pressure, but she also knew that he gobbled it down greedily when she wasn't there, or when he didn't think she was watching.

She knew the exact spot on his face, below his mouth, about a quarter inch to the right, where he inevitably (always! maddeningly!) got a piece of food stuck to his stubble. She knew the mess he would leave
190

around his plate, the grains of rice and random cast-aside peas, how he would gulp the remains of his glass of soda and bang down the glass, tongue clicking against the roof of his mouth, followed by a deep and appreciative, "Aaah."

When they first married, she had found it charming, adorable even, that he ended each meal with such satisfaction, but after watching him repeat this performance meal after meal, year after year, it had begun to annoy her. Why such deep sighs of relief after every meal? He ate this well every day. Did everything have to be such a production? Did every bite have to end with such drama?

But then the annoyance gave way to an appreciation for comfortable familiarity. Somehow, she was soothed by watching him go through this routine, soothed by the intimacy inherent in knowing exactly what he was going to do and how he was going to do it, and when. She smiled to herself as she internally conducted the orchestra of sounds and movements he made in her head, smiling each time he delivered a line or hit a note.

She waited for him to finish. It was 10:30 and she was tired and thinking that by now she should be in her pajamas, washing her face and getting into bed. But she had stayed dressed to wait for him, thought that he saw her so little, she should at least look pretty when he did, the way her mother always made sure to look pretty for her father.

Sitting across from him she tried to look pretty. Did he notice? Or was he too exhausted from the combination of too many legal briefs and too few hours of sleep to see. She wondered how he was even capable of working that much.

"How was your day?" she asked.

"Long," he said. "Hard. Like every other day these past few months. I keep thinking we're getting close to the end, at least of the worst parts, but this case is a living testament to Murphy's Law. Anyway, I don't want to talk about the case. I'm tired of the case. I want to spend time with my wife."

He took her hand in his. "How was your day?" he asked.

She smiled and nodded her head. "It was fine. Uneventful, which is good."

They sat in it silence, holding hands, looking into each other's eyes, half smiling, both tired, both wanting to go to bed, but afraid of saying it for fear of hurting the other.

Earlier as she watched him eat, she knew she could conduct the sounds of his chewing and sighing, predict with laser-accuracy where on his face tidbits of food would fall, and she brought the same clairvoyance to predicting the conversation they would have should she begin by asking, "Nathan, why do you love me?" He would freeze, then jerk his head back, then ask her why she needed to know, and wasn't it enough that he did love her, and then an awkward silence would come between them, which she would have to break by cracking a lame joke.

So she didn't. When he moved closer and kissed her, she kissed him back, and when he half lifted her out of the chair, one of the first steps to get her upstairs, she went with him.

She wanted to talk, to know if their relationship was still solid, to know if it really was just about the case, to ask how much longer he could reasonably expect her to accept him as an absentee husband. But he wanted to make love, so they made love. Even as they did she wondered if he really wanted to. Did she? Or were they both doing it because they hadn't done it in a while and figured they should? A stab at intimacy, an effort at connection.

Obligatory sex. Not particularly good sex, but not bad either. Just overly familiar. Him, on top of her, intermittently making eye contact. Her, under him, hands on his back making moaning noises. Not really moans of pleasure, just making the noises she made while she had sex, enjoying the feeling of him, the closeness with his body, the idea that they were actually doing something together at the same time and in the same place, but hardly in the throes of passion.

Mind elsewhere, on the navy pleated skirts and white blouses she had to buy Lauren for school because what she hadn't outgrown, she had either ripped or stained, and all the school supplies she would need for both Lauren and Jack, erasers, pencils, and then for all the art projects, construction paper and pipe cleaners and glue sticks and crayons. And little Sarah would need a new winter coat, unless Marcelle could find Lauren's old one, which was still around somewhere, wasn't it?

She was tired and wanted to sleep and the pillow under her head had slipped out from underneath her so that her neck was twisted at an uncomfortable angle, but she could see from his facial expressions that he was almost finished, so it seemed simpler to just wait than to stop him and readjust. And she wondered if she had time to work on her own orgasm and then she decided she didn't really care whether she had one anyway. He was squeezing her breast now, so she knew he was close, so she grabbed his behind hard like he liked and he came and he kissed her.

Then he rolled off her, careful not to leave a wet spot, and she reached for the baby wipes she kept by the bed to clean up, and got up for her usual after-sex pee because she was prone to urinary tract infections. Then came the mandatory cuddle, the exchange of "I love you"s and then she rolled over to go to sleep, feeling as far from him as she had the night before when she had gone to sleep alone.

Was this what he meant, "spend some time with my wife?" Come home, get laid, pass out?

Was this the most she could look forward to for the rest of her life?

I'm twenty-eight years old. This can't be as good as it's going to get.

An hour later, Marcelle was still awake, and the sound of Nathan softly snoring was driving her mad. Quietly, she slid out of her bed and, tiptoeing down the stairs, found herself at her kitchen table again. Putting the kettle on the fire, she prepared mint tea, and, again, reaching under the sink to the box of steel wool, removed the pack of cigarettes she had been craving earlier.

Thinking of Chris, she found herself aroused; it was a feeling that surprised her. Was she ever aroused anymore? Did she ever feel sexual?

Eleven years and three kids later, when was the last time she just felt horny? She didn't know. She loved touching Nathan, holding him, snuggling into his chest. But when was the last time she wanted to throw him down and rip his clothes off? When was the last time she wanted him to push her against a wall and take her violently?

Had she ever wanted that with Nathan?

Sex with Nathan was always so sweet. She had been his innocent virgin wife, and he had been gentle and caring, kind and loving, the way a husband should be. But maybe also completely boring.

She had fantasies for what she wanted Chris to do to her, and none of them were sweet. They were all violent, and dirty, the kinds of things a woman who had been raised as she had been wasn't supposed to do. Ever. The sex she wanted from Chris wasn't ladylike, or elegant, or appropriate; it was nasty and slutty and characteristic of the woman her mother had spent every breath in her body trying to prevent Marcelle from becoming.

Was this who she was becoming? And if this was who she was becoming, why was this happening? Were they right, all the elders of the community, in marrying girls off young before they had the chance to have these thoughts? Or did they make it worse, pushing girls, inchoate women, into marriage before they had a chance to learn these things about themselves.

When she was younger her mother had drilled it into her head, "No sex before marriage; no self-respecting man wants a woman who isn't a virgin."

She and Ruby joked about hearing the collective sigh of relief of the older generations as another young girl was moved to safety before she could spoil everything for herself.

"I just want to see you settled," they said, as though marriage meant the end of all trouble, as though nothing bad could befall you once you were in the arms of a spouse.

But now, what about now, if she sinned now, now that she was settled, wouldn't the penalties be so much worse? Now, that she had so much more to lose? A husband? Three children? A whole family? A whole life?

What price would she pay for committing the sins she had never had a chance to commit earlier? But what price had she paid for never having the experiences she now longed to have? Thinking of her own daughters, Marcelle wondered if it was fair to burden them with the same expectations Sarah had placed on her.

What would she tell her daughters? What would she tell Lauren? Already at nine, she was stubborn and headstrong, but even when Marcelle's frustration with her was at its peak, she could not help but admire her. Lauren demanded what she wanted, didn't subsume her desires to those around her or the expectations placed on her by her parents.

Sarah blamed Marcelle for it, telling her she wasn't strict enough, was too indulgent, gave up too quickly. Like it was possible to fight with Lauren. She was a force of nature, heiress to her grandmother's iron will.

Is it strange to admire a nine-year-old?

Great mother I am, jealous of my daughter.

But it wasn't jealousy. It was mostly pride. Because Lauren was smart. Not just regular smart, like all parents think their kids are smart. Lauren had something special. Lauren could see to the heart of a problem, find an answer and then stick to it no matter how hard anyone tried to convince her she was wrong. She knew she was right.

And so how could Marcelle fight with her, when half the time Lauren could come up with a logical argument for why she was right? Marcelle was no match for a child who combined Sarah's stubborn will with Nathan's analytical mind.

Marcelle loved watching Lauren read on the couch. She always had a book in her hand, had a voracious appetite for them, cracked the spine of one as soon as she closed the cover of another, without pause, constantly soaking up everything within her reach.

Her school sent a recommended summer reading list home, asking that students read at least two books over the summer and write two paragraph summaries of each book. Lauren was going into fourth grade, but she had read the fourth grade list last summer along with the third grade, and by the time the summer was over, had read the fifth grade list and was most of the way through the sixth.

I will not push her into marriage, Marcelle promised herself.

She will go to the best college she can get into, no matter who I have to fight for that, no matter what Nathan says.

I might be stuck here, but my daughter will soar, one voice said.

But at what cost? another asked.

Angie knew something was up. When they met for their weekly coffee catch-up session, Angie told Marcelle about the romance that had sprouted between her and Evan.

"There's something different this time," she said. "We've been seeing each other for three weeks and we still haven't had sex. He wants to wait, he said. He doesn't want to rush things. I've never been in a situation like this before. I don't know what it means."

"Maybe that he respects you?" Marcelle offered.

"Or that he's gay," Angie laughed. "But seriously, he invited me to his parents' summer home in Cape Cod for Labor Day weekend. He says it's no big deal, that he always brings a friend, but I think I'm the first female friend in a while. Can you imagine him introducing me, the Sicilian Slut, to Mr. and Mrs. Wasp? They're going to freak out!"

But the outrage on Angie's face couldn't hide the smile, the inner radiance, the frightened but hopeful feeling she tried to hide under her bravado.

Marcelle put her hand on Angie's and squeezed. "They'll love you. How could they not?"

Angie smiled and squeezed back. "Do you think this could be real?"

"Only one way to find out."

"It would be so nice, to have what you have. The husband, the kids, the white picket fence. God, I never thought I'd say that."

Marcelle felt happy, but then embarrassed. She smiled, but then looked down.

"What was that look?" Angie asked.

Marcelle shook her head and pulled her hand away.

"No, seriously. I have to ask you this. Maybe I shouldn't, but I have to. What was that, the other day, with Chris? Look, I'm not going to judge you. Lord knows, I have no right to do that. I just want to make sure you know what you're doing."

"I'm not doing anything, Angie. Not a thing."

"I believe you, but that's not what it looks like."

"What does it look like?" Marcelle glared.

Angie shrugged and opened her hands. "It looks like something's going on."

Marcelle shook her head. "But he knows I'm married."

"And you think he cares because?" Angie looked her right in the eye. "A guy like Chris isn't going to let a little thing like your husband stop him. Trust me. I know the type. I have a lot of, you know, 'experience' with the type. Just be careful."

"I'm not going to do anything, Angie," Marcelle said, maybe a little too forcefully. "I'm just flirting. That's as exciting as it gets for me."

Angie shook her head again. "Well I'm pretty sure that's not what he thinks," she said. "And Marci," she continued. "Marci, look at me. If you're sure you don't want to go there, I think it might be better if you stayed away."

Chapter Ten

Marcelle was humming when she arrived at Sarah's house. Normally, she sang children's songs to baby Sarah, but today she was singing one of Sarah's favorites, an Edith Piaf song, "*Non, Je Ne Regrette Rien.*"

"You look so pretty, again, today," Sarah exclaimed upon opening the door. "Are you going somewhere later?"

Marcelle shook her head. "Just felt like looking nice," she replied.

"It's so nice to see you looking like this all the time," Sarah said, searching for clues. "Getting your nails done, your hair straight, your make-up so nice. I don't know what's come over you, but I'm very happy."

Marcelle just smiled as she put the baby down and assembled the baby-gate to keep her in the kitchen. She took wooden spoons out of the drawer and plastic bowls out of the cabinet.

"'Poon!" baby Sarah said, giggling and banging the spoon on the floor.

Marcelle smiled. "That's a new word," she said to her mother. "She said it yesterday for the first time." Marcelle held up a spoon and a bowl. "Spoon," she said, putting another spoon down. "Bowl," she said, placing the bowl on the floor.

As Marcelle smiled lovingly at her baby, Sarah informed her that they were making sambousak that afternoon. Sarah kept a list of Syrian pastries taped to her freezer door, and when she didn't have a Tupperware full of any of them, she became anxious; anyway, the holidays were in three weeks and they would need double portions of everything to serve their family.

As Marcelle walked into the kitchen, she noticed that her mother had already made the dough. It seemed Sarah could never wait until Marcelle got there, and always had half the work done before her daughter arrived.

The dough, yellow and buttery, kneaded wheat and semolina flour, sat in a basketball-sized mound in the middle of the table. On the

198

table was a tortilla press and another bowl containing shredded mozzarella cheese mixed with egg and salt. Cookie sheets lined with parchment paper sat on the counters.

Despite years of cooking, it annoyed Sarah that Marcelle still couldn't prepare any of the intricate dishes on her own. She always came after Sarah had started, missing some key step, never making anything from start to finish.

"I thought we should make a double recipe," Sarah said, "so we'll have about a hundred and sixty pieces. Do you think that will be enough?"

Normally, Marcelle would have told her mother she was crazy, that a hundred and sixty pieces was too much, that they always made more food than could be humanly consumed, but today she just smiled and said, "Whatever you want, Mommy," before walking to the sink to wash her hands.

Sarah chatted as Marcelle dried her hands on a kitchen towel, going over menu lists for each meal, who would be attending, when they were invited out, what they were bringing when they were guests at meals hosted by her cousins, what she thought Marcelle should serve at the meals she was hosting in her home, wondering out loud if it was going to be enough food, or too much food, or if all the picky eaters in the family would be satisfied by the menus. Usually, that conversation made Marcelle nervous, wondering how she was going to get everything done in time.

"Don't worry so much, Mom," Marcelle said, still smiling. "No one's ever left a holiday meal hungry in this family. I doubt this will be the first."

Still humming, she took baby Sarah, who had laid her little head down on the floor, still clutching a spoon, into her mother's room for a nap. On the way back to the kitchen, she went to her mother's record collection to select the soundtrack to their afternoon.

Sarah was shocked when she heard French music coming in from the living room. Edith Piaf was her favorite. It reminded her of Cairo, of her own mother, who loved listening to Mademoiselle Piaf on her phonograph while she got dressed. Marcelle usually picked out Arabic records, usually Oum Kalthoum, almost always *Enta Omri. Enta Omri*—"You Are My Life"—was the most famous song of the most famous singer to come out of Egypt. The live performance on Sarah's record was over an hour long, a mournful, melancholy tune that evoked loss and the pain of unrequited love. Marcelle could listen to it over and over again, the music stoking her misery, the sound of desert longing resonating in her unhappy soul, often bringing her to tears at the song's climax. How different was one diva from another, the Egyptian one singing of sorrow, and the French one called the voice of the sparrow, singing rich, happy tunes about *"La Vie en Rose."*

"Since when do you like this?" Sarah asked as Marcelle returned to the kitchen. "I was sure we were going to listen to *Enta Omri* again."

Marcelle smiled that same smile that was starting to make Sarah nervous. "I don't know. I felt like listening to something romantic rather than something depressing for a change."

Sarah raised an eyebrow and stared at Marcelle. It had always bothered Marcelle that Sarah could do that. Raise one eyebrow and not the other. Marcelle couldn't, and it seemed unfair that her mother was allowed the full range of emotional expression allowed by only raising one; like she had been cheated out of her birthright because she couldn't mirror her mother in that way, could not suggest the mix of bewildered mocking contempt and scorn allowed by that gesture. That she would never be able to convey those to her daughter, or that she would never be allowed to respond to her mother with the same gesture.

Today she laughed and kissed her mother on the forehead. "Let's get to work, shall we?"

Sarah muttered something in Arabic, and again Marcelle laughed to herself. For so many years she envied her mother's command of languages, when she could only speak one plus a collection of Arabic phrases that she probably mispronounced.

The women got to work, first rolling the dough into small balls. Once they filled a tray with balls, Marcelle flattened them in the tortilla press. Sarah then filled them with cheese and dipped them into a plate of sesame seeds and pinched them closed, her fingers expertly creating a scalloped edge around the half-moon-shaped pastries. Marcelle had given up on pinching years ago, as Sarah's always looked so perfect and uniform, and Marcelle's looked mangled and childlike.

"Mom," she said, "I'm almost thirty. I think it's time I learned to pinch, no?"

Sarah's eyes shot up. Again, she raised one eyebrow. "Sure," she said, taking the tortilla press. "Go ahead. Whatever you want." Again, she muttered something under her breath, though this time it sounded like French.

Marcelle took the cheese-filled shell and used her thumb and forefinger to pinch the dough shut, curling it over and pinching it again. Usually she was frustrated when she tried but this time she was patient, creating the scallop carefully, moving her fingers slowly and enjoying the pretty embellishment she was creating. She stopped to admire her work.

"Not bad," she said smiling.

Sarah studied the sambousak. "No, not bad at all. Keep practicing till you can do it twice as fast."

Marcelle nodded. "I will. Also, next time, I think you should let me make the dough. Don't you think it's ridiculous that I've been married for ten years, but every time I want to make sambousak, I have to come here?"

"Well, if you hate coming here that much..." Sarah began.

"Don't be silly, Mommy," Marcelle replied. "It's just that I'm a grown woman. I should be able to do this myself."

"Yes," Sarah said, "you should be able to. You just never seemed very interested in knowing how before." Something is wrong, Sarah though to herself. Something is very wrong here. I have to find out what it is.

Sarah continued, "What's going on with you? You're not acting normal. You've been acting funny for the last few weeks. What is it? All of a sudden you have make-up on, you're dressing beautifully, you're getting your nails done. What is it? Did Nathan say something to you? No, it can't be; Nathan wouldn't say anything, and even if he did, I know you,

you'd be like you are with me: angry, resentful. You'd look like a mess on purpose just to spite us. No, something's going on. What is it?"

"Nothing's going on, Mom. I just felt like looking pretty."

"For no good reason? Marcelle Salama Hazan, I have known you your whole life, and the only time I have seen you feel like looking pretty was when you first started dating Nathan."

Shock passed over Sarah's face as the words came over her mouth. Suddenly everything made sense. She dropped a ball of dough on the table.

"Marcelle, you wouldn't. You couldn't. I didn't raise you that way. No. Not my daughter. No way."

Marcelle flushed. How could she possibly know?

"Mom," she said, collecting herself, continuing to pinch as though she were entirely unperturbed by her mother's suggestion, "I have no idea what you're talking about."

"Marcelle, look at me," she said. Marcelle had always been bad at hiding when she did something wrong. "Put the sambousak down and look at me."

Marcelle looked up, praying her eyes would not betray her.

Sarah searched in them for evidence.

"I don't see any guilt," she said, "which means one of two things. Either you haven't done anything yet, or you have no shame. If I did anything right in my life, it was instill you with a proper dose of shame."

Sarah stood up. She paced the room. Marcelle watched anxiously.

"I'm going to tell you something now, a terrible family secret, something that happened in Egypt. Now you listen to me, and you listen good. You had a cousin, Fortunee, back in Egypt, my mother's sister's daughter. I know, you never heard of her, and the reason you never heard of her is that we disowned her. Disowned, Marcelle, do you know what that means? Because she brought shame on the family. Fortunee was young, maybe in her early thirties when this happened. She was married to an older man, fifteen years older than her, but he was a good man, and they had five children together. Five children, Marcelle, and she ruined

202

all of their lives. Do you know what she did? She ran off with a neighbor, a Coptic man from a good old family, who had been her neighbor her entire life.

"No one paid attention to the signs, but they were there. He came over for tea in the afternoon when her husband was working. He sent flowers to the family for Shabbat. Of course he was married as well, and his wife, such a fine lady, that our family should shame her that way!

"Do you know that Fortunee's daughter was of marriageable age when this happened and no one would touch her? Before her mother ran off she had so many suitors, so many families who wanted her for their sons, but after, with such disgrace, no one would touch her. Everyone thought, well if her mother could do something like this, what must she have been teaching her daughter all of these years? And your poor cousin! Graciella was her name; she tried to kill herself. Your poor uncle loses his wife and comes home to find his daughter bleeding to death in the bathroom. He went insane with grief. The family was ruined. They had to send all the children to live with family members in Italy so they could escape the stain on the family name.

"Marcelle, are you listening to me? By then Fortunee wanted to come home, to fix what she had done, but your uncle wouldn't have her. And you know the laws. The rabbis forbade it. A woman can't go back to her husband after she's with another man."

"That's a really terrible story, Mom, and I feel horrible for her children, but I have no idea what this has to do with me."

"Marcelle, you can lie to yourself all you want, but you can't lie to me."

Marcelle stared at the floor. Sarah resumed rolling balls of dough. For as long as Marcelle could remember, Sarah's response to stress had been to work harder.

Suddenly Sarah stopped. She sighed deeply and folded her hands in her lap, staring at her fingers as she squeezed them together. Marcelle saw tears in her eyes.

Finally, she looked up at her daughter, looked her straight in the eye. Marcelle tried to avert her gaze, but having seen her mother cry only once before in her life, she could not.

"I know that I'm hard on you, Marcelle," Sarah said, a tear sliding down her cheek. "I know that. But it's only because I love you; it's only because sometimes I think you sell yourself short and you need to be pushed. You have everything, Marcelle," here she stopped to grab her daughter's hands for emphasis, "everything I ever wanted, everything I lost and never thought I would have, it all came so easy to you and you've never appreciated it."

Another tear slid down her face, and she wiped it away with the back of her hand. She grabbed Marcelle's hand again and continued, "I know you've always wanted to go to school, and I understand that you were angry about waiting so long for that to happen. But this? Marcelle, this is much worse than being unhappy, and this is much worse than being ungrateful. This is dangerous. This is risking everything. How could you live exactly the life I begged God for every day, and then just throw it away? I won't let you."

Marcelle held her mother's gaze as long as she could, but finally withdrew her hand and looked down. From the corner of her eye, she saw Sarah wipe her face again.

"I haven't done anything wrong, Mom, I swear. I haven't done anything to throw my life away."

Collecting herself, Sarah resumed flattening dough in the tortilla press. "But you're thinking about it," she said, folding the dough in half and stuffing it with cheese. "And don't you think," she said, her voice hushed, her tone low, "that if I noticed something, Nathan will, too? What will you do then?"

Chapter Eleven

He had lied to her. It was clear. As soon as she realized that he had lied to her she should have left. She knew she should have left. But she didn't.

Partially, she was drunk. When he had ordered a Long Island iced tea, she ordered one as well (what did she, who only drank wine on Passover, know about what went into drinks?). And after taking her first sip, and tasting how awful it was, she resolved to chug it quickly and order something less vile, rather than admit she didn't like it.

He had told her to slow down, not to drink it too fast, that it was stronger than she thought. Why didn't he instead tell her to order something that wouldn't get her that drunk that fast?

Because he wants me to get that drunk that fast.

The semester was finally over and they had finished handing in portfolios and taking exams. After their last class, Chris had suggested they all go out for a drink to celebrate. Marcelle never went to bars, but, because Angie and Evan were standing there when Chris said it, she assumed they were coming as well.

No, she had done more than assume. When Chris told her when and where, she had asked with whom, and he had told her they were coming. She knew it. Because though part of her wanted nothing more than to go out with him alone, at night, like on a date, the rest of her knew it was crazy, and never would have agreed to it.

Though of course I could have asked Angie myself.

And there she was, in a bar, decidedly not sober, out with a man who wasn't her husband, when she realized that he had never invited them, and had allowed her to get completely drunk.

You should leave.

But I don't want to leave.

But what if Nathan saw you here?

Nathan won't see me here; he's home watching the kids.

You left your husband home watching your kids so you could meet with your boyfriend?

He's not my boyfriend and nothing's going to happen because there are tons of people around, and I'm not doing anything wrong, just having a drink, and leave me alone already, damn it!

And while she should have felt rage at Chris, should have demanded to know why he lied to her, she instead pretended she was still expecting Angie and Evan to show up, or that she had known all along that they weren't going to, and didn't really care.

Looking around, she saw a world she had never been in. Marcelle watched a girl across the bar, young, pretty, big hair and small clothes. She was talking to two guys, one tall and broad and good looking, and the other medium height, wiry and dark. The girl clearly favored the smaller, darker man. She laughed loudly at his jokes. She hit his arm every time he said something funny, leaned into him, looked him in the eye. It was so clear that she wanted him. Clear, even, to the tall blonde guy, who had been trying to curry her favors, but had finally realized, by reading the motions of her body, that she wasn't interested in him.

It was so easy to read the girl's intention on her face; she wanted to sleep with the smaller, dark man. Anyone in the bar looking at her could tell. What did people in the bar looking at Marcelle think?

Oh God, what if someone sees me? What if someone tells Nathan?

But she had told Nathan the truth, or had told him the truth as far as she had known it to be, that she was meeting a few friends from her class after the final. Of course, she had told him they were going to a restaurant.

And here she was in a bar, alone with a man who definitely wanted to sleep with her.

It was amazing that at twenty-nine years old, in New York in 1989, she had never experienced this before in her life.

Because Nathan, had, of course, wanted to sleep with her when they were dating. But he hadn't just wanted to sleep with her; he had wanted to marry her first, sleep with her second, and have her bear his children, third.

Chris only wanted sex from her.

206

Had anyone in her life before just wanted sex from her?

Her mother's how-to-be-a-lady training always taught her that to be wanted that way was disrespectful. What did it say about her that she found it more intoxicating than the Long Island iced tea she had just downed? What did it say about her that, upon realizing all of this, she remained exactly where she was while still pretending she didn't know it?

There, at Zeo's, a bar in Bay Ridge, everything Marcelle knew about who she was, and what a woman was supposed to be, came into question.

How could it be here, in this bar? Why was it not in the sacred space of synagogue, where she would be sitting in only a few weeks' time, standing before God, asking to be forgiven, admitting all her sins? It wasn't the sound of the shofar, blown during prayer, that prompted these questions. No, it was Rick Astley singing, "Never Gonna Give You Up" in a smoke-filled room, crowded with people. Neon lights blinked in the window, their garish colors reflected off the black glass-topped bar. They sat on 1960s mod-style chairs, vaguely reminiscent of the Korova Milk Bar in Kubrick's *A Clockwork Orange*.

"You must be a magnet for men," he said, and she laughed, imagine that, and had an image of herself posing like Marilyn Monroe.

"You're crazy," she said, brushing it off and loving it at the same time.

"I couldn't take my eyes off you the first time I saw you. You were sitting in front of me in class. I remember you had your hair in a bun, with a pen sticking through it. When I asked you if you had a pen, you handed me yours, and when you turned around, you took your hair down and shook it out cause that was the only other pen you had. Your hair smelled like lavender."

She smiled. She had forgotten about that.

"I was going to drop that class," he said, his hand grazing her knee. "I kept coming because I wanted to see you. I couldn't stop thinking about you. I kept smelling lavender."

His hand felt warm on her knees, and she felt warmth shoot up her leg, between her legs, to her breasts and all over her body.

"We have a connection, don't we?" he asked. "Don't we?"

She looked down, at his hand, now on her thigh (what if someone sees?).

"I'm married, Chris. I have kids."

"I'm not asking you to leave them. I'm just asking if you feel it, too."

Still looking down she nodded her head, watching his hand rise from her thigh and to her face, where he caressed her cheek, pushing her hair behind her ear.

"You're amazing," he said. "In a world full of trashy women, you're a lady. So feminine in everything you do. And so open, and Marci, Marcelle," he lifted her chin so her eyes made contact with his, "so alive."

What was he saying? Words she had longed for. From Nathan, but Nathan wasn't here and he was. And as his words flooded over her, so did the six varieties of alcohol in her Long Island iced tea, and her body felt warm and gelatinous, like it had been freed of something, and she felt her emotions flying all around her, simultaneously happy and angry and grateful and bold.

And then, all of a sudden, sad.

She felt herself choking back tears. "I've felt so dead for so long, so much like everything was planned, and nothing had anything to do with me, and I was just going through with it, and I lost myself, Chris. I've been so dead."

"No Marci," he said, "you radiate life in everything you do. You're amazing. I've wanted my whole life to meet a woman like you!"

Like me? Like who?

What is this?

What the hell is going on here?

She looked up at him through her tears. "What do you want from me?"

Before he answered, she noticed her watch and nearly fell off her chair. How could it already be 10:30? Where had the time gone? What had they even been talking about? Why did she feel as though everything around her was liquid, like she couldn't hold on to it, like everything was too loud and too bright and too fast, and yet so slow at the same time, so free and suspended in a sort of fearless freedom, but still it was 10:30 and she had kids, and there was a babysitter. Oh God. No babysitter. Nathan! And she was drunk!

"I have to go," she said. "I told Nathan I'd be home by now."

"You're in no condition to drive," he said.

"What, and you are?"

"Yeah, I only had one," he said.

"I also only had one," she said.

"Yeah, but this isn't the first drink I've ever had. Come on, I'll drive you home."

"What about my car?"

"You'll get it tomorrow."

"No. I need to drive my car. I have to go to my mother's tomorrow," she said.

"Marci, you have children. What if you get into an accident? Who will take care of your children?"

Despite her drunken haze, the irony was not entirely lost on her; the man who lied to her and got her drunk to take advantage of her invoked her children to get her into his car. Scylla or Charybdis; monster or whirlpool? Which was worse? Which was which?

He dragged her to the car and she followed.

He started the engine, but didn't move the car, and she said, "Please, please take me home."

"Wait," he said.

"I will," he said.

"But first, please, just kiss me."

"No!"

"Just kiss me. Just once. Before I leave for Senegal."

"No!"

"Please, Marci, please."

His hand was back on her face, under her chin, guiding her closer and closer to him.

"Just. One. Kiss."

He kissed her. And to her surprise, she kissed him back. He moved closer to her, kissing her, grabbing her body, pulling her head back by her hair, exposing her neck and kissing her neck, violently. Kissing down to her breasts, as his hands pushed up her torso—hard, hurting her—until he grabbed her breasts from underneath and pushed them up, so her cleavage spilled out of the v-neck of her shirt. And brought his face down to her breasts and kissed them, and back up to her neck to her mouth, pulling her down so he was on top of her and holding her down and kissing her mouth and grabbing her face and kissing her.

"I want you so bad," he growled, "I've wanted to rip your clothes off from the minute I saw you."

And she was kissing back, and grabbing his body, her initial resistance gone, grabbing his head, her fingers in his hair, and holding his body down on hers, kissing him, electric shocks in her body, feeling warm and wet between her legs, an intense feeling that redefined desire.

He grabbed her hand and guided it down his body to the hardness in his pants, pressing her hand up against him.

"Do you feel that? Do you feel how bad I want you?"

Her desire doubled and she shivered with arousal.

"Do you want me, too?" he asked, his hands on her hips, moving to her waist and fumbling with the button on her jeans.

"Let me feel how bad you want me."

He undid her top button and pulled down the zipper and pressed the palm of his hand on her stomach pressing down towards her panties.

Oh God. Oh No. I can't. I can't. No. No.

"No," she said. "Stop. Chris. Stop. I don't want to do this. Stop." And she grabbed his hand and pushed it off her, and pushed him off her and sat up abruptly and shook her head.

"I can't do this. I don't want to do this. I need to go home. I have to go home."

"But Marci, I love you," he said, still trying to kiss her. "I love you," he whispered in her ear.

Marci, I love you. The words rang empty in her ears, compared to their richness when Nathan spoke them. Marci, I love you. His cheap

210

words lay bare, a ruse to get her to this moment, to this tawdry imitation of love, this empty longing, this simulacrum of intimacy. It was disgusting; it made her feel dirty. She was disgusted with him. She was disgusted with herself.

She fumbled with the latch on the door to the car.

"Unlock the door."

"Marci, wait."

"Unlock the fucking door now!"

"Okay, but Marci, wait, don't be mad, don't be upset, I just..."

"You just what? You just wanted to lie to me? To get me drunk? To fuck me and then go to Senegal and ruin my life? You think I'm the kind of woman who cheats on her husband? And then goes home to her husband and kids and pretends like nothing happened? Just goes about her life like she didn't just betray everything she believes in? That's not who I am! That's not the kind of woman I am!"

"I never thought..."

"No, you never thought about anything except about how to get in my pants. You selfish, immature, lowlife piece of scum! I can't believe I actually thought you cared about me. How stupid could I be? You never cared about what was going to happen to me after all of this. You only though about you and your dick," she screamed, as she pulled the handle and opened the door.

Violently, she pushed herself out of the car. She stopped for a moment before slamming the door, turning around and leaning back in.

"And by the way, Chris, you think you're so smooth, but that wasn't it at all. I guess the mother in me just found your puppy dog pathetic-ness endearing."

She slammed the door behind her and wobbled off to her car, praying, please God let me make it home safe tonight, please God, let me make it back home to Nathan. She drove carefully, slowly, terrified of crashing, praying all the way, whispering, I'm sorry, I'm so sorry, I've learned my lesson and I'll never do anything like this again.

Nathan was sitting on the living room couch, remote in hand, when she walked in the door.

"Where have you been?" he asked. "It's after midnight. I've been worried sick."

If Marcelle had been sober she would have apologized profusely and begged for his forgiveness. But she was still emboldened by the liquor so she yelled back.

"Oh you're worried that I get home after midnight? You don't know where I am? And it bothers you? How do you think I feel every night? You waltz in whatever time you feel like it. How do I know where you've been?"

"I've been at work!"

"Doing what? With who? How many hours a day can a person work!"

"Is that really what you think?"

"I don't know what to think! You're never here. We maybe have sex once a month. What the fuck am I supposed to think?"

"Are you drunk?"

"So what if I am?"

"So I watch the kids all night so you can go out and get drunk with your friends?"

"Are you having an affair?"

"What?"

"You heard me. Are you having an affair?"

"What? No! How could you think that?"

"Why are you never home?"

"How do you expect me to pay for all this? For this house? And the car and all your fancy clothes and our nice vacations and that diamond bracelet on your wrist?"

"Who needs it? Whoever said I wanted all of this? Whoever asked me what I wanted?"

"What do you mean you don't want this? When did you ever tell me you didn't?"

"You just assumed. Everyone makes assumptions for me, but no one ever asks me what I want. I don't even know what I want. I just know what I don't want. And I don't want this. I'm going to bed."

She stomped up the stairs, unaware that she was acting like a child, unaware that she had turned her own guilt into accusations against Nathan.

Until she woke the next morning. Until she saw Nathan's form asleep beside her. Until she realized the images flooding her mind were not from a dream. Until she thought she might have found an answer to the question, "Who are you," and the answer was a plea, a cry, "Not this!"

But then who?

Part Four: 1992-2001

Chapter One

Nura Anteby Abadi couldn't have been older than twenty-seven. Yet as Marcelle watched the young mother sink into her chair, she seemed ancient and weary, as though life had gone on too long. She seemed lost inside her oversized tee-shirt, her tiny, too-thin legs peeking out, clad in black leggings. Her brown eyes sunk into her face, peering out from skin so darkened by exhaustion it looked bruised. A deep crease cut through the smooth skin of her forehead and frown lines framed a mouth that had clearly once been quite pretty.

Marcelle wore a light cotton sweater and a pleated plaid GAP skirt that was technically Lauren's. She brewed a cup of tea and placed a plate of her mother's kaak on the table. Nura dipped her kaak into the tea, nibbled on it, complimenting the flavor and telling Marcelle it reminded her of home. Marcelle smiled in return and waited for her to talk. Nura and her family had been over for Shabbat lunch a week earlier, but with so many children in and out of the kitchen, it had been difficult to talk. Marcelle had sensed that Nura needed to open up and invited her over for the tea and kaak they were enjoying now. They sat together as a Sarah McLachlan CD played softy in the background.

"When we left Syria, I knew it would be difficult. We sacrificed a lot to come here. But it seemed worth it. For my children. But I didn't know it was going to be this hard. No. I didn't know at all."

Marcelle nodded sympathetically, patting Nura's hand.

"We're nine people living in a two-bedroom apartment," she said. "There's no room to stand. And my husband, thank God he found work, but I never see him. He works two jobs because how else can I feed everyone?"

Marcelle wanted to help. She had a solution but she didn't know how to offer without offending. Should she just say it? Or let Nura keep talking, hoping for an opening?

Marcelle already knew Nura's story. It was the story of the last 4,000 Jews to leave Syria, when Hafez Assad finally yielded to international pressure and issued travel visas to all the Jews who wanted to leave. Before then, any Jew able to obtain a visa had to leave at least one family member and a significant amount of money behind to ensure his return. Those who escaped did so knowing their family members would be tortured by the Muhabarat, the secret police, as punishment. But in April of 1992, after years of intense lobbying, Hafez finally dropped the restriction, and though he didn't explicitly allow the Jews to emigrate permanently, he also did nothing to make them return.

The Syrian community in Brooklyn organized quickly upon learning the news. They would absorb a large number of people, find them housing, jobs, places in school. Though many of the Jews had been financially comfortable in Syria, they would have to leave most of their assets behind.

Nura left Damascus with her husband and three young children. Her two brothers and two sisters came as well, and, as their parents were dead, all lived with her. Their caseworker tried to find them a bigger apartment. Recently, the caseworker had placed Nura's oldest brother in a job, a welcomed development that considerably eased their situation.

"Even with that," Nura said, "we are still struggling. But I know that it will get easier. We are so lucky mush'allah to have so many people trying to help us, people like you. We are so lucky to have a place to live. I must be patient. I know it will get easier. But Marci, I am so tired. Sometimes it's hard to feel lucky."

"Well," Marcelle said, clearing her throat and steadying herself. "That was why I invited you over. I was wondering if I could help even more."

Nura looked at Marcelle, a mixture of hope and shame coloring her face.

"Well, it's about Toufiq. Nathan and I...well, we were thinking maybe Toufiq could come live with us."

Nura continued staring but said nothing.

"So you could have more room."

Silence.

"And one less person to look after."

Nura rubbed her temples.

"And so he could have time to devote to his studies," Marcelle cleared her throat, taking Nura's hand in hers. "So that he could go to college."

Here Nura lost it. She dropped her forehead down to the table, pressing it into the hand that still held Marcelle's and cried. Was she angry? Embarrassed? Relieved?

"Nura?" Marcelle asked. "Are you okay?"

Which Marcelle knew was a stupid question, because of course she wasn't okay. She sat awkwardly, still clenching Nura's hand, gently squeezing to offer support.

Marcelle first met Nura's fifteen-year-old brother Toufiq in the English class she had volunteered to teach for the new immigrants in the Community's high school. Though Marcelle had not yet completed her degree in English and Education, the Community's high schools had hundreds of students to absorb, and they took help from any who offered. Three days a week after school, Marcelle helped twelve boys refine their English diction and grammar. Most of them had studied some English in Syria, but they were far from fluent.

The boys in Marcelle's class were rowdy and wise-cracking, often breaking into song, sometimes dancing and clapping in the middle of class. She let them laugh and play jokes, constructing her lessons around games, as long as they spoke English. Though Marcelle couldn't speak much Arabic, she understood it and could translate useful idioms and sayings into English.

Toufiq Anteby barely took part in the shenanigans. Reticent and quiet, Toufiq watched, as though trying to take up as little space as possible. He pressed his slight, wiry frame into the corner, so as not to be noticed, but his dark eyes took everything in, his thin lips smiling slightly at his classmates. She encouraged him to join the lessons to no avail. He answered questions when asked and was unfailingly polite, but kept himself outside the crowd.

One afternoon, she decided to do an exercise on family structure. She had them take turns at the blackboard, drawing their family trees, relaying anecdotes about family members.

When Marcelle called Toufiq to the board, she felt tension in the room, saw anxiety on her students' faces. Toufiq tensed, smiled his cryptic smile, and adjusted his kippah on his short, dark curly hair before coming to the front of the classroom. He wrote the names of his parents and of his five siblings, his brother-in-law and his nieces and nephew. He told a story about his younger brother and sister, and then explained that they all lived with his oldest sister, Nura, and her family. Normally, Marcelle would have asked about his parents. She'd heard many stories of big families temporarily splitting up to live with relatives while they got their lives sorted out. Everyone was in the same neighborhood, so though the situation wasn't ideal, it was hardly tragic. But there was something tragic on Toufiq's face, in the collective breath-holding of his classmates while they hoped Marcelle would not push.

She just smiled, corrected his grammar, and said, "Thank you, Toufiq. Your family sounds lovely."

After class, she called Ruthie, the social worker who was her class's liaison. She had to know, if for nothing else to avoid embarrassing him.

"That story's a really sad one," Ruthie informed her. "Their mother died in childbirth with the youngest daughter. Toufiq was nine. The father had an older widowed sister with grown children who came to help. But about four years later, he was picked up by the Muhabarat and never seen again. The children lived with their aunt until Assad let them out. The aunt wanted to stay in Syria. She didn't want to leave without knowing what happened to her brother."

The story tormented Marcelle; it was so similar to her own family's tragedy. She lay awake at night, unable to sleep. She wanted to help, but didn't know how.

She decided to invite her students to her house for Shabbat, one family per week, so that Toufiq would not feel singled out. She asked his family first. It took several phone calls to his sister, insisting over Nura's protestations that it wasn't too much, and that she didn't need any help.

"But we're so many people," Nura said.

"I have a big table," Marcelle replied.

Finally, they came. When Marcelle met Nura, she was shocked. The girl looked ragged and worn down. As she helped Marcelle in the kitchen, Nura pretended to be optimistic. "Haim just found work," she said, referring to her oldest brother. "And soon Toufiq will leave school and go to work as well."

She sliced a cucumber for salad. "It breaks my heart," she continued. "He's so smart. Nobody in our family went to university because it was very hard for Jews to go, but also my father was lucky that he had a good business. But Toufiq, he wanted to study engineering. In math, he's a genius."

Marcelle knew he placed out of high school math and was taking Advanced Placement calculus and chemistry. He would be devastated.

Later that night, as she and Nathan were lying in bed, she said, "I want to help. What can I do?"

"You are helping," he replied.

"I want to do more."

"What more can you do? You're teaching them English. You're welcoming them into your home with your family."

"That poor girl. Poor Toufiq," she said, shaking her head.

Nathan just shrugged. He rolled over, burying himself under their down blanket, as if to end the conversation.

Marcelle gently shook his shoulder and continued, "Imagine if you hadn't been able to go to college. If you had to work in an electronics store instead of reading Plato."

"That's what our parents did," Nathan said. "That's what your father did."

"I know. But my father wanted to own his own business. He didn't want to be an engineer."

218

Nathan sat up and huffed. "Marci, what do you want to do?"

Marcelle shrugged, "I mean, the boy has no parents."

"Marci," Nathan said, cocking his head and making eye contact with her. "What do you want to do?"

She rubbed her eyes and then her face. "What if he lived with us?"

"Are you crazy?" he asked, leaning into her. "Anyway, what would that solve? She needs him to work so they can have money."

"She also needs space. And one less mouth to feed. What if he works part-time while he does whatever he needs to do to get ready for college and lives here? He can give her whatever he earns, and we can take care of him."

Nathan shook his head. "They'll never agree to it."

She noticed he didn't say he'd never agreed to it, so she pushed on.

"Why not? Lots of families in the community are taking people in."

"They'll never agree to it," Nathan repeated.

"He's not even sixteen," she continued. "He's too young to have his dreams crushed."

Nathan rolled his eyes and rolled over onto his side again. "Ok, fine," he said. "If it makes you feel better, talk to his sister and see what she says. There's no way she's going to agree."

He pulled the blankets up over his head. The conversation was over.

But Nathan was wrong. When, over tea, Marcelle made her offer to Nura, Nura wept with relief.

"I feel so terrible," she said. "He's my brother, he's my responsibility. But I have so much cleaning and laundry to do, and we have no room. I'm so overwhelmed, all I do is scream at everyone. I'm a terrible person."

"You're not a terrible person. You have an awful lot of responsibility, especially for someone your age."

Nura cried harder. "I'm just so tired. I know there are women who can do this. I've seen the women in my family do this. But I'm just not as strong as they were."

Nura shook her head and thought for a moment. "Why are you being so kind to me?" she asked.

Marcelle told her the story of Sarah's family. Nura nodded her head.

"It seemed like a way I could honor my grandfather. I know it will make my mother happy."

Nura smiled. "We have to ask Toufiq, of course."

"Oh, absolutely," Marcelle replied. "But you're the oldest, so I wanted to clear it with you first."

Toufiq was shy about the arrangement at first. Had he been adopted or cast aside? Still, he agreed, and Marcelle readied her family for the changes. At first, she considered having Toufiq share a room with Jack but then decided against it. The poor boy had been uprooted so many times, at least she could give him a little privacy. Instead, she informed Lauren and Sarah that they would be sharing a room.

Lauren, who was a freshman at the high school, was not pleased about this boy moving in with them, and threw a fit upon learning that her nine-year-old sister would be her new roommate.

"But she goes to bed at 9:30. Where am I supposed to study?" Lauren yelled. "I have no place to talk on the phone in private."

"Lauren, the boy's mother is dead, his father has been missing for five years and is probably also dead, he lost everything he had and is living in a strange country with strangers. Could you show just the slightest bit of human compassion?"

Lauren was silent for a second and then burst into tears.

Marcelle was ready to yell when Lauren cried, "I'm disgusting."

Marcelle hugged her. "No you're not. Sometimes it's not so easy to do the right thing. Don't feel bad. Just do something nice for him. You're always bugging me to let you go to the city. I'll let you take the train to the Village one afternoon if you take him with you."

Lauren looked excitedly at her mother.

"You're welcome," Marcelle said.

Marcelle and Nathan expected some difficulties in their household as Toufiq settled in, but the transition was deceptively simple.

Imagine, Marcelle, thought, a fifteen-year-old boy moves into my house and there is no disruption. But that boy had a quiet charm, finding a way to relate to each member of the family. He played backgammon with Nathan. He practiced his English by reading Sarah stories. He loved that loud angry music Lauren insisted on blasting in her room. He let Jack teach him to play basketball.

The year before, for Jack's birthday, Nathan had installed a basketball hoop over the garage, but he was always too busy to play. Jack invited friends over sometimes, but Toufiq was there every day, and always agreed to play. Marcelle wondered if she should tell Jack to leave Toufiq alone, but the boys seemed to genuinely enjoy themselves.

One Sunday afternoon, late in October, a few short weeks after Toufiq moved in, Marcelle sat in the kitchen with her daughters, watching out the big bay windows, as her husband, son and this new boy played basketball in the backyard. As Marcelle showed her daughters how to stuff grape leaves, putting rice in the center, and folding the corners of the leaves in before rolling them like cigars, Nathan showed Toufiq how to block the ball, as Jack faked left, then threw it neatly into the basket.

Toufiq tousled Jack's hair, and Nathan put his arm around both boys.

"Don't worry," Jack said. "You'll be shooting like Jordan in no time."

Toufiq saw Marcelle smiling at him through the window and blushed. Then he waved.

Such a fine boy, she thought. We're lucky to have him.

Chapter Two

When Toufiq moved in, in the fall of her sophomore year, Lauren was sure she was in love with Ricky Shalom. Then again, so was every other girl in school. Ricky was tall, with dark blonde hair and intense blue eyes; he looked more Irish than Syrian. He was captain of the basketball team and co-captain of the debate team with Lauren. He was a senior and he was perfect.

Lauren was still fifteen, and by Community rules, she wouldn't be allowed on an official date till she turned sixteen that April. Still plenty of girls her age had boyfriends, the couples hanging out in groups because they weren't allowed out on their own.

Ricky lived a few blocks from Lauren and often offered her a ride home after debate practice. Before Toufiq moved in, she relished those moments alone with Ricky, but after, she felt like a jerk leaving school with Ricky knowing Toufiq was going to have to take the bus, so she started asking Ricky if he would drive Toufiq home, too.

Within a few weeks, Ricky got a message Lauren wasn't trying to send, and decided she wasn't interested. Instead, he started driving Jaime Dweck, a very pretty junior, and soon she saw them sitting together at lunch every day, holding hands in the hallway.

"That should have been me," she said, glaring at Jaime, while she ate lunch in the cafeteria with her friends Lily and Rachel.

"He's not that great," said Lily. "He's totally full of himself."

Lauren rolled her eyes.

"I think the one you did get is a much better catch," said Rachel, a mischievous smile on her face.

Lauren rolled her eyes again.

"We're not together!" she said.

"Well you're the only one who thinks so," Rachel continued. "You should be."

Everyone in school assumed Lauren and Toufiq were a couple, a myth he did nothing to dispel. In fact, he encouraged it, often joining her and her friends at their lunch table, meeting her after her classes so he could walk through the halls with her, letting his hands graze hers.

She supposed her actions helped the rumors as well. They studied together, went to parties together. She dragged him to high school basketball games, trying to force him to have a little fun. He was so serious. She knew things had been hard for him, and she wanted to help him enjoy being a kid.

Often on Saturday nights, she opened the door to his bedroom to find him sitting on the floor, papers all around him, studying. She was amazed by his spartan living space. No posters adorned the walls, no clothes piled up on chairs and in corners like they did in her room. Toufiq kept his room neat and tidy. Save a few pictures of his family, and one of his parents holding him as a baby, Toufiq did nothing to make it his.

"There's a basketball game tonight," she said one night. "I'm going with Lily and Rachel. Come with us."

"I don't know," he said, gesturing to his papers. "I really have to study for our history test on Monday."

Lauren felt sorry for him. Days at their yeshiva high school didn't end till 5:30, and then Toufiq worked three nights a week and most Sundays. He didn't have lots of time for homework, but she knew he wanted to come.

"No problem," she said. "I was going to make a review sheet for the test tomorrow. We can study from it together tomorrow night when you get home from work."

He was torn; she could see it in his face. Toufiq didn't like to take anything from anybody without giving something in return.

When he first moved in, it drove Marcelle crazy. He lived with them for months before he took food from the fridge without being offered and only because Marcelle yelled at him.

"Toufiq," she finally said, "this has to end. I can't remember everything. You're giving me more work by making me offer you every time. Do me a favor and make my life easier. Just take!"

Lauren employed the same strategy. "Come on, you're doing me a favor. We have no one to drive. I'm being the bad influence so I have to make it up to you."

He stared at her for a moment, smiled and closed his book.

She often caught him staring at her, smiling. If those looks came from anyone less sweet, they would be creepy. As they studied together, both at home and at school, she would look up from her books, chewing on her nail, to catch his gaze fixed on her, to see him blush as her eyes met his.

At first, she ignored the displays of affection. She thought of him as a brother. But little by little, she found herself holding his gaze, blushing and smiling back.

One night, Lauren and Toufiq were studying for their AP Government exam. Toufiq was especially interested in the subject because he hoped to take his citizenship exam.

They sat on the floor of the room Lauren shared with Sarah. The walls were ivory and the carpet was pale pastel green. Lauren and Sarah had decorated by drawing flowers in magic markers around the door post and in a border around the ceiling. On a shelf in the corner sat Lauren's prized possession, an Aiwa 5-CD changer stereo system that her parents bought her when she broke 1450 on her PSAT. Smashing Pumpkins played as they studied. In another corner, Sarah played with her Beanie Babies.

"I want to listen to Toufiq's music," she said.

Lauren rolled her eyes. "Did you put her up to that?"

Toufiq shrugged and half-smiled. "Who, me?" he asked. "Never."

"Come on," said Sarah. "I want to hear Habibi!"

"It's called Nour-al-Ain," Lauren said, switching to the Amr Diab CD.

"You know what I mean," she said.

"You're a big sneak," Lauren said, smiling at Toufiq.

"It's not my fault she likes good music," Toufiq replied.

As the sounds of Arabic pop filled the room, Sarah stood up and danced the way her grandmother danced at weddings, flicking her wrists and shimmying her hips. Toufiq clapped his hands and ululated. Sarah danced over to the other side of the room, and Toufiq stood up and danced with her.

Lauren rolled her eyes and Toufiq laughed again. Then a serious expression settled on his face as he quickly picked up the textbook. "Okay, Lauren, explain the process for passing a constitutional amendment."

"You're impossible," she said. She stood up and stretched. "Enjoy your dance party. I'm going downstairs for a snack."

As she left the room, she heard her little sister giggle. She turned to see Toufiq twirling Sarah around and dipping her. It made her want to kiss him.

The thought disturbed her. It kept worming its way into her head, but that night, she wanted to push Sarah out of the way, jump on top of him and plant her lips onto his. She wanted to feel his arms around her, to bury her head into his chest, to lay down next to him, feeling the heat of his body on hers. She loved every time he fake-accidentally brushed up against her, loved the electric jolt of energy that passed between their barely touching skin, as they sat side by side, staring at each other but never verbally acknowledging what was transpiring between them.

She shuddered, trying to push the feeling away. She took a deep breath.

"Are you okay?" Toufiq asked.

She nodded and hurried out of the room.

What could she do with these feelings? They lived together: Dating him was out of the question. It would be too awkward, seeing each other all the time, knowing everything about each other. What would happen when they had a fight? Would he overhear her on the phone telling her girlfriends how mad she was? And what if they broke up? There would be no escape.

Though she wouldn't date Toufiq, Lauren also wouldn't date anyone else. In a community where a woman is considered marriageable by age eighteen, sixteen is a magic number. A sixteen-year-old girl is officially on the market, and her friends and family will introduce her to all the eligible young men they know to help her find her husband.

The summer after she turned sixteen, she went to parties with her friends on the Jersey shore, just as her parents had, and though she met boys and flirted with them, she could never bring herself to go out with any of them.

How would that work? When they came to her house to pick her up, would Toufiq stare longingly from the landing above the stairs as some boy introduced himself to her father? Would he stay in his room, waiting till she got home, hoping to eavesdrop on whatever she told her friends afterward? How could she do that him? She wouldn't.

Instead, they hung out with each other. They went to concerts in the city, used bad fake IDs to get into small clubs to hear live music. While her friends went to fancy restaurants and trendy nightclubs with older boys, she and Toufiq ordered grilled cheese sandwiches and coffee in diners and wandered around the Village. Sometimes they held hands on the street, and sometimes, in poorly lit corner booths, she snuggled up next to him, and he put his arm around her and they held each other contentedly. But there was a line, and they didn't cross it. They didn't kiss. They didn't talk about their feelings. It was too risky and that was something they both intuitively understood.

Marcelle watched her daughter fall in love and was concerned. In retrospect, it seemed obvious that two teenagers living in such close confines would develop a romance, but of all the potential problems she had anticipated when Toufiq moved in with them, this particular one had never seemed a real possibility.

Nathan, of course, had already planned the wedding. He clued her in one night when they were watching _The X-Files_. Toufiq came home from work, and Nathan asked him to join them.

"Thanks, but I can't," he said. "Lauren gave me this book to read two weeks ago. If I don't finish it soon, she's going to kill me."

Nathan put his arm around his wife and hugged her closer. "They remind me of us," he said.

"Let's not rush them," she replied, making a mental note to talk to Lauren. "They're just kids."

"You were her age when we met," Nathan said.

Marcelle sighed. "Lauren isn't me," she said. "And anyway, we don't know what her intentions are."

Nathan shook his head. "She'd be crazy to let someone like that go."

Nathan sat on the couch smiling, probably imagining a lifetime of basketball games in the back yard. Marcelle's brow furrowed.

In the two years since she had started teaching ESL, Marcelle completed her degree and began her first year as a full-time freshman English teacher in the high school both Lauren and Toufiq attended. She knew Lauren was likely less than thrilled to have her mother in school with her all day and tried to make it up by always giving Lauren and Toufiq a ride home.

On a cold afternoon in November, Marcelle decided it was time for a serious conversation with Lauren. She watched them walk to the car dressed in what was essentially the yeshiva student uniform, Toufiq in a navy parka, khaki pants and loafers, Lauren in a black pea coat, knee-length jean skirt and thick tights under her black Doc Marten boots.

After she dropped Toufiq off at the cell phone store where he worked, she turned to Lauren and said, "I have to ask you something."

Lauren fidgeted in her seat.

"Can I change this?" she asked, referring to the Celine Dion CD playing in the car. "Aren't you embarrassed to listen to this sappy crap?"

"Fine," Marcelle said. "But none of that screaming music you listen to."

"No Soundgarden?" Lauren said.

Marcelle shook her head. "Ugh," she said. "How about that Tori person? She mostly sings."

Lauren took Tori Amos's *Pretty Good Year* out of the glove compartment, sliding the CD into the player.

"Put that back in the case," Marcelle said, pointing to her Celine Dion CD. "I don't want it to get scratched."

"It might make it sound better," Lauren replied.

Marcelle snickered.

"Go ahead," Lauren said.

"Go ahead, what?" Marcelle asked.

"Go ahead and ask me." Lauren waited for Marcelle, annoyed. "What's going on between me and Toufiq."

"How did you know?"

"Mom, you are the most obvious person," Lauren laughed.

Marcelle looked at her daughter, her beautiful, green-eyed daughter, and, not for the first time, was shocked at what a woman she was becoming.

"He has real feelings for you, Lauren," she said, careful to keep her voice soft, careful not to accuse.

"I know," she said. She gathered her long, light brown hair into a bun and wound a rubber band around it.

"He told you?" Marcelle asked, shocked.

Lauren shook her head. "He doesn't have to."

"And you?"

Lauren shrugged and looked out the window. It was already dark at 5:30 and she watched people walk down Avenue P, pulling their coats up over their faces to protect against the cold.

"Lauren?"

"I have real feelings for him, too."

"You have to be careful," Marcelle said.

Lauren nodded her head. "I know."

"Because if you broke up, he'd probably move out. There's a lot at stake here," Marcelle continued.

"Mom, I know," Lauren said. "That's why we're not together. And anyway, we both want to go to college. Even if we wanted to get married, it would be years away."

Marcelle nodded. "Better not to rush into anything."

They stopped at a red light. Marcelle looked at Lauren who was looking out the window at a girl she knew from high school, who had been a senior when she was a freshman.

"Is that Sari Cohen?" her mother asked.

Lauren nodded. "Sari and her baby," she said.

The light changed to green. Marcelle looked at the road ahead of her. "Just don't lead him on," she said.

But she wasn't leading him on. He was the only one who knew about California. He was the only one who listened as she daydreamed about Stanford, about Berkeley, about getting as far away as possible from New York.

One Saturday night, when her parents were out, Lauren stayed home to babysit, and Toufiq stayed in to keep her company.

They sat in the living room, Toufiq stretched out on the couch and Lauren curled up in her favorite club chair. She pulled her legs to her chest, propping her face on her knees as she talked.

"My mother said I should go to the best school I get in to. I mean, I didn't tell her where I wanted to go, but she didn't say I couldn't go to California."

"Why California? Why not stay in New York? Then we could be in school together." He hugged a pillow to his chest.

"So come with me to California," she smiled. She knew he would never leave his family.

"I don't understand why you want to be so far away."

"I don't understand why you don't."

"I've seen a lot, Lauren. Life is good here. Why leave someplace good?"

"Well, I haven't seen anything. I want to know what the outside world is like. And I need to get away from here for a while."

Toufiq swallowed hard, clutching the pillow. He cleared his throat. "Well, then, I hope you get what you want."

She stared at him, but he was looking towards the window. Was that sarcastic or serious?

She buried her face back in her knees. "I hope you do, too," she whispered.

In the months to come, as they prepared for their SATs in the spring of their junior year, Toufiq succumbed to the stress.

"I'm so nervous," he said on a Saturday afternoon in April, as they walked down Ocean Parkway on their way home from synagogue.

Young families and senior citizens sat on the benches that spread across the length of the avenue, enjoying the weather on that warm, sunny morning. The Community had several synagogues on Ocean Parkway, and as Lauren and Toufiq made their way down the avenues they saw many people they knew: family members, schoolmates, family friends.

"The whole reason your parents took me in was so I could get a good education. What if I let them down?"

Though Toufiq aced the math sections on the practice exams they took constantly, his verbal scores were mediocre.

She grabbed his hand to stop him.

"Hey," she said. "Look at me."

He turned to her. She smiled. Then she hugged him.

"It's your second language. It's pretty amazing that you're doing as well as you are. Besides, with those math scores, you're going to be fine. Whatever happens, it's going to be okay."

She linked her arm with his and they continued walking home. That was a mistake. The old ladies sitting and young mothers jogging saw them and made assumptions and spread those conclusions to anyone who would listen. Within days, the gossip brigade decided they were engaged. People came up to her father during prayers to congratulate him.

"So, I hear you're getting married," her father said to them the following Shabbat over dinner. He sat at his chair at the head of the table, grinning like the village idiot, Lauren thought.

Toufiq blanched.

"Nathan!" gasped Marcelle.

"Mabrouk!" Jack yelled. He was sitting next to Toufiq. Jack leaned over to tousle his hair.

Sarah, who sat next to Lauren on the opposite side of the table, elbowed her older sister and giggled. "So now I can have my own room?"

"What are you talking about?" Lauren asked.

"Toufiq," Nathan said, wagging his finger, "if you want to marry my daughter, you have to ask me first."

Lauren looked across the table at Toufiq. He was sweating.

"Dad, seriously, we have no idea what you're talking about," she said.

Nathan continued, that awful smile still on his face. "Abe Fallas told me his mother saw you two holding hands on Ocean Parkway. You know that's basically like announcing your wedding to the neighborhood."

"God, I hate those people," Lauren exclaimed. "I guess I should never touch my stomach in public either. Wouldn't want people to think I was pregnant."

Marcelle sighed loudly, and put her hand on Lauren's, trying to calm her.

"Lauren, you know that's how people here are. If you don't want them talking about you, don't give them a reason."

"First of all, we weren't holding hands. Second, I don't care if they talk about me," Lauren said. Marcelle could see the rage rising in her face.

"Well, you're my daughter, and I do," Nathan said, no longer amused.

Marcelle caught Nathan's eye from across the table. She shook her head, telling him to stop.

Nathan ignored her. "As for you, young man," he said, turning to Toufiq, "she doesn't listen to anyone, but I expect more from you."

Toufiq started down at his plate. Lauren though he might cry from shame.

"Though I would hardly object to the courtship," Nathan continued.

Sarah giggled. "Toufiq and Lauren sitting in a tree," she sang.

"Sarah, shut up!" Lauren yelled. Then she turned to Nathan, "Dad, honestly!" she said. "It's bad enough you're embarrassing me, but do you have to do this to Toufiq? I'm not going to sit here and watch you humiliate him." She stood up and stormed away from the table.

"She gets that from your side," Nathan said to Marcelle. "No one in my family runs away from the table like that."

Toufiq focused on his peas, trying to catch his breath. Jack patted him on the back. Marcelle thought he might faint. She tried to ease the tension.

"So you must be excited about Haim's wedding," Marcelle said, referring to Toufiq's older brother. Toufiq looked up and tried to smile.

"Seriously, Toufiq," Nathan continued. "I think you and Lauren would be great together."

"Nathan!" Marcelle said. Jack and Sarah both giggled.

"I honestly don't know who else is going to put up with her," Nathan said. He cut a piece of roast and put it in his mouth.

In her room, Lauren cried into her pillow, taking deep breaths to stave off the sense of suffocation overcoming her. Everything felt inevitable, all her choices already made, as though her life had already been lived and she was simply repeating it, acting out the consequences of someone else's decisions. Her entire future lay mapped out, as though she were a character in a play with no agency of her own. She knew the plot well: a wedding next year, a baby two years later, and another two years after that.

Maybe they'd live in the city for a year or two while Toufiq went to school. Oh, she might go to school, too, but why bother taking it seriously when she would drop out once the baby was born? And then of course, they'd have to move back to Brooklyn so her mother could help once she had their second child. That was what everyone did, right?

And it would be easy. Toufiq was already part of her family, and his family treated her as though they were already engaged. She might be happy. Everyone thought she should be happy. Everyone else would be happy. But what if everyone else's happiness hinged on forfeiting her own?

She couldn't ignore the growing restlessness, the anxiety, the feeling from deep within that she couldn't accept this prefab life, these pre-made choices, this life unlived, the world unseen. Though they were technically in New York, in reality, the Community was like a small town, and she longed to be someplace where no one knew her, no one knew her great-grandparents back in the old country, and she could act, could experiment, could try new things without everyone knowing, and everyone talking, without those details forever entering the catalogue of information people stored away about her and her family.

But even as she wanted out, she wanted a clear map of the way back in. She wanted to know Toufiq would be there when she came back, to know her scary sojourn into the outside world would have a neat and tidy end, a house on Ocean Parkway, entertaining her in-laws on Shabbat. She wanted to watch Toufiq tuck their children into bed at night; she wanted to argue with him whether to take the kids on their vacation or go alone to have time for themselves. To be out in the world with no anchor was too frightening, too hard to even fathom.

Eventually, she believed she would make everyone happy, but it had to be on her terms, on her timeline. If Toufiq was the one, he still would be after college was over, and if he wasn't, better to find out now than five years and two babies from now.

What lay in front of her was hers to decide, and she wasn't going to let anyone do it for her. She had to get out.

Chapter Three

Marcelle fingered the thick envelope and wondered what she would tell Nathan. For months, she had been preparing for the fight, but she hadn't expected it to come so soon.

Stanford. She had been admitted into Stanford. As proud as Marcelle was, she was furious with Lauren for not telling her she applied. How did she pay the admissions fee? Marcelle never wrote her a check, and Nathan certainly hadn't.

It was December. Which meant she had applied early. Which meant she was bound to go. One thing was certain: her daughter had balls.

What was she going to tell Nathan?

Marcelle knew it was her fault. She knew she should have seen it coming.

"Apply to the schools you want," she had said. "There's no reason to fight with your father till you see where you get in."

She should have realized that Lauren would do something like apply early to the school he was most likely to reject.

Of course, Nathan had been pushing his alma mater, Columbia. And indeed, another large envelope bearing Columbia's insignia was in the mail as well, only it was addressed to Toufiq. Nathan would be so pleased. He had written the boy a long letter of recommendation, had personally called everyone he could influence into securing a full scholarship. She wondered if he had been successful. Surely Toufiq's family could not afford the tuition, and though he was practically their adopted son, she didn't know that she could pay for two private colleges at the same time. It didn't matter though. Toufiq was proud. He wouldn't accept their money. He would go to the best school that gave him a free ride. She smiled, thinking of how far he had come.

When Lauren walked in the door, her cheeks red from the cold, she found Marcelle sitting at her kitchen table with a cup of coffee, leafing through a magazine as though nothing had happened. Marcelle could see the anticipation on Lauren's face.

"Look what came today," Marcelle said, tossing the envelope to Lauren.

She saw the excitement jump into Lauren's face and then fall when Lauren realized she was holding an envelope from Columbia.

"Oh. Wow," Lauren mustered. "Toufiq's going to be so happy."

"But you applied early to Columbia, too," Marcelle said. "It's odd that they didn't send all the letters out on the same day."

"Oh. Uh. No. I changed my mind at the last minute," Lauren said, setting Toufiq's acceptance package onto the table.

"Where's the rest of the mail?" Lauren asked.

"Why, are you expecting something?" Marcelle asked, trying too hard to be casual.

"Yeah. No. Um, nothing, I just wanted to look."

"For what? The cable bill?'

"Why are you torturing me?

"Oh, are you looking for this?" Marcelle asked, holding up the envelope.

Lauren shrieked and jumped up and down. "I can't believe I got in! I can't believe it!"

Marcelle stood and hugged her. "I'm very proud of you. But you should have warned me."

"I thought you'd stop me."

Marcelle sat back down and gestured Lauren to join her. "Probably. Your father's going to be pretty upset. It's going to be a hard sell."

Lauren remained standing. She was too anxious to sit. "But you're okay with it. You'll help me?"

"I don't know, Lauren," Marcelle said, gripping her mug. "I have mixed feelings about this. I want to support you but Stanford is far. Realistically, how often are you going to be able to come home?"

Lauren stood silently, biting her lower lip and sticking her hands in her pockets.

Marcelle looked hurt. "That's part of the point, isn't it?"

Lauren fidgeted.

"Well, if I figure that out, so will your father. It's going to be an ugly fight."

"But you'll help me?" Lauren pleaded.

"I'll do the best I can. I was already preparing, but I thought I'd be fighting with him to send you to Harvard or Yale. You know, somewhere where you could come home a lot. That was going to be part of my argument. You really should have let me know."

"I'm sorry."

"No, you're not. And I have to tell you, I'm angry." Marcelle stared at her daughter until Lauren met her gaze. "But I'm still really proud of you."

She sipped her coffee. "You're going to have to help me, you know. This is a team effort. You must be on your best behavior. You have to convince him he can trust you. Stop picking fights with him. Don't give him more reasons to say no."

"He can't really stop me," Lauren said.

Marcelle could see the defiance rising. She laughed. "Lauren, it costs $30,000 a year. How are you going to pay for it otherwise? You're going to mop floors in the cafeteria? Somehow, I don't see you doing that. We have about a month. Let's see what we can do."

Later that night, Lauren heard her parents fighting while she studied in Toufiq's room. Sarah was already sleeping, and Jack was loudly playing Super Mario brothers on his Nintendo.

She opened the door quietly, crept to the landing and sat, resting her head against the banister.

"Are you crazy?" she heard her father yell. "You think I'm going to allow my daughter to move to California? It's bad enough you want me to let her dorm. Those people have no morals. All they do is have sex and do drugs. You don't know what goes on. The things I saw my friends do at parties. The things that went on in their dorm rooms."

She heard her mother's voice, muffled, muted, so that she couldn't hear what her mother said. But then her father yelled again.

"No, Marci. No. Absolutely out of the question. She can go to Columbia. She can go to Barnard. She can go to NYU. But she is not leaving my house until it's with a husband."

Lauren hugged her knees to her chest, trying not to cry. Toufiq came out and sat beside her, trying to console her.

"It's not over yet," he said. "You knew it was going to start out this way. Your mother's on your side. Just give her a little time."

"I don't know what I was thinking," she said. "She's never going to be able to change his mind. What can she possibly say?"

Downstairs, Marcelle asked herself the same question. She sat at the kitchen table, clutching a mug of tea while Nathan paced around the room.

"I can't believe we're fighting about this," he said. "I can't believe she convinced you that this was acceptable."

"She didn't have to convince me, Nathan. I made myself a promise a long time ago that I wouldn't hold her back. That I wouldn't make her choices for her, the way my choices were made for me. I'm not going to force her into anything."

Nathan stopped pacing and turned to face Marcelle. He leaned his back against the wall and tilted his head back, resting the crown of his head on the wall, too. Then he stood up straight and rubbed his temples.

"You say little things like that all the time, and every time you do, it hurts me. I don't feel like we were forced. I knew I wanted to marry you. I was ready. We may not have had the easiest beginning, but what came next, the last twenty-one years, more than half your life, they've been good years. Maybe not every minute of every day, but overall, they've been good. At least I think so. Don't you?"

"Of course I do, Nathan," she said.

He walked over to the table and sat down next to her. "So then, what is this?"

"I wanted to see the world, Nathan. I wanted to travel. There were so many things that I wanted to do, and I never got to do any of them," she said.

"What are you saying? That you regret marrying me?"

"No, Nathan, of course not," she said, taking his hands in hers.

"You never told me anything," he said. He stared at the wall.

"Stop it," she said, her voice tender. "Look at me. Please. I never said I regret marrying you. I just wish we waited a little longer."

Nathan continued staring at the wall and rubbing his temples.

Finally, he said, "Until you said you wanted to go back to school, you never told me what you wanted. You just sulked around the house being mad at everyone, god knows why. I never stopped you from doing anything."

She reached across the table to touch his face. "I love you, Nathan. I'm happy I married you. But I was too young. You just said yourself, I wasn't the most the pleasant person to be around for a while."

He kept staring at the wall, kept avoiding her gaze.

"Nathan," she said softly, "you're not listening to me. If we had gotten married a little later, if I had a little more time to be me before I became a mother, we could have avoided those bad years. Things could have just been the way they are now from the beginning."

Nathan thought for a moment, and nodded. He looked back at her and she smiled at him.

"We're happy now," she said. "We're good. Right? I know I'm happy."

He nodded.

"I'm sorry, Nathan. I didn't mean to hurt you."

He nodded. "I'm fine," he said. She raised her eyebrows and bit her lip.

"Really," he repeated, "I'm fine."

He took a deep breath. "But, Marci, we're losing sight of the argument. This isn't about us. Okay, so you don't want her pushed into marriage and motherhood too soon, but nobody's marrying her off. I just don't want her moving across the country by herself. Nothing you say is going to convince me that's a good idea."

Lauren would never know what her mother said to change her father's mind. Years later, Marcelle had no idea either. But that was because she wasn't the one who convinced him.

One night, after Marcelle and Nathan commenced another screaming match regarding their daughter's future, Nathan retreated to the den and poured himself whiskey. Nathan rarely drank, but the stress of the constant battling drove him to alcohol that night. As he sat on the black leather couch in front of the television that he didn't turn on, Toufiq poked his head in the room. Nathan invited him in and offered a drink. Toufiq poured himself two fingers of whiskey and joined Nathan on the couch.

"What did I do wrong?" Nathan asked.

"I don't know what you mean," Toufiq replied.

"How did I raise such a rebellious daughter?"

"She's not trying to rebel. She just wants something different. If she were your son..."

"But she's not my son. She's filled your head with that garbage, too? You know how this community is. Can you imagine the things people are going to say about her? And who's going to marry her after she lives away for four years?"

Toufiq paused and stared at the empty television screen.

"I would," he said quietly. "If she would have me, I would."

Chapter Four

Lauren and Toufiq were kissing in his bed when the new millennium began. She was home for winter break during her junior year, and he had grown tired of waiting.

Toufiq had finally moved out of her parents' house, into an apartment a few blocks away that he shared with his younger brother, Solomon. He worked part-time at a financial services company. They had initially hired him to help them with Y2K compliance, but they were so impressed by his smarts and his work ethic that they offered him a full-time position when he graduated. He had a semester's worth of AP credits from high school, and had decided to take classes over the summer so he could graduate early. Finally, he would have his own money. Finally, he would be able to build a life.

He wasn't a boy anymore. Financial independence transformed him. He wasn't meek and he wasn't shy and he didn't want to wait for the things he wanted.

She wasn't expecting it, when he showed her around the apartment, around the kitchen, into his bedroom. She realized, as he led her into his room, that this was the first time they had ever been completely alone together. When they lived in her house, someone—a parent, a sibling—was always there, always waiting to walk in on them, and Toufiq would have never disrespected his hosts by dishonoring their daughter. But this was his house and this was his room and in it was his bed.

He came up behind her, slipped his arms around her waist. He kissed her neck and she leaned back into him. He pushed her on the bed and fell on top of her, flipping her over so she was facing him, and stared deeply into her eyes before he grasped the back of her head and pushed her lips up to meet his. He kissed her with the passion of a man who has been waiting five years for that kiss and she kissed him back.

She expected his kisses to be tentative and sweet, to be kind and gentle. But they were rough and bruising and hungry and she loved them. She expected his hands to stay on her face, her back and maybe her hips,

240

but they were pressing into her, moving up her shirt, grabbing at her breasts.

"Toufiq," she said, gasping for breath, "What are you doing? Stop."

"You don't want me to stop," he said, pressing himself into her.

She giggled. "Well, not everything." Her lips met his again. "But watch your hands."

He was a really good kisser. She wondered whom he had been kissing, but then pushed the thought out of her head. She had been kissing people, too. In the last two and a half years, there had been a few guys she had hung out with, a few she had hooked up with, but she had never gone all the way.

Lauren didn't necessarily believe in waiting for marriage, but she also didn't want to lose her virginity to someone she didn't care about. But when she found someone she cared for enough, and they got to the point when it seemed a good idea, all she could think about was Toufiq. Lauren didn't know a lot about sex, but she did know it was probably not wise to sleep with one boy while thinking of another. So she waited, trying to make sense of her emotions. Until it hit her: she knew there was a lot Toufiq could deal with, but a bride who wasn't a virgin wasn't one of them. She couldn't risk losing him. And knowing she was afraid to lose him made her realize her feelings for him had gone beyond childhood crush, that even though they had never discussed it, he was clearly waiting for her. And she, too, was waiting for him.

They spent three hours in his bed, kissing and groping.

Finally, she said, "Toufiq, I have to go."

"Don't leave."

"Would you like to tell my father where I spent the night?"

He smiled and nodded, getting off the bed to grab his coat and car keys so he could drive her home. They sat in the car outside of her house. As she reached to open the door he said, "I've wanted to do that for years."

She smiled slyly. "Me, too."

"You know I'm waiting for you," he said.

She looked down and exhaled deeply.

He turned to her. "Lauren?"

She fixed her gaze on her boots. "I know."

He shook his head. "You don't want me to."

She looked up from her boots to him. "I don't want to promise anything. I don't know how we are together."

"You know exactly how we are together. And the only thing we didn't know, we found out tonight."

She smiled again. "That was awesome."

"You're home for a whole month," he said, running his hand up her thigh.

"Toufiq!"

"You want to know how we are together. Let's find out. The summer's only five months away, and after that, it's less than a year."

He looked so hopeful. And what he said made sense. But she wasn't ready to let go yet, she wasn't ready to give in to him.

"Come on, we just rang in the new millennium together. It's perfect. A new age for the world, a new stage for us."

She smiled. She often forgot what a romantic he was. She cleared her throat. "I was thinking of going to Paris this summer."

He took his hand off her leg and stared at the steering wheel. "Paris," he whispered. "So now you need to go to Paris."

"Come with me," she said. "Imagine how wonderful it would be."

Toufiq shook his head. She could hear the frustration in his voice. He took a deep breath and exhaled loudly through his nose. The same thing her father did when trying to calm himself.

"How am I going to go to Paris, Lauren? I need to work. I'm not going to turn this job down."

"Tell them you'll start a month later. Come with me in June."

"Sometimes I think you live in a dream world."

"Well, sometimes I think you don't dream enough. Don't be such an old man. Live a little. Don't you want to see things?"

Toufiq shook his head again. "Please stop making me feel bad for all the things I can't give you."

"Toufiq…" she trailed off. "I'm sorry."

"Lauren," he said, caressing her face. "I love you. I have always loved you. I just want to be with you already."

"I love you, too," she said, weaving her fingers into his. "That's never been the issue."

"The issue is that it's never been the right time," he continued. "It can finally be the right time."

"I live in California."

"Not for much longer."

She pulled away from him. "I'm just not ready to start this. This is it. This is the rest of our lives. Forever."

"Yeah," he said, nodding his head. "Isn't that the point?"

"I need some time before I can jump into it," she said.

"Jump into it?" he asked. "Are you kidding? I've been in love with you for five years!"

She pursed her lips and folded her hands in her lap.

He flicked the switch on the car door, unlocking it, turning away from her. "I'm not going to wait forever, you know."

She grabbed the handle and pulled. "I never asked you to wait."

And like a spoiled bratty child, she slammed the door and ran in the house, and felt angry and aroused and exhilarated and guilty.

Sarah never could get used to her granddaughter living in California. Lauren was already in her third year of college and still Sarah woke up some mornings unable to believe her daughter had let her granddaughter move so far away.

The things people said bothered her, too. Of course, she was proud to have a granddaughter who attended such a fine school, but she was embarrassed when people said, "Really? She lives by herself in California?" Some of her ruder friends continued, "I would never let my daughter move that far away." Sarah smiled and brushed them off, but it upset her. Why should anyone have anything bad to say about her family, about her wonderful granddaughter, Lauren?

What bothered her the most, though, was the change she saw in Lauren. Each time she returned home for a break, it seemed she had moved further from them. When she spoke, she no longer sounded like she was from New York, instead pronouncing words like "orange" and "vanilla" in that funny West Coast way. She no longer used the Arabic slang that was popular among her generation in the Community. But there was more. One Shabbat, Sarah caught her turning off the light in the bathroom, gasping and turning it back on, like she had forgotten she wasn't supposed to use electricity on Shabbat and was more concerned with her parents finding out than sinning before God.

Sarah worried. An oblivious Marcelle was too busy reveling in stories of her daughter's adventures, and Nathan acted like he had given up. She felt Lauren slipping away. Clearly, someone had to do something.

When Lauren was home, Sarah contrived to spend as much time with her as possible, to remind her who she was, and what their family was about. On the first Sunday of Lauren's winter break, Sarah invited Marcelle and Lauren to have lunch with her in the health food café she loved on Kings Highway.

Sarah looked at her pretty girls, Marcelle in a pastel twin-set and a grey knee-length straight skirt with a slit up the side, and Lauren in boot-cut corduroy jeans and a chunky turtle-necked sweater.

Lauren was talking about her plans for the next year, when Sarah interrupted her to ask, "How much more school is there?"

Lauren looked surprised. "I told you Nonna, I have a year and half left."

Sarah shook her head. "It's such a long time to be away," she said. "Isn't there any way for you to finish early?"

Lauren knit her eyebrows together. "I guess I could finish a semester early if I took summer session, but, um, actually, sorry Mom, I was going to ask you and Dad later, there's this internship in Paris I was interested in..."

"Mmm, Paris," Marcelle said, a wistful smile on her face. "I've always wanted to go to Paris. Maybe one day. What kind of internship is it?"

244

But Sarah wasn't interested in the internship. She could feel the anger rise to her face. She knew she should keep her mouth shut. Eddie would tell her to keep her mouth shut, but Rosette would tell her to speak up. So she did.

"What do you mean, Paris? What kind of craziness is this? Go to Paris with your husband. Not as a young girl by yourself. Finish school early and get married. Toufiq will take you to Paris."

Lauren was used to the insinuations that she would marry Toufiq. Everyone assumed she would, and she probably did, too. Except that Toufiq was barely speaking to her at the moment, and their New Year's celebration had left her very confused. Angry as she was, she knew there were rules that couldn't be broken, and one of those rules was that she didn't talk back to Nonna, no matter if she deserved it, no matter how wrong she was. Lauren forced her face to freeze in an awkward smile, trying to mask her rage.

Marcelle, however, had no such self-control. Something inside her snapped. Something she had pushed down long ago stirred as she saw a situation that felt too familiar and tried to protect her daughter from falling into it.

"Mom!" she said, her voice a rough whisper. "Why would you say something like that to her? They're not engaged. They're not even boyfriend, girlfriend. Maybe something will happen between them and maybe something won't, but it's not up to us to decide."

Sarah huffed. "If they're not boyfriend and girlfriend, I'm Marilyn Monroe."

Lauren put her elbow on the table, dropped her head into her hand.

"Mom, why do you have to embarrass her like that?"

Sarah was incredulous. "Why is this embarrassing? We're talking about her future. We always talk about the future."

Marcelle hissed. "Keep your voice down! The whole restaurant doesn't have to hear this conversation. And we're not talking about her future. You're deciding it for her."

"Well, somebody has to step in. You and Nathan just let her do whatever she wants."

Lauren wanted to crawl into the salt shaker and hide. "Can you guys please stop talking about me like I'm not here? I'm right here."

Sarah looked at her. "I was talking to you, ya rohi. I was asking why you feel you have to wait so much longer. Why you don't just come home and marry Toufiq. But your mother here had to interrupt us to yell at me."

"Really, Mom?" Marcelle said. She leaned back in her chair and folded her arms over her chest. "So much for a nice lunch with my mother and daughter," she muttered.

Lauren felt like she was going to vomit. She caught Marcelle's gaze, her eyes pleading. Marcelle nodded. "Baby, you can leave if you want."

Lauren nodded and stood up hastily. Before leaving she kissed the top of Sarah's head. "I love you, Nonna," she said. "I just can't have this conversation with you."

She grabbed her coat and ran out of the restaurant, not even stopping to put it on.

"You're too free with her," Sarah said, shaking her head. "You have to be her mother, not her friend."

Marcelle sighed loudly. "Sometimes a mother can also be a friend. Sometimes a mother can actually listen to what her child wants instead of telling her what to do."

"Are you saying I never listen to you? You know that's not true."

"You know what? I don't want to have this conversation with you, either."

Marcelle stood up and went to find the waitress. Sarah overheard her excusing them, explaining that Lauren felt sick, handing the woman a tip for taking the trouble to bring them menus and water.

At least she's polite to strangers, Sarah thought. As least I got that right.

The waitress waved to Sarah, and Sarah faked a smile and waved back.

As Sarah and Marcelle gathered their coats and bags Sarah said, "You're right. The whole restaurant doesn't need to hear us have this conversation."

Marcelle didn't answer. They walked out of the restaurant.

"We'll talk in the car," Sarah said. There was never any parking on Kings Highway, so Sarah had picked everyone up.

Marcelle shook her head. "You know what Mom? I suddenly feel like walking."

Sarah shook her head. "Are you crazy? It's twenty degrees out."

Marcelle glared. "Good," she said. "It'll help me cool down."

Lauren had walked home too, the cold stinging her skin, the skin that had forgotten what real cold felt like after living in California. She walked in the door, grateful no one was home and she could have a few minutes alone.

She put water in the kettle and rummaged through the pantry for a hot chocolate packet. She needed something soothing. Lauren was already raw when her grandmother stuck her finger in the wound, already confused, already didn't know what to think.

She needed to talk to someone, and the only person who could possibly understand was her mother. So when Marcelle walked in on that cold day after the disastrous lunch, Lauren barely let her take her coat off before asking her, "Mom, how did you know?"

"How did I know what?"

"With Daddy? How did you know you were ready? And wasn't it weird, having known him most of your life, and having your whole family know him and love him? How did you separate what they wanted from what you wanted?"

And then Marcelle wondered, does a mother tell her daughter she got railroaded? Does a mother tell her daughter that she never really had a chance to decide?

"I don't know what's better," Marcelle said. "To have too many years to think about it or to be so rushed you don't have a minute to breathe."

"How will I know when I'm ready?" Lauren continued.

"Do you love him?" Marcelle asked.

"Of course, I do. And I don't know what I'm waiting for. I just know whatever it is hasn't happened yet."

"Look, sweetheart, of course there's a large part of me that hopes you'll end up with Toufiq, but only if it makes you happy. You're the one who'll have to pick up his dirty socks for the rest of your life." Lauren smiled.

Marcelle smiled back. "Finish school. Move back to New York, and then you'll figure it out. You don't have to decide this second."

"How can Nonna be so sure?" Lauren asked, sulking into her hot chocolate.

Marcelle put her arm around Lauren, pulling her close. "It's not Nonna's decision. She thinks everyone's marriage is as perfect as hers and Nonno's. I think their lives were so hard they didn't have any energy left to have problems between them, you know? All that external pressure bound them together."

Lauren relaxed her head onto her mother's shoulder. "He's becoming impatient. He finally told me."

"It's understandable. But if you're going to be together, you'll have the rest of your lives. You don't have much more time to be on your own. Make the most of it."

They sat quietly for a moment in their embrace until Lauren broke away.

"Thanks for standing up for me," she said.

Marcelle sniffled. "Your grandmother needs to learn to think before she talks. As she's gotten older, she's lost her filter. I don't know if she stopped caring or she just can't help herself."

"Should I apologize for walking off?" Lauren asked.

"No," Marcelle replied. "She needs to learn not to meddle so much."

Lauren chuckled. "Good luck with that."

Marcelle smiled, too. "Well, we can at least keep from encouraging her."

Sarah was still fuming when she pulled into her driveway. Imagine not being able to have a simple conversation with her own daughter and granddaughter. Why was everyone so sensitive? Since when were they a family who couldn't talk about things? Had she been so out of line?

She feared Lauren was going in a dangerous direction. As someone older and wiser who loved her and wanted what was best for her, wasn't it Sarah's responsibility to stop her before she could get hurt? To prevent her from making mistakes?

She decided to call Rosette.

"You shouldn't have brought it up in the restaurant," Rosette said. "And maybe not in front of Marci. If you want to talk to Lauren, do it in private. Invite her over, just the two of you. This way, she'll be more relaxed."

Sarah agreed. She called Lauren's cell phone. She didn't risk calling the house phone and having an angry Marcelle answer. Lauren didn't pick up, so she left a message.

"I'm sorry for embarrassing you in the restaurant," she said. "I really wanted us to have a nice time. Why don't you come over so we can spend some quiet time together?"

Lauren played the voicemail for Marcelle. "Into the lion's den?" she asked.

Marcelle laughed. "Go. This is behavior we should encourage."

Lauren went the following day. Sarah started nice enough. She asked Lauren to help her make baklawa. They had done this many times before, and Lauren slipped comfortably into the chair at Sarah's kitchen table.

Sarah succeeded in luring Lauren into a false sense of security, and Lauren laughed, telling Sarah stories about the various groups on campus. Sarah was especially fascinated when Lauren described the Goth kids.

"But why?" she asked, shaking her head as she brushed butter over a sheet of filah dough. "Why would people want to make themselves so unattractive on purpose?"

"They must think it's attractive," Lauren said, shrugging. "I don't know."

"And you?" Sarah asked, continuing to butter and layer filah until she had a stack of seven sheets. She passed the stack to Lauren. "Why do you love being around such strange people?"

Lauren spooned a row of chopped pistachios onto the dough. "It's nice for a change," she said. "Everyone here is exactly the same."

"Everyone here is not the same," Sarah said, swirling her pastry brush in the butter.

Lauren turned the corners of the sheets in, folding them over the nuts and rolling everything into a log. "Don't get offended, Nonna. What I meant was that everyone here has the same values, the same ideals. We all agree on what's right and wrong."

"Of course," Sarah said, working on the next stack. "How is this a bad thing?"

Lauren looked up at her, pushing her hair off her face with the back of her hand. "It's just nice to learn that other people see the same things differently. It's nice to be exposed to new ideas."

"But why?" Sarah said, her hands stopping for a moment. "Why is that important? Why do you want your head filled with all that garbage?" She looked up at Lauren, then buttered another sheet, and passed the stack to Lauren. "These people, they don't know what's important. They hate their families. They complain because they have to spend a day and a half with their parents once a year on Thanksgiving. They don't have children, they don't stay married. What can you learn from such people?"

Lauren laid the nuts out again, working slowly, deliberately, formulating her answer. Finally she said, "Things here aren't so perfect either, Nonna. A woman has to fight to be educated. And if she leaves home, people say terrible things about her. I have heard some crazy things people have said about me, mean things that aren't true, just because I don't want to be the same as everyone else."

"A woman's reputation is important, Lauren," Sarah said.

Lauren put her spoon down. "Why? What is so important about it? And why is a man's reputation not important? Men in this community do whatever they want with whoever they want, and then they turn around and get married, and no one says a thing, but if a woman so much looks at a man who isn't her husband, everyone has to talk."

"I don't like that people are talking about you," Sarah said, the pastry brush in her had hand flying over a sheet of dough.

Lauren clutched her spoon. "Well, I don't care. If they have nothing better to do, let them talk."

"Does Toufiq care?"

"Nonna!" She stabbed the spoon into the bowl of chopped nuts.

"You don't want to scare him away, Lauren," she said, passing another stack to Lauren, noticing the stack that remained unfilled. "What if he changes his mind?"

"So what if he does?" Lauren said, standing up from the table. "I'll die an old maid? Honestly, Nonna, are we really going to measure my worth by the man I can trick into marrying me?"

Lauren gathered her things. As she put on her coat, she said, "I thought we were going to have a nice afternoon together. I really believed you when you said you were sorry, but now you've called me over here just so you can make me feel guilty about doing what I know is right for me. I don't understand. I have to go."

As soon as Marcelle came home from work, she saw Lauren sitting on the couch in the den, eyes glued to the screen watching *Buffy the Vampire Slayer.*

"How did it go?" she asked.

"I don't want to talk about it."

"What did she say?"

"I don't want to talk about it."

Immediately Marcelle called Sarah.

"What did you say to her?"

"It's none of your business."

"She's catatonic in front of the TV. What did you say to her?"

"Marci, I'm allowed to have a conversation with my granddaughter without you interfering all the time."

"You think I interfere? I wonder where I learned that."

"I can't talk to you. It's impossible to talk to you. It's impossible to talk to anyone in your family. And I'm not going to listen to you mock me. I'm your mother. Show some respect."

Sarah hung up angry, but the anger soon turned to anxiety, a feeling that nothing was in her control.

Marcelle and Sarah usually spoke daily, but after their argument over Lauren neither woman called the other in days. Tuesday went to Wednesday and Wednesday into Thursday, and still they had made no plans for the coming Shabbat.

On Thursday night, while she was cooking the Shabbat meal, she saw her mother's number on the caller ID. Finally, she thought. But when she answered, it was her father.

"I'm sorry, *ya binti*," Eddie said. "We're not coming this week. Your mother said she isn't feeling well."

"She isn't feeling well?" asked Marcelle, as she stirred a big pot of cumin-flavored beans in tomato sauce. "Or she just said she's not feeling well."

"What can I say?" Eddie said. "You know how she is."

When Nathan came home from work at 10:00, he heard the *Alabina* CD blasting from the kitchen. Over the sounds of the Spanish-Arabic fusion, he heard Marcelle slamming cabinets and swearing loudly. When he kissed her hello, she practically snarled.

"Whoa!" he said, lifting his hands and backing away. "What did I do?"

"Sorry," she said. "My parents aren't coming this Shabbat because my mother isn't talking to me."

Nathan smiled. "What did you do this time?" he asked.

She slammed a metal spoon into a pot. "Why is it always my fault?"

Nathan lifted his hands again. "Come on, I don't mean it that way. What does she think you did?"

Marcelle told him about the disastrous lunch and the phone fight that followed.

"You know, she's twenty years old. You don't have to fight her battles for her."

Marcelle nodded. "I just don't want my mother pushing her into doing things she doesn't want to do. Not like she did to me."

Nathan turned the volume down on the CD player.

"Marcelle, I thought we worked through this. I thought we were okay."

Marcelle put down the spoon and walked over to Nathan. She cupped his face in her hands and kissed him lightly on the lips, then circled her arms around his neck and hugged him.

"We *are* okay, Nathan. We are way better than okay. This isn't about us. This is about my mother imposing her will on people."

Nathan hugged Marcelle back. "Well, I'm not getting involved with this one. This is best left between parent and child."

She bristled at the word. Her mother still treated her like a child. We are always children to our parents, she thought, and in that thinking there was anger, and that anger still bristled at her mother.

Finally, almost a week later, Sarah summoned Marcelle to her house. That's what she does, Marcelle thought, she commands and I obey.

True to form, Sarah was full of orders when Marcelle walked in.

"Sit down," she said. "I want to know why you're so angry with me. I've been thinking about this all week and it doesn't make sense for you to be mad at me for talking to Lauren. I've always spoken my mind with her. Something else is bothering you. I want to know what it is."

"There's no reason to have this conversation. It doesn't matter anymore."

"No," Sarah said, standing up and facing Marcelle. "I think this conversation is long overdue."

Marcelle turned away from her mother, and stared out the living room window. It was one of those January days when the light glows off the snow and it's so bright it's almost blinding.

"Marci," Sarah said. "You've been angry with me for years. Either talk to me like the grown woman that you are or get over it."

Marcelle snapped around and faced her mother.

"Really?" she yelled. "Really? Get over it? You're right I should have said that to you twenty years ago. Your father wasn't at your wedding. Get over it. What does that have to do with me? Get over it. Why do I have to get married because you feel guilty that you forgot your father was alive all those years? Get over it. Why do I have to pay the price for that?"

"What are you talking about?" Sarah said, sitting back down on the sofa and waving her hands. "What does my father have to do with any of this?"

Marcelle remained standing. "You pushed me into marriage. You felt guilty about your father and you made me marry Nathan to ease your guilt. And you never thanked me. And you never apologized. You sacrificed my happiness for yours and you've never acknowledged it."

Sarah raised an eyebrow, then shook her head. "I didn't make you marry Nathan. You kept telling me how much you loved him. I didn't make you do anything. And even if I did, it's not like your life turned out so bad. You have a husband who loves you. You have an enormous house, beautiful children. You never had to try for any of those things."

"I wanted to go to college." Marcelle practically stomped her feet.

Sarah raised her eyebrow again. "You went to college!"

"Ten years after I wanted to, and only because Sofia intervened!"

"So what, Marcelle?" Sarah said, folding her arms over her chest. "You didn't get exactly what you wanted when you wanted it? You're not a child. Sometimes you have to wait for what you want, but if you get it in the end what does it matter?"

Marcelle put her hands on her hips and shook her head. "That's not the point. You never listen to me. You have never listened to what I wanted. You have always told me what I should want. What you would want. You have never allowed me to have my own wants."

"Marcelle," Sarah said, arms still folded, using her exasperated voice, "when you said you wanted to go to school, I said go. I called Nathan. I watched your children. I changed my whole schedule around to give you what you wanted. But still you're angry."

Marcelle felt her lip quivering. She felt her eyes fill with tears. But she didn't want to cry. She didn't want to give her mother any more reason to think she was a child. The million times she had told her mother off in her head did nothing to prepare her for the real thing. She had perfected her argument, had laid out a case for why her mother was wrong, but now that the conversation was happening in reality, all she could say, the only response she could muster, was a choked and angry accusation, "You made me get married and I wasn't ready."

Exhausted, Marcelle sat down, running her hands over the upholstery on the sofa, staring straight ahead.

Sarah couldn't believe what she was hearing. She made Marcelle marry Nathan?

"I can't believe you think I forced you to marry Nathan." She turned towards Marcelle. "We talked about it, Marci, you told me it was getting serious."

Marcelle continued to stare ahead. "I told you that it scared me because I wasn't sure. Because I didn't know how to be sure. One minute you tell me to take my time to figure it out, and the next minute you tell me I have to marry Nathan because it'll make your father happy."

That wasn't how Sarah remembered it at all. But the memories from that time were never clear, rather they were images and blasts of strong emotions. Had she really done that to Marcelle?

"I've known for a long time you were upset with me," Sarah said, her eyes focusing on the candy dish on the coffee table in front of her. "But I never would have guessed why."

Marcelle faced her mother. "Why else did you think?"

Sarah threw her hands up. "Because I wasn't there for you when the wedding happened. Because I was so crazy with grief that I left you to figure things out on your own. And then, when your brother got married, I was more available to Sofia than I ever was to you."

"That's why you think I was angry?" Marcelle said, standing up again. "Because you were grieving over your dying father at a time that was inconvenient for me? Because I'm jealous for your attention? Well, if I was angry before, now I'm just offended. It's nice to know you have such a high opinion of me."

Marcelle paced the living room floor. Anger replaced pain, and with anger came clarity, and with clarity the words she had practiced in her head hundreds of times, the words she had promised herself she would one day speak. She stopped pacing, put her hands back on her hips, and turned to Sarah.

"It may not seem this way to you, but I made a huge sacrifice for you. I made a major life decision that I wasn't ready to make in order to make you happy. And you never thanked me. Not once. You never acknowledged that I put what you wanted first. You acted like any feeling I had on the matter was immature and ridiculous.

"I know you weren't in your right mind then, but eventually, you went back to yourself, and you ignored my unhappiness, deciding that I was a spoiled brat instead of trying to see things from my perspective. And instead of empathizing, you criticized me. You criticized everything I did. Because I was never you. Because you were trying to fix your life in mine. Well, I'm not going to let you do that to my daughter."

"And what do you think," Sarah said, raising her eyes to Marcelle, lowering her voice to the tone that was far worse than a yell. "That you're so much better than me? You're not trying to fix your life in Lauren's?"

Midway through dinner, Sarah realized she had been yelling at Eddie for the previous five minutes, but couldn't remember why.

She stopped mid-sentence.

"Why was I yelling at you?" she asked him.

Eddie laughed. "I was wondering the same thing."

Sarah slumped in her chair.

"Bad day?" he asked.

"Marcelle came over to talk to me. It didn't go well."

"What happened this time?"

"I don't want to talk about it."

"So you feel guilty." She smirked. "Sarah, I know you. Feeling guilty makes you angry. Every time you feel bad about something you did to someone else, you yell at me for no reason. It's called deflecting."

She smirked. "And where did you learn this? Oprah?"

Eddie smiled. "Dr. Phil was on today."

Sarah glared. "Is that what you do all day at work? Watch TV? If you're bored, I have plenty of things you can do around here."

Eddie smiled at her again. "Why don't you just apologize?" he asked.

"She thinks I made her marry Nathan. She says she wasn't ready and I pushed her."

"Ah," Eddie said, nodding his head.

"You knew this?"

"I talked to her about it back when."

"Why didn't you tell me?"

"Sarah, no one could tell you anything then."

Sarah slumped into her chair and rubbed her temples.

Eddie rubbed her back and kissed her head. "Just tell her you're sorry. She doesn't expect you to be perfect, you know. She would just like it if you sometimes admitted that you're wrong."

Sarah thought for a while. Then she stared at Eddie again. "She told you that?"

Eddie stood up, holding his empty plate and tea cup, leaning over to take Sarah's. He put them both into the sink. He walked back to Sarah and kissed her on the head. "Just call her. Don't defend yourself. Don't explain yourself. Just tell her you're sorry. Call her now. I'll load the dishwasher."

Sarah went upstairs and sat staring at the phone.

Eddie came up after *Who Wants to be a Millionaire.*

"Did you call her yet?"

She smiled sheepishly. "No."

He yawned. "It's getting late. You came up over an hour ago."

"Has it been that long?" she asked.

Eddie shook his head. "Stop stalling and call her."

She looked at the clock. 10:30. Marcelle would be getting ready for bed now. Nathan joked that her bedtime routine took an hour. She changed into her pajamas and applied an anti-aging mask on her face, then drank a cup of tea while reading whatever novel she was consuming. After half an hour, she washed her face, brushed her teeth, and read in her bed for another fifteen minutes. If Nathan didn't ask her to turn out the light, she would probably stay up all night.

Marcelle was drying her face when the phone rang. She rushed over to the caller ID box on the phone beside the bed. Her mother. Ugh. Probably calling to yell at her again. She steeled herself and answered the phone.

"Hi, Mom," she said.

"Marci?" Sarah asked.

"Yes?" Marcelle answered.

"I'm sorry," Sarah said. Those were not words Marcelle expected.

"For what, Ma?" Which one of the many things?

"I'm sorry I pushed you into marriage."

"That wasn't the point…"

"Marci. Let me finish. I'm sorry I didn't listen to what you wanted. I'm sorry you had a hard time."

"Thank you. Thank you for saying that."

"I mean it. I never thought of it from your side. I never thought what I did hurt you."

"Again, thank you."

"But I have to ask you, not because I need to be right, but because I want to know, are you so unhappy with the way your life turned out?

Marcelle sighed. "No."

"Then do you think we can let go of this? What's the saying, 'All's well that ends well'?"

Marcelle nodded her head. "I can try." Then she furrowed her brow. "Now I have to ask," she continued, "where is this coming from?"

"Your father and his stupid Dr. Phil."

Marcelle laughed in spite of herself. "What would Daddy have done in a time before television?"

"God only knows," Sarah replied.

"Well, I'm grateful to Dr. Phil today."

"Yes, well..." Sarah trailed off. "Still tell me you wouldn't love to have Toufiq as a son-in-law."

"Okay, Ma, I'm hanging up now. Goodnight."

Marcelle climbed into her bed, rested her head on her pillow, and gathered her blankets around her. Her mother's words hung in her mind: Could she finally let this go?

Honestly, wasn't it time?

Chapter Five

Immediately after her college graduation, Lauren went to Israel. She stayed for the summer, visiting all her second cousins, her grandmother Sarah's siblings' grandchildren. She emailed Toufiq almost daily from internet cafes, describing her hikes in the Negev, her evenings on the beach in Haifa watching the sun set into the Mediterranean. Though he had been angry when she told him about the trip, he wrote back that he couldn't wait to see her, that he was counting the days till she got home.

They had the same fight every time they saw each other. They would start fooling around in his bed, he would tell her wanted to start their life together, she would inform him of some new plan for some new trip. Still, she promised him her summer in Israel was the last time she would be away, that they could start their relationship for real when she got back.

But when she did come back, she put off seeing him. She returned his many phone calls during work hours, when she knew he couldn't talk. She made excuses. She was moving into a studio apartment in Park Slope. A few days later, she was starting her new job. The following week, she was sick. Finally, she made plans to see him, but she was afraid for that day to come because she knew what was coming with it.

She had a job at Reuters and he had been working at Cantor Fitzgerald for the last year. They could afford to marry. They could support themselves. They could rent their own apartment, and in a few years they could buy a house. Toufiq, the immigrant from Syria, orphaned by chance and by the Muhabarat, would be the paragon of the American dream, with his fancy financial services job, and his childhood sweetheart American wife. He had earned that. She could give it to him.

The morning before she was set to see him, she stood on the subway platform at 4th Street and 9th Avenue, waiting for the F train to take her to work. Looking south, she could see the train tracks lead her back home, to McDonald Avenue and Avenue P, where Toufiq got on the

260

train, blocks away from where they grew up. But then looking north, far off in the distance she could see the Manhattan skyline, the beckoning of steel and glass, the towers that rose to the sky, like two fingers extended and retracted, summoning her. But summoning her to what? To the city and all the glamour and excitement it offered, or to Toufiq, who worked on the hundred and eighth floor, who was offering her a life.

She was still not ready to start that life, but it wasn't fair to put it off any longer. It had gone on for too long. That night, they would have a conversation. She would tell him she wanted to slow things down. He would tell her he wouldn't wait anymore.

When Lauren got off the train at 42nd and 6th, and walked an avenue over to Times Square on that sunny Tuesday morning in September, she found her coworkers standing in a big crowd in the streets.

"Is this another of those stupid fire drills?" she asked her friend Kristi, who was staring up at the enormous TV screen on the corner of 7th Avenue and 42nd Street.

Kristi shook her head. "A plane crashed into the World Trade center," she said, shaking her head.

"How? What do you mean?"

Kristi pointed up at the Reuters screen, which displayed an enormous image of the burning tower. "I don't understand either," she said. "I got here two minutes ago, and saw everyone looking up. So I looked up. And I saw the tower on fire."

Toufiq. I have to call Toufiq.

Lauren rummaged through her bag, looking for her cell phone.

It was just past 9:00. What time does he get to work?

Just then she heard a scream that grew to a collective howl.

Another plane. The other tower. It wasn't an accident.

Lauren looked up the screen, fixated on the image of a second plane crashing into the second building. He worked on one of the top floors. Please God, tell me he doesn't get in till 9:30.

Finally, she found her cell phone, but everyone in Manhattan found theirs at the same time, and Times Square was filled with terrified people cursing at busy signals.

"I have to go upstairs," she said to Kristi. "I have to use the phone.'

"Are you crazy?" Kristi said. "We're in Times Square, Lauren. We could be next."

Lauren started to tremble, holding her phone in hands, staring blankly at it. "But he works there. He's on the hundred-and-something floor. I have to call him."

Kristi nodded, pulling Lauren into a hug.

"How could this happen?" Lauren asked. "Who could do this?"

On the corner, a line formed.

"Look, there's a phone bank," Kristi said. "Wait on line for the payphone."

So Lauren got on line, behind eight other dazed New Yorkers, staring at the cell phones, staring at the burning towers and crying.

"It's busy," the man in front of her said. "The phone's busy. I can't get through."

"Where are you calling?" said another woman.

"Cantor," he said, his voice cracking. "My wife works at Cantor. She's pregnant."

Another man, someone he had never met, put his arms around him. "My daughter just got out of culinary school. She works at Windows on the World."

"My friend works at Cantor," Lauren said. "Maybe we can try another number. Maybe he can tell us if your wife is ok."

Slowly they organized themselves, forming groups according to where their loved ones worked, sharing phone numbers, trying to get through to anyone who might answer, while others tried numbers on their cell phones.

The man with the pregnant wife got through.

"Can you take the stairs?" he was crying. "I know it's a long a way down, but someone can help you. You have to get out of there."

He sobbed at her reply. "No, I don't want you to do that. No. Please. I love you," he sobbed. "I love you.'

Lauren didn't want to interrupt him, but she had to know.

She touched his shoulder, "Please? What is she saying?"

He nodded his head. "I'm sorry," he said. "She said the stairs are blocked off from the fire. HR is telling them to go to the roof so that helicopters can come pick them up."

"Can you ask her if she knows Toufiq Anteby?"

Again, he nodded. He picked up the receiver. "Maddy?" he asked. "Maddy? Madeleine? Maddy? Please answer." He moaned.

"The phone went dead."

The group trying Windows on the World wasn't getting any information either. The phone kept ringing and ringing and nobody answered. In her frustration, one woman hurled her phone into the street. They all turned to see it splinter on the asphalt.

Someone she didn't know pulled on her sleeve. "My husband," she sobbed. "I need to reach my husband."

A collective scream rose through the crowd, as fear curdled inside the belly of everyone who watched. "Another one," someone screamed. "They hit the Pentagon!"

And if the Pentagon wasn't safe, what was?

A woman in front of Lauren reached her sister, another woman screamed and slammed the phone down. Most of the people in Times Square stood frozen on the street corners, staring at the images on the television screen, as though watching a movie, a trailer of an alien invasion in which the towers ultimately fall and the Statue of Liberty splashes into New York Harbor before the directors shift to a scene in Paris, where the Eiffel tower gets shot down, too.

Everyone waited for someone to tell them what to do. Should they return to their buildings? Should they go home? Should they stay where they were?

Overhead they heard fighter jets, and an announcement on the television screen informed them that the US military sent the jets to protect the skies above New York from further attack.

Some people filed into their office buildings and Lauren did the same.

The phone lines in her office were working. She called her mother.

"Thank God you called," her mother said. "I was worried sick."

"I don't live or work anywhere near the Twin Towers," she said.

"You could have had a meeting. I don't know. Anyway, thank God you're okay."

"Mom," she said, her voice sticking in her throat. "Have you heard from him? Has anyone heard from Toufiq?"

"He sent your father an email. All he wrote was 'Thank you'."

Lauren dropped the phone. Email would have never occurred to her. She logged on to her account. And there it was, in her inbox, a note from him

She stared at the letters that spelled out his name: Toufiq Anteby.

"I've waited seven years to ask you, and if it has to be by email, so be it," he wrote. "Lauren, will you marry me?"

That was it. Just two sentences. A question that would haunt her for years.

Lauren, will you marry me?

He tried to ask her in person, but she never let him. For the last two weeks, since she moved back to New York, he had wanted to see her, and she had been avoiding him because she knew he was going to propose and didn't know how she was going to respond, and didn't want to humiliate him with silence when he said:

Lauren, will you marry me?

But that wasn't all. It was more selfish than that. Because when he formally asked the questions they had so long discussed, she would have to make a choice immediately. To commit to being his, or to lose him forever. He had waited, as he promised her all those years ago, but he wanted to start a family, and if it wasn't with her, he would move on. Surely, they'd still be in each other's lives; they were practically related. But what wife would allow her husband to spend hours on the phone consoling the woman he had loved for years? No, it was either commit, or lose him—a decision she didn't want to make. So she didn't see him, so she didn't have to respond to the words he needed to speak, the words that would make her choose:

Lauren, will you marry me?

It meant picking a life, deciding between the life she was about to start, as a young career woman in the small studio apartment she had sublet in Park Slope or as a young wife, moving back to the Midwood neighborhood where she had grown up. She had exhausted his patience and there would be little of it left when he asked her in person what he had been forced to email:

Lauren, will you marry me?

Without thinking, she wrote him back.

"Of course I will."

But it was an act of cowardice really. What else do you write to a dying man? "I need more time to think about it?"

Once again somebody screamed, "Oh my God! The tower fell!"

She ran up to the roof of the building. From that roof, they had a clear view of downtown. She needed to see it herself. One tower was on fire. A gaping hole filled the skyline where the other tower had been. Plumes of smoke rose and a cloud of grey matter spread through the air, filling it with the incinerated molecules of the man she loved and countless other innocent people who had done nothing but show up for work that morning. And there they were, ground into the particles that filled the air, into the rubbish that flooded lower Manhattan, as one of the greatest symbols of American prosperity imploded and spilled all over the streets.

And somewhere in that implosion was Toufiq.

But maybe not? But maybe he was in the other tower? Maybe he worked on the side of the remaining building that wasn't engulfed in flames. And maybe he had found a staircase and maybe he was on his way down. And maybe as he ran down a hundred or so flights, he thought of his email—Lauren, will you marry me? —and maybe as he ran for his life, he thought of how she would respond. And maybe he would find an internet café, or maybe even make it home and turn on his computer to find her email, her response—Of course I will.

But the answer lay in scene she saw unfold before her, or rather collapse, as the second tower, the one that held the last shreds of her hopes came tumbling down as well, just fell, just sank, as though it were suddenly swallowed by quicksand, sank directly down, as though an elevator shaft had opened up to lower it. And like that, it was gone. The iconic skyline, the symbol of her city: Gone.

And with it her future.

And with it Toufiq.

She stood immobilized on the roof of her office building, staring at the smoke, shaking her head back and forth, whispering, "No." Kristi found her there, took her by the hand, leading her back to her desk, where Kristi put all of her things—wallet, cell phone, keys—into her handbag and said, "Lauren, it's time to go home."

Time to go. Time to walk the ten miles back to Brooklyn, as the subways had been shut down and the bridges and tunnels were closed to cars.

On that beautiful Tuesday morning in September, on that clear sunny day, Lauren walked with thousands of New Yorkers who evacuated their office buildings and flooded onto the streets. Looking around, she felt as though she were in a zombie movie, a post-apocalyptic nightmare, the end of the world as we know it. She felt fear clogging the streets, questions hanging over everyone: What now? What will life be like now?

Somewhere down by City Hall, before the pedestrian path to the Brooklyn Bridge, where the air was thick with ash, where somewhere in the back of her mind Lauren knew she was breathing in particles that once comprised Toufiq, her legs gave out underneath her. She sank, straight down to the ground, and sat in the middle of the street to cry. A woman she didn't know, a plump redhead in her mid-thirties who was wearing a navy wrap dress and had taken off her shoes and was walking barefoot through the streets, sat down next to her, took her hand, and started crying, too.

Another woman, a tiny black woman, probably in her sixties, sat down next to them both and held their hands.

"Jesus loves you," she said. "It may not look like it today, but the Lord is always watching over us."

From a shop across the street, an Indian shopkeeper brought them bottles of water. A young man who worked at the deli brought out sandwiches. Somehow, the fear and pain and grief brought out everyone's kindness, and the people of a city maligned as the rudest on earth showed the humanity they hid under their exteriors.

Lauren loved New York as she had never before loved it, loved it as fiercely as she had hated it when she had vowed to leave it behind for California.

The elderly black woman unwrapped a sandwich and handed each crying woman a half. "Eat something," she said. "You're not doing anybody any good by starving."

When she saw them each take a bite, she waved and continued walking.

Lauren wiped her face and managed a half smile at the redhead, who tried to smile back.

"My fiancé," she said.

Lauren thought of Toufiq, of lying in his bed, holding each other, talking about how their life would be when they finally began it. "Mine, too," she said.

She and the redhead sat arm in arm in the street until they were strong enough to stand and continue walking home, and as she walked over the bridge crossing from Manhattan, the place of her dreams, to Brooklyn, the place of her birth, she thought of what she had called him. "My fiancé." Of course he was the one. What had she been so afraid of?

And with that knowledge came agonizing pain that turned into guilt that turned into self-loathing and a sense of suffocation and a need to flee.

But there was no place to go, so she walked.

And she walked.

And she walked some more.

For three hours, until she arrived in her parents' house to find Toufiq's sister sitting with her mother in the kitchen. Marcelle held Nura in her arms as Nura's body heaved with sobs.

Upon seeing Lauren enter, Nura rose from the table to hug her.

"He couldn't wait to marry you," she said. "How I wanted to have you as my sister."

Lauren clung to Nura, but Nura soon broke their embrace. She took a small black felt pouch of out her pocket. Inside was a diamond ring, a round center stone set in a platinum art deco flower.

"My father gave this ring to my mother after she gave birth to Toufiq. It was her favorite. He was going to give it to you. He would have wanted you to have it."

Lauren shook her head as tears slid down her face. Marcelle remained at the table, holding her hand over her mouth, trying to stifle a sob.

Nura took Lauren's hand, placing the ring on the fourth finger of her left hand, but the ring was so big it slid off. Nura thought for a moment, then slipped in onto Lauren's middle finger instead. Lauren put it to her lips and kissed it. Then she sank to the floor and buried her head in her knees.

Nura sat down beside her. "He loved you so much," she said. "You don't know how happy you made him."

Marcelle sat on her other side, putting her arms around her daughter, rubbing her hand on Lauren's back.

I never made him happy, Lauren thought, crying into her knees. All I did was make him suffer.

Part Five: 2011

Chapter One

She needed to move. Stuck, tied down in situations outside her control—these things were never good. The first thing to do was change. For now, her music. Last night, she downloaded the new Rihanna, the latest Black Eyed Peas, Kanye, stuff she would never admit to enjoying except when she ran, because whatever kept her moving was allowed.

She synched her iPhone as she quickly changed into her running clothes, her stretched-out sports bra and worn-in sneakers and tattered Stanford gym shorts.

As she disconnected the iPhone from her laptop she saw the time: 6:12. She was two minutes late.

Move!

She ran out of her hotel room. The elevator door opened, and there stood Travis Miller.

Damn it.

"Good morning, Lauren," he said.

"Morning, Travis," she replied.

"Off for your morning run?" he asked.

"No, I'm dressed like this at 6 a.m. to go pumpkin picking."

"Ha, ha. Smartass Yankee."

Lauren looked at the elevator panel and watched the numbers get lower, mentally willing it to go faster.

"So," Travis began again, "feel like having a running partner this morning?"

Damn, she thought, the man doesn't give up.

"Because," he continued, "I found a new route I think you'll like."

"No, thanks. I think I'm just going to run along the river today."

"Miss 'I never run the same route twice'?"

"Well, I haven't done that one in a while."

"I get the feeling you're avoiding me."

The elevator dinged as it reached the ground floor. That took long enough.

"Lauren?"

"Travis, you should trust your intuition," she said, jogging out the elevator and away from him.

Lauren worked as a consultant, and her current project, reducing costs for a utility company, was two weeks from completion. Then she would leave Memphis, in time to be home for Passover. Thinking of home, she felt a swell of anxiety rise from her stomach, but she pushed it back down.

Not now. Deal with it when it comes.

For now focus on the run. Focus on moving to a six-minute mile. She was fifteen seconds shy now and angry it was taking her so long to advance. A six-minute mile shouldn't be that hard.

Go! Move! Faster! Go!

She ran down the street until she reached the promenade and began her jog along the Mississippi. Though she had been running along the promenade to avoid Travis, in truth, she never tired of watching the great river rushing down. She loved its strength, its force, its will to constant motion, constant change juxtaposed by its permanence.

The river inspired her; its speed lent urgency to hers. Yes, she thought. I'll run here for the next two weeks. Pushing herself harder, she passed all the other joggers. They are joggers, she told herself; I am a runner; I am faster; I am better. The thought made her proud. I am the fastest runner out here today. Until a man in blue shorts and a Texas Longhorns t-shirt breezed past her, almost effortlessly.

Travis. Slowing himself down all this time, allowing her to believe she was setting the pace, and he was trying to keep up. To hell with him, she thought.

Her watched beeped. It was the halfway point; she turned around and ran back. Travis passed her so she needed to run faster: she had something to prove. Moving with great speed, she astonished herself. Her feet had wings; she was flying on the pavement. Fifteen seconds shaved easily off her time just by being angry. Maybe she should start running with him again.

No. It needs to be over now, before things get too complicated.

He passed her again, this time bumping her slightly, throwing her off.

Goddamn it! He must be running a five-minute mile. And now he would make it back to the hotel first and she would have to talk to him again in the elevator. Shit. Shit. Shit. Great start to the day.

Yet, she began to smile. He knew just how to get to her. Because even as she reminded herself why their affair needed ending, she watched the way his body moved with appreciation. Watching his large muscular frame, his beautiful rounded ass, his sculpted arms pumping back and forth, pushing him faster, warmed her inside, made her smile despite herself.

As predicted, he stood waiting in the hotel lobby.

"A little slow out there today, weren't we Yankee?" he said, as they waited for the elevator.

"And you, Hillbilly, must have had a miracle happen, Mr. Slowpoke, Mr. 'Oh Lauren slow down I can't keep up,' suddenly runs a five-minute mile. What the hell was that?"

"Oh, I don't like to spend it all at once, if you know what I mean."

Lauren rolled her eyes and walked into the elevator. Travis followed.

"Don't tell me you don't miss me," he said, moving closer.

"Travis, I don't want to do this anymore," she said, sliding to the corner furthest from him.

He moved closer, stroked her hair with his hand. "I know I've missed you," he said.

She turned away. "I don't want to have this conversation again. I already explained it to you."

"But it doesn't make any sense," he said, kissing her neck, working his way to her face and then her mouth.

She felt herself go warm again, enjoying his kiss, enjoying the game even more. She pushed him away.

"Have dinner with me tonight," he said, kissing her forehead.

"No," she shook her head as she tilted her face toward him.

"Jimmy Knight is performing on Beale Street." He ran his hand down her cheek and kissed her again.

"No." God, he's good.

"I already have two tickets."

"No." And smart.

"I'll be at your room at seven."

"I won't be." Maybe it could just be fun again.

"I'll see you there."

"You wish," she said, as the elevator dinged, opening to her floor. Walking out, she thought, tonight calls for the red dress.

Chapter Two

Lauren met Travis at the hotel bar a few days after she arrived in Memphis. She was flirting with a salesman from Louisville, Kentucky, when this very attractive, tall blonde man started sending her drinks. At first, she ignored him, sending his drinks back, but after she noticed the tan line where the salesman's wedding band should have been, she excused herself and smiled her most winning smile at Travis.

"Why the change of the heart?" he asked, as he sauntered over.

"He's married and hiding it. A girl has to have some morals," she replied.

"So I'm safe in assuming that," he pointed to the flower-shaped diamond ring she wore on her middle finger, "does not represent any kind of matrimonial commitment?"

She looked down at her ring, weaving her thumb between her pointer and middle fingers, rubbing it.

"This? No. It once was. It's sort of a family heirloom."

"Well, now that we have that out of the way, do you want to get out of here?"

She stepped back and raised an eyebrow. "And go where?"

"I know this great blues bar..." he smiled.

"Sounds tempting," she said, "but I have to be up really early tomorrow. Maybe another time."

She could tell by the shock on his face that Travis was not used to having women turn him down. Which was exactly why she did it.

She felt his eyes on her as she exited the bar. She knew he would figure out who she was, how to find her. And he did, sending flowers to her room, bearing a card that read, "Saturday night. 7:00 pm. Meet at the bar." He didn't even sign it. He knew she'd know it was him.

When she walked into the bar at seven-thirty that Saturday night, the two women standing next to him were clearly disappointed as he bid them farewell. In an exaggerated motion, he brought his wrist to his line of sight and studied his watch. Then he looked up at her, grinning as she walked towards him.

"Do you always keep everyone waiting?" he asked, as she leaned on the barstool next to him.

She raised her eyebrows and shrugged. "Seven wasn't a good time. And you didn't leave me any way to get in touch with you."

Again, he grinned. She knew exactly who he was; she knew exactly how to play this.

Over dinner, he told her more about himself. Travis Miller was thirty-six and for the last three years, he had been building his record label, specializing in blues, bluegrass and country music; he was in Memphis looking for new talent. He employed two scouts, but finding new music was his favorite part of the job. When he wasn't combing bars, looking for musicians, he lived in Dallas, where he had been born and raised.

Lauren had never heard of him or his label, but she googled him the next morning. She knew a successful man when she met one, so she wasn't surprised to learn that he was highly regarded in the music industry. Travis didn't name-drop the famous musicians pictured with him on his Facebook page. It lacked manners and if Travis lacked anything, manners were not it.

"And you?" he asked.

"Lauren Hazan. Thirty-one. Consultant. Native New Yorker. Live in hotels, in whichever city has the most interesting project."

"What do you mean you live in hotels? Where do you go when you're not working?"

"Wherever I want. It costs me less to pay for a hotel room in New York than it does to keep an apartment."

"That's so sad," he said.

She shrugged again. "It doesn't make me sad."

Over the next few weeks, he showed her everything he loved about Memphis. They went dancing in country bars. Travis was a goofy dancer, all big movements and hammy faces, but he was so confident, so comfortable in his own skin, that it was sexy.

He took her to blues bars. She knew a little about the music from Uncle Charles, but the experience of live performances was intoxicating:

she could see why Travis enjoyed it. She loved the sex that pervaded the air. The seductive music, the smoke-filled room, the old black man on the guitar, his cigarette- and-whiskey voice singing about his baby, about his broken heart, never failed to turn her on, to stir her longing, to move her deeply in a place she rarely allowed herself to go.

He took her for great dinners, too. Lauren had been kosher till her mid-twenties, so seafood was still a novelty. She remembered her first bite of shrimp, at age twenty-five. Someone asked her why she kept kosher, and she was shocked that the only reason she could conjure was that she always had been. When the Lord didn't smite her as she bit into her first piece of unclean food, she realized she didn't actually care about religion anymore, she'd just been holding onto it out of habit. She also realized she really loved shellfish. So on nights that followed particularly grueling days of work, when Lauren just wanted to order room service and eat dinner in her pajamas, Travis could easily talk her into going out with promises of shrimp and scallops and crawfish.

"Come on," he'd say, "this town has such great food."

At first, she thought their relationship was like the rest of her road relationships—an extended hook-up, a little fun, a new diversion in a new city. Lauren liked men. She liked sex. And her job and her lifestyle didn't really allow for long-term entanglements. She kept her feelings under control on these flings, never letting them grow deep. Most of the men she met on the road wanted the same thing, a little companionship, no commitment.

But not Travis. Travis wanted to hear all her stories, wanted to tell her all of his. He treated their affair like it could turn into something real. He looked at her like he wanted to know her. No one had looked at her that way since Toufiq. It was unnerving and she wasn't sure she liked it.

One Tuesday night, after some live music and late-night catfish and chips, he lay on his bed naked, watching her get dressed.

"Why don't you ever spend the night?" he said. "It's going to take you the same time to go to your room tomorrow morning as it is now. Just stay with me."

"If I stay," she said, slipping her arms through her bra straps, and closing the clasps behind her, "you and I both know I'm not getting any sleep. I have a tough few days coming up. I can't show up for work exhausted."

"Please stay."

"I can't."

"Tomorrow?"

"Sorry."

"Fine, then. Friday night. You're not working Saturday. Spend the night with me. We'll order room service in bed."

She turned to him and smiled. "You don't give up, do you?"

"Never," he flashed his boyish grin, again. "Not till I get what I want."

As she slipped her skirt back on, she said, "I feel like I should tell you no just to teach you a lesson."

"Nah. I'd just go after you ten times harder."

"Really? That sounds fun." She giggled and then put a serious expression on her face. "I'm sorry but I have to wash my hair on Friday night."

"You're kidding," he said, folding his arms over his chest.

She shook her head. "Yeah, and on Saturday, I have to let my hair dry, so that's out, too."

He sat up and grabbed her arm. "You have got to be kidding. You're going to waste a whole weekend on this?"

She giggled again. "You asked for it." She pecked him on the forehead before leaving his room.

Lauren expected Travis to inundate her with phone calls and text messages, but he didn't. She was shocked not to hear from him at all. She started to worry she had angered him: surely, it was clear she was just playing. She stopped herself from calling him to smooth things over several times. No, she told herself, he's playing me back. He's seeing if I'm serious; he's making me sweat. Give it a few days. See what he does.

She had last seen him Tuesday night, and despite her heavy workload, she could not get him out of her mind. Lauren was good at focusing, at channeling all her energy into her work; it was why she was so successful in her career. But she knew she was distracted. She worked twelve and fourteen hour days that week, forcing herself not to think about him. But she kept checking her phone, kept checking her email. Nothing.

When she finally got back to her hotel at ten o'clock on Friday night, she heard commotion coming from her floor. As she exited the elevator, a woman looked her up and down, and then looked at a man standing in front of the elevator bank. He shook his head, "no," and the woman turned away from her. Lauren rounded the corner to walk to her room and saw people standing in the hallway, pointing and talking, two of them policemen and one security guard. As she got close to her room, she saw crime scene tape stuck to her door.

"What is going on?" she asked.

"Sorry, Ma'am. Police business. You can't go in there."

"But that's my room. All my stuff's in there."

Another man, this one dressed in a suit, and wearing a nametag that identified him as a hotel employee said, "I'm sorry Ms. Hazan, but we have another room all ready for you. Someone will come by and tell you if and when you can retrieve your personal items."

The security guard and hotel employee led her to the elevator, where they went down a few floors, and led her down the hall to a room she had been in before.

Travis stood outside, grinning and then laughing as he saw the expression on her face morph from bewilderment to understanding to anger to laughter.

"You're insane!" she said, slapping him on the arm.

He grinned. "You asked for it."

She grinned back, shaking her head.

"Everyone likes a good prank. Anyway," he said, reaching for her waist, pulling her towards him, "I told you I always get what I want."

Those words could have been creepy or possessive or objectifying, but when he said them, his voice was soft, the expression in his face open. He held her and looked into her eyes, and the twinkle in his eyes just barely concealed his longing, his vulnerability.

She broke his gaze, but then she laughed.

"How did you pull that off?"

"Most people are romantics at heart, Lauren. You tell them you're trying to woo a woman, and they're inclined to help. Also, I know a great costume shop."

"You are seriously crazy."

"You'll stay with me this weekend?" he asked, his playful expression gone.

"The whole weekend?"

She planned to protest further, but the look in his eyes, the sincerity, the earnestness, stopped her.

"Yes," she said. She nodded her head. "Yes. I will. Yes."

But that weekend wasn't all he wanted from her.

They sat in a coffee shop on Sunday, drinking late afternoon lattes when he dropped another bomb.

"I've got to go to Chicago next weekend," he said, holding his coffee mug with both hands.

"One of your other lovers needs attention?"

He laughed. "You think I have the energy for another lover? No, I'm going to my cousin's bar mitzvah. Why don't you come with me?"

"You're Jewish?" she asked, raising an eyebrow.

"Sure am. Is that so shocking?"

"No. You just never mentioned it. And you look so...corn-fed."

"So? Corn's kosher, last I checked."

"You know what I mean."

"Yes. But that's beside the point. Come with me. My family will love you!"

Lauren shrugged and mentioned something about checking her work schedule. He wanted her to meet his family?

"You work too hard," he said. "Come on, it'll be fun."

She forced a smile onto her face as she felt her heart race. She excused herself and went to the bathroom, where she gripped the sink and forced herself to take long, slow, deep breaths.

In through the nose, out through the mouth.

She looked into her eyes in the mirror.

You may not lose your shit in a coffee shop.

In through the nose, out through the mouth.

You will calm down. You will be fine.

Finally, her breathing returned to normal, and she stared at her face again, this time wetting a paper towel with cold water and pressing it to her forehead. The ring on her middle finger winked at her. She pressed that finger against her lips and took another deep breath.

Days later, she pushed her guilt down into her stomach and called him and lied, saying she had to work all weekend. From his voice, it was clear he was crestfallen. The guilt fought its way back up.

He flew to Chicago for the weekend, texted her pictures from the party, one of the bar mitzvah boy, another of him dancing with his aunt, the rabbi, trying to make her sorry she hadn't come. Every message from him intensified her nausea. She couldn't sleep. She ached for him. These feelings weren't part of the plan.

By the time he returned, she stopped taking his calls.

Why let herself fall if she was only going to end it? Better to get out early. Only it wasn't early anymore.

Chapter Three

After a week of trying, Travis finally convinced Lauren to see him again.

And by six-fifteen that Friday night, Amy Winehouse was singing, "You Know I'm No Good," as Lauren set her long brown hair in large rollers. Sitting in front of her vanity mirror, powdered and rouged, she applied eyeliner to her large green eyes. Cat's eyes, everyone called them, her grandmother Sarah's eyes.

Just then the phone beeped—a text from Travis that read: "Be there in 30 min." She noticed the time. It was almost Shabbat.

With one eye done and one eye undone, Lauren called her mother.

"Hi Mom," she said.

"Hi, baby, how are you? I haven't heard from you in a few days. I was worried about you."

"I'm okay," Lauren replied. "Just working hard."

"It's not too much for you?" Marcelle asked.

"It's good to have things to focus on," she said, staring into the mirror and finishing her eye make-up.

Marcelle paused for a moment. Lauren could hear her take a deep breath. "Sweetie, don't get mad at me," Marcelle continued, "but sometimes I wish you would focus a little less on work and a little more on your personal life."

"Mom..."

"I'm done. I just worry about you."

"I told you," Lauren said. "I'm okay."

"No more...episodes?"

Lauren knew she should never have told her mother about the panic attacks, but the first time she had one, after realizing how close her parents had come to real danger, she needed to hear her mother's voice.

Nathan had surprised Marcelle with a trip to Israel in January, over her yeshiva high school's winter break. When he did, she begged

280

him to spend a few days in Egypt, so she could see some of the places her parents had described for so many years. They stayed in a hotel in Sarah's old neighborhood, Zamalek, ate éclairs in Groppi Gardens, went to the Bassatine Jewish cemetery in a futile search for Nonna Terra's grave. Sarah later told Lauren how disappointed she was to learn how dirty and rundown the city she once loved had become.

Marcelle and Nathan were in Egypt only days before the protests began in Tahrir Square. They arrived home in time to watch the riots on TV with Eddie and Sarah, who were both unsure of how to feel about revolution overtaking their homeland for the second time in their lives.

Lauren watched streaming footage from Al-Jazeera's website in her hotel room. At first, she was inspired, impressed by a people held down for so long rising up to overthrow their corrupt rulers. She was annoyed with her pessimistic grandfather, who only spoke about the dangers of a power vacuum after Mubarak was gone. She listened to her grandmother daydream about the recreation of the Egypt of her youth.

But as the days went on, and the protests turned violent, Lauren listened to pundits discussing the ramifications, the possibilities of renewed radicalism in the Middle East. Anxiety struck, and Lauren sat on her bed, clutching her chest, feeling like her heart was exploding.

She called her parents' house in hysterics.

"We're fine," Marcelle reassured her. "We left Egypt before anything even started."

"But what if you had gotten stuck there? What if something happened to you?"

"But nothing did," Marcelle said, her voice soft and reassuring. "And anyway, all the tourists got out safe. Even the Israeli ones."

Her grandmother had been at her mother's house when Lauren called. Sarah picked up the phone.

"Rohi, why is this upsetting you so much? This is like déjà vu for me, and I'm okay."

Lauren's chest kept heaving, her mind going into dark, ugly places, places she had done everything to erase from her consciousness.

"But what if something happened, Nonna?" she repeated. "What if they had gotten hurt?"

"But they didn't. They aren't in Cairo anymore. They're safe and sound in New York," Sarah said.

A question formed in Lauren's mind, one she didn't say out loud: Since when is New York safe?

That Friday night, as she fished through her closet for the red strapless dress she was wearing on her date with Travis, she lied to her mother. "No, Mom. No more episodes. Really, I'm fine."

"Okay," Marcelle said. She made her voice casual. "What are you doing for Shabbat?"

Why does she ask the question when she doesn't want the answer?

"The usual, room service and a book," Lauren said, taking the rollers out of her hair.

"Well, you'll be home in two weeks. I can't wait to see you."

"I know. I miss you, too, Mom."

"Oh, and sweetie, call your grandmother. She hasn't been feeling well."

There was a loud knock at the door. Lauren glanced at the clock. It was seven o'clock and she wasn't ready.

"What was that?" Marcelle asked.

"It must be room service, let me go."

"Okay. Shabbat Shalom, honey. I love you."

Another knock at the door.

"Shabbat Shalom, Mommy. I love you, too."

Shit. Shit. Shit.

Travis banged on the door. "Lauren, I know you're in there. I can hear you."

"I told you, I'm not coming."

"I'm not leaving until you open the door, woman."

"Travis, go away," she said as she rushed to pull out the last few hairpins.

282

"Just open the door, Lauren," he said, knocking again.

"I have to think about it," she said, fluffing her hair.

"I'm counting to twenty and then I'm leaving," he said.

"Count to a hundred," she said, slipping into her red dress.

"Thirty-five, thirty-six, thirty-seven," she heard outside her door, as she put on her shoes and grabbed her handbag and wrap.

"Sixty-nine, seventy," he yelled, as she put on her lipstick and crammed it in her bag.

He was in the high nineties as she checked her appearance in the full-length mirror in the bathroom.

"One hundred. Fine, I'm leaving. The blonde I met at the bar today said she'd love to come."

She heard him walk away, counted to three and opened the door.

"Hey, Travis," she said.

He turned around. She stepped out of her room, closing the door. He stared at her, his mouth opened slightly.

"Worth waiting for?" she asked, walking toward him.

"You have to make everything difficult, don't you?" he asked. She smiled and shrugged.

"You look gorgeous," he said. "And all for me."

She laughed. "It's not for you. It's for Jimmy."

"Fine, whatever you say."

He had his hand on the small of her back as he led her out of the hotel and into a cab. Leaning into him, she breathed his scent. Again, she felt herself go warm, and again she suppressed the feeling.

When they arrived at the restaurant, the host led them to Travis's favorite table by the window and almost immediately, a waiter appeared with two glasses of champagne. He called ahead. He always did.

"Are we celebrating something?" she asked.

"Being alive," he said. She smiled.

He kept the conversation casual, telling her about a new band he just signed. He wanted to start recording them as soon as he got back to Dallas, but he was going to have to push it back a few days so he could spend Passover with his family.

"Are you going to New York for the Seders?" he asked.

She nodded. "My presence at major Jewish holidays is non-negotiable."

"My parents are like that, too. Are you close to your family?" he asked.

She pondered the question. Could you be close to people you rarely saw? Did speaking to them often count? She nodded again.

"Me, too," he said. He sipped his wine. "Where will you go after?"

"Don't know," she said. "I have to find another assignment."

He nodded, but didn't speak. She felt the obvious question form in his mind, and was grateful he didn't ask. Instead, he changed the subject, telling her about the friends they were meeting that night at Jimmy's Joint. He told her funny stories about them, a group of musicians who had known each other for decades, a rowdy group of pranksters who had hazed him horribly before admitting him into their crew.

But even as he laughed and joked and turned on his charm, she could sense his reservation, could feel him trying too hard to keep the banter light. Her stomach twisted as she forced herself to be as bright and casual as he was pretending to be.

But later, in the bar, after the band played, when the musicians came to sit with her and Travis at their table, there was no pretending.

"This must be that lovely Lauren you keep telling me about," said Jimmy Knight.

Travis glanced at her, and when he saw her smile, he smiled broadly as well.

Then Skinny Mike, the bassist with his dark skin and grey beard, said, "So now I understand why we ain't seen you none the whole time you been here." He kissed Lauren on the cheek. "I forgive you. I understand."

Normally Lauren would have loved the attention, would have loved knowing she had one up on him. Just two weeks earlier, she would have reveled in it, later teasing him mercilessly that he must be falling in love with her. But since she knew he was, instead of making her feel powerful and sexy, it just made her feel ugly and suffocated.

Travis rose from the table to greet another member of the band, shaking his hand vigorously, and slapping him on the arm.

"He's crazy about you, you know," Jimmy said, when Travis was out of earshot. "I seen a lot of women come in here with Travis, but none he talks about like you."

She forced a smile onto her face, and Jimmy squeezed her hand. She looked up at Travis and found him looking at her. He was practically beaming. She downed what was left of her bourbon, and excused herself.

Lauren was only planning on getting some air, but once she was outside, she needed to flee. She looked around and saw the street was closed off and she would have to walk two blocks to find a cab. She found herself running down the street, jumping into the intersection, trying to hail a cab. After several futile minutes, she felt someone grab her arm.

"What the hell was that?" Travis said.

"What was what?"

"Why did you walk out?'

She didn't say anything.

"Lauren, you embarrassed me. I work with these guys. I don't deserve that."

She looked away from him.

"Lauren, what do you want from me?"

She wasn't sure. The wine and bourbon flooded her body. Her legs were gelatinous. They couldn't support her. She looked into Travis's eyes—Travis who was lovely and patient—and was overcome with self-loathing. She did something she hadn't done in ages: She cried.

Stunned, Travis hugged her.

"I'm disgusting," she said.

"No, you're not," he said. "It's okay."

"It's not okay. I don't know why I keep acting like such an ass."

"It doesn't matter. Let's get out of here."

"No, let's go back. We'll pretend I had to make a phone call."

"I love Yankee women. You're so drunk you can't stand, but you're still thinking clearly. Let's get you back in there and get you some water."

Travis laughed and Lauren felt less terrible. She leaned into him and they walked back to Jimmy's arm-in-arm.

Lauren was dreaming of water. She stood beside a rushing river, trying to fill an empty bottle. She kept drinking from the bottle and refilling it, her thirst refusing to slake. Then a butterfly landed on her chest, flapping its wings against her skin. But the butterfly morphed into an angry black bird and the fluttering turned into pounding, and she awoke with a start grabbing her chest to stop the pounding wings.

Her heart still pounding, she looked at the nightstand. The clock read 3:00 a.m. She needed to pee. Her head was spinning. She was thirsty. Pressing her hands into the end table, she lifted herself to standing and looked down at Travis's naked body sprawled out on the bed. He opened his eyes and smiled, opened his arms, beckoning her back to bed.

She turned away and bent down to look for her dress. Inhaling deeply, she rummaged through the pile of sheets and pillows strewn over the floor.

"What are you doing, baby?" he asked. "Come back to bed."

She didn't answer, continued searching. She found the strap of her hand bag and pulled on it, but her leg got caught in a sheet and she lost her balance and fell. She grabbed hold of her knees and forced another deep inhalation.

Travis laughed. "Seriously, Lauren, what are you doing?"

He shimmied off the bed and held her to him, helping her sit. He unraveled the sheet from her leg and pulled her back to him. She relaxed into him as he kissed her neck, moved his hands down her shoulders to her breasts. The familiar stirring began inside her. But then an unusual stirring began as well.

"Oh shit," she yelled, grasping her mouth, springing up, jumping over Travis and leaping for the toilet.

286

She didn't make it.

But at least she got to the bathroom, where she threw up all over the floor. Travis followed in seconds, holding her hair back with one hand, her with the other.

"We have to watch how much we let you drink, don't we?" he said, brushing stray strands of hair off her cheek.

"I'm thirty-one and I just threw-up all over your bathroom floor. This is humiliating."

"It's fine. We'll get this all cleaned up and put you back to bed."

"No. I'll clean it up, and then I'm going home."

"Where? To New York?" he laughed. "I think it's a little late for a flight."

Lauren reached for a stack of folded towels.

"Let me help you," he said.

"No." She pushed him towards the bathroom door. "Please."

He left and she locked the door. She wiped the towels over the floor, dumped them into the bathtub and turned on the hot water. Then she sat, her naked body cold on the tile floor, hugging her legs to her chest, resting her head on her knees, sticking her thumb between her fingers, rubbing her ring.

What is happening to me?

She shivered and rubbed her hands up and down her legs.

"Lauren?" Travis tapped lightly on the door. "Honey, what are you doing in there? Why is the door locked?"

"Please leave me alone," she said.

"Lauren, honey, let me in. Let me help you."

"Just give me a minute. Please?"

She was too ashamed to face him. She looked at her reflection and was frightened. She saw black make-up smeared on her face, her hair tangled, her eyes red.

Clean yourself up. Get it to together.

She washed her face, gargled, ran Travis's brush through her hair until she looked presentable. The cleaning calmed her. Finally, she was ready to come out. When she opened the door, Travis stood open-armed, waiting to pull her back to him. She pushed past him.

"Please," she said. "I can't breathe."

She kneeled on the floor beside the bed where she found her dress, shoes, bag and wrap. She kept her back to him as she dressed herself.

"You don't have to go, Lauren," he said.

She slipped on her shoes.

He rested a hand on her hip. "Please stay."

She shook her head, avoiding his eyes.

"Why are you always running from me?"

Chapter Four

The next morning, she woke to a knock on the door.

"Come back in a few hours," she said.

"It's not housekeeping. It's me. I brought you some food. Open up."

Does he ever stop? Can't he just leave me alone?

But she got up anyway. She walked over to the door, opened it without undoing the chain.

"Hey," she said.

"I'm not a murderer. You can undo the chain."

"I'm a mess. I feel awful and I want to sleep."

"Fine. Just let me in. I'll leave the food on the table and then you can get back into bed."

"I haven't even washed my face yet."

"So go wash your face. Take your time."

She undid the latch. Because she was too tired to argue with him. Because she knew he wasn't going to go away anyway. Because it was easier to let him in than to make him. Anyway, who cares why?

She opened the door and immediately turned around to go to the bathroom, where she washed her face, brushed her teeth, and combed her hair. And sighed.

"Coffee?" he asked.

She nodded yes. He poured her a cup. Skim milk and Splenda. Then he opened a dish. An egg white veggie omelet. Whole wheat bread. Salad instead of potatoes on the side. He opened the other one. Steak and eggs. Potatoes and bread. Breakfast for a real man.

"I don't even know if I can swallow."

"Try."

She curled up in his lap, nibbling a slice of toast. He stroked her hair. "I wish you hadn't run out last night."

"I'm sorry. Me, too."

"Why do you keep running away from me?"

"I don't know."

He continued stroking her hair. He took a deep breath, sounded like he was about to say something but stopped himself. Then he did it again, that sharp intake of air, the slightest beginning of sound coming from his throat. Again, he stopped.

Finally, he said, "Lauren I have to say something to you."

"Travis, I'm sorry," she said, sitting up to face him.

"No, let me talk. I don't really know how to say this, so just listen."

She felt the nausea rise, her chest pound.

"This game we started playing," he said, "it was fun. And I never expected it to go further than that, but when I was in Chicago...I couldn't stop thinking about you. And when you stopped talking to me..." he looked towards the far corner of the room, then back at her. "Anyway, I don't want to play anymore. I want to be with you. I love you."

She shook her head.

"That wasn't the response I was hoping for," he said.

She took a deep breath. She ran her thumb over her middle finger. Finally she said, "I'm not good at loving people."

He laughed. "That's ridiculous!"

She shrugged. "It is what it is."

"I call bullshit," he said. "Do you love me?"

She looked away from him.

His boyish grin returned. "I know you do," he said.

She shook her head, but the corners of her mouth turned upwards in spite of herself.

"I wouldn't have said it if I thought you didn't," he continued.

She leaned back, away from him, still unable to speak. Then she laughed and covered her face.

"Tell me you love me," he said, grabbing her hands, pulling them off her face.

"No," she said, falling back onto the bed.

"Tell me you love me," he said, laying down next to her and planting wet kisses on her face.

"Ew, you're slobbering all over me," she said, laughing and wiping her face onto the blanket.

"Tell me you love me," he said, kissing her on the mouth, his hands in her hair.

She closed her eyes and kissed him back.

"I love you, Lauren," he whispered, kissing her softly. "Now tell me you love me."

She opened her eyes and looked into his. His face was open, honest, hiding nothing. He was exposed, a naked display of emotion, but in that exposure he was strong, and in his vulnerability, he was powerful. She wanted to feel powerful. She wanted to be strong.

"I love you, too," she whispered.

He grinned like a kid on Christmas morning. Then he pounced on the bed and tickled her. "I knew it! I knew it! I told you I always get what I want." He looked down at her again and smiled. "God, I am so in love with you."

She pulled him down on top her, guided him inside of her, and gave herself to him for the first time without holding anything back.

For a moment, she thought she could be happy.

Later, they curled up in her bed, watching *300* on Pay-Per-View.

"This is my favorite movie," she said.

"I know," Travis said. "This is the second time you've made me watch it."

"Wait, wait, this is my favorite part." She sat up and affected a British accent. "'The thousand armies of the Persian Empire descend upon you. Our arrows will block out the sun.' 'Then we'll fight in the shade.' I love that. Do you know that's in the original Herodotus?"

He laughed and kissed her. "You're such a dork. But that's why I love you."

They lay in bed, limbs tangled together, for the rest of the day. They made love twice, and by the evening, Travis suggested they go out for dinner. Lauren didn't want to leave the room, but Travis convinced to her to shower and see how she felt after.

When she returned to the room, he lay on the bed, watching the news.

"Hey sexy," he said, watching her run her towel over her wet hair.

But Lauren didn't hear him. What she did hear was the newscaster saying, "The instability in Yemen could lead to a strengthening of Al-Qaeda."

She stood transfixed.

"Hey, are you okay?" he asked.

"Turn off the TV," she said.

"Sure, babe, one second. I just want to know the score on the game."

"...And further attacks on U.S. soil," the pundit continued.

"Travis," she said, her voice low, her tone even, "turn off the fucking TV."

He looked over at her, but her eyes were glued to the screen. Without saying a word, he hit the power button on the remote.

"Lauren, are you okay?"

She held her hand over her stomach and walked back to the bathroom. Just then, her phone rang. She paused for a moment, then continued to the bathroom and closed the door behind her.

"Hey, it's your mother," he shouted through the door.

"I'll call her later," Lauren shouted.

"Can I answer it?" he yelled.

She opened the door and ripped the phone out of his hand.

"No!" she said, pressing ignore.

He stared at her, quizzically. She turned around, walked back into the bathroom, and slammed the door.

The phone rang again. Her mother, again.

Huddled in a corner in the bathroom, she answered. But the echo in the bathroom made it hard for Marcelle to hear her, so she went back into the room, where Travis stood staring at her, clearly confused.

"Where were you before?" her mother asked.

"In the shower. I'm on my way out," Lauren answered.

"Where are you going?"

"To meet some friends for a drink."

Travis mouthed the word "liar."

"You have friends there?"

Lauren rolled her eyes.

"People from work, Mom. I'm already running late," she said.

"Let me talk to her," Travis whispered.

Lauren shook her head and whispered, "Absolutely not."

"What did you say?" her mother asked. Travis tried to grab the phone out of her hand. She swatted him away.

"I'm sorry, Mom. I can't talk now. I'll call you later."

She turned the phone off and looked at Travis.

"What the hell?" she said.

"I wanted to say hello to your mother," he said. "Mothers love me!"

"I'm not ready for you to talk to my mother," she said, putting on her bathrobe, and sitting on the bed.

"Why not? You're the first woman who hasn't wanted to introduce me to her parents."

"Stop rushing me. Stop pushing me into things I'm not ready for," she said.

Travis sat down next to her and took her hand in his. "Why are you so upset about this?"

Lauren stiffened, felt her hands sweating. "Because I don't need my mother to know there's a man in my room. I don't need to give her the details about the man I'm currently screwing."

"Or, it's 8:00. I can be the man who's taking you to dinner. You couldn't tell her that?" He tried to look into her eyes, but she fixed them on the carpet.

"No. I couldn't," she said, still looking down.

"No?" he asked, dropping her hand. "Why not?"

She took a deep breath and lifted her eyes to stare at the wallpaper. "Because I don't want to tell her yet." After another deep breath, she faced him. "Why don't you give a shit about what I want?"

"I don't give a shit about what you want? What are you even talking about?" He looked away, paused and looked back at her. "Is that what I am? The man you're currently screwing. Even after today?"

She rolled her eyes. "Travis..."

He stood up. "I wanted you to meet my whole family in Chicago and you won't even tell your mother you're dating me?"

"I knew it," she said, throwing up her hands. "Here we go."

"What does that mean?"

"Nothing," she said, eyes back on the wallpaper. It really was an ugly color, an almost urine-like yellow.

"No," he said, standing directly in front of her. "It doesn't mean nothing, or you wouldn't have said it."

She looked up at him. "You're acting like a chick. I thought I was the chick."

"Irregardless..."

"Irregardless is not a word, Hillbilly."

Clearly taken aback, he yelled, "Do you have to be such a bitch all the time?"

"Evidently, I do," she said, folding her arms across her chest.

"I don't have to stand here and be ridiculed," he said, leaning over her.

"So leave!" she yelled. "It's not like I'm the one chasing you."

Travis stared at Lauren for a while, his mouth agape. She sat on the bed, hugging her knees to her chest and pulling her robe tighter. The defiant expression she wore softened when she saw the pain in his face.

"You just said you loved me," he said, staring into her eyes.

She stared at her lap. "I told you I suck at loving people."

"I understand you don't want to make a commitment. I get that. I don't know where I want this to go, either. But when you love someone, there's a certain level of kindness, of respect, that you treat them with. At least, I do. But not you. I don't know what love means to you. But if this is it, I don't want anything to do with it."

He watched her, waiting for a response. She said nothing. He shook his head.

"This isn't what I'm looking for. I've done this already and I'm too old to do it again. I thought there was something real underneath all the games. I should have known better."

She watched as he gathered his clothes. He dressed himself, every so often looking at a spot on the wall or the floor and nodding his head, as if agreeing with himself. He sat on the bed and tied his shoelaces. She stared at him and said nothing. He stood up. He stared at her as he would a puzzle that might reveal itself if he only looked hard enough. She said nothing. He broke his gaze and walked to the door. He didn't turn around as he went out. She heard the door click, listened as his footsteps grew fainter on the carpet in the hallway

She took the flower shaped ring off her middle finger and spun it on the end table like a top.

Chapter Five

At noon on Monday, Lauren looked up from her desk to see that most of her co-workers had gone to lunch and once again no one invited her. She had been shocked by their hostility initially, but soon realized she was the youngest person on the team and the one who made the most money. But she got in before they did, and left after they did, and was always willing to do the grunt work no one else would. Honestly, if they were going to be that lazy, at the very least they could appreciate her for picking up the slack.

Lauren's boss called her into his office. Most of her co-workers were scared of Ned, but Lauren had just been promoted, so she knew she had nothing to fear.

Lauren sat in the chair opposite Ned, admiring his tall broad frame, his all-American good looks, short blonde hair and blue eyes. She thought, not for the first time, that she probably would have slept with him long ago if he hadn't been her boss. Or married.

"I've been telling Devon about you," he said, referring to the company's CEO.

She smiled. "I figured you had a lot to do with the promotion."

"You deserved it," he said.

"Thank you. I really appreciate your confidence."

She twirled her pen between her fingers while waiting for Ned to continue.

"But that's not why I called you in here. This project is over at the end of the week. I know you're off for Passover for a few days, but I'm going to Dallas on an oil company account. It's high profile, a career-building move if it gets done right. I want you to be my second-in-command."

Lauren dropped her pen. Then she cleared her throat. Dallas. Where Travis lives.

"Is there something wrong?" he asked.

"No."

"Spit it out."

"I heard some people talking one day. I'm always on your team. I've been promoted twice. There are people who suspect some, ahem, extra-curriculars, if you know what I mean. I don't want people talking that way about me."

"Who thinks that?" he asked. "Claire?" He faked a smile and waved at Claire, who was standing on the other side of the glass wall that surrounded his office, pretending to make photocopies. "Please. She's lucky she still has a job. You get twice as much done as she does with a fraction of the complaining."

Ned scratched his arm, something he often did when he was deep in thought. "To hell with her. You keep working with me because you're consistently the best person on my team. Everyone who looks at your job evaluations, especially your client evaluations, would see that. Don't let an idiot like Claire hold you back."

"You don't understand, Ned. You're a man. People don't automatically assume that because you're attractive you're sleeping your way to the top. I work too hard to have that stigma attached to me."

"Oh, yeah?" he laughed. "You think I'm attractive?" He bumped his arm into hers.

"Ned, everyone thinks you're attractive. But don't change the subject."

"No, wait, let's change the subject for a minute."

"Ned, I used to do HR consulting. I know my sexual harassment statutes," she said, laughing and bumping his arm with her own.

He scratched his arm again. "Fine. Just think about it. I'm going to send you the project description. I need an answer in a week."

Lauren returned to her desk and finished the spreadsheet she was to present to her team at their end of day meeting. She had gone over the numbers three times and was amazed at the waste companies permitted. By changing two suppliers and eliminating a few redundant positions, she had been able to increase their profit margin by almost 2%. It was ridiculous that no one in their management team had seen what was so obvious to her.

Lauren's phone vibrated. She jumped, and dug through her bag to find it. She made a habit of ignoring calls and emails when she was working, delaying correspondence till she finished a task so as not to interrupt her thought process. Also, she hated talking on the phone. Communications were so much simpler in this era of text messages and emails, where a few words sufficed and banal pleasantries could be done away with.

But that Monday, she dug through her bag to see who was calling: her sister Sarah. She hit ignore. Sarah had called a few days earlier, so Lauren knew it must be important. But Sarah was hard to get off the phone once she started talking so Lauren finished her presentation before calling her back.

She didn't like others hearing her conversations, so she took the elevator downstairs and stood in the warm April air as she found Sarah's number in her phone and hit send.

The phone rang three times and Lauren felt relief when the answering machine picked up. "Hi, you've reached Sarah and David Dayan," said her sister, in a sing-song, annoyingly chipper voice.

Lauren was leaving a message when Sarah answered.

"Oh, hey, Lauren. I just walked in," Sarah said. Ugh.

"How are things?' Lauren asked, as she looked for something to occupy her hands. Maybe I should take up knitting. Like Madame Defarge.

"Really good. How about you?"

"Fine. The usual. Working. How's David?"

"Great. Working hard. Well, not like you, but you know, hard for normal people."

"Very funny. How's school?"

"Right." Sarah took a deep breath. "I have to tell you something. I wanted to wait till Passover so I could tell you in person, but then I thought someone else might tell you by accident, so I'm just going to tell you now."

"Is everything all right? Did you drop out of school again? Sarah, just because you're married doesn't mean you shouldn't finish your degree."

"I don't like school. I only went cause Mommy made me. I don't want to work and I don't have to, but that's not why I dropped out."

"What if something happens to David? What if he leaves you in twenty years? What are you going to do then?"

"Lauren, stop lecturing me and just listen. This is good news, okay. I'm pregnant!"

"Oh. Oh my God. Wow."

"You can at least pretend to be happy for me, Lauren."

"I am. It's just. You're so young."

"Half my friends from high school already have kids. I'm not that young."

"Yeah, in your world."

"My world. It used to be your world, too. You can at least be happy for me."

"Okay. You're right. I am happy for you. I really am."

"Not everybody wants what you do, Lauren. I'm happy. I love David. I want to have this baby. I don't give you a hard time about your ridiculous life, you can at least be supportive of mine. You know what, forget it. I'll see you next week."

Sarah hung up.

Lauren felt awful. She felt antsy, like she needed to move, like she couldn't go back to her desk. She wanted to run, but she already ran that morning and she had work to do. She had to steady her nerves. She needed to talk to someone who understood her. She called her brother, Jack.

"Why does God hate me?" she asked.

"You spoke to Sarah?"

"Why couldn't I be born into a normal family?"

"You're normal?"

"Why do girls get married at twenty-two and pregnant at twenty-three?"

"To piss off their spinster sisters."

"Fuck you."

"I missed you, too. Where are you? I haven't heard from you in two weeks."

"Still in Memphis."

"Still screwing the cowboy?"

"It's complicated. Still not screwing the girl next door?"

"Looks like I will be, soon enough."

"Not you, too."

"I was planning on proposing a few days before Passover."

"God hates me."

"Maybe. But I love you. And you have a wonderful way of congratulating people. Sarah just texted me. She's pretty upset."

"Why does she text you? She insists on talking to me!"

"You have a wonderful way of making people feel loved."

"Whatever. I have to go back to work."

"'Mabrouk, Jack. I'm sure you and Joy will be very happy together. I always liked her for you.' Think you can say that, Lauren?"

"Mabrouk, Jack. I'm sure you and Joy will be very happy together. I always liked her for you. Is that better?"

"Yes. Thank you. When do I get to see you?"

"Never. I'm going to kill myself as soon as we hang up."

"Funny. Just make sure you save the night before Passover. We'll go to that wine bar you love."

"To toast the loss of my brother."

"You're such a drama queen. Now, I guess you can get on with killing yourself because I have to go back to work."

She laughed. "I love you, Jack."

"I love you, too, you heartless bitch."

By the time Lauren left work she wanted a cigarette more than she had wanted one in the entire two years since she quit. Usually, when she had a craving like this, she did some yoga breathing, but she wasn't feeling particularly zen, so she decided to get a glass of wine or three at the hotel bar. And who should be sitting there when she walked in but Travis and a bleached-blonde with bad roots. She was hanging off his arm, laughing too loudly at what he said, wearing too tight clothes with too big hair.

They were seated at the bar, an old-fashioned mahogany affair, the kind of bar that may have once been in a high-class brothel, a little too ornate, a little too formal, suggesting some kind of easy sexuality, the kind of easy sexuality this girl was draping over Travis's arm.

She sat in an outside seating area, under the heat lamps, not technically in the same room, but positioned so she could look straight through the glass partition, could have a great view of Travis and his date. Someone had left an old copy of *The Economist* with a picture of Mahmoud Ahmadinejad on the cover. Lauren remembered her father's furious reaction when Iran's President had been allowed to speak at Columbia. It was the first year since he graduated that he didn't write a check to his beloved Alma Mater.

But Lauren didn't want to read about yet another person who wanted to erase Israel from existence. She wanted something vapid, something mindless telling her how to wear her hair or how to know if that guy *really* liked her, or how to have the best orgasm imaginable. Or something she could read with *schadenfreude*, like Lindsay Lohan entering rehab for the tenth time, or one of Charlie Sheen's drunken rants.

A waiter came by to take her drink order, and she asked if she could order a copy of *Cosmopolitan* from the newsstand. As the waiter left, Lauren tried as hard as she could not to look at Travis. Who she noticed was trying not to look at her either.

She finally pushed him too far and now she had to sit and watch him with that sleazy blonde. The waiter returned with a glass of red wine and a glossy magazine. Lauren ordered another glass as well as a pack of Marlboro Reds. She used to smoke lights, back when, two years ago, she had last smoked. But tonight, if she was going to have a cigarette, she was going to have a real one. Anyway, she was only going to smoke two and throw the pack away.

The clock on the wall read seven-fifteen. She knew she should go to her room to sleep. Why she stayed and watched was beyond her. Why she watched his hand on the small of some other woman's back, why she watched that woman look at Travis in ways Lauren had never dared—the blonde's eyes screaming, "let me have your babies," when all Lauren screamed was "get away from me"—defied logic.

She flipped through the pages of *Cosmopolitan*. "The Truth About Your Biological Clock," it read. The truth about my biological clock, thought Lauren, is that my sister will have enough babies for the both of us, so why bother. Looks like my brother and his little virgin, too.

Her sister pregnant. Her brother engaged. It was impossible not to imagine what her life could have been, how different her married life would have been from the life she was living now. She looked at her ring, rotating it with her thumb so she could press the diamond into her palm when she closed her hand over it.

She looked up again. Travis had his back to her. As well he should. He would not be coming after her anymore. She had put an end to that. And he was already at the bar when she arrived, so he wasn't the one who should leave. She should leave. Except she couldn't bear the thought of being alone in her room. Not after what happened there this weekend. Despite the warmth from the heat lamps, Lauren pulled her jacket around her body.

The waiter arrived with her cigarettes and matches. She packed them against the inside of her wrists, a feeling of exhilaration coming over her. This was the first time in two years and no better time than now. She tore off the top of the cellophane wrapper, ripped out the fire retardant paper, pulled one out and put it between her lips. Then she struck a match on the matchbook, lit her cigarette and inhaled.

Lauren guzzled her second glass of wine. She should have ordered shots. She should have sat in the corner with a bottle and a shot glass like some down-and-out gambler who's just lost his last dime. She lit another cigarette. At the bar, Travis smiled at his slut-for-the-night. He looked at his watch, downed the rest of his whiskey, and put on his jacket. Then he helped his lady friend into hers. Always the gentleman.

As they prepared to leave, Lauren wondered if he would look her way before walking out. He was with another woman, and she sat on the patio, drinking by herself. His way of saying he was over it. Her way of saying she was sorry.

He did look, and when he did, he looked confused. His eyes met hers. But you don't smoke, his expression said. She held his gaze as she put the cigarette to her lips and inhaled. There's a lot you don't know about me, hers replied.

Travis and his date walked out. Lauren called the waiter over and ordered another glass of wine.

"Wait, hold on," she said to the waiter. "Just bring the whole damned bottle."

By ten-thirty, she looked down at the ashtray in front of her and saw at least ten cigarette butts. She held her hand over her mouth as her stomach lurched. Twice in one week?

She staggered out of the bar and up to her room, the elevator ride endless, the hallway interminable. She kicked off her shoes and dropped her clothes in a pile at the foot of her bed. Then she fell into bed and passed out.

Later, she found herself awake and confused. Then she realized the phone was ringing. Travis?

"I'm so sorry. I'm sorry. I'm so sick of being sorry," she said.

"Uh, Ms. Hazan?" the voice said.

"Oh, um, yeah?"

"This is Nicky from the bar. Sorry. I didn't mean to wake you. You forgot to close your tab."

"Oh."

"It's all right. We'll just add it to your breakfast bill tomorrow."

She put the phone back on the receiver and looked at the clock on the nightstand. Twelve-twenty. She was drunk and she wanted Travis. She dialed his room.

"Mmmmm, Hello?" he said. She remembered the blonde at the bar. Was he alone?

"It's Lauren. I have to tell you something."

"Yeah? What's that?"

"Why I keep pushing you away. It's because of 9/11."

"Is this is a joke? Because of 9/11? Why don't you blame it on Halliburton? Dick Cheney made you do it!"

"No, Travis, listen. I know you're not Toufiq, but..."

"What the hell is toofy? I'm sorry I'm not toofy enough for you."

Lauren's words got caught in her throat and she sobbed.

"I'm sick of your crying. And I'm sick of your excuses. Do me a favor and don't call me anymore, okay?" He hung up.

She sobbed harder. And then she felt that familiar rumbling. Oh no, she thought, running to the bathroom. Here we go again.

Chapter Six

Sarah didn't even have a belly yet. Though four months pregnant, her tiny little frame hadn't gained a single visible pound. And Sarah could eat. She ate everything she felt like eating and always had. Whole pints of ice cream topped with crushed Oreos, mozzarella sticks, deep fried Chinese food, while Lauren ordered hers with no sugar, no oil, no cornstarch and brown rice. Sarah just kept eating. Lauren was certain that two weeks after giving birth, Sarah would be back in her skinny jeans.

On the couch, a scene of repugnant affection took place before Lauren's eyes. David, her brother-in-law, sat holding his pregnant wife in his arms. Sarah sat between his legs, her back on his chest, resting her head on him. One of David's hands lay on Sarah's non-existent belly and the other held a chocolate-covered macaroon in front of her mouth that she delicately nibbled, while he delicately nibbled on her neck. Sarah giggled.

Opposite them, in the big leather club chair, her legs tucked beneath her body, crunching on a baby carrot, sat Lauren. Just looking at Sarah made her want to go for a run. Or smoke a cigarette. Or break something made of glass.

As the feeding progressed, there was a knock on the door. Jack jumped to answer it, eager as a baby seal. In walked Joy, radiant in a white wrap dress with a pink and green floral print. She looked so pure, so virginal, so much like a porcelain doll.

Sometimes Lauren wondered if her sister was as sweet as everyone thought she was, or if, in reality, she was a devious little shit. Because her timing was just a little too perfect. She could have waited until no one else was in earshot, unless she was purposely trying to humiliate her sister, revenge for the way Lauren handled the news of her pregnancy.

In front of both of their parents, Nonna, Nonno, Jack and Joy, Auntie Sofia and Uncle Charles, Sarah said, "So Lauren, are you seeing anyone? Because if you're not, David has a friend for you."

Touché.

Immediately, everyone in the room stared at Lauren, who made the face she always made when asked that question—rolling her eyes, pursing her lips and exhaling deeply through her nostrils—then ignored it, returning to the important task of crunching on her carrot.

And then it started.

Nonna: "Lauren, rohi, why don't you answer your sister? Why not meet this boy?"

Mom: "It would be nice if you started dating someone, honey."

Dad, to Mom: "See, I told you if we sent her to college in California she'd never come home, never get married."

Uncle Charles: "Just meet the guy. What do you have to lose?"

Auntie Sofia, to Uncle Charles: "Leave her alone, you don't know what this is like."

Dad, to David: "What business is he in? Who are his parents?"

David, to everyone: "A nice Egyptian boy. You know his parents, they pray at our synagogue. He went to Columbia, Dad, like you. An investment banker. Very smart. Maybe even smarter than her."

Then laughter.

Mom: "Lauren, it could be very nice if you met someone."

Nonna: "At least try, honey, maybe you'll like him."

Dad: "Lauren I want you to meet this boy. Just go out with him once."

Nonna: "Don't you want to get married, Lauren, to have children?"

Mom: "Mom, stop, of course she wants to get married. She just hasn't found the right guy."

Awkward silence.

Nonna: "Well, how's she going to find the right guy if she won't even look?"

Auntie Sofia: "Guys, stop. You're ganging up on her and it isn't fair."

Nonna: "Ganging up on her? We're her family. We want what's best for her."

306

Dad, laughing: "Maybe I'll talk to his father in synagogue tomorrow."

Lauren: "While you're at it, why don't you give him four camels and a donkey to seal the deal? Oh, wait, I'm really old. You might have to up it to six camels and two donkeys. Sorry."

Sarah: "Lauren, why do you have to get so mad? We're only trying to help."

Lauren: "Well I don't want any help. Especially not from someone so stupid she can't even make it through one semester at community college."

Sarah burst into to tears. Goddamned crybaby. Lauren grabbed her coat and ran out the door, slamming it behind her. Sofia followed.

Lauren sat on the front steps, head in her hands, between her knees, hyperventilating, trying to breathe. Sitting next to her, Sofia put her arm around her niece.

"Why don't we go for a walk?"

"Why do I bother coming home? Why would any sane person do this to herself?" Lauren asked.

"I know what this is like," Sofia said. "Especially now, at this point in your life. They mean well, but they can be so cruel. But once you're married, once you have children," Sofia had four, "it's the most wonderful place in the world. You'll find happiness here if you want to. I did."

"But what if that never happens?"

Sofia held her hand and led her down the block. It was cool for an April night, a welcomed contrast to the steam building up inside her.

As angry tears fell down Lauren's face, Sofia said nothing, just put her arm around Lauren's shoulder, pulling her close.

When they returned to the house, it was like nothing had happened. The women were in the kitchen preparing for the meal. Her father and David played backgammon on one table, and Jack played her grandfather on the other. As they played, they talked about the revolutions taking over the Middle East.

"You people are so optimistic because you haven't seen this before," said Eddie. "It starts out full of hope, but then wait and see who takes over."

"Why wouldn't they want freedom as much as we do?" asked Jack.

"It's not about what they want," Nathan added. "It's about who's strong enough to take over."

"The people won't stand for another dictator," Jack said.

"Yeah," Eddie huffed. "That's what they said in Iran."

"We should go help," Sofia said to Lauren.

Damn. Now I have to apologize to Sarah. But Sarah wasn't in the kitchen when she walked in, and neither was Nonna. Just her mother and Joy.

"Joy," said Marcelle, "why don't you go sit with Jack inside. You just got engaged, you'll have plenty of years to help me in here."

Joy took the hint. Sofia did, too.

"Lauren, help me prepare the Seder plate," Marcelle said, slicing celery on a cutting board.

The Seder plate: Celery and salt water to remember the tears their ancestors cried in slavery; bitter herbs for their bitter lives; haroset, crushed dates and walnuts, representing the mortar the slaves turned into bricks; the shank bone, reminiscent of the Pascal lamb; an egg, round, without beginning or end, signifying eternity, the endless cycle of life.

They put a serving of each on salad plates.

"You're going to have to apologize to your father. You know he won't tolerate that kind of disrespect."

Lauren nodded, spooning dates onto the plates.

"I mean it, Lauren, you can't talk to him like that."

"Why is he allowed to talk to me like that?"

Marcelle slammed her knife down.

"We're your parents. We gave you everything. We deserve some respect!"

Marcelle took a deep breath to collect herself. She continued, "Why do you have to make everything difficult? I have always been on your side, Lauren. When you wanted to move to California for college and your father resisted, when you refused to move home after school, when you decided to live in hotel rooms and only come home twice a year. I told everyone, 'Let her find her way. Let her figure it out for herself. We shouldn't force things on her. She knows what's right.' But you don't even appreciate that! I call you all the time, and you shut me out.

"It's like being a part of this family is a burden to you. You're miserable from the minute you walk in the door and then you can't wait to leave. I miss you. I look forward to you coming home and then you act like this."

Marcelle wiped her hands on a kitchen towel. "You have everything I ever wanted and you've never appreciated it."

The look Lauren shot at Marcelle was practically a sneer.

Sitting around the table, they read the story of Passover from the Haggadah. To free them from bondage and end their enslavement, God took the Israelites out of Egypt. The Israelites were forced to work endless hours in the heat of the unblinking sun, building palaces and pyramids for Pharaoh while they lived in rude huts, to throw their sons into the Nile lest they beget a boy who would one day grow into a man who could unite and free the slaves.

God smote Pharaoh with the ten plagues for his insolence and his cruelty and his refusal to recognize Him, and freed the Israelites from this backbreaking labor, from their enslavement, from forced infanticide. He then brought them out of Egypt in such a hurry that the dough they used to bake bread did not have time to rise. He created a new nation that, four thousand years later, still told the tale of these great miracles.

How odd, Lauren always thought, sitting with her Egyptian-born grandparents, to celebrate this holiday, this exodus from Egypt, when they themselves had been exiled from Egypt, had been forced out of a homeland they had loved. How strange to celebrate freedom from bondage, when they had lived pleasant lives in Egypt, the hard labor beginning only after they reached their new promised land.

And how surreal, the Seder this year, celebrating their biblical homecoming, evoking their modern displacement, while watching the regime whose first rulers had initiated their own exodus, as it unraveled, driven out of Egypt by the citizens that regime used to rule.

Lauren wanted to ask her grandparents how they felt that night, but knew it was best if she didn't say anything to anyone. She was quiet, only reading from the Haggadah when called upon. Her father ignored her. Sarah stared at her plate as David rubbed her back. Jack tried to hide how mortified he was at Joy's first holiday with his family. Joy smiled and tried to be polite. Her mother, grandmother and Auntie Sofia kept the banter light and inoffensive. Uncle Charles told a funny story. No one addressed Lauren. Lauren addressed no one.

Marcelle studied her daughter. What if Nathan was right? What if they had lost her? What if it was too late? What if it was her fault?

Across the table, Lauren studied herself. I did it again, she thought. My mother worked so hard for this night and I ruined it. I ruin everything. Travis is right: I treat the people I love like shit.

The night was over and it was time for the guests to go home. Marcelle tried to convince her parents to sleep over, but Sarah clucked and shook her head.

"We only live a few blocks away. We can walk. Lauren will help us," she said.

Sarah looked lovingly at Eddie. "Your grandfather drank too much wine," she said. Eddie laughed, singing, "When Israel was in Egypt-Land."

Sarah laughed. "You know it's his favorite holiday."

"Let my people go," Eddie thundered.

They both laughed and Lauren smiled. She grabbed her coat and slipped her arm around her grandfather.

"Let's go, Nonno."

They walked in silence, except for Eddie's singing. When they arrived at her grandparent's house, Sarah said, "Come inside for a few minutes. I might need help getting him into bed."

But Eddie walked straight upstairs. As Sarah poured him a glass of water, she said to Lauren, "Will you light my narghile? I want to smoke before bed."

Lauren nodded, and Sarah followed Eddie upstairs. Lauren knew where everything was—the narghile, the coals, the tobacco. Lauren had packed the pipe for her many times before. Sarah had left the fire on the back left burner of her stove. Lauren placed the coal on the fire, put the tobacco in the bowl, and filled the chamber with water. When the coal turned red and began to crack, she took it off the flame with the tongs and placed it on top of the tobacco. She thought of taking a puff to make sure it was ready, but instead waited for her grandmother to offer.

Lauren sat on the couch in the living room, waiting for her grandmother to come down. Sarah had filled her bookcases with framed pictures of her children and grandchildren, weddings, brises, bar mitzvahs, Lauren's college graduation photo. She crossed the room to look at the one from Jack's bar mitzvah. Toufiq stood in the corner of the picture. He had been shy about being in the photo, but Nathan had insisted he was part of their family, had taken Toufiq by the hand, and stood him between himself and Lauren, told him to smile.

Sarah returned to the room and sat on the couch. Lauren sat next to her. Sarah held the narghile's mouthpiece and took a long, slow inhale, then passed it to Lauren. As Lauren brought it to her lips, Sarah looked at her hand, noticing the diamond ring.

"You still wear that?" she asked.

Lauren nodded.

"Maybe it's time to stop," Sarah said, gently. "It's been ten years, rohi, you can't mourn forever. You know he would want you to be happy."

Lauren nodded. After Toufiq died, it was all anyone talked about. They treated her like a widow, tiptoeing around her, always ready with tissues, with kind words, but she steeled herself, refusing to be made into a spectacle, never answering anyone's questions, never responding to their sympathy. It drove her to leave New York, to be away from the constant mourning. When she announced she was leaving, taking a new job that would require her to be out of town much of the year, they were angry with her, but anger was easier than pity. And soon everyone stopped talking about him. Despite her protest, despite the defenses she erected, her grandmother always saw through to her grief, though she was kind enough not to mention it.

"I worry about you. I worry that you push us all away."

"That's what I do," Lauren said, her voice barely a whisper. "I make people love me, and then I push them away. Everyone would be better off if I just stayed gone."

"Oh, hush," Sarah said, slipping her arm around her granddaughter. "Enough of the self-pity. Enough with the excuses."

Lauren leaned into her, feeling the comfort of her grandmother's love.

Suddenly, Sarah sat up and put her hand to her chest, clearing her throat.

"Are you okay?" Lauren asked.

Sarah cleared her throat again, patted her chest.

"All that matzah," she said. "It gives me indigestions. This," she pointed to the narghile, "is an excellent *digestif*."

From an end table, Sarah picked up a picture of herself, her brothers and their father, taken in Israel when she was in her late-thirties.

"We took that one right before he died. A few months after he came back to us," Sarah said. "Life happens too fast. You never get to say the things you want."

Lauren nodded.

"I wish you weren't so unhappy," Sarah continued. She put her arm around Lauren again. Lauren stared at the floor.

Sarah took a long drag from the narghile. "Lauren, I understand what it is to lose someone you love. You know my mother died when I was young. For years, all I wanted was to have one more day with her. And then my father was imprisoned and we thought he died, too. And all

I wanted was more time with him. Then half my brothers moved to Israel after I came here with the other three. Then your grandfather and I couldn't have children. All I wanted, all of that time, was to be with my family, to have my own family, and it seemed like everything God threw my way went against that.

"But I had your grandfather, and other people who loved me, and I made a decision to cherish what I had instead of crying over everything I lost. And then I had two babies, and then I got my father back for a little while, and I see my brothers every few years, and now I'm old, and I've lived a hard life, but I'm happy. I have my family around me, and I'm happy. So it pains me to watch you running away from all the love you could have in your life if you would just let it in."

Lauren felt tears form in her eyes and covered her face, choking them back.

"I don't want to be the victim of a tragedy. I don't want to be an object of pity."

Sarah stroked her back and pulled Lauren towards her.

"I understand, angel. But if you define yourself against something, you're still letting it control you."

When Lauren got back to the house, everyone was asleep but her father. He sat in his armchair, reading the newspaper, drinking mint tea. He looked up as she walked in. She held his gaze, then lowered her eyes, ashamed.

They stood in silence, he looking at her, she biting her nail, feeling like she was sixteen and caught coming home after curfew.

Finally, Nathan broke the silence. "This was why I didn't want you to leave," he said. "I knew you'd never come back."

She stood, speechless, chewing on her thumbnail.

"If Toufiq had lived..." he said, his voice trailing off.

She froze where she stood, felt her gut clench, her windpipe close. She heaved and grabbed at her chest.

"But he didn't, did he?" she whispered.

He looked at her and shook his head. He ran a hand over his eye and looked back down at his paper. She waited a moment, then slowly walked upstairs. She heard the paper crinkle as he turned the page.

Lauren lay in bed that night, unable to sleep, her grandmother's words filling her mind. All the love she could have in her life if she just allowed it to enter. She had been grieving for too long. It was time to move on.

But when she thought of moving on, the only thing she could think of was Travis.

Travis, I miss you. Have I pushed you too far?

But she had another chance. An assignment in Dallas. Six months in his hometown. He told her he would be there, had a new band to record.

She texted Ned, accepting the Dallas assignment.

So she could get Travis back.

The only question was how.

Chapter Seven

Standing in front of Plywood Records, Lauren remembered something her grandmother once told her. "Don't chase after men," she said. "A lady always waits for the man to come to her."

Well, I'm not a lady, Lauren thought, and there's no chance he's coming after me.

She thought of her grandmother again, of all she had managed to overcome, of the happiness she had found in her life. Lauren made a mental note to call her. Tonight, she promised herself. For now, she stared at the studio door and forced herself to go in. She moved towards it, put her hand on the knob, then let go and hurried away, back across the street.

Just as she had done yesterday.

And the day before.

Originally, she planned to arrive in Dallas a week before the assignment began. A week would give her enough time to find him and hopefully smooth things over before she was too busy with work. She hadn't counted on her cowardice. As she waited for the traffic light to change, she knew if she didn't force herself to go in, she was doomed to repeat the process until she started working and no longer had free days. Showing up at his house was out of the question. Who knew what she would find there?

This was her third day in Dallas. This was her third time at the studio. This was her third failure. Enough failure. It's time to go.

She walked back down the block, and back up to the studio doors. She held the knob in her hand. She felt sweat beading on her palms. She felt her chest tighten. She wanted to flee.

And then she made up her mind: she was sick of running. Memories of hours on planes and on lines at airports flooded her mind. Different cities and hotel rooms, different offices, different teams, different projects all coagulated into one force and the force screamed, "I don't want to run anymore."

Using that force, she pulled the door so hard it almost broke off its hinges. The receptionist gasped.

"Oh my God," she said. "Ya'll don't have to pull that hard for it to open."

"I'm here to see Travis Miller," Lauren said.

"Do you have an appointment?"

"No," Lauren said. "But will you tell him Lauren Hazan is here?"

The receptionist explained that he was in the recording studio and could not be disturbed. Lauren said she would wait. The receptionist, who introduced herself as Melissa, laughed. "He might be in there all day."

Having come this far, Lauren was not about to let some fake blonde with fake boobs stop her from going in.

Lauren wondered what was funny and then realized what a spectacle she was. What if she wasn't the first woman to come barging in, desperate to see Travis? What if she was just the next in a long line of lovers, demanding to have him back?

Lauren asked if they could send someone to tell him she was there, if only to see how long she should wait. Melissa obliged and Lauren wrote him a note. "I'm here. I need to see you. Please come out and talk to me."

She sat in the reception room, trying to occupy herself by leafing through the pile of celebrity gossip magazines: sex in relationships, sex outside of relationships, babies, divorces, cheaters and new couples. Nothing different, she thought. Their lives are made of the same nonsense as ours, they just have better clothes.

She stood up and smoothed her skirt before sitting back down again. Choosing her outfit had taken hours: a pink linen skirt, a white cotton sweater, long brown hair worn down her back. She looked like a schoolgirl: innocent, sweet. Would she fool him?

Plywood Records was a small studio, with one recording room in the back. The waiting room was painted pale blue. "A calming color," he explained when describing it. The walls were covered with photographs of musicians, many of them with Travis. She had heard of almost none of them. Framed single records were everywhere, the platinum or gold ones displayed in the center of the wall at eye level, impossible to miss.

It reminded her of Graceland. He had taken her on one of their first dates. She had not wanted to go, but he insisted, saying that every American should see it once. Plus, he offered her the musician's tour: that was when he told her about his recording career.

"I had one album that went platinum," he said, "and a second that went plywood. So I named my label after that."

Walking around the jungle room, Lauren wrinkled her nose in distaste.

"So this is what happens when white trash gets rich," she said.

"One day you'll see my place. Then you'll really know what happens when white trash gets rich," he laughed. It was then she nicknamed him Hillbilly.

She waited forever, glancing up at Melissa every so often to see her chewing on her hair in between answering phone calls.

"Y'all are persistent," she said, after an hour passed.

Isn't y'all plural, Lauren thought. She smiled. "How long do you think he'll be?"

"I told you, he might be in there all day."

"But you gave him my note."

"Sure did."

"Did he read it?"

"Yes."

"Then I'll wait."

Another hour, filled by an entire magazine devoted to the cast of *The Jersey Shore*, went by and Travis still didn't come out.

Lauren looked up Melissa. It was two o'clock. "He has to eat, doesn't he?" Melissa smiled back at her and shrugged.

Twenty minutes went by, then twenty more. After three hours, Lauren got ready to leave. She took a business card out of her wallet and wrote her contact information on the back. Just then he came out from the back room. He looked surprised to see her but didn't acknowledge her immediately. He gave Melissa the band's lunch order and sent her out to get it. After Melissa left the office, he turned to Lauren.

"I didn't think you'd still be here."

"Well, I am," she said, standing up.

"This is not a good time for me."

"When is?" She moved closer to him.

He stepped back. "What do you want from me?"

"Have dinner with me tonight."

Travis looked her up and down. "How long did it take you to pick out that schoolgirl outfit?"

Lauren laughed. "Three hours. Will you please have dinner with me tonight?"

He nodded. She hugged him. He kissed her forehead and walked back into the studio. That was easy, she thought.

They had dinner at Del Frisco's steakhouse that night. Travis looked gorgeous in a white button down shirt, jeans, a big buckled belt and cowboy boots. Lauren went for sexy innocent in a knee-length pencil skirt and snug sweater. She was amazed at how naturally the conversation flowed. He cracked jokes about the recording session with the band. She told him about her newest project. Travis listed several bands she actually knew who were performing in the area over the next few months. She imagined them going to concerts together, sitting on a picnic blanket in the park, drinking wine, feeding each other cheese and fruit. No part of her wanted to move: she wanted to dive inside him.

"I love you," she said, interrupting him mid-sentence. She realized she had no idea what he was talking about.

He grinned. "Choose your words carefully," he said.

She started to explain her behavior in Memphis, but he stopped her. "It's all in the past. No need to talk about that now."

They went home together after dinner. She begged to see his house, but he swore it was a mess so they went to her hotel room.

They made love for so many hours it seemed like her body would break, and yet the smell of him, the feel of his weight on top of her, his arms holding her down, his lips, kissing, biting hers, energized her so that she could not have enough of him. Every time they finished, her hand found its way to his body and began stroking him, caressing him, loving him, until he was ready to go again. And he did. Four times. Until finally she disentangled herself from him and said, "God, I'm going to sleep like a baby tonight. All night. Next to you."

He sat up. "Sorry, babe, but I have a really early morning tomorrow. I should go home."

"You always said it's going to take the same amount of time to get home in the morning as it will now. Why don't you stay here with me?" She smiled at him, kissing his chest.

He gently pushed her off him. "Wish I could, but I gotta go."

She couldn't contain her disappointment. She tried. She didn't say another word as he dressed himself. He leaned over the bed and kissed her forehead.

"This was fun, babe. Sleep well."

She grabbed his face and angled it so her lips met his. She kissed him slowly, softly. Looking in his eyes she asked, "When can I see you again?"

He pulled back. "I don't think that's going to happen."

She sat up and pulled the sheets against her naked body. "Why not?"

"You're more than I can handle. I'm happy I got to see you tonight, though." He made his way to the door.

"You can't just leave me here like this. After tonight!"

He took a long hard look at her as he opened the door. "Well, I guess now you know how it feels, don't you?" He slammed the door behind him.

Not so easy, after all.

She thought she would be angry. She waited for the panic, for the throbbing heart, the tightened chest, the pounding in her ears, but what came, when the blinding pain subsided, were stabs of grief.

Leaving Egypt

All the years she refused to cry over Toufiq, and all the times she pushed her feelings back down into her gut, had been like drops of water on a rock, dripping and dropping until finally the rock eroded, until finally it cracked in two.

Lying in the fetal position on the floor of a hotel room still heavy with the scent of the only man she had been able to love since she lost the man who was supposed to be the love of her life, Lauren was too worn down to fight, too tired to run, too weak to put on her armor, and she wept.

And she didn't hold it in, and she didn't push it down, and she didn't stare at her reflection, forcing herself to get a grip.

No. On the floor of the room, she wept for Toufiq, for the promise of his life, for the dream he almost lived. She wept for the life they never had, the quiet moments, the intimacy of a shared Sunday morning, for coffee in bed with the crossword puzzle. She wept for the Shabbat dinners she never cooked him, for the Friday nights she never lit candles in their home, for the Kiddush he never recited at the head of their table, a husband blessing the meal for his wife.

She wept for the babies she had been too scared to bear him in their youth. She wept for all the bedtime stories she had never heard him read their kids, the petty arguments they never had over whose family to go to for the holidays.

She wept for all the times he never whispered "I love you" into her hair, in his Arabic-inflected English, before they went to sleep. She wept for the way he whispered her name, prolonging the first syllable, rolling the "r."

She wept for her virginity, saved for him all through college, and then squandered on the first man who paid her attention after he died because she needed to make it meaningless, to make all the intimacy she never shared with him mean nothing with all the lovers she fucked and never cared for.

She wept for Travis, the only man she'd made love to, the man who had just left her. The first time sex meant anything, she ruined it out of habit.

320

She wept for the emptiness of her life, no friends, no family, just work and hotel rooms and airports and strange cities. She wept because she had no home. She wept because she had exiled herself.

Alone and naked on her hotel room floor, Lauren needed a connection, a lifeline, someone to ground her and confirm her existence.

The only person she wanted was her mother.

Marcelle was wide awake at her kitchen table when Lauren called at her four o'clock in the morning. She hadn't been able to sleep. She was worried. Her mother kept losing her breath, kept refusing to see a doctor, and her daughter, her eldest daughter, whom she loved and worried about, was leaving them and might never come back.

A phone ringing at four a.m. is never a good thing, but Marcelle was relieved to hear Lauren's voice, then heartbroken to hear the pain in it.

"I ruin everything," Lauren sobbed. "I don't deserve to be happy."

"Slow down, baby, take a deep breath," Marcelle said. "Tell me what happened."

And Lauren told her everything: how she loved Travis, how she lost him.

"And the worst part is that I deserve it," Lauren said. "For what I did to Toufiq."

"No, baby," Marcelle said. "No. You didn't do anything to Toufiq. You loved him."

"I rejected him again and again. I hurt him. He died hurting for me."

"No, baby. You didn't reject him. All you asked him was to wait. And Lauren, Lauren, honey, are you listening? Even if you hadn't asked him to wait, even if he'd proposed and you said yes, he still wouldn't be here, baby. He would still be gone."

Marcelle heard Lauren whimper on the other line. She had never understood why Lauren had changed so drastically after Toufiq. She understood now.

"Lauren, are you there?" she asked.

"Mm hmm," she whimpered again.

"This new man, this man you love, it's not too late. Go back and find him. Tell him what you told me. If he's worth anything, he'll understand. Baby, when you want something, you have to fight for it."

She could hear Lauren nodding, and whispered to her to get some rest, that things are always clearer in the morning.

When they hung up, Marcelle sat alone in her kitchen, watching the room slowly grow lighter. She rummaged under the sink in the brillo box where she kept her hidden cigarettes. Smoking one, she prayed for Lauren.

And prayed Travis would take her back.

Chapter Eight

Lauren was too exhausted to fight, so she channeled her energy into her work. She decided to make her time in Dallas count, working sixteen-hour days, following Ned's advice to treat this assignment as a career-making opportunity. When one of their team members caught a stomach virus, she took on all of his work in addition to hers.

"Go home," Ned yelled at her one night, when, at eleven o'clock, she was still in the office.

"You're still here," she replied, barely lifting her head from her papers.

"Because I'm taking a few days off," he continued. "You're young and beautiful. Go out and have a life."

"No," she said. "I'll just screw it up. Better to stay here." She gestured at the mess around her, the papers, the empty cups of coffee, the leftover pizza crusts.

She saw him shake his head as he left. At least I'm good at my job, she thought.

After a few more sixteen-hour days, she finished everything she could do without Ned. When she called to ask for more work, he said, "Lauren, I'm on vacation. Do you know what that is? When you take time to do something other than work."

She didn't know what to do with the time, except think. She hated thinking.

Three weeks had passed since Passover and, though she had made amends with her mother, she still hadn't apologized to the rest of her family. She had to stop putting it off. It might be too late for Travis, but she couldn't let the same thing happen with her family, too. It was time to make amends.

Her father first, because that was the call she dreaded most. If she got that out of the way, the rest would be easy.

She dialed his office.

"Hi, Daddy," she said. "It's Lauren."

"This is a nice surprise," he said. "You never call me."

"Because we always end up fighting when I do."

He paused. "Well, I guess that's what happens when you put two headstrong people on the phone together."

"I'm calling to apologize."

"All right."

"You're not going to make this easy are you?"

She could hear him shaking his head.

"Okay, then. I'm sorry for being so disrespectful. Especially in front of our guests. I know better than to talk to you and Mommy that way."

"Thank you, Lauren, I appreciate that. But that's hardly the problem."

She waited: this was why she never called.

"The problem is that every decision you make takes you further and further away from us. We don't even know you anymore."

She mumbled the usual excuses.

"I went away, too, Lauren. None of my brothers went to college. But when I was done, I came home. Your mother told me if we didn't let you go, you'd feel trapped and you'd hate us for it. So we let you go. And you hate us anyway."

"I don't hate you," she said, hurt by the suggestion. "It's just hard to be home sometimes."

"You can't run away from things because they're painful. You have to face them and move on. I loved Toufiq, too. He was a son to me. But I didn't run away from this house and the rest of my family because I lost him. You're making yourself lose everyone else, too."

"I'm sorry, Daddy.'

"I don't want your apology, Lauren. I want you to do something about it."

She remembered feeling comfortable. She remembered when all she wanted was to sit at the table with her mother and grandmother, to help with whatever they were doing. How different things were now from when she was a girl. She used to love Passover, when there was so much to do, they really needed her help, didn't just pretend to give her things to make her feel useful. She used to help them clean the rice. Sephardic Jews could eat rice on Passover, but only if they checked it three times before the holiday began.

They sat at the kitchen table, lined with a paper tablecloth and a plastic tablecloth over the paper. Sarah, with the most careful eye, began with a big pile of rice, spreading a small amount of it on the table with her hand, moving the grains from the pile towards her. With her hand, she separated the grains, picking out any that looked deformed, looking for stones, or pieces of wheat or any other grain they may have accidentally mixed in with the rest. When she had taken the discards out of the pile, she passed the rice onto Marcelle. Marcelle looked at the pile, and in the same way, moved the grains in front of her, accepting most, rejecting some, until, satisfied, she passed the rice onto Lauren. By the time Lauren picked through the rice, there was little to discard, and yet she found things, probably because she was looking to find them, felt she had to remove something, and took those grains from the pile as well. They picked through fifteen pounds of rice at least, passing the pile from mother to daughter, mother to daughter.

Now her sister Sarah helped in her place.

Her father was right. Saying sorry wasn't enough. She needed some sort of larger gesture, she needed to forge a connection. Opening her laptop, she looked online. All she had was money, but her money could buy things, and those things could speak louder than words. She sent "I'm sorry" gifts: for Sarah designer maternity jeans, a few fun maternity tops, a t-shirt that read, "I'm not fat, I'm just pregnant." Sarah would know what she meant. For Jack and Joy, she sent guidebooks about Vietnam and Thailand, as she overheard them talking about a honeymoon in Southeast Asia. For her grandmother, the collected works of Oum Kalthoum on CD, because she still listened to the music on old records that constantly skipped.

A gift wouldn't do for her parents, so she emailed Ned, asking for two weeks off that summer. Her family would be on the Jersey shore. She called her mother to say she would be joining them. Her mother was overjoyed.

Still, that time was months away, and stuck in Dallas, her primary mission failed, her assignment not over for another three months, she felt as alone as the proverbial princess locked in a tower. Except that in this case, she was her own evil stepmother.

Weekends were the worst. On Saturday morning, she spent half an hour in a staring contest with her running shoes, which ended with her throwing them back in the closet and ordering chocolate chip pancakes and a side of hash browns because she couldn't decide between salty and sweet.

Her father's words hung in her head—you can't run away every time things get difficult.

She thought back to an afternoon with Travis.

"You don't fool me for a second," he had said. They were sitting on a bench near the Mississippi. He had been downtown, near her office, and met her for lunch. He packed a picnic for them. They sat on a blanket, Travis in jeans and a Drive-By Truckers T-shirt, Lauren in a suit. She sat with her legs folded to the side, and he slipped off her shoes and rubbed her feet while she nibbled on pesto pasta. He poured Pinot Noir into plastic cup, handed it to her and poured another for himself.

"Cheers." He clicked his glass into hers. "To figuring you out. You pretend to be so tough, but it's all a load of bunk. I'm wise to you."

Someone who knew her that well could not possibly be finished with her. There still had to be a chance.

She eyed the running shoes she had just thrown back in the closet, called down to room service to cancel her order. She put on her sneakers, decided she was tired of running.

She grabbed her iPhone, googling Travis, seeing he was listed. She put the address in the navigation system in her car, and let it lead her to his house. It was nine-thirty on Saturday morning, and God knew whom she would find there. She didn't care. It was time to end the games, time for the drama to be over.

When she arrived at his house, she jumped out of the car and ran up his front steps. She rang the doorbell. He didn't answer. She banged on the door. He still didn't answer. His car was in the driveway. He must be asleep. She banged harder. She rang the doorbell ten times.

What if someone was there?

What if he was just in the shower?

She didn't care. She kept banging, kept ringing.

Finally, he came to the door, his eyes sleepy, his hair tousled, wearing a white cotton bathrobe.

"Lauren, what the fuck?"

"I need to tell you something."

"I don't want to hear it," he said. He tried to slam the door, but she hurled her body against it, stopping him. Her shoulder throbbed from the impact, but something, maybe her forcefulness, maybe the determination on her face, made him stop and open the door.

And while he waited for her to speak, while he rubbed his eyes, trying to open them, squinting in the bright morning light, she felt it start again.

And in front of Travis, in the moment when she needed to be lucid, when she needed to make a case, when she needed all of her powers of persuasion to convince him to take her back, she felt that pressure on her chest, felt her eyes pop from her head, and began gasping.

She clutched the doorpost for support, sure she was about to fall. Her vision clouded, everything going black and blurry, as she held on and fought for breath.

She felt Travis grip her shoulder, felt him pulling her to the ground, where he sat her on the stoop, and she dropped her head between her knees and struggled for air.

"Do you need a paper bag?" he asked, sitting down next to her.

She didn't respond.

"Isn't that what always works on TV? Breathing into a paper bag?"

She managed a smile and looked over towards him.

"Panic attack," she gasped.

"I noticed," he replied.

"Been having a lot," she said between breaths.

"Shh," he said, rubbing her back. "Let yourself recover first."

She nodded and leaned into him, feeling the warmth of his body, her hand brushing against the soft cotton of his bathrobe. How ironic to be the happiest she'd been in weeks while also feeling as though she were dying.

After a few moments of sitting on his front steps, the door to the house still open behind them, he said, "Come on in. Let me get you some water."

They stood up and he led her inside. The house was a single-story ranch, with an open plan kitchen, living and dining area. From a large skylight, the morning sun flooded the room.

He sat her on a dark brown leather sofa and put a glass of water on the mahogany and wrought iron coffee table in front of her. As he did, she noticed the matching bookcases on the wall facing her, thinking Travis had really good taste.

She felt her breath return to normal and took a sip of water. She placed the glass down on the table and smiled up at Travis. He didn't smile back. Finally, he sat in the loveseat opposite her, waiting, almost annoyed, for her to speak.

She took another sip of water, circling both hands around the cool glass, then pressing the glass against her forehead.

Finally, she said, "I have to tell you something."

He nodded and rotated his wrist, motioning for her to get on with it.

She took a deep breath and covered her mouth with her hand. She stared at the floor, noticing the Spanish-style terra cotta tiles. She didn't usually like this burnt orange color, but it worked nicely in this room.

"Lauren? You were saying?"

She looked up and saw exasperation in his face. She glanced around the room.

"My bag. Where's my bag?"

"What bag?" he asked.

328

"My handbag. I need to show you something." She stood up and walked around the room. "Did I leave it in the car?"

He walked towards the door.

"No," he said. "It's right here."

He picked it up and held it out to her. She walked over to where he leaned on the wall next to the door. She stopped, standing just inches away from him. She wanted to put her arms around him, to pull him into her, to move past this moment without having to go through it. But whatever tenderness he still felt for her had been used up during her episode. If she wanted more, she would have to earn it.

She looked up at him. He held her gaze for a moment. His face twitched and he turned his face away from hers. From her handbag, she took out her wallet, and from her wallet, she removed a picture, and that picture she unfolded, revealing the image of a happy young couple in love. She handed the picture to Travis.

Marcelle had taken the picture at Toufiq's brother Solomon's wedding, just a few months before Toufiq died, when Lauren was twenty-one and Toufiq twenty-two. Lauren wore a black cocktail dress and Toufiq wore a tuxedo. He stood behind her, arms wrapped around her, his cheek resting on the top of her head, her body leaning back into his chest. They both smiled widely at the camera.

"This is Toufiq," she said. She waited for the chest pains, and was surprised when instead she felt calm. She cleared her throat, feeling strong and composed as she spoke. "I fell in love with him when I was sixteen. He died in the World Trade Center. You are the only person I've loved since."

Travis studied the picture, and Lauren studied Travis. He held his expression, not allowing any emotion to register, except for an involuntary twitch in his lip.

She was aware of every atom of air in the foot of space between them. She could smell the faint remains of last night's cologne on his skin. He wore Creed's Green Irish Tweed, a woodsy, manly scent that she loved.

He looked up from the picture, but said nothing.

"I've been afraid. Of losing you. Of you dying. Of you leaving me. Of any of the million bad things that can happen if I let myself love you. I've been protecting myself."

Travis continued to stare at Lauren. His lip twitched again. The space between them seemed to solidify, turning into liquid, then a futuristic gel that would soon harden into a wall.

She forced herself to continue. "But it's too late. Because I already love you. And I've already lost you. And what hurts the most is that I never even got to have you. And I'm sorry. I'm sorry I hurt you. I was so busy protecting myself that I never thought of what I was doing to you."

Travis nodded, eyes fixated on the picture. He looked at Lauren, and then at the picture again. He watched as she ran her hand over her eyes, wiping away fresh tears.

Finally, Travis cleared his throat. "So, that ring?"

She nodded. "It belonged to his mother. We were going to get married. He never had the chance to ask. His sister gave it to me the day he died."

Travis nodded his head.

"I don't want to lose you," she said. "I'll do anything not to lose you, too."

He continued to stare at her, still not moving towards her, his face still twitching as he tried to maintain control.

She inched closer to him, and when he didn't step away, she inched closer again. Then she put her hands on his hips and leaned herself against him, pressing her chest against his, resting her face on his shoulder. Her hands moved from his hips to the center of his back until her arms wrapped around him. His arms remained by his sides.

"I love you, Travis," she whispered into his robe. "And I'm so sorry."

She felt his arms move from his sides. He held them suspended in the air, deciding whether to embrace her or push her away. She tightened her grip around him, pressed herself into him harder. Finally, she felt his hands rest gingerly on her back, felt those hands apply more pressure until he was holding her tight, until he ran his hands up her back and pulled her head off his chest and angled her chin up towards him and kissed her. Her arms circled his neck and she kissed him, too.

When he finally separated his lips from hers, he rested his forehead on hers, his blue eyes looking into her green eyes. He held her gaze, and she held his, neither breaking away, until tears formed in his eyes and he said, "So this time it's for real?" And she bit her lip, and let her own tears fall, and stared into his eyes, nodding her head again, repeating, "This time, it's for real."

From then on, whatever time Lauren didn't spend working, she spent with Travis. They took the time to date each other, going to dinner, to museums, having picnics at the park. They continued what they started in Memphis, except that this time, the only games they played involved cards or dice.

This time they talked about their pasts, telling stories about their families. He told her how angry his father had been when he went into the music industry. She told him how badly she had ruined Passover at her house. He told her about his three older brothers who beat him up throughout his childhood. She told him about her brother's engagement and her sister's baby.

After six weeks, Travis suggested that, since she stayed at his house so many nights, she stay with him for the remainder of her project. First she declined, but three weeks later, decided to give it a try.

Living with him felt as natural as breathing.

Every night, after work, she ran home to be with him, ran home to the gorgeous stillness of their life together. They cooked dinner together, took long showers, made love in every room of the house. They spent Saturdays curled up in bed with the phone turned off, the TV off, listening to Travis's endless playlists of Little Walter, BB King and Etta James.

Some nights they made fajitas, on others they made stir-fry. One day Lauren went to the Middle Eastern market in Plano and cooked him her grandmother's famous stuffed grape leaves. She met his brothers, his friends, his co-workers. He wanted her to meet his parents.

As he integrated her more and more into his life, she tried to imagine him with her family. She tried to see him having Rosh Hashana dinner with them. She tried to imagine him dancing with her to Arabic music at her brother's wedding, or sitting in the men's section in synagogue, with a kippah on his head, during her nephew's circumcision. She tried to imagine her father's reaction upon hearing that his aunt was a rabbi.

Lying in bed, she and Travis watched *The Daily Show* every night before going to sleep. His head rested on her lap, and she stroked his blonde hair, curling the longer strands between her fingers. Rooted in this bed beside him, she felt grounded, at home and at peace, like if she never left she could know happiness forever, like she might know the peace that had eluded her all these years.

He dozed on her lap, one hand thrown over her body, resting on her hip, holding her, securing her for himself. He always fell asleep before she did, as though he had no cares, no worries to keep him awake at night, whereas she, who was finding peace, found that peace transient, as some deeper nagging in her gut told her that she was not finished yet.

Could she stay here? Or would she always be looking for something else, something better, one more thing? She was tired of seeking, yet something remained unfinished.

Tired of thinking, Lauren turned off the bedside lamp. Travis felt her stir, and whispered, "Come here, my angel."

Readjusting her pillows, she curled over on her side and he nuzzled into her back, one arm thrown over her body holding her close to him.

As though he's still afraid I'll leave, she thought.

But this time it wasn't about leaving; it was about what she needed to do to make this real. This relationship, as it lived in its own vacuum, wasn't real. Even as she had the physical proofs that it was real, his arms around her, his body beside her, their everyday life spent next to each other, it was not real, did not count, did not resonate, until her family knew about it and accepted him. She knew it. He knew it. It was a fact of her life she could no longer ignore, a fact she no longer wanted to ignore.

Every time she called her family she put off telling them. Her family had accepted her apologies, and she spoke more regularly to all of them. But she left out the part about Travis.

Though they would accept him, he was so foreign to them, so alien to the way they lived, that wouldn't she in effect be exiling herself anyway?

But wasn't that what she wanted? To be exiled? Hadn't she put herself in exile all this time, for the past ten years, doing everything possible to get away? She yearned for home.

Sitting at the Seder watching Sarah and David, and Jack and Joy, she was so envious that they had found their place within the lives they had grown up in; when she had been offered that option—a life in the Community with Toufiq—it had scared her. Could she find her home outside the only one she'd ever known?

Even Marcelle had been able to find herself within her home. When Lauren was in college, she looked down on her mother, only a teacher, while her friends' mothers were judges, bankers, ran companies. But her mother had managed to fulfill herself, to earn two degrees, to do what she really loved, a job she was proud of, without giving up her family or her identity. Why couldn't Lauren learn from her mother?

She was different; there was no ignoring it. The only options were to lie to herself and pretend, or to be honest with herself and live the way she was living. It was why she had blown up at Sarah, perfect little simple Sarah who never wanted anything outside her grasp. Who never wanted to be anything other than exactly what she saw around her. Sarah didn't have to try.

Why did everything have to be so easy for Sarah and so hard for Lauren? As they read of forced exiles, of strangers in strange lands at the Passover Seder, Lauren had sat at the table, a native of a land that would always be strange for her, wondering if she would ever arrive at the Land of Milk and Honey, if a promised land existed for her. Or was she doomed to die like Moses in Sinai, leaving the land of his birth but never reaching the land of his dreams?

Where would a life with Travis leave her? Exile in Sinai or home in the Holy Land? Lauren, ever the outsider, never felt more at home than she did in Travis's bed, in Travis's arms, but, who was she kidding, she didn't belong in Dallas.

Where did she belong? Pregnant and cooking in a kitchen in Brooklyn two doors down from her mother? Driving her SUV to pick her kids up from pre-school, the neighbor's kids, too, on carpool days? Making menus for the holidays, buying ingredients for Shabbat, having lunch with her high school girlfriends once a week in one of their houses, ten blocks from hers, playing mahjong like her grandmother?

There was no place where she fit. Home was her history, but not her present. Travis was her present, but not her history. Where was her future? She was a different person in each different place, one Lauren with Travis, another with her family. Her life with Travis ignored her past, but that same past defined her present.

Defining yourself against something is still being controlled by it.

How to fit them together, present and past? And where else to find a future than at their meeting point?

Travis had to meet her family. If for nothing else, to help her solve this.

Keeping him from her family was hurting him.

He kept asking, "Did you tell them?"

She kept saying, "No."

He was losing his patience.

She knew he deserved better.

Where was the future?

A question she didn't want answered, yet.

Chapter Nine

Missing her home, Lauren prepared a dinner that encapsulated its flavors. In Travis's stainless steel and glass kitchen, she prepared her grandmother's mechshe leben, scooping out baby zucchinis and stuffing them with a mixture of rice and chickpeas, flavoring it with mint and butter. She prepared a yogurt sauce, dicing cucumbers, and crushing garlic, sprinkling in more mint.

The call came when she sautéed the flesh of the zucchini that she had scooped out, mixing it with egg and cheese to turn into a quiche, the taste of her childhood.

Cooking happily, Lauren ignored the ringing.

A few minutes later, her phone rang again.

She added allspice.

Two minutes later the phone rang again.

The zucchini bubbled, the cheese melting, forming a perfect texture.

Three phone calls in five minutes. It had to be important. Leaving her sauté pan, she ran to the living room to fetch her phone.

It was Jack.

"Nonna's in the hospital."

Sarah had been reading the newspaper on that Tuesday evening, popping antacids into her mouth to stave off the growing indigestion. She turned the page to a news story about Egyptian protestors who had been beaten by the police, and as they recounted the tales of their torture, cigarettes burned on their flesh, caning on the soles of their feet and armpits, the burning in her chest turned to pounding and the pounding to choking. She dropped the paper and clutched her heart. She looked for the phone, but she had left it in the living room. She grabbed the corners of the table and tried to catch her breath.

Eddie walked in to find her slumped over the table and called 911.

Nonna was dead. There were endless conversations Lauren put off having with her until the time was right, until she knew what to say. There were so many things they had discussed in Lauren's head in the three months since the Seder. Lauren bitterly regretted keeping those conversations theoretical. A need for her family overtook her. She experienced that need viscerally, her hands shaking, her heart beating erratically, her skin hurting from needing to be touched. Nonna was gone but the rest of them were still there. There was still Nonno and Jack, still her father and her sister, the remaining Sarah, but especially her mother: Lauren needed her mother.

Travis came up from behind her. He heard her screaming from the other room. She had been screaming at Jack. Why didn't anyone tell me, why didn't anyone call me? She would have gone to New York immediately. She would have made a list of everything she wanted to say, everything she wanted to reveal, everything she needed her grandmother to know about her, and armed with the immunity that death provides, would have confided everything. And now it was too late.

In life, Lauren had been afraid to discuss Travis with her grandmother. Every night, Lauren had looked at the clock on the nightstand and thought of calling Nonna to tell her how happy she was, to ask her what to do about this man she loved so much. Every night she wanted to say, "I know he's not one of us, Nonna, but he makes me happy, and that's enough, right?" and every night she had been too afraid and had put it off for another day.

Every night some part of her, the same part of her that had pushed Travis away for so long, had known it was not how her grandmother would respond that scared her, rather what she would say. Somewhere in her deepest self, Lauren knew that what she told Nonna would reveal her intentions for this relationship. There was no way to lie to Nonna, no ruse she could not see through. And once again, because of her cowardice, her need to maintain the appearance of bravery, Lauren lost an opportunity. With Travis, she had been able to make amends. This time, there was no going back. Nonna was dead.

Travis's arms encircled her while she had these thoughts, and he squeezed her closer to him as tears found their way out of her eyes, spilling down her face. She told him what happened. He moved her over to the couch so she could sit. He kissed her head. He made her tea. The room blurred.

Waking in a small puddle of drool, she looked frantically for Travis. She wiped the saliva from her face, her cottony tongue unable to formulate sound, her body too exhausted to stand. Remaining on the couch, she flipped the wet pillow over and stared at the rug till he returned. When he did, it was to tell her he had called her brother to arrange details, and then booked them both on a flight to New York the next morning.

Lauren wanted to hug him with gratitude; she also wanted to scream that this was not the time to meet her family. This was not the time for her to explain his presence, and his background and his place in her life to the grief-stricken people he would be meeting the next day. And just as the words began to form in her mouth he said, "I can stay in a hotel if you want me to, but I'm coming with you regardless." She cried and grabbed him harder.

Lauren knew she would need her mother. She was not prepared for how much her mother needed her. Her mother asked her to stay in the house and she complied. An hour before the funeral, Lauren found Marcelle standing in front of her closet, staring.

"I can't get dressed," she said, eyes wet with tears. "I can't decide."

"Come, Mommy," Lauren said, sitting her mother on the bed. "Let me help you. You need something nice enough for the funeral, but you're going to be wearing it all week, so we need something comfortable." Selecting a grey a-line skirt and black v-neck top, Lauren asked, "How's this?"

Marcelle nodded.

Lauren placed the clothes on the bed beside her mother.

"Come, Mommy, lift your hands up," she said.

Marcelle complied. Lauren slipped the shirt over her mother's arms and head and onto her torso.

"Stand up, Mommy. Here, lift this leg. Good. Now this leg. Okay. Let's zip you up. Stockings?"

Marcelle shook her head no.

"Shoes," Lauren, continued. "Flats are better, right? Right. Here we go. Give me this foot, Mommy. Good. Now this foot. Okay, now we're going to brush your hair."

Like she's my child, Lauren thought. Like I'm repaying her for all the times she did this for me.

"You look very nice," Lauren said.

"Nice. Huh," Marcelle replied. "Am I supposed to look nice? How am I supposed to look?"

Lauren shook her head. "I have no idea."

Marcelle stared into space.

"Mom. Mommy? You okay? I think we have to go now. You ready?"

Marcelle nodded. Lauren helped her up, held her hand, and led her down the stairs and to the car, where her father was waiting.

It's my grandmother's funeral. The phrase repeated in her head; if she kept telling herself would it make it real?

Lauren held her mother's hand as Eddie ended his eulogy and Uncle Charles began another.

"I should have written something," she said to her sister Sarah.

"Write for the arayat," Sarah replied. "You'll have more time to think about what you want to say."

Sitting in the front row, she turned her head to see who had come. The synagogue was packed, people standing in the back, more trying to come in. She noticed Travis sitting in the back, by himself, in the men's section.

Her mother turned around to look.

"Which one is he?" she asked.

Lauren raised an eyebrow.

"Jack told me he came with you," she said.

Lauren described him. Marcelle nodded.

"I'm happy you have someone here. It would've made Nonna happy."

Lauren was amazed by her sister Sarah. There was so much to prepare for the shiva: arranging food for the mourners; buying food for those who came to pay respects; renting chairs so they had a place to sit; buying plastic plates and spoons, napkins, coffee urns, tea; cutting fruit and arranging cookies and pastries. Sarah gracefully organized everything within an hour, delegating to everyone who wanted to help: Lauren, Auntie Sofia, Marcelle's best friend Ruby. Everyone but Auntie Rosette.

"You're not a young woman anymore," Sarah told her. "Your job is to comfort my mother, my grandfather, my uncles. Leave the rest to us."

Auntie Rosette huffed, but Sarah was firm.

Kissing her, Sarah said, "You've done so much for so many years. Let us do this, please?"

Rosette relented. "You're just like your grandmother."

The shiva was mayhem. It confounded Lauren that this was a religiously mandated way to mourn. When all she wanted was to be alone, she had to find the wherewithal to be a polite hostess to the endless throngs of neighbors paying their condolences. It seemed as though her grandmother had known everyone in the Community. Cousins, in-laws, friends, women from the market, boys who had grown up on her block and were used to her feeding them freshly baked pastries, sometimes in return for shoveling snow from her driveway, usually just because she felt like it. Many times, Lauren became angry with visitors for laughing, only to overhear them telling Sarah stories, repeating funny things she had said. There were so many stories she had never heard, so much about her grandmother she had never known.

Leaving Egypt

As the days went on, strangers took Lauren and her sister Sarah aside and told them how much they had loved and respected their grandmother. The money she had lent to one woman. The time she made all the food for a shower herself because the bride's mother died and none of her relatives were willing. They discussed her volunteer work at the Community charity, the cookbooks she had compiled, the Chinese auctions she had planned, the fundraisers she had worked on for the Community school and synagogue.

Sitting on pillows on the floor were her mother, her grandfather, her uncle Charles, and Nonna's brothers, Uncles Zaki and Jacques. They wore the same clothes they had been wearing for days, the same ones they would wear until the shiva was over, collars ripped by a Rabbi the day the shiva began. They were not allowed to bathe, but Marcelle cheated just a little by using baby wipes on her body, and soap and water on "the important parts." Nonno, Uncles Charles, Jacques and Zaki all had three-day-old shadows on their faces, and they would not shave until thirty days had elapsed. Around them, chairs lined up in rows for visitors to sit. Three times a day, her father ensured that a minimum of ten men came for prayers, the number required to recite kaddish, the mourner's prayer. Lauren, her sister, her aunt and cousins made sure there was always something for them to eat. Signs posted on the walls printed prayer times, and Sarah's Hebrew name, so any time a visitor ate or drank they recited a blessing in her name, helping her soul to ascend just a little bit higher in heaven.

One night, they stayed up late listening to Jacques and Zaki tell stories about their baby sister, how she used to wave her wooden spoon at them, scolding them, insisting on proper behavior. How they would fall for it until one of them remembered she was the youngest and sent her to her room.

In the middle of the laughter, Marcelle began to sob, and Nonno succumbed to tears as well.

Auntie Rosette held Marcelle who held her father's hand. "She missed her parents. She missed my Elie. Be happy for her. She's with them now."

340

The days went on, and Lauren resented the shiva less and less. Despite her instinct to be alone, she appreciated having so much work. Feeding, cleaning, buying, organizing, and providing for the mourners kept her too occupied to think.

Caught up in her family, Lauren knew she was ignoring Travis. He worked from his hotel room, trying to keep busy. Lauren knew he was waiting for her to tell him it was all right to come.

By the third day she called him.

"It's calmed down a lot here. I think now is a good time."

He arrived within the hour.

Meeting her mother, he said, "I'm sorry for your loss. And I'm sorry I'm meeting you under these circumstances."

Marcelle smiled. "Knowing what a pain my daughter can be, I'm glad I'm meeting you at all."

Travis laughed and Lauren flushed.

Lauren busied herself cleaning and replenishing the trays of food while they talked. She noticed Jack had joined the conversation, she noticed Jack laughing, patting Travis on the back. Standing in the walkway to the kitchen she watched them, her lover, her mother and her brother, despite the tragic circumstances, seeming to enjoy each other's company.

Could this be happening? Could this be real? It was almost too perfect.

Her father interrupted her. Grabbing her arm, he pulled her into the kitchen.

"I thought I got through to you the last time we talked," he said.

"You did," she said, raising an eyebrow. "What do you mean?"

"Him. He's just one more step away from us."

"He's Jewish, Dad."

"Dear God, Lauren, it wouldn't even occur to me that you'd bring someone who wasn't into this house. He's not one of us."

Travis walked over and introduced himself.

Nathan shook his hand, but ended the conversation abruptly.

"What was that about?" Travis said.

"Later," she answered, shaking her head.

That night, Lauren tried to sleep in her old twin bed in her parents' house; she couldn't. She went downstairs to find her mother smoking her Nonna's narghile in the living room.

"I didn't know you smoked that thing," Lauren said, sitting on the couch next to her mother, waiting for her turn.

Marcelle exhaled and passed the mouthpiece to Lauren. "Lauren, honey, I suspect there's a lot we don't know about each other."

They smoked in silence for a while, sharing the narghile that had travelled so far, from Syria to Egypt to America, providing solace and connection to five generations of women in their family.

"She loved you very much," Marcelle said. "She was so proud of you."

"I wish I'd been closer to her. Like you were. You were always so close to her."

"No, not always. Not till I was older than you are now."

"Really?" Lauren asked.

Marcelle nodded.

"Why not? What happened?"

"Nothing in particular. It just took me a while to figure out who I was and what I wanted. And once I knew that, she was able to see me on my own terms. And then I could see her on hers, too. You know what I mean?"

Lauren knew. It was what she wished for. To be seen for the person she was. Did she see her mother that way? Had she ever tried?

Marcelle held her daughter's hand. "It's never too late for that, you know."

Lauren squeezed, and looked at her mother. "I hope not."

"Think you'll be able to sleep?" asked Marcelle.

Lauren shook her head no.

"Would being with him help?" Marcelle asked.

Lauren looked up shocked.

"Honey, he's not what I would have chosen for you, but really I just want you to be happy. Do you need him tonight?" Lauren nodded as she exhaled.

"Then go to him," Marcelle said. "I have your father to comfort me. I'll think of something to tell him."

Her mother called her a cab so she could spend the night in a hotel room with her lover. What was the world coming to?

Marcelle waved her off as she got into the cab, but not before hugging her with an urgent, "I love you."

She arrived at Travis's hotel in Park Slope. She crept into bed with him. He was asleep but he woke when he felt her beside him. He pressed his stomach into her back, his knees into the curve of her body, his face into her fanning hair. He pulled her smaller body close to his large one. Still mostly asleep, he muttered, "I love you, my Lauren." Hearing those words, she fell asleep, too.

The next morning Travis returned to Dallas; they agreed it would be best for now.

Each night, after everyone left, Lauren worked on her speech for the arayat, a ceremony used to mark the end of the mourning period. Loved ones gathered on the last evening of the shiva to read the book of Psalms, to eulogize and to pray. Lauren struggled, trying to capture her grandmother in a just a few words. Recalling their last conversation, she wrote about the difficulties of her grandmother's early life. How she had overcome a series of tragedies and, by her sheer will, had created the life she wanted to live for herself, finding balance between her traditions from Egypt and life in this new place, New York. She had stayed among her own. She had married her children among their own. She rooted herself deeply in her new home—all the people who came to pay condolences were a testament to that. She had lived well, integrity intact, surrounded by those she loved. She had left Egypt, but Egypt had never left her.

As she sat in synagogue again with her mother and sister, she heard Jack recite her words; by their custom, women were not permitted to address mixed company in synagogue. Her hands held those of her sister and mother. They took strength from the blood they shared, the blood passed to them from the woman they now mourned.

Jack finished reading. People sniffled and blew their noses. Various relatives turned around to smile at her. Beside her, her mother grabbed her hand and kissed it. Tears in her eyes, looking into her daughter's, Marcelle said, "You did right by her."

At that moment, Lauren understood what her grandmother had been trying to tell her for so long. A message so simple, Lauren had added layers of mystery to it, always trying to overcomplicate life. And dear Nonna, so stubborn, so insistent that Lauren get the point, had literally died making it.

Lauren still didn't know where life was going to take her, or how many more mistakes she would make until she got there. But she knew one thing was certain: she could always, always go home.

Acknowledgments

There are so many people I would like to thank for their support:

My amazing mother and stepfather; my father who I know is looking down at me with pride; my siblings, Monique, Jaime, Shlomo, Jessica and Alissa. Special thanks to Joey H. for the beautiful cover.

My writing group; Lev, Laura, Holly, Robin, Stella, Dan, and my personal readers; Joey S., Diana and most especially Lauren, who read more drafts of this book than anyone should ever have to.

The many people who have loved me throughout the years it took me to write this: Lauren, Chaim, Ruby, Joey, Alie, Daphne, Lisa, Anu, Elizabeth, Camille, Jaime, Andrea L., Simon, Mickey, Andrea P., Cara, Ellie, Karen, Jill, and Joe.

So many thanks to Kate Lee, whose guidance and edits were indispensable in shaping this book into a story worth telling.

Made in the USA
Middletown, DE
23 December 2022